VISIBILITY

Boris Starling has worked as a reporter on the *Sun* and the *Daily Telegraph* and for Control Risk, a company which specialized in kidnap negotiation, clandestine investigations and political risk analysis. He was one of the youngest-ever contestants on Mastermind in 1996 and went to the semi-finals with his subject: the novels of Dick Francis. Boris studied at Cambridge and currently lives in London. His first novel, *Messiah*, was adapted into a major BBC TV drama series, starring Ken Stott. Boris currently lives in North London.

Visit www.AuthorTracker.co.uk for exclusive updates on Boris Starling.

Also by Boris Starling

Messiah
Storm
Vodka

BORIS STARLING

Visibility

HARPER

Harper
An imprint of HarperCollins*Publishers*
77–85 Fulham Palace Road,
Hammersmith, London W6 8JB

www.harpercollins.co.uk

This paperback edition 2007
1

First published in Great Britain by
HarperCollins*Publishers* 2006

A catalogue record for this book is
available from the British Library

ISBN-13: 978 0 00 711948 6

Set in Meridien by Palimpsest Book Production Ltd,
Grangemouth, Stirlingshire

Printed and bound in Great Britain by
Clays Ltd, St Ives plc

For Charlotte

Acknowledgements

Three days before this book was published in the UK, my sister Belinda died. She was 34, and her first novel had just been accepted for publication. Her myriad of qualities as a sister and friend aside, she had always been my most perceptive and constructive critic. Every manuscript I sent her came back with pages and pages of notes, every single one valuable and accurate – sometimes uncomfortably so! She was every bit as fantastic an author as she was a critic, and though her career has been ended almost before it started, perhaps in years to come she'll be bracketed alongside Margaret Mitchell and Harper Lee, women who wrote one immortal novel each and called it a day right there.

At HarperCollins, Julia Wisdom has the patience of a saint, and Anne O'Brien the eyes of an eagle. They are brilliant editors, and every time I read their notes I realise how lucky I am to have them.

At A. P. Watt, Caradoc King is quite simply the best agent a writer could ask for.

Much, perhaps too much, of a modern author's research can be done online, but now and then we have to emerge blinking into the sunlight. My investigations for *Visibility* took me to Tower Bridge, where I was royally looked after; special thanks to Claire Forrest, Charles Lotter and Dave Savage.

Thanks too to the guides at Highgate Cemetery, one of London's most beautiful parts, and sadly too one of its most under-resourced. The Friends of Highgate Cemetery do a grand job, but they will always need people with time or money to spare to aid them in maintenance. Please help them if you can.

Most of all, thank you to Charlotte, who is the best thing that ever happened to me.

4TH DECEMBER 1952

THURSDAY

The fog was coming, without and within.

On the far side of the river, the first smoky tresses were stroking the rooftops with fingers as slim and elegant as a concert pianist's. If a man had watched for a while, he would have seen the mist crawling slowly across the cityscape, its purposeful stealth that of a prowling cat.

And if a man had watched for a while, he might have felt the first hazings in his head, a gauze which would make the world opaque and through which he would have to reach for his very thoughts.

The fog had come before, but rarely with such purpose. Londoners were nothing if not survivors, however, and they knew when trouble was ahead. Certainly they needed no warning from the weathermen to brace themselves for a bad one.

New Scotland Yard was a riverside riot of turrets, crenellations, and people; a Gothic extravagance that swallowed thousands of worker bees every morning and spat them out again come dusk. Overcrowding was a permanent endemic; the place had grown like Topsy, with new buildings added every few decades to ease the strain, but the problem remained resolutely unallayed. Bounded by the Thames in front and Whitehall to the rear, New Scotland Yard's room for expansion was running out fast.

Shifts in the Metropolitan Police's Murder Squad came in threes: the morning, 6 a.m. until 2 p.m.; the afternoon, 2 p.m. until 10 p.m.; and the night, 10 p.m. until 6 a.m. On the days when Herbert Smith, once of the British Army, latterly of MI5, and now a member of said Murder Squad, was scheduled for the afternoon slot, he liked to lunch beforehand with no company save for that afforded by a pie, a pint, the *Evening Standard*, and *The Times* crossword. He frequented a pub off Smith Square, which at ten minutes' walking distance from the Yard was at least twice as far as any of his colleagues were liable to venture, even those adventurous enough to seek grounds more exotic than those of the staff canteen.

This day, he read Milton Shulman's film reviews in the early edition of the *Evening Standard*, making a mental note to go and see *The Narrow Margin* at the London Pavilion ('an exciting journey' wrote Shulman), and to miss *The Road to Bali*, on at the Plaza and succinctly dismissed as 'a cul-de-sac'. Herbert usually found Shulman's opinions pretty accurate, though as he only ever went to the cinema on his own, he had never discovered whether this was a majority opinion or not.

The *Standard* duly read, he polished off three-quarters of *The Times* crossword – particularly proud of decoding *Writing implement dripped red ink?* (7) as 'N-I-B-B-L-E-D' – and found without surprise that forcing himself into the office was a genuine physical strain.

It was not that he wanted to stay in the pub – he was not a big drinker – but simply that anywhere was surely better than another afternoon in the office.

There, in a nutshell, was the contradiction at the heart of working the murder beat. Days in the Yard, cramped, airless and noisy, were dreadful; but to get out of there, someone had to have been killed, and Herbert had seen enough violent death in his time not to wish for more of it.

And, if he was to be honest, cramped, airless and noisy weren't the half of it. No one else on the Murder Squad seemed to mind the conditions, but then no one else on the Murder Squad felt as though their presence was at best tolerated and at worst resented.

Herbert was not One of Them. He hadn't done his time in the ranks, and he was still learning how to do things the Scotland Yard way. As far as his colleagues were concerned, therefore, his time at Five might as well have been a sojourn in the inner circles of Hell. Suspicion between arms of the law was always bad; when an espionage service was involved, it was exacerbated tenfold.

Of the five men round the table when Herbert walked into the office, only Tyce and Veal acknowledged him, and only Veal did so with anything that approximated a greeting in recognised English. Tyce gave a curt nod. The others, Connolly, Tulloch and Bradley, glanced at him as though he were something the cat had brought in, and turned their attention back to the matter at hand; that matter being the case of Christopher Craig, an unlovely, manipulative psychopath, and Derek Bentley, an illiterate, impressionable epileptic, who had broken into a warehouse in Croydon the previous month.

The police had arrived. Craig had drawn a gun. Bentley had shouted: 'Let him have it, Chris.'

A plea to surrender the weapon, or an exhortation to murder?

Craig, clearly taking it as the latter – assuming that he had listened to Bentley at all, which given their relationship seemed unlikely – had shot two policemen. Detective Constable Frederick Fairfax was hit in the shoulder, painful but not too serious. Police Constable Sidney Miles was killed.

Killing a policeman was so far beyond the pale as to be invisible. Bentley and Craig were due to stand trial at the Old Bailey the coming Tuesday, the ninth, and there was not one man in Scotland Yard who felt anything other than that they should both be convicted of murder.

No, that was not quite true. There was one man

who felt otherwise, one man only – and that man was Herbert.

The problem, as far as Herbert was concerned, was this. The death penalty applied only to those over eighteen. Craig, who deserved to hang as much as anyone Herbert had ever encountered, was only sixteen. Even if he was found guilty, he would not be executed.

But Bentley was nineteen, and he would surely swing; even though his mind was that of a child, even though he had not fired the fatal shot, and even though he was less Craig's friend than his plaything.

Uniquely amongst his peers, Herbert felt that Bentley had been asking Craig to hand over the weapon; for if Herbert was sure of anything, it was that he knew a victim when he saw one.

He had expressed these thoughts to his colleagues once, and they had made it clear that once was once too many.

So now they hunched round a table and discussed the trial next week; specifically, what they termed strategy for their appearances in the witness box, and what the cynical would have called getting their stories straight.

Herbert's colleagues departed to continue their discussions in the pub sometime around dusk, leaving Herbert marooned in the office while another afternoon exodus ebbed and flowed around him. From the window, he saw that the fog was thickening now, diffusing the street lamps into haloes of dull gold. People scurried beneath with collars up and chins down.

He sensed a communal disillusion with the weather. The previous day had been magical, one of those winter days which made one believe sincerely that England was God's own country: skies of lapis lazuli, air so crisp that it fizzed on the way down to one's lungs, and a cheerful sunshine dappling lightly through bare branches. Now there was only filthy, moist grey shot through with traces of sulphur.

Bradley and Tulloch returned about six, realising that, much as they might have been tempted to, they could not in all conscience leave Herbert minding the fort indefinitely. Not that there was much to do; the steady trilling of phones throughout the afternoon had dwindled to a trickle by the time they came back, and the call at eight o'clock was the first in more than an hour.

Neither Bradley nor Tulloch showed much inclination to answer it.

Bradley did not even move; he might have been a stone Aztec, Herbert thought, forever phlegmatic and unflappable, completely unreadable even to as adept an observer as Herbert.

Tulloch, cut off midway through a rant about whichever aspect of modern society had most recently attracted his ire, clicked his tongue angrily, as though the call had been made purely to irritate him. He tended to treat all crimes as a personal slight, or at least an institutional one, as if the very existence of the police force should have been enough to stop the forces of lawlessness and disorder in their tracks.

Herbert let the phone ring a few times for form's sake, and then picked up.

'New Scotland Yard,' he said.

'Is that the Murder Squad?' A young man's voice, breathless with excitement.

Herbert felt a brief twinge in his gut; apprehension and excitement tangling.

'That's right.'

'This is Sergeant Elkington, in Hyde Park. I've got a floater in the Long Water.'

Elkington stumbled over the word 'floater', as if its use implied a casual machismo that he did not really possess.

Herbert sighed. Fogs always brought death; people who couldn't see where they were going and tipped off walls or into rivers, usually. Had Herbert been a betting man, he would have considered an accumulator; that this floater, as Elkington had so unconvincingly referred to it, had had a few drinks inside him when he had walked into the water, and that he wouldn't be the last.

Herbert looked at his colleagues, rolled his eyes, and made a drinking gesture.

Bradley stared back, his expression altered not a jot. Tulloch ground his teeth in silent fury at the world.

Herbert wondered why he bothered. A simple human connection, that was all he was trying to establish. Perhaps the day he stopped trying was the day it would happen.

He turned his attention back to Elkington. 'Any reason you're calling me . . . ?'

'Sergeant Elkington,' Elkington repeated, in case Herbert hadn't got it the first time. 'No more than the usual. Just taking precautions.'

Herbert now knew exactly the kind of policeman Elkington was: the Janus sort, always looking to cover his behind so that if anything went wrong he had already and demonstrably passed the buck, all the while squinting forward through ambition-slitted eyes, so that if anything went right he was in position to claim as much credit as possible.

The biggest excitement in the Hyde Park police station was locking the park gates every night. Herbert was sure Elkington wouldn't be there long; he would get himself transferred as soon as possible, treating every case as a possible key to the door which led out and up.

Herbert considered a moment. Neither Bradley nor Tulloch would want the case. They had wives and children, and they needed a new case this late in the day like a hole in the head. At best, it would be a false alarm; at worst, a serious drain on their Friday, possibly their weekend too.

A cold, foggy night; a warm room for once mercifully quiet.

10

No contest.

'Where's the body?' Herbert asked.

'By the Peter Pan statue,' Elkington said.

Herbert told Bradley and Tulloch where he was going, and promised to call in the moment he had something concrete. 'Any time after ten,' Tulloch said; meaning Herbert could call as much as he liked, once the night shift had come on and Tulloch had gone home. He wasn't joking.

Herbert took a car from the pool and almost immediately regretted it. The fog was already thick enough to make driving difficult, and Herbert lost his way twice, even on roads he was sure he knew like the back of his hand. Headlights were little use; they simply bounced back off the thick particles of mist.

Eventually, he parked round the back of the Albert Hall and completed the journey on foot, his breath billowing in lung-shaped plumes around his head as he hurried forward against the cold.

Elkington had ensured that the scene was lit by flaming torches, as though it were some sort of pagan funeral. The edge of the water was blotched with ice, and covered in what looked like a thin film of powdered graphite. Herbert wondered for a moment where this film could have come from, and realised with a start that it must have settled there from the fog. What other particles the mist was carrying, and what was settling inside his lungs every time he inhaled, scarcely bore consideration.

The Long Water was a dammed river; effectively a lake, therefore, without a current. The floater was a few yards from shore. It was lying face down, as corpses tended to, with its limbs and head hanging lower than its torso. Perfectly motionless, it could have been a jellyfish.

Elkington looked even younger than he sounded, cold-reddened cheeks smooth beneath a pile of dirty blond hair.

'I've touched nothing, sir,' Elkington said. 'All I've done is call you and seal the scene; twenty yards in every direction.' Twenty yards was already beyond the limits of visibility; Elkington's gestures indicated nothing but fog. 'That's correct procedure, isn't it, sir?'

Herbert had been dead right about the kind of person Elkington was. His initial deduction now seemed less inspired guesswork than impeccable snap judgement. Still, he reflected, at least it was a pleasant change to have someone look up to him, after the stonewalling indifference he faced back at the Yard.

'That is indeed,' Herbert said.

'The way you would have done it?'

'Don't tell me – you've always wanted to work in the Murder Squad.'

'As a matter of fact, sir, I have.'

'Then you can start by telling me who found the body.'

'I did.' If Elkington had put his hand up and started shouting *Me, sir, me, me*, it would not have surprised Herbert in the slightest. 'When I was doing my rounds.'

'You were alone?'

'No, sir. I was with Flew and Hare. Here, sir.'

He indicated the constables either side of him. Flew had a neat, slightly effete face framed by a mass of curly black hair. Hare's nose kinked halfway down before setting off at a tangent to its original course; broken and badly reset, Herbert thought. Like Elkington, neither looked old enough to be shaving yet, let alone policing.

Herbert nodded at Flew and Hare, and they waded into the water with a synchronicity of which twins would have been proud.

Elkington made a sign of the cross, which Herbert might have found touching had Elkington not checked first to see whether he was watching.

There was an autopsy unit at Imperial College, less than a mile away on Exhibition Road. The pathologist, a small man whose glasses were as round and shiny as the top of his head, was waiting for Herbert in the foyer.

'Rathbone,' he said simply.

Rathbone, Elkington, Flew, Hare; didn't these people have Christian names?

Herbert and Rathbone shook hands.

'Right then, right then.' Rathbone's voice rose and fell in twittering ululations. 'Let's get on with it, yes?'

There would soon be a backlog, he explained

en route to the autopsy room; pedestrians hit by cars travelling too fast in the murk, elderly people for whom the extra pollution would prove too much.

Herbert supposed it lucky that the body had been found before the rush.

It could not have been in the water long, for it was still recognisably human, more than enough for Herbert to imagine what the man must have been like in life.

He rattled through the alphabetical checklist that had been drummed into him during Five's surveillance training. A for age: mid-twenties. B for build: medium, as far as he could tell under the man's dark suit, which took him neatly on to C for clothes – white shirt, crimson tie, dapper black shoes, no hat. No surprise in any of that; men invariably wore a jacket and tie, whatever they were doing and wherever they were going. Strange not to have been wearing a coat in this weather, though.

No Distinguishing Marks. Ethnic Origin: Caucasian. F for Face, in this case somewhat cherubic, even through the post-mortem swelling. No Glasses, at least none still hooked over the ears; and, since he was dead, no chance to ascertain his Gait. His Hair was blond and floppy. He carried no Items.

All this had gone through Herbert's head in less than a second.

Rathbone stripped the body quickly and efficiently until it was laid out in inglorious nudity

14

on the examination table. Herbert supposed that pathology, with all its emphasis on the clinical and chemical, was intended to sanitise death. Here, it seemed to have exactly the opposite effect, making it even more revolting than Herbert had thought possible.

'You understand,' Rathbone said, 'that drownings are usually suicides or accidents, yes? There are plenty of easier ways to murder someone.'

'I understand.'

'And it's very difficult to tell whether someone was drowned at all, as opposed to being immersed in water post-mortem, yes? Let alone whether they were drowned voluntarily or against their will.'

'All I'd like you to do is to tell me how he died, and who he was.'

'Well, ha ha, I'm no alchemist, Detective Inspector . . . ?'

'Smith.'

'First things first, yes? Let's find out how long it's been there.'

It's, Herbert noticed, not *he's*. Well, that was only to be expected. If he had had corpses coming across his table as though on a conveyor belt, he would probably have tried to regard them as objects rather than human too.

Rathbone took a thermometer and rolled the body on to its side. It stared at Herbert with bulbous eyes in which he read accusing disappointment. The corpse's cheeks were swollen and its skin wrinkled,

15

like a washerwoman's hands. Drained of colour, its face seemed to leach into the air.

Rathbone pushed the thermometer towards the rectum, and stopped.

'What?' Herbert said.

Rathbone placed a hand on each of the dead man's buttocks, pulled them apart, and nodded for Herbert to come closer.

Herbert thought of several snappy replies, all of them inappropriate.

He stepped forward, looked, and winced.

The man's backside was a disaster zone; red raw, swollen into puffy ridges of flesh, and criss-crossed with scratch marks.

'Raped?' Herbert said.

Rathbone shook his head. 'Not tonight. Many of these marks are several days old.'

'Homosexual, then. And practising.'

'Very.'

All things being equal, Herbert would rather this particular can of worms had remained unopened. Homosexuality was illegal – 'gross indecency contrary to Section 11 of the Criminal Law Amendment Act 1885', as the law had it. Like most things illicit, it was also widespread, albeit necessarily furtive.

Every queer therefore lived with the same question: who knew? Among their own, they were usually safe; but, if caught, they faced chemical castration, the introduction of female hormones for what the law saw as their abnormal and

16

uncontrollable sexual urges. Oestrogen would make them impotent and obese, their looks suffocated in a welter of fat, their touting reduced to receiver status only.

As King George V had famously, or infamously, said about homosexuals: 'I thought men like that shot themselves.'

Herbert had no particular beef against homosexuals, certainly not by the prevailing standards of intolerance. He simply did not relish the prospect of poking around a closed community trying to find a truth that was liable, like many deaths, to end up being petty and sordid.

Rathbone busied himself around the man's rear end for a few moments.

'No trace evidence,' he announced at length. 'No body fluids.'

'You mean he'd taken a bath since his last, er, last . . .'

'Encounter?'

'Exactly.'

'Probably. But the water in the park could have washed such evidence off, yes?'

'The Long Water has no current. It's like a millpond tonight.'

Rathbone pursed his lips and nodded. 'Unlikely, then.'

He inserted the thermometer into the corpse's rectum, waited a few moments, extracted it and read off the digits.

'Eighty-eight degrees.' He looked at his watch.

'It's half past nine now. Normal body temperature is ninety-eight degrees. Bodies in water cool at about five or six degrees an hour, twice as fast as they do in air, yes? But these measures are approximate. Very generally, therefore, I would estimate the time of death at between half past six and eight o'clock this evening.'

In other words, not long before the body had been found; eight o'clock was when Elkington had phoned.

'You might want to go outside for this next part, yes?' Rathbone said.

'I'm not squeamish.'

Rathbone shrugged – *suit yourself* – took a small handsaw, and began to slice at the cadaver's right shoulder.

He was right. Herbert did want to go outside.

After a small eternity while Herbert waited in the corridor, Rathbone popped his head round the door and beckoned him back inside.

Herbert followed him through, and almost immediately went straight back out again. The subject – see, Herbert was already beginning to think like Rathbone; hard not to, when they were in a glorified butcher's shop – had been sliced open in three neat cuts, a perfect Y from shoulders to sternum and sternum to waist.

Rathbone picked up a lung. Patterned in marbles of grey and crimson, it shifted over the inside of his forearms, an outsize bladder which gave the disconcerting impression of being alive.

18

It looked far too big to have ever fitted inside the dead man.

Rathbone placed the lung in a metal tray, picked up a knife, and sliced into it. Dirty water spurted from the gash.

How Herbert managed not to vomit, he had no idea.

'As I thought.' Rathbone seemed pleased. 'Fluid.'

'I can see that.'

'No, no. Fluid, which you get only when air and water have been actively inspired. Passive flooding of lungs with water – in other words, post-mortem – looks quite different, yes? And see –' he indicated above and around the dead man's mouth – 'the froth? Fine and white? Must still have been breathing, yes?'

Rathbone tripped over to a set of scales and lifted a small bag from the bowl. 'The stomach. Pretty full.'

'He had just eaten, then?'

'A few hours before. Perhaps a late lunch. Shepherd's pie and cabbage, at a guess. Also weeds, silt and dirty water. Lake water. Not the kind of thing you get even in the most disreputable of restaurants, yes?' By the time Herbert realised that Rathbone had, in his own way, cracked a joke, the pathologist had moved on. 'When the victim's dead before entering the water, very little matter gets as far as the stomach. What you find is usually confined to the pharynx, trachea and larger airways, yes?'

So the corpse, whoever he was, had drowned, rather than being placed in the water after his death.

Accident, suicide, or murder?

He had drowned in shallow water, at a point where it was easy to enter the water, but equally easy to walk out again. It was therefore unlikely to have been an accident, unless he was dead drunk, which seemed improbable given the time frame involved; drunks tended to die later in the evening.

Rathbone would test for alcohol, of course, but both he and Herbert were thinking the same thing: the corpse did not have the look of a drinker.

Suicide was always a possibility, especially in the winter, when long nights and unremitting gloom could drive the heartiest of fellows to despair. Every suicide involved a great deal of resolve – Herbert had no truck with those who glibly dismissed it as the coward's way out, as he imagined that few things involved more courage than the decision to kill oneself – but drowning oneself in a still, shallow body of water took more determination than most. There were many easier methods, especially for men, who tended to prefer the more violent methods of exit.

Which left only murder.

Rathbone wanted to run more tests, so Herbert found a phone and rang the Yard.

'Yes?' Tulloch's voice was even more loaded

with rage than usual, and when Herbert glanced at his watch he saw why; it was ten to ten.

He batted away a pang of childish pleasure at inconveniencing Tulloch. 'It's Smith.'

'What do you want?'

'To tell you about the dead man.'

'Couldn't you have waited? He's not going anywhere, is he?'

'No, but I am.'

Tulloch sighed. 'Right. Tell me what you've got. And keep it short. Name?'

'Unknown.'

'Cause of death?'

'Drowning. Probably forcible.'

'Probably?'

'The pathologist's running tests as we speak.'

'Is there anything you *do* know?'

'He was a homosexual.'

'Your ideal case, then.'

Herbert chose to ignore this last remark. 'There's not much more I'll be able to do tonight, so I'll come in tomorrow morning after breakfast and take it up from there.'

'And put in for overtime, no doubt.'

The last time the topic of overtime had come up, Herbert remembered, Tulloch had contended that the whole system was skewed. The men who needed the money for their families were the ones who couldn't afford the time to make that money, he said; in contrast, the ones who had the time to spare had nothing to spend the money on.

21

Herbert had suggested that he do the time and Tulloch take the money. Tulloch had thought that a splendid idea.

'Well,' Tulloch continued, before Herbert could answer, 'everyone else here's too busy to waste time on a poof in the drink, so you're more than welcome to it. You'd know their haunts better than us, that's for sure. What about the scene?'

'I've sealed it off, of course. I'll have a proper search done in the morning, when there's enough light.'

'Gordon Bennett,' Tulloch said. 'We *have* taught you something after all.'

And he hung up.

South Kensington tube station was more or less at the bottom of Exhibition Road, so Herbert managed to find it by the simple expedient of walking straight, dodging the hardened drinkers who had headed for the private clubs after lunch – membership on the spot for five shillings – and remained there as afternoon slid to evening, nursing their cut-price whiskies and bemoaning their luck. South Kensington and Earls Court were full of such places, never-never lands of clipped moustaches, army-style overcoats and old school ties.

Seven years on from the war, they were still weary, still clinging to their Micawberish feeling that something would turn up. War veterans were prematurely and preternaturally aged, their careers ripped apart by the conflict; many of them had stepped aside so as not to get trampled underfoot by younger men desperate to fill their shoes.

Herbert found a Piccadilly Line train heading east almost at once. The tube system was still free from fog; strange days indeed, he thought, when those malodorous and claustrophobic tunnels were cleaner and brighter than the real world above.

He sat in a near-empty carriage, flicking through the notes Rathbone had given him. There was little of surprise and even less of encouragement within them.

That the blond man had been drowned against his will was now almost beyond doubt. Threads of wool, presumably from his killer's clothes, had been found under three fingernails on the right hand and two on the left. His right hand had also been clutching silt and weeds, presumably fixed in a cadaveric spasm.

Rathbone could have written most of what followed in Greek for all the sense it made to Herbert, but, whatever he said, Herbert was happy to take his word for it.

Bilateral haemorrhages on the shoulders and chest followed lines of muscle bundles and were therefore consistent with violent tearing, itself indicative of a struggle. Such symptoms could be confused with putrefaction, but extravascular erythrocytes provided histological proof of a true haemorrhage. Moreover, petechial haemorrhaging inside the eyelid and on the eyeball itself were indicators of excessive pre-mortem adrenalin, as were the abnormally high histamine and serotonin levels. Such indicators were all consistent with murder.

It was Herbert's patch all right.

Since homosexuals were proscribed by law, it followed that they had an underworld. As Tulloch had insinuated, Herbert knew full well where the gates to this particular Hades were; the queer pubs, in the first instance, such as the Fitzroy Tavern on Charlotte Street, the Golden Lion on Dean Street, and the Duke of York on Rathbone Street, where the landlord, whom a Five report had once superfluously described as 'eccentric', liked to cut off customers' ties and display them as trophies.

The Fitzroy was especially notorious, not just for the marines and guardsmen who packed in there on Saturday nights looking for a quick pick-up, but for the eclectic quality of its straighter clientele; Dylan Thomas (who apparently liked to pick fights with the guardsmen), the hangman Albert Pierrepoint, and the Satanist Aleister Crowley had all drunk there, Crowley evidently inventing his own cocktail of gin, vermouth and laudanum. When the police had raided the place and the landlord been charged, the court had heard that 'there can be very little doubt that this house was conducted in a most disorderly and disgusting fashion'.

Failing all other leads, Herbert would trawl such establishments, hopefully with a name for the dead

24

man and a photograph of him which did not include a mortician's slab and a face rendered puffy by drowning.

Before then, however, would come the usual, tedious routes to finding out someone's identity. Dental records could be checked, fingerprints matched, public appeals launched; all involving a level of manpower the police could ill afford. The force was desperately short of men, particularly in towns and cities, and had been so ever since the war. Too many young men had died for it to be otherwise.

Herbert alighted at Green Park. Advertisements greeted him like old friends: *Good Mornings Begin With Gillette*. The pubs were closing; through doors pushed briefly open, he heard the usual landlord banter. 'Arses and glasses!' 'Haven't you got homes to go to?' and 'Let's be having the company's glasses,' all pronounced with the tired, ersatz flourish of the provincial actor.

The journey had taken ten minutes, and yet it was like going from one world to another. South Kensington and Mayfair might have been continents apart; London could change faces in a heartbeat, a street.

Where there had been sad sacks, now there were men a decade their junior, the generation who had not been sent away to fight and who consequently brimmed with energy and vigour; spivs with padded shoulders and pencil moustaches, who winked with conspiratorial jauntiness as they checked the time on their Cartier watches and lit cigarettes with gold-plated lighters.

Some called them conmen; they themselves would say that times were changing and, perhaps as never before in Britain, the race was to the swift. The pubs they frequented had once been the preserve of the domestic servant seeking ale and dominoes. Now they were crowded out by wide boys and posh girls.

It was change, all right; whether it was progress was a different matter.

Herbert fancied a nightcap before closing time, but one glance through the window of the Chesterfield pub put him off going in there. The place was brimming with Five officers, most of whom he recognised, and most of whom were also doubt-less drunk and loudly discussing matters of national security.

Five's oppressive regime and culture of secrecy had with grim inevitability fostered an endemic culture of excessive drinking. The Chesterfield was almost an official service watering-hole, so much so that it was known within Five as Camp Two. Camp One was the Pig & Eye Club on the top floor of Five's HQ, Leconfield House, established precisely to avoid too many people decamping to the pub; but the woeful lack of atmosphere within the club ensured that decamp they did.

This was, as if Herbert needed any reminding, the outfit charged with defence of the realm.

He walked through Shepherd Market, a curious enclave of passageways which sprouted pubs, bistro restaurants, galleries, antique shops and brothels in more or less equal quantities. Herbert lived in the heart of the Market – his flat gained in the desirability of its location what it lacked in size – and as he approached his front door he saw through the fog that someone was standing on the pavement outside.

'You look like how I feel,' a female voice said, when he was close enough to make out her features. 'Anything I can do to help?'

Herbert smiled. It was Stella, the doyenne of Shepherd Market tarts, universally known as 'the Auld Slapper', a name bestowed with affection or bile according to whether one had come across her sunny side or her dark one. She could be piercingly understanding and bitterly funny, but behind the façade, the set of her mouth and the waves of dullness in her eyes betrayed her.

Tonight, her make-up looked as though it had been applied by a plasterer. Dark roots streaked through her badly bleached hair. Business was clearly slow.

Propriety should perhaps have prompted Herbert to rebuff her, politely but firmly. Corporeal weakness had him following her gloomily upstairs.

Stella was the nearest thing Herbert had to a friend; seven years older than him, perhaps she was in a strange way the elder sister denied to an

27

only child. She was also, rather unimpressively, the extent of his sex life.

That part of proceedings was over in short order, as usual. Stella made her habitual crack about the oldest profession in the world encountering the second oldest, and Herbert made his equally customary reply that he was no longer a spy, and that even if he had ever been one, he could not possibly have told her. It was a routine as old and sagging as the bed on which they had bounced with a distinct lack of lustre.

He dug a couple of pound notes from his pocket and handed them over. He always paid; if he was to be in debt to her, he wanted it to be for her companionship rather than her services. Correspondingly, she never feigned ecstasy, and he would no more have wanted her to do so than he would have expected the grocer to hand over his shopping with piercing yells of fake rhapsody.

Dressed again, Stella stroked Herbert's cheek with the backs of her fingers.

'Be careful what you wish for,' she said.

This was one of her favourite sayings, and he knew how it finished.

'Because it might just happen, right?'

'Right,' she said. 'And we wouldn't want that, would we?'

Herbert's flat was nothing to shout about; a small kitchen area with a porcelain sink, a wooden draining board, and a small cupboard in the coolest part of the larder which served as the next best thing to a refrigerator. The pictures on the wall of the living-room were plain and the furniture even plainer; most pieces carried the 'Utility' mark, designed for newly-weds and those whose homes had been destroyed by the war. How they had ended up here was anyone's guess, and Herbert was not much inclined to try and find out. They had come with the flat, and that was that.

There was one bathroom, with the lavatory cistern high on the wall and a sit-up bath which would have cramped a pygmy, and two bedrooms, both small enough for the single beds within them to look large. Herbert had one room; his mother Mary had designs on the other, on the grounds that she was ill and needed constant looking after, but Herbert had so far resisted. Living with one's mother was for serial killers, queers and Italians only.

He wondered how long it would be before he succumbed; for she *was* ill, of that there was no doubt. He had taken her to Guy's Hospital that very morning with a recurrence of breathing difficulties, and the fog would hardly be doing her any favours.

He phoned the hospital, sat through stretching minutes as his call was passed from one ancient switchboard to another, and finally got through to the duty nurse on Mary's ward, who told him that his mother was asleep and that her condition was unchanged.

29

He said he would visit tomorrow, and the nurse promised to pass the message on.

Having piled the fire with extra coal, banked it to ensure maximum warmth, checked that the windows were sealed tight against everything which came from outside, Herbert was left alone with the silence.

He thought of his colleagues finding warmth in the press of their wives' bodies and the glow of protection over their children which every man carried in him like a birthright, and reflected, not for the first time, that of all the truths he sought in his work, the most indisputable was also the easiest to find; that it was precisely *because* he was alone that he could afford to seek, and that he was alone not because he had chosen to be but because every turn his life had taken had ensured it.

5TH DECEMBER 1952

FRIDAY

Herbert turned the radio on and then up, to drown out the clattering of the milkman in the street below. The newsreader said that Jomo Kenyatta was being tried in Nairobi for association with the Mau Mau. Imprisonment would not harm Kenyatta's political prospects, Herbert thought; the British authorities in India had locked Nehru up during the war, and he had not done badly since. Had Herbert been a betting man he would have put money on Kenyatta eventually running the place.

Unexciting news came and went in unexciting tones. Herbert listened for a while, summoning up the enthusiasm to move; then, with a huge effort, rolled out of bed, stumbled over to the window and pulled open the curtains.

The fog had thickened into a greasy, heavy swirl which was condensing in oily drops on the window-panes. It had hardly been worth the trip.

He should have been a bear, he thought; any

self-respecting grizzly would have taken one look outside and hibernated until April.

He was not due back on duty until two o'clock that afternoon, but he had told Tulloch he would be in after breakfast. True, he owed Tulloch nothing, but he felt obligated to the man in the Long Water, whoever he had been. In death as in life, anonymous or otherwise, he deserved the best the Metropolitan Police could give him.

Herbert rang the Hyde Park station, where Elkington, keener than a factory full of mustard, was already at his desk. Herbert asked that Elkington bring a police diver and meet him by the Peter Pan statue in an hour.

Elkington could do it in half an hour, if that was better.

No, it was not better. An hour was fine.

The weatherman came on the radio to announce that London had suffered a temperature inversion during the night. The air near the ground had grown colder, effectively trapping itself beneath the lid of warmer air above. Unable to rise vertically and with no wind to disperse it laterally, this shallow layer of low-lying, dense, frigid air was now totally inert.

The Port of London Authority had announced that all navigable sections of the river were fogbound, and that river traffic had ceased in its entirety.

A perfect day for hunting murderers, in other words.

*　　*　　*

It was breakfast time, but day and night were pretty nebulous concepts when the fog was so dense. It was noticeably more opaque than last night; dirtier, too. Herbert thought of all the millions of domestic fires which would have been lit in the past few hours, of the power stations which stood sentinel on the Thames at Barking and Woolwich and Deptford and Battersea and Fulham, of all the vehicles belching smoke as they crawled blindly round town; and when he peered closer he was sure he could see streaks of amber and black in the mist.

Back in Kensington Gardens, he walked straight past the Peter Pan statue without noticing. Only when he heard the muted splashing of the fountains at the top of the Long Water did he realise that he had gone too far. He turned round and retraced his steps on the landward side of the path, holding his right hand out like a blind man's cane so as not to miss the railings around the statue.

Elkington was already there, together with an assortment of others, Flew and Hare among them.

'Terrible, this fog is, absolutely awful,' Elkington said with relish. 'Coppers are abandoning their Humbers for bicycles or their own two feet. The river police have tied their boats up and are doing their patrols on shore. The smash-and-grab men will be harvesting fast, sir, mark my words.' He could hardly have sounded more thrilled.

For his part, Herbert could have done without Elkington's particular brand of *schadenfreude* this morning. 'Where's the diver?' he asked.

'Right here, sir.' Elkington pointed to a young woman alongside him. Herbert could have sworn he saw a flourish in the gesture; and then he was no longer thinking of Elkington at all, as his entire attention was focused, almost against his will, on the woman.

It was not that she was beautiful – although she was certainly that – more that she seemed so exotic, so incongruous, in this freezing fog-bound city. Her skin was olive beneath hair black as night; Herbert saw almond eyes, a nose the elegant side of aquiline, lips like lightly-plumped pillows. She was short and slender, but something in her carriage suggested a wiry strength. She could have been a Biblical queen, brought early to her throne. She looked to be in her early twenties.

'Detective Inspector Smith, meet Hannah Mortimer,' Elkington said.

Hannah put out her hand for Herbert to shake, and missed his fingers by three inches. Her eyes were staring without focus at a point over his left shoulder.

'It help me if you say something,' she said.

The foreign undercoat to her accent – Eastern European, he thought – could not entirely disguise the hint of insolence in the statement. Elkington stiffened in proxy embarrassment; Herbert stifled an absurd desire to laugh.

'How do you do, Miss Mortimer?' he said.

Her sightless eyes swivelled slightly towards his

face, as though she were a radio astronomer picking up return signals.

'I know what you think,' she said.

'What?' Herbert asked.

'You wonder how blind person can be diver.' He said nothing; it was exactly what he *had* been thinking. 'My answer is very easy,' she continued. 'River and lake beds are filthy dirty; most of the time, you can't see a thing. You want to find things, you must feel for them. So your sense of touch must be accustomed. There are many blind divers, in actuality.'

She invariably emphasised the first syllables of words, Herbert noticed, irrespective of their proper pronunciation – *acc*ustomed, *act*uality, *won*der.

'I'm sure there are,' Herbert said mildly. 'OK. I want you to look for –' he caught himself, and stumbled over the next words – 'I mean . . .'

'You can use words like "look" and "see". I know what they mean. For me, is no bother to hear them.'

Herbert was glad that she could not see the rouge of embarrassment on his cheeks; the flush was too deep to pass off as reaction to the cold.

'So, you want me to find – what?' Hannah asked.

'Anything that might tell me who the man was, or why he was killed.'

Sheathed in a bulky wartime diving suit with heavy boots and a metal helmet, Hannah stepped into the Long Water as easily as a seal would and vanished from sight.

Herbert turned back towards the statue.

Peter Pan stood atop a bronze tree stump which swarmed with fairies, squirrels, mice and rabbits. His right hand was raised, as though hailing a cab; in his left he clutched a set of pan pipes.

Herbert remembered the layout from the previous night. The statue was bounded from behind by an array of flowerbeds and shrubbery, and from in front by the Long Water.

The water was cordoned off by a railing, presumably for the safety of the children who congregated at the statue. Either side of the railing were sections of hedges and small trees. The body had been found beyond these, where the path gave directly on to the water, presumably for launching small boats in the summer.

Random sounds floated past Herbert, distorted and lacerated by the fog. He heard voices, engines, footsteps, though he could tell neither from which direction they came, nor indeed whether they even existed outside of his imagination. Perhaps they were caused by atmospheric interference, like static on a radio set.

Splashings from behind the curtain of mist were for him the only proof of Hannah's existence. Herbert could not see her; twice he almost shouted, asking if she had found anything, before realising she would not hear him from under her huge brass helmet.

Tinker Bell stretched lovingly up from the tree stump towards Peter. A pair of fairies embraced; a sprite chatted with a squirrel which squatted on its haunches with its paws clasped out front.

Herbert called Elkington, Flew and Hare over.

'Right,' he said. 'We're going to search this place top to bottom. I'll take the area round the statue. Flew, you take the grass to the north; Hare, to the south. Elkington, you search the path and shrubbery by the water. Divide your sectors up into grids and do it methodically: up, down, left, right, like you're mowing a lawn.' He looked at them each in turn. 'What are you looking so boot-faced about, Flew? Worried you're going to crease your uniform?'

Other detectives might have thought themselves above crawling around on all fours, but Herbert was happy to get down and dirty with the juniors. He knew that if one wanted something done, nine times out of ten, the best way was to do it oneself.

He started in the immediate vicinity of the statue. Within minutes, the knees of his trousers were dark with dew. When he wiped his face, small strands of grass clung to his cheeks like a beard.

He stamped his feet, wiggled his fingers inside his gloves, and hoped that clenching his teeth would let the oxygen through and keep the sulphur out.

The flowerbeds were next. He picked his way through clumps of winter weeds and felt the heaviness on his shoes as they came up trailing chunks of mud.

He gathered the others together after half an hour; too soon for them to have finished their searches, but Herbert could sense they were flagging, and a break would keep their minds fresh and minimise the chances of them missing anything.

They pooled discoveries: a used condom, a sodden copy of yesterday's *Daily Express* – the best possible use for it, Herbert thought – an empty tin of Spam, and a box of matches.

Elkington had found the majority of items, of course; all of them irrelevant.

Herbert heard a sudden chatterbox of sounds, all from Hannah: snapping her fingers, humming, clicking her tongue, anything to get an echo, be it the sharp, distinctive click of a building or a tree's softer sigh.

He would have thought that smooth, open spaces would be easiest for her, but he saw that in fact they were the most difficult; in a park there were few orientation marks, and hence few ways for her to tell where exactly she was.

Satisfied that she had found the right place, Hannah pulled off her helmet and shook her head.

'Nothing,' she said.

'You've finished?'

'You joke? What it is, I've found nothing *so far*. You ask me to search this water; that's what I do. I have made less than half the job. Go and have a cup of tea, if you want. I come and get you when I find something.'

Hannah's damnation of weakness and self-pity

40

stung Herbert. For the second time in as many hours, he was glad that her blindness prevented her from seeing the flush which rose ashamedly to his face.

Herbert was no stranger to patience. He had spent much of his life waiting, with no guarantee of success and with only his own thoughts for company. This was no different. He watched Hannah clump back to the water.

'Come on,' he said. 'Back to work.'

Five minutes became ten; ten became thirty; thirty became an hour.

Then, suddenly, thrillingly, Herbert saw a patch of undergrowth torn flat, the earth beneath dotted with footprints.

He caught his breath, dropped his shoulders, and took his time.

The footprints were jumbled, their indentations overlapping as they twisted in different directions and pressed down to varying depths. He could make out at least two separate sole designs; there might have been more, but it was impossible to be sure.

Twigs had been snapped and leaves crushed across an area perhaps eight foot by three; large enough, in other words, to have been caused by a prone man, especially one who had been moving, perhaps struggling.

A ring glinted dully in the gloom. Herbert picked it up. Gold, no inscription, entirely ordinary. Not the corpse's – there had been no ring marks on his fingers. It could be something; it could have belonged to the killer. But it was probably nothing; it might have been here for days, weeks, months, years.

Hannah appeared again, and this time she *was* holding something. In the haze, Herbert thought at first that it was a dead animal. Only when she handed it to him did he see that it was a tweed overcoat.

The overcoat whose whereabouts he had pondered at the autopsy? He hoped so.

He turned it over and over, noticing as he did so two things.

Firstly, it was exceptionally heavy. It was water-logged, of course, but even that could not account for the weight. When his hands gripped at uneven lumps inside the pockets, he realised the reason: stones, packed hard to weigh the body down.

Secondly, the coat was torn in several places; specifically, at the collar, the left armpit and cuff, and on the right outside pocket.

'Was the lake bed sharp?' he asked.

Hannah shook her head. 'Not especially.'

Then the rips in the cloth would probably have come from the dead man's struggle with his killer, or from trying to take his coat off to avoid drowning; or both. The Long Water was a lake, so there was no current which could have separated body from coat post-mortem.

If the victim *had* managed to get the coat off, therefore, he would have been at the end of his tether when doing so; too weak to do anything after that except slump back into the cold water, this time for good.

Elkington, Flew and Hare watched as Herbert laid the coat flat on the ground and began to search through it.

There were five pockets – two on the outside flanks, one at the breast, and two inside – and each had been stuffed with stones. He pulled them out and sent them skittering across the path.

No name tag inside the collar. Not surprising. They were not at school any more.

In the right-hand inside pocket, Herbert found something hard and flat. His first thought was that it felt like an identity card, but it could not have been; such cards had been abolished earlier in the year.

When he brought it out, he saw that he had been both right and wrong.

It *was* an identity card, but a university rather than a national one. It was laminated – hence still legible after a night in the water, rather than reduced to pulp – and it announced its holder as a graduate student of King's College, London.

More importantly, it gave Herbert a name: Max Stensness.

'You have something?' Hannah asked.

'We do indeed. A name. Thank you very much.'

She punched the air in delight. 'Is my pleasure. Maybe you come to dinner tonight?'

She ran the two sentences together, as though they were part of the same thought process, and

43

it took a second or two for Herbert to take stock of what she had asked.

'I couldn't possibly,' he said.

Hare made a noise that was part cough and part snicker.

'What else do you do?' Hannah asked.

Flew had covered his mouth with his hand. His shoulders were heaving, and he was making small trumpeting noises into his palm.

Herbert pointed at Hare and Flew. 'You two, take the coat over to Scotland Yard, and get it logged as evidence.'

They scurried away like miscreant pupils from a headmaster's study, openly laughing long before they were out of earshot. Herbert noticed that Elkington had discreetly stepped a few yards away; clearly the man had some redeeming features after all, he thought.

Herbert turned back to Hannah.

'Well, for all you know, I could be going home to my wife and children.'

'Do you?'

'No.'

'Good. Then you can come to mine. Number 14, Frith Street, in Soho. Top bell.'

Herbert toyed briefly – very briefly – with the idea that this was some kind of pass. Not that he would have known one if it had hit him in the face, for it had been so long since he had been intimate with a woman who did not charge for her services. Nor did he think that someone like Hannah would have been in the remotest bit interested. He was twelve or fifteen years her senior, for a start.

It had clearly been a social invitation, therefore, which in itself was as rare as a sexual advance.

Herbert wondered if this was what learning a new language felt like.

'That would be nice.' Was that what one said? It was what he said, at any rate. 'I'd like that.'

'Good,' she said, taking his elbow and giving it a quick squeeze. 'Maybe you give me your name, too.'

'Oh.' He laughed. 'My name is Herbert.'

The fog seemed to be congealing by the hour. It was also becoming appreciably more noxious. By the time he and Elkington reached King's, Herbert's throat felt as though someone had scoured it with bleach. He hawked hard to clear the taste, and found that what came up was laced with black streaks.

If the fog was having that effect on him, Herbert thought with a shudder, imagine what it was doing to his mother's elderly, asthmatic, bronchitic pair of bellows.

King's was nestled between the Strand and the Thames, tucked up next to Somerset House in the lee of Waterloo Bridge. At the main entrance, Herbert and Elkington paused to let a crocodile of schoolchildren past. The boys were wearing shorts, even in this savage cold; long trousers were as infallible a sign of adolescence as a broken voice. A couple of lads clutched *Eagle* comics, the covers screaming paeans for Dan Dare. One of the girls was carrying a copy of *Girl* magazine.

Herbert had heard of neither; the language of children was not his.

There were teachers at either end of the line and in the middle, all very young and looking understandably anxious at being unable to see more than half their charges at once.

Inside the main entrance of King's was a small office, and here they found a porter who was at least as old as God, and quite possibly older. He was huddled next to a two-bar electric fire, reading the *Daily Express*. He was holding the pages so close both to his face and to the fire that at any moment Herbert expected man and journal to go up in flames.

'Terribly sorry, sir,' the porter said, standing up and putting the paper away in one movement, like a schoolboy caught with contraband. 'Didn't see you there.'

Herbert flipped his warrant card. 'Detective Inspector Smith, New Scotland Yard.'

The porter practically snapped to attention.

'And Sergeant Elkington, Hyde Park,' Elkington said.

The porter glanced at him, instantly calculated who fitted where on the food chain, and turned back to Herbert. 'What can I do you for, sir?'

'You can tell me who works in Max Stensness' department.'

'Certainly, sir. Mr Stensness works . . .' The porter held the last word a fraction longer than necessary, watching for Herbert's reaction, waiting to see if he had got his tenses right. When Herbert gave him nothing back, he went uncertainly on: 'He works with Dr Wilkins and Dr Franklin.'

'And where would I find them?'

'You go out of the door here, turn left, first right, second door on the right, down three flights of stairs, take the fourth set of swing doors and follow the signs which say "Biophysics" and "Medical Research Council".'

Herbert nodded his thanks.

He and Elkington left the porter's office and followed the directions, soon finding, with a grim sense of inevitability, that they were lost.

The only people they could see were a pair of men in white coats who, even at ten paces, smelt strongly, and somewhat incongruously, of fish.

Herbert approached them and said, more in hope than expectation, 'I'm looking for Dr Franklin and Dr Wilkins.'

'Sure,' said one of them. 'I'm going that way myself; I'll show you.'

Up close, the smell of fish was all but overpowering. As they walked, the man saw Herbert sniff in surprise, and laughed. 'Oh, don't mind me. Too much cod roe, that's the problem. There's no showers here, so when they overdo the roe, me and Geoff end up stinking like a couple of Billingsgate porters.'

'What on earth do you use the roe for?' Herbert asked.

47

'It's those lot in the lab where you're going; they use it, not me. Something to do with their experiments. They did try to explain it to me once, but they might as well have been talking Greek, for all the sense it made. Sometimes they want roe, sometimes it's meat from Smithfields: calf glands, you know, the ones butchers sell as sweetbreads. We were there this morning – Smithfields. Awful, it is, this fog, there's cattle there for the show and they're dropping like flies. Lovely beasts, too: Red Polls, Galloways, Lincoln Reds, Shorthorns, all so fattened up they can hardly breathe, just like humans can't if they're too porky – no offence, if there are any bloaters in your family. They were giving the animals whisky, you know, to keep their airways open. Whatever works, I s'pose. Poor things.'

He opened a pair of swing doors, and ushered Herbert and Elkington into a small laboratory. It was spotlessly clean; they must have been too far below ground for the fog to have penetrated from outside.

A workbench cluttered with apparatus ran along the two walls to their left. The third wall, across the other side of the room, gave on to an even smaller storeroom. The fourth wall had a tiny window looking on to a light well; not that there was much light today.

A man and a woman, both wearing white laboratory coats which made them look like doctors or cricket umpires – or fish-bearing university technicians, come to think of it – were standing in the middle of the room.

The woman was in her early thirties, and she was not conventionally pretty – her face lacked a certain definition, and she had a pronounced widow's peak – but her figure was trim, and her dark eyes were steadily watchful. The man was perhaps a few years older, with large square glasses perched on a prominent nose and a weak chin which receded apologetically into his neck. They were arguing.

'All I'm saying, Rosie –' the man said, with a tinge of old maid peevishness.

'Rosalind,' she said. *Ros-lind*; two clipped syllables. 'Not Rosie.'

'All I'm saying, *Rosalind*, is that you might consider sharing your research like everyone else.'

'And what *I'm* saying, Maurice,' she snapped back, 'is that there's a convention in science: when you've done a lot of work and got some experimental data, you should have the first chance of interpreting it.'

'Rosalind, I am your superior, and –'

'You are *not* my superior!'

'I'm senior to you.'

'That doesn't make you superior. When it comes to X-rays, in fact, you're a positive *amateur*.'

Maurice mumbled something, took off his glasses as though he did not wish to see too much, and turned half away, evidently fatigued by the very confrontation which seemed to energise Rosalind so.

The fish man turned to Herbert. 'Doctors

Franklin and Wilkins. At each other's throats, as usual.'

He disappeared back into the corridor.

Herbert stepped towards the warring scientists. He introduced first himself and then Elkington, if only to stop the wretched man butting in again. *Rosalind Franklin, Maurice Wilkins. How do you do, nice to meet you, what terrible weather* . . . And an instant, mutual stiffening when Herbert revealed his provenance. Policemen seldom ventured into the bowels of the science department, and their presence was rarely a harbinger of good news.

'I think you'd better sit down,' Herbert said.

Wilkins subsided into the nearest seat, an upright wooden chair which backed on to the workbench. Rosalind tipped her head back slightly, an infinitesimal movement which only someone like Herbert, accustomed to and experienced in watching people, would have noticed.

'I prefer to stand,' she said.

'You know Max Stensness?' Herbert asked.

'I do.' Rosalind's voice seemed a fraction louder than the norm, as though she were taking marriage vows.

Wilkins nodded his assent.

'He was found drowned in the Long Water last night.'

'Dear God,' Wilkins said.

Rosalind's mouth formed a perfect 'O', visible for the split second before she clapped her hand to it.

'Would you excuse me?' she said, and walked quickly from the room.

Herbert looked at Wilkins, who stared blankly back. Rendered speechless by shock, Herbert thought; perhaps, more accurately, by the introduction of disorder into a world where order was all.

Herbert heard a muffled sob from outside, followed by the unmistakable hoot of a nose being blown; then Rosalind was back in the room, eyes slightly reddened but otherwise in control. Herbert had a feeling that he had seen all the emotion she would display today.

'Drowned?' Rosalind said. 'Impossible.'

'Why so?'

'Max hated water, absolutely hated it. He couldn't swim a stroke.'

No wonder Stensness had ripped at his coat, Herbert thought. No wonder, too, that the autopsy had shown such elevated levels of serotonin and histamine. Being in the water would have been torture enough.

'Dead? He can't be,' Wilkins said vaguely.

'Well, he clearly *is*, Maurice,' Rosalind snapped, 'or else the Inspector wouldn't have come here.' She turned to Herbert. 'So how can *we* help you?'

'What was it that Max did here?'

'He's an assistant,' Wilkins said.

'He was *my* assistant,' Rosalind added, to clarify. She had got the tense right first time, Herbert noticed; incredibly rare, when dealing with people who had just been told that someone they knew was dead. He addressed himself to her.

'Which entailed what?'

'Helping *me* with *my* experiments, collating data, collaborating on reports.'

'In what areas?'

'Crystallography, mainly.'

'And what were his qualifications for this?'

'He was a doctoral student. Studied at the University College Medical School.'

'The PhD slave boy handed over in chains,' Wilkins said.

'Were you friends, or colleagues?' Herbert asked.

'Does there have to be a difference?' Rosalind replied.

'There doesn't have to be, but there often is.'

Rosalind pondered this. 'I liked Max, if that's what you mean,' she said at length.

'Did you ever see him outside work?'

'I had him round to dinner a couple of times.'

'And you, Dr Wilkins?'

'No, no – she's never invited me.'

'No; did *you* ever see Max outside work?'

'Oh. No. He works much more with Dr Franklin than with me.'

That distinction, Herbert felt, covered a multitude of divisions between them.

He turned back to Rosalind. 'How much did you know about his private life?'

'Very little.'

'Anything about his romantic life, for instance?'

'There's a reason why private lives are called private, Inspector. I didn't pry.'

'All right. You say you had him round for dinner; did he ever reciprocate?'

'Just last week. He'd moved house a few days before, up to Highgate. A few of us went round as a sort of housewarming.'

'Did he live alone?'

'No. He had two flatmates.'

'Do you know their names?'

'Er . . . Stephen is one, I think. The other . . . Noel? Nick? Something like that.'

'Family?'

'Sir James and Lady Clarissa.'

Herbert stifled a sigh. Knighthoods meant Establishment, and Establishment, more often than not, meant connections, and pressure, and trouble. He turned to Elkington.

'Elkington, go find a copy of *Who's Who*, will you?'

Elkington nodded and hurried off, delighted to be of service. Herbert turned back to Rosalind.

'And when did you last see him?'

'Yesterday afternoon. Around five o'clock.'

'Here?'

'No. At a conference.'

'You, too, Dr Wilkins?'

'Yes, indeed.'

'What was the conference about?'

Rosalind reached down to the workbench,

picked up a pamphlet, and handed it to Herbert. He read the front page.

THE LONDON BIOCHEMICAL CONFERENCE
THURSDAY, 4TH DECEMBER 1952

Held under the joint auspices of the Royal Society
and the International Congress of Biochemistry
(Hon. Chairman: L. C. Pauling)

THE ROYAL FESTIVAL HALL, LONDON S.E.

Herbert remembered the Royal Festival Hall from the previous year's Festival of Britain, with its Skylon and its Dome of Discovery; ostensibly harbingers of a new age of scientific progress, but with rationing higher than it had been during the war and the conflict in Korea at its height, the Festival had felt less like a genuine national celebration than a lollipop jammed in Britain's mouth to keep the grumblers quiet.

Shame the conference hadn't taken place today; the Hall had been the first building in the country to have had air conditioning integrated into its construction, and with that air being washed and filtered however many times an hour, it was probably the only genuinely fog-proof place in London.

'What was he doing when you saw him?'

'Eating.'

'Tea?'

'Leftovers. He said he hadn't had time for lunch.'

'Do you remember what he was eating?'

54

'Shepherd's pie, I think.'

'You're very observant.'

'It's my job to be.'

Five o'clock, Herbert thought. Stensness had been found dead at eight, possibly killed as early as half past six, according to Rathbone's calculations. Whatever he had done in the intervening period, it could not have been much.

The library was not far away, for Elkington was back with *Who's Who* within minutes, his thumb marking the page featuring Sir James Stensness.

Herbert laid the tome flat on a table and skimmed the entry for Stensness Sr.

Sir James's gong had come, like so many, after a lifetime in Whitehall playing dresser to an ever-changing cast of ministers: Private Secretary and Under-Secretary at the Ministry of Education, Deputy Secretary at the Ministry of Works, Permanent Secretary at the Ministry of Supply during the war, and then at the Board of Trade, his last stop before retirement. Educated at Charterhouse and Brasenose; married Clarissa Carter; one son, Maximilian Aloysius; a member of the Travellers' Club; a keen racquets player; and an address in Kensington.

'Is there a phone anywhere?' Herbert asked.

'Down the hall, third office on the left,' Rosalind said.

Herbert beckoned to Elkington, and together they found the office and the phone. Herbert dialled the Yard.

'Murder Squad.' It was Tyce, the senior officer.

'Smith here. I've got the dead man's name: Max Stensness. And listen, I don't know what Tulloch's told you, but Stensness's father is Sir James; quite a senior mandarin, by the look of things.'

'I don't give a stuff if his father's the King of Siam.' If there was ever a serious republican movement in the country, Tyce would be at the vanguard, Herbert thought.

'I could really do with someone else to help me on this.'

'Smith, I haven't suddenly magicked a squadron of detectives into existence. We're as stretched now as we were last night. Get some of the bods from Hyde Park to do your legwork.'

Herbert looked at Elkington. 'That's what I'm doing.'

'Good. Keep me posted.'

Tyce was as curt as Tulloch, but without the latter's vengeful bile. It was not that Tyce actively disliked Herbert; more that he regarded him as being on some sort of eternal probation, where every case was a test not only of his skills but of his character. If he was to impress Tyce enough, Herbert thought, he would be in.

There were several aspects of his job that Herbert found objectionable. Autopsies were fairly vile; most murderers were hardly charm personified; and there was the nagging sense that, however well he did his job, it would never be enough, because he was primarily trying to find culprits of crimes already committed rather than stopping future offences.

As far as Herbert was concerned, however, all these paled into insignificance when set against the one thing he truly hated having to do: breaking the news of a murder to the victim's family.

There was no easy way; the only easy way was not to do it in the first place.

One had to judge pretty much instantaneously the type of people one was dealing with: those who needed soft-soaping and a long lead-in to the dreadful news, or those who appreciated it when one spoke plainly and got straight to the point. Even when one got it right, of course, one still had to deal with the initial blast of shock and anger, as often as not directed straight at the messenger himself.

Herbert could have sent Elkington, of course – if the man really wanted to join the Murder Squad, then this was where his apprenticeship started – but that would have been to shirk his own duty.

So instead he had sent Elkington up to Max's home in Highgate – 43 Cholmeley Crescent – with instructions to secure the place and see if he could find anything which might pertain to the murder. Herbert would join him there when he had finished with Sir James and Lady Clarissa.

They lived in Edwardes Square, in a tall, thin house with a pub on one side and rather pretty communal gardens across the road. As a detective, Herbert was not in uniform, but Sir James knew there was trouble the moment he opened the door; his antennae for danger had doubtless been honed to perfection by years in the corridors of power.

'Yes?' he said, eyebrows curling up on themselves in suspicion.

Herbert introduced himself and asked if he could come in.

Sir James paused for half a beat – Herbert wondered whether he was going to ask him to use the tradesmen's entrance – before taking a pace backwards and allowing Herbert through.

They went straight into the study; no offer of tea, no sign of Lady Clarissa, and no small talk about the fog. A straight talker, Herbert decided.

'I'm afraid your son Max was found dead last night,' Herbert said.

Sir James's head jerked back a fraction, and that was the extent of his shock – the visible extent, at least. He had not been a mandarin for nothing, Herbert thought.

'How?' he asked.

'Drowned. In the Long Water. We're treating it as murder.'

'No one would have wanted to murder Max.'

'You don't know if he had any enemies, undesirable friends, anything like that?'

'Max was a scientist, Inspector, not a criminal.' Sir James tapped his fingers against the desktop. 'He'll have to be buried immediately, of course.'

'Sir James, I can appreciate your anxiety, but

please understand that, while the case remains open, your son – your son's body, I should say – is evidence, and therefore must be treated . . .'

'Listen to me, Inspector. My wife is very ill. She has, at most, a couple of months to live; more likely weeks, perhaps even days. I have to look after her twenty-four hours a day. I am not going to let her go to her grave with her son still in a mortuary. Do you understand?'

Parents should never outlive their children, Herbert thought; it was not in the natural order of things. 'I am doing all I can to find your son's killer, Sir James.'

'That is as maybe, Inspector; but your department are not, are they?'

'I'm sorry?'

'They send me an Inspector.' Sir James rolled the word out of the side of his mouth, as though it were a bad smell. 'A single Inspector; no one higher. I would imagine there are plenty of victims who get better treatment than this. Is my son less important than them?'

All men were equal below the turf, Herbert thought.

'Sir James, if you are unhappy with my assignment, please ring Detective Superintendent Tyce at New Scotland Yard . . .'

'Young man, I will ring the Commissioner himself. Now, if you're going to look for my son's killer, you won't find him in here; so you may go.'

*   *   *

59

The station attendant at High Street Kensington said the next train was five minutes away. Herbert sat on a platform bench and read the conference pamphlet Rosalind had given him.

The speeches and panel discussions were as esoteric to a layman's eyes as he would have expected; science really was a different language, he thought. He flicked through the pages, reading little and understanding less, until he reached the list of delegates at the back.

Each delegate was listed, along with his institution and country. There had been about a hundred people there, representing a healthy selection of nations. British apart, there were Americans, French, Swiss, Canadians, Swedes and Portuguese.

Speakers were marked with an asterisk; there had been six sessions, four of them individual lectures, the other two panel discussions. The topics looked suitably obscure; manna for the scientist, Herbert thought, but anaesthetic for the layman.

He was halfway down the list, skipping through the list of British delegates, when his gaze, attention, and heartbeat skidded to a halt pretty much simultaneously.

De Vere Green, Richard. University of Cambridge.

Herbert knew Richard de Vere Green, and he knew too that he was not affiliated to the University of Cambridge, at least not officially. De Vere Green's institution was altogether closer to home. He had been Herbert's boss at Five.

* * *

Elkington and Highgate could wait; Herbert took the underground back to Green Park. Someone had left a copy of the *Express*, and Herbert flitted idly through the classifieds and the promotional contests – *Win a car! First prize a Humber Super Snipe, worth £1,627. Second prize an MG Midget, £825* – before turning to the gossip column, spiritual home of those whom he envied and despised in equal measure.

Lord Beaverbrook had declared that the gossip column was the most important part of the paper, and had therefore decreed a list of those never to be mentioned favourably. No one knew for sure who was included, but prime suspects included Charlie Chaplin (suspected communist), Noël Coward (queer) and Paul Robeson (a bit of both, not to mention the colour of his skin).

The *Express* was a dreadful paper, which was one of the main reasons Herbert liked it, and its interest lasted precisely the length of an average tube journey, which was recommendation enough for any journal. Today, however, he read the *Express* primarily to avoid thinking about de Vere Green, an exercise which proved predictably futile.

At Five, Herbert had been a Watcher. No, he had been *the* Watcher; the best surveillance operative in the entire service. Being a Watcher was like playing the drums; almost anyone could do it, but very few people could do it well.

In the opinion of all those qualified to make such a judgement, Herbert had been outstanding. His eyesight and hearing were both very good, he

61

was a quick thinker and capable of reacting well to the unexpected, and he was endlessly patient, a master of the gentle art that was doing damn all convincingly.

And he was the nearest thing to an invisible man. He was neither dwarf nor giant, not revoltingly ugly nor sickeningly handsome, midway between beer barrel and string bean. In short, he was the kind of person one would pass in the street without noticing.

Many people were just different enough from the norm – whatever that was – for a stranger to notice them, even for a couple of seconds.

Not Herbert. He was entirely nondescript, exceptional only at being unexceptional.

It was not hard to imagine what *that* could do to a man's psyche.

But back to de Vere Green – and back, too, to Donald Maclean.

May 1951, eighteen months ago. Five had been tailing Maclean for months, looking for fresh evidence of his treachery; they already had enough to hang him several times over, but their proof had been gained from coded messages sent to and from Soviet stations and decrypted under the Venona programme.

To seize Maclean on such evidence would have been to alert Moscow that their ciphers had been cracked, which would have caused more problems than it solved. So the order had gone out: catch him with his fingers in the sweetie jar.

Maclean was followed in London only; the Watchers were called off every night when he boarded his train back home to Tatsfield, on the border between Kent and Surrey. De Vere Green – at that time head of A Branch, under whose auspices surveillance fell – had decreed there was no point in following Maclean further than Charing Cross.

Outside London, Soviet officials' movement was restricted. They were therefore unlikely to venture forth for contacts that could just as easily have been made in town. Besides, Tatsfield was a small village; it would have been virtually impossible to watch Maclean there without attracting attention.

It was de Vere Green's call, and it was, notwithstanding everything that happened later, exactly the right one.

Six foot four, and wearing a shabby tweed coat and crumpled trilby at a time when the fashion was for Anthony Eden homburgs, Maclean was easy to follow. He knew that Five were on to him, too, though he probably thought they should have been embarrassed at having to tail a member of the upper classes. 'I'm in frightful trouble,' he would tell people. 'I'm being followed by the dicks.'

Alcohol made him indiscreet. Herbert once got close enough to him in a pub to hear Maclean say, 'I'm working for Uncle Joe. I'm the English Hiss.'

Friday, 25th May, was Maclean's birthday. That lunchtime, the Home Secretary had signed an order authorising his interrogation, to begin the following Monday. As he arrived at Charing Cross to catch the 5.19, Herbert was immediately struck by the change in Maclean's demeanour. Usually he walked with his shoulders hunched and his hands jammed into his pockets, but that evening he seemed to walk down the platform with a spring in his step. The brim of his hat was up all round and he was wearing a jaunty bow-tie. He seemed in good spirits, for once.

Then Maclean turned and waved, and Herbert knew. *He knew*.

Maclean could not have been sure exactly where his shadows were, but he waved anyway, before leaping easily on to the train. Perhaps he thought he was being stylish, but Herbert thought it arrogant; idiotic, too, in what it revealed.

Herbert went to the nearest phone box, barged an old lady aside without ceremony, and rang de Vere Green, who was off to the country and did not want his weekend disturbed.

'Dear boy,' he said, 'don't be so ridiculous.'

Herbert persisted. Something was up; de Vere Green had to send men down to Tatsfield immediately. Hang the expense and the likelihood of the surveillance being blown.

'You cannot have heard me,' de Vere Green said, steel beneath his tongue as the suave Establishment bonhomie vanished. 'There is nothing to worry about. He'll be back tomorrow morning, fear not.'

Saturday was a half-day in Whitehall. Herbert met Maclean's usual train, and there was no sign of him; nor on the two subsequent services.

Detention at ports and airports needed the Home Secretary's permission, and there was no way to get *that* without going through endless stifling strata of gradism and bureaucracy.

The deputy branch assistant director would pass it up to the assistant branch director, who would hand it on to the branch director, who would take it to the deputy director-general of the entire service, who might or might not give it to the director-general himself, who might mention it to the Home Secretary when they next met over a whisky, but only if he remembered in between praising the beauty of the minister's teenage daughter and discussing prospects for Laker and Lock down at the Oval.

And when a decision *had* been made, it would be passed back down the ranks with the same excruciating slowness, a trickle of water rolling slowly through hanging gardens, and the chance to act would have vanished.

In six years at Five, the most sensible words Herbert had come across had been scrawled in an anonymous appendage to a memorandum: 'This case is of the highest possible importance, and therefore must be handled at the lowest possible level.' It was laughably, sickeningly true.

Anyway, the weekend came and went, with the great and the good doing things that were no doubt both great and good. The panic started on Monday, by which time Burgess and Maclean were halfway to Moscow. They had taken a midnight ferry on

Friday from Southampton to St Malo, where they had met Russian intelligence officers who had given them false papers and a route via Vienna.

During the search of Maclean's office, Herbert found a piece of his doggerel:

> Dared to leave a herd they hate,
> Dared to question church and state.
> Sodden straws on a rising tide,
> They know they've chosen the losing side.

Naturally, there was an inquiry; naturally, it was a farce; and, naturally, there was a fall guy.

No, said de Vere Green, none of the Watchers had contacted him that Friday evening to apprise him of their suspicions.

Yes, of course he would have expected them to; particularly Mr Smith, who had operational command and with whom lay all tactical responsibility. Maclean had *waved*, and still Mr Smith had not thought to tell de Vere Green.

No, he would not have expected it of such a respected professional.

Yes, he agreed; such incompetence was staggering, and must be punished.

Throughout all this, de Vere Green looked straight at Herbert without turning a hair.

It was Herbert's word against his, and de Vere Green was higher up the greasy pole; he had been in the service for thirty years, having joined straight from Oxford; he was One of Them.

Five was no place for a fair hearing. Arguing one's case was seen to imply lack of judgement. 'Because I say so' and 'It's always been done this way' were stonewall discussion-finishers. External overviews were out of the question, for 'security reasons'.

Even as the Empire crumbled, everyone in Five was clinging with sticky fingers to their own little spheres of influence.

But equally, there was a reluctance to dismiss Herbert for fear he would make a nuisance of himself with the press or some such. Besides, Five were never decisive enough to sack anyone; one left only to tend one's garden in retirement or be interred six feet beneath it.

So Herbert was offered a post in Vetting, a new department created on Attlee's express order to prevent further treason. The words 'horse', 'stable door' and 'bolted' sprang pretty much unbidden to mind. At least he was spared the formalities of a leaving party; in Five these tedious affairs were known, with manifest irony, as OBJs – short for O! Be Joyful.

Vetting fell within C Branch, Security. The remit was to examine the backgrounds of all civil servants with 'regular and constant access to the most highly classified defence information' and 'the more highly classified categories of atomic energy information'; but since most Whitehall departments believed that they and only they should meddle in their colleagues' affairs, Vetting's role was relegated more or less to that of applying the rubber stamp.

The process went as follows.

The internal security departments at each ministry would forward completed copies of the standard questionnaires, along with a full curriculum vitae, a declaration of links to extremist organisations both left and right, and two referees.

Vetting would check the Registry files to see what, if anything, Five held on each candidate, and then send a standard letter to the referees – some of whom, it transpired, had not seen their particular applicant for a decade or more.

Then Vetting would conduct a pointlessly anodyne 'interview' with each nominee, pen a laconic *nothing recorded against* on his application, and recommend him for clearance, which he had enjoyed anyway while they had worked through the endless backlog of cases.

Even when Vetting did turn up a bad apple, very little was done about it, particularly if the contender in question had gone to the right school. If a chap was one of us, reasoned de Vere Green and his ilk, why bother to put him through this beastly snooping? They had their special ties and their inscribed cufflinks, and they could do no wrong.

If the intelligence services had been as adept at spotting spies and traitors as they were at discerning who was one of them – and, just as importantly, who was *not* one of them – then this country would have been impenetrable, then and evermore.

But they found it impossible to believe that anyone from the upper classes could be anything other than loyal to the institutions into which they had been born and raised. Besides, no one wanted McCarthyism on this side of the Atlantic.

The sheer futility of it was enough to make a man weep. Not least because all this was taking place after Burgess and Maclean – *because of* Burgess and Maclean, in fact – and if ever two people could prove that breeding meant nothing, it was them. They would both have sailed through the very procedures that their treachery had sparked into existence.

The pair of them seemed destined to cast a long pall, not only over Herbert's life but over that of the country as a whole. Gone was the unquestioning innocence of the pre-war world, where the upper classes had been pre-ordained to lead, unquestioned in their fitness to do so.

Now there prevailed a strange mixture of democratic optimism, Cold War chilliness and tutting prejudice, especially against homosexuals, whose cause Burgess had almost single-handedly set back thirty years. Within months of his defection, prosecutions for sodomy and indecency were running at five times what they had been before the war.

Then, a few months later, the cards of yet another internal reshuffle landed with de Vere Green taking over as head of C Branch. It was hardly ideal, but then again even Herbert could see that Five would have been a one-man band had it allowed itself to take account of every feud under its roof.

If anything, de Vere Green seemed to have got worse in their brief time apart. His talents for politicking and ingratiation had now wholly eclipsed whatever soupçon of administrative efficacy he had once boasted, and he impressed the staff of wherever he worked mainly by his terror when called upon to take a decision.

They lasted a week together. De Vere Green went out of his way to appear pleasant to Herbert, who in turn went even further out of his way to annoy him, all the while trying to pretend that the work they were doing was in any way meaningful.

Finally Herbert did what the faceless powers had no doubt been angling for all along, and resigned. De Vere Green must have seen it as a capitulation, and a shockingly easy one at that; when Herbert broke the news, he actually started, and in doing so inadvertently jabbed the letter-opener into the soft webbing between his left thumb and forefinger.

Herbert watched as a perfect globe of blood appeared on his skin as if fully formed; it was a moment before he realised that the unholy scream of pained terror he could hear was coming from de Vere Green himself.

'Do something,' he gasped between howls. 'Get a cloth, for God's sake.'

Herbert looked again at his hand. The cut seemed a nasty one, though not especially serious; certainly not one which merited his yelling the house down. This was de Vere Green, Herbert reminded himself; one of those Englishmen who probably cared more for his dog than his wife, if indeed he had one.

Several people had already appeared at the door of his office, excitedly aghast. It occurred to Herbert that they might prove good witnesses if de Vere Green tried to claim he had been the one to stab him.

And then Herbert turned on his heel, side-stepped the gathering throng, and walked quickly from the building. He should probably have been ashamed, but he was not. Not in the slightest.

New Scotland Yard could hardly offer him a post quick enough; they were desperate for recruits, and much of his work at Five had been sufficiently akin to their own disciplines – one of the reasons Six looked down so much on Five was that they saw them less as spies than as plodding policemen, country cousins to their urban sophisticates – to allow Herbert to come in at a much higher rank than usual; though, as he had discovered, what the top brass decreed and what those on the shop floor thought of it were two very different things.

At last Herbert was free of Five, free of being a menial man doing a boring job in a humdrum organisation, an outfit of such crashing incompetence that it denied its own existence even while fuelling the fantasies of young men nationwide. He was free of de Vere Green, with his hail-fellow-well-met veneer and his endless capacity for intrigue, for de Vere

Green intrigued at all times, everywhere, in all places, and with everybody.

He was free of it all. And now he was right back in it.

He went via his flat, to make a couple of phone calls in privacy.

The first was to Rosalind Franklin at King's.

He described de Vere Green to her – a whipped cream of whitening hair, a face a shade or two of purple darker than seemed entirely healthy – and she identified him immediately as a man she had seen talking to Stensness during one of the breaks.

Herbert asked her three times, and each time she was adamant. There could not have been that many people who looked like de Vere Green, she said.

And even fewer who would want to, Herbert thought.

The second call was to Tyce.

Herbert didn't want to mention de Vere Green. Tyce knew their history, and Herbert feared that the case would be taken away from him, staff shortage or not. Or, perhaps even worse, he would be retained on the case, but kept in limbo as it became bogged down in endless layers of bureaucracy while the Pooh-Bahs at Leconfield House and New Scotland Yard thrashed things out between themselves.

Tyce was many things, but he was no fool, and he sensed more or less instantly that Herbert was keeping something back. So Herbert told him.

'Stick it to those bastards,' Tyce said. 'Don't let them walk all over you, you hear? You're one of us now, Herbert, so behave like one. Think where your loyalties lie. Good man.'

Well, Herbert thought. Whatever he had been expecting, it hadn't been *that*.

In Tyce's own, roundabout way, it had sounded suspiciously like a vote of confidence.

One lived and learnt.

De Vere Green's reaction to Herbert walking through the door of his office in Leconfield House was entirely predictable; a blizzard of bonhomie.

'Dear boy!' He was rising from his desk before Herbert was more than a pace inside the room. 'What a pleasant surprise! I was just thinking that I needed something to cheer me up in this beastly fog, and blow me if you don't appear like an angel sent from heaven! Not that I imagine too many people refer to the gothic monstrosity where you work as in any way celestial. Sit down, sit down. What brings you to my humble inferno?'

De Vere Green sometimes spoke as though he had swallowed a thesaurus, refusing to use one word where ten would do. Herbert had once heard him say 'individuals with access to conspicuous wealth in their own right' to describe rich people.

De Vere Green's chin had cloned itself during a slight migration south, and his smile fell a fraction short of his eyes.

'Max Stensness was drowned last night,' Herbert said simply, watching him hard.

'Who?'

The man was a pro, Herbert had to give him that. De Vere Green had not flinched; if he had, Herbert had not seen it, and Herbert was trained to see such things.

'Max Stensness. Young man, blond. Worked at King's College.'

'Dear boy, I've never heard of him.'

'That's strange.'

'How so?'

'Because you were seen talking to him yesterday afternoon.' Herbert pulled the pamphlet out of his pocket and dropped it on de Vere Green's desk. 'The London Biochemical Conference, Royal Festival Hall.'

'My dear fellow, how can I have been seen talking to him when I don't know who he is?' His tone was one of perfectly reasonable, mild bewilderment. Despite himself, Herbert began to wonder whether he might be mistaken.

'Son of Sir James Stensness. One of the scions of Whitehall.' De Vere Green shrugged; Herbert pressed on. 'I've just been to see two of his colleagues. They gave me this –' He tapped the pamphlet. 'Your name was on it, on the delegate list. I described you to them. One of them said she'd seen you talking to him.'

'You know scientists, Smith,' de Vere Green said. 'If it's not at the other end of a microscope, they don't know which end is up.'

'I never said they were scientists.'

'Who else are they going to be, at a biochemical conference?'

If it had been a slip, de Vere Green had covered himself expertly. Herbert conceded the point, and switched tack. 'What were *you* doing there anyway?'

De Vere Green tapped his nose. 'You know the drill, Smith.'

'And the affiliation to Cambridge University?'

'Again, ask me no questions, Smith, and I'll tell you no lies.'

'But that's the thing, Richard.' Herbert felt a strange sense of liberation; finally out of the Five hierarchy, with all its connotations of Gentlemen and Players, he could use de Vere Green's Christian name with impunity. 'Max Stensness is dead, so I *have* to ask questions. And if you lie to me, I'll just keep asking them.'

'You can ask all you like, but I'm bound by Acts of Parliament, Smith.' The emphasis was unmistakably on Herbert's surname; the class divide was still alive and kicking, at least as far as de Vere Green was concerned, and the bonhomie had been dialled back a notch. 'As are you, if you recall.'

'You're not immune from the law of the land.'

'Dear boy, that sounds like some kind of threat.'

'Ask Sillitoe. He'll back me up.'

De Vere Green winced slightly, as most of Five's officers did when someone mentioned Sillitoe – Sir Percy of that ilk, a policeman to his bootstraps, now halfway through his sixties and with the genial, bluff face of a kindly grandfather. With his erect bearing, Sillitoe had always reminded Herbert of Wavell, the soldier who had been the penultimate Viceroy of India; an altogether too simple, too straight, too decent soul to prosper in the muddy waters where the intriguers hunted.

As Five's Director-General, Sir Percy was, in contrast to the majority of his peers, busy trying to reduce the organisation's powers rather than augment them, for fear that Britain would become a police state. Five's officers could not make arrests, nor did they have the expertise to gather evidence that would stand up in court.

The Metropolitan Police could, and did, respectively.

'How can we act legally when our work so often involves transgressions against propriety or the law itself?' de Vere Green asked.

'Propriety and the law being mutually exclusive?' De Vere Green made a gesture: *Don't be naïve, Smith, we're men of the world*. Herbert continued. 'Richard, we can go round and round, but the fact remains: I have a dead man, and you were seen talking to him a couple of hours before he died.'

'Your witness must have been mistaken.'

'You're quite distinctive, you know.'

'And I tell you, she was mistaken. Whose word do you trust?'

'Do you really want to know the answer to that?'

De Vere Green flashed Herbert a look of shamed

malevolence; he could witter all he liked about the greater good of the service and the public interest, but he was nowhere near stupid enough not to see Herbert's grievance and the reasons for it.

'She'll come and do a physical ID, if need be. And since you wouldn't allow her in here, we'd have to do it down at the Yard. Lots of people down at the Yard, Richard.'

This was the crux, and they both knew it full well; despite his flamboyance and bluster, de Vere Green was, like all spooks, part of a vampiric breed that shunned the light and thrived in the shadows.

If he had to stand and fight, then he would want to do so on his own terrain; and that meant giving Herbert something, a morsel even, to keep the policeman in the spy's cave.

As far as Five was concerned, the darker the better, as though they were bats.

'Max Stensness was one of my informers,' de Vere Green sighed.

There were three levels of files within Five.

The lowest, Nominal Indices, were open to all officers.

Y Box, next up the scale, were Top Secret, requiring special clearance.

The most sensitive, Held Files, were not kept in Registry at all.

De Vere Green was gone ten minutes, and returned with Stensness' file; a Nominal Index, he

a sliver of disdain, implying that
had been small beer.

rt opened the file.

Stensness, born Kensington, 17th November
Parents, Sir James and Lady Clarissa. Graduate
student at King's College, London, working in the
field of crystallography. Marital status: single. Address:
14 Cadiz Street, Walworth, London S.E.

Walworth was hardly one of London's more
salubrious areas. That was often the way with
Establishment children, Herbert thought; they either
conformed completely, or rebelled completely.

Herbert opened his mouth to put de Vere Green
straight – Rosalind Franklin had given him the
address in Highgate where she'd attended
Stensness's housewarming only a week before –
and then thought better of it. Two could play at
withholding information.

Member of the Communist Party of Great Britain.

Herbert sat up straight, and read on.

Stensness, along with fifty thousand other card-
carrying Reds, had been exposed as a member of
the CPGB by Operation Party Piece, one of Five's
more notable successes. A few months earlier, a
team of enterprising operatives had broken into the
CPGB headquarters in Covent Garden over a
weekend and photographed the entire membership
list, which included thirty Labour MPs. Also
included in the haul had been a statue of Lenin –
there were hundreds, the operatives said, so one
would never be missed – and an intriguing lump

of metal which, following intense and prolonged examination, had turned out to be a toilet ballcock.

The dossier contained a photograph of Stensness participating in a rally and waving a banner quoting Lenin: *The state is the instrument by which the economically dominant group in society exercises power*.

As far as snappy slogans went, Herbert thought that Gillette could have taught Lenin a thing or two, but anyway.

He looked up from the file and at de Vere Green. 'If Stensness was a party member, why was he informing for you?' he asked.

'It's all there, if you keep going. He went to the Soviet Union this past summer, some kind of cultural shindig, you know the type.'

'What did his father think of that?'

'As little as possible, I should imagine. Anyway. While he was there, he saw the kind of beastly place that the "workers' paradise" –' de Vere Green's fingers described quotation marks in the air – 'really is. Came back a changed man. Offered to inform. Decent of him, I thought.'

'Decent' was not the word Herbert would have used, but he knew that there were only two sides in espionage: us and them.

'How did Stensness know where to find you?' he asked.

'We have other men in place within the Party, of course. There are channels through which such information can be passed. He came to me that way.'

'What kind of information was he giving you?'

'Again, it's all in there. Party activities. New members. That kind of stuff.'

Reports in de Vere Green's fluid handwriting were attached in loose leaf. Herbert flicked through them. Rumours of a strike here and a demonstration there; a trade delegation looking for Moscow's approval; a clandestine diatribe against the atom bomb. It all seemed pretty standard stuff.

Too standard, in fact, to be dealt with by someone of de Vere Green's seniority.

'I like to keep my hand in, dear boy,' de Vere Green said in answer to Herbert's unasked question. 'It's something I press for at every departmental meeting, in fact; almost every officer should maintain some contact with the grass roots.'

The only time de Vere Green came into contact with grass roots, Herbert thought, was when he bent down to examine the carcass of a pheasant he had just blasted from the sky.

Not to mention, of course, that the very qualities that had made Herbert a good follower – specifically, his invisibility – would have mitigated in every way against de Vere Green being a successful field agent. The Great Wall of China was less noticeable than he was.

Unless – and this was in no way beyond Five – they let de Vere Green operate on the grounds that, since no one in their right mind could possibly believe de Vere Green a spy, that was conversely the best cover of all.

'How many other informers do you handle?' Herbert asked.

'Three.'

'Can I see their files?'

'No.'

'Why not?'

'Because they're not relevant to this case.'

'I think you should let me be the judge of that.'

De Vere Green shook his head. 'Dear boy, you should just concentrate on solving your own mystery, not anyone else's.'

Herbert felt the muscles in his cheeks tighten, as though he was using them to crack nuts. De Vere Green's jaunty condescension could still bring his blood to the boil at double speed.

Herbert exhaled through his nose and, with some effort, kept his voice calm. 'How often did you and Stensness meet?'

'That depended on how much material he had for me.'

'On average?'

De Vere Green made a *moue*. 'Once a month. Once every three weeks, perhaps.'

'Where did you meet?'

'You remember your tradecraft, Smith.'

The usual places for agent and handler to cross paths, in other words: parks, darkened alleys, the far corners of pubs, anywhere where they could cloak themselves in furtiveness.

'Did you ever go to his house?'

'Don't be absurd.'

81

'You weren't friends, then?'

'Friends?' De Vere Green gave the word a yard of clean air. 'Lordy, no.'

And there it was; take a man's information, and despise him for it.

'You never met any of his friends?'

'Dear boy, these weren't social occasions.'

'His private life?'

'Was private, I presume.'

There was no mention of Stensness's sexuality anywhere in his file.

On one level, this was odd. Post-Burgess, Five considered homosexuality the very worst of the seven character defects, the others being profligacy, alcoholism, drug-taking, unreliability, dishonesty and promiscuity.

Red and pink, Herbert had been told during his Vetting days, red and pink; it was a short step from one to the other. Sodomy equalled heresy, and heresy equalled treachery; whether you were a commie or a bugger, or both, you had chosen to set yourself above society's clear and unmistakable judgement, and if you could do that, you could do anything. You had lost all mental control. You might love the enemy.

But equally Herbert knew another golden rule of Five: if ever a situation could be explained either by conspiracy or cock-up, the latter invariably won the day. Five's image as the acme of domestic espionage services would have been laughable had it not been so tragically wide of the mark. Behind the masks of powerful, heroic crusaders were phalanxes of bumbling loafers.

Five was a place where everyone seemed to smell of failure. The shadow of the war still hung heavily over Britain, and nowhere more so than Leconfield House. During the war, most fit and dynamic young men had opted to join the fighting services, forcing Five to recruit – how to put this charitably? – more idiosyncratic characters from the law and the theatre, from Fleet Street and Oxbridge.

The good ones were merely dim and dreary, or harmless eccentrics; the bad ones were venal and pernicious. Nepotism was not so much an unspoken principle as official policy. It was widely said in Leconfield House that the answer to the question 'How many people work in Five?' was 'About half.'

Run a security service? Herbert thought. This lot couldn't even run a bath.

That Five had not uncovered Stensness's homosexuality was therefore no surprise.

'What were you talking to Stensness about at the conference yesterday?' he said.

'I asked him if he had anything new for me,' de Vere Green replied. 'He said he hadn't, but there was a party meeting coming up so he'd get back to me in the next week or so.'

'Did you know you were going to see him at the conference?'

'Not at all.'

'So what you were talking about was nothing to do with the conference?'

'Correct.'

'Was it a shock?'

'Was what a shock?'

'To see him there.'

'Nothing in this business is a shock, dear boy.'

The fog crawled past. It was a grey, obscene animal, a deep-sea predator, drifting with the minutest slowness, draping itself round Leconfield House's gun ports which had been installed during the war in anticipation of Nazi parachutists landing in Hyde Park and marauding down Curzon Street. Rumour had it that they were still manned on Sundays in case a mob from Speaker's Corner decided to go on the rampage.

The occasional passer-by loomed suddenly out of the gloom, was dimly visible for a few moments and then melted once more back into the murk. The world seemed to have shrunk to a circle barely a cricket pitch's length in diameter; beyond that small clearing of clarity, armies could have been massing without Herbert's knowledge.

Herbert stopped by his flat, found Cholmeley Crescent – the street on which Stensness had lived – in an *A to Z* map of London, memorised the names and layout of every street within a half-mile radius, and set out for the tube again, this time with a copy of *The Times*. In the time it would take him to get up to Highgate, he could do nine-tenths of the crossword.

He took the Piccadilly Line to Leicester Square.

A sequence of letters (5,4); C-H-A-I-N M-A-I-L.

Not quite enough room for a Yankee in the colony (5); K-E-N-Y-A.

At Leicester Square, he changed for the Northern Line.

Turned over French bed in a French town (7). A French bed: *lit*, and backwards – 'turned over' – made *til*. That left a four-letter French town into which 'til' would fit.

Herbert flicked through the names of French towns in his head. Paris, Marseilles, Avignon, Bordeaux, Lille . . . All more than four letters.

Lyon fit, but he could find no way in which 'til' could be inserted to make a word.

Then came Lens, and he had it: L-E-N-T-I-L-S.

Cycling coppers; the first four times as good as the second (5,8); P-E-N-N-Y F-A-R-T-H-I-N-G.

A day for football in Yorkshire (9); W-E-D-N-E-S-D-A-Y.

Herbert was not so absorbed in the crossword that he did not observe his fellow passengers from time to time; and so it was, somewhere between Euston and Camden Town, that he realised he was being followed.

There were three of them, all men, dressed in blacks, greys, dark blues and browns; the usual urban camouflage of Fifties man, but to Herbert's eye, in this particular place and at this particular time, colours that were determinedly – perhaps too determinedly – neutral. Two of them were sitting on the opposite side of the carriage from him, at an angle of ten and two o'clock respectively; the third was on his side of the aisle, about four seats along.

It was this configuration that had given them away, for they had used the exact same one on the journey from Green Park to Leicester Square. Plenty of people had changed trains with him, but for the same three people to take up the same three positions in the same carriage as him on both occasions was beyond coincidence.

He wondered where they were from. An espionage service was the most obvious possibility; Five, of course, given Stensness's role, though the dead man's political leanings meant that the MGB, Soviet foreign intelligence, could not be ruled out either. Or perhaps the followers were strictly criminal elements, come to protect a part of Stensness's business about which Herbert as yet knew nothing. He wondered whether Elkington had found something at the destination, or whether old man Stensness was somehow involved. Though, if he was, it would not have been directly, assuming he had been telling the truth about looking after Lady Clarissa twenty-four hours a day.

Questions, Herbert thought; questions.

Of one thing, however, Herbert was certain: these were amateurs. Professionals would never have let themselves get burnt like that, especially so early in the surveillance; they could only have picked him up this morning because it would have been impossible to tail anyone in the fog last night.

At least they did not seem to be togged out in pantomime get-ups such as false beards, which were not only more trouble than they were worth but also tended to be easily detectable under the intense lights of a train or restaurant.

At Highgate station, Herbert tore off *The Times* crossword, put it in his pocket, and disembarked as planned. He was relying for orientation on what he had memorised from the *A to Z*, and wanted to stick with what he could remember.

The three men followed him off the train, all but signalling to each other as they moved. Whichever outfit they represented needed to buck up either their training or the quality of their recruits, and fast.

God Almighty, Herbert thought; he was beginning to sound like de Vere Green.

The cleanness of the air took Herbert by surprise. All of a sudden, it was a perfect winter's day, cold and crisp. He gulped down lungfuls which felt impossibly pure after the filth of the smog.

It was the height that was making the difference, rather than the distance from central London; visibility was no better at Kew than at Kingsway, after all. Highgate was several hundred feet above the river, and the fog was low-lying. The residents here, and round Parliament and Shooters Hills too, must have wondered what all the fuss was about.

Herbert's route took him down Archway Road, past a smattering of shops and cafés, and then right down Cholmeley Park, into a labyrinth of comfortable suburbia. He stayed on the left side of Archway Road until it was time to cross; not at the pedestrian beacons, which might have forewarned the trackers, and not until there was traffic approaching, which gave him a reason to take a long look both ways, and in doing so to size up what was happening behind him.

A Hillman Minx and a Vauxhall Wyvern closed on him, and on each other, at slow speed. He looked up the hill, down the hill and up again, giving himself enough time to see that his three escorts had arranged themselves in the classic pattern for foot surveillance – 'going foxtrot' as the trade term had it.

The first man was about twenty yards behind him, and would be designated 'A' for Adjacent. Herbert mentally christened him Alf.

A further twenty yards behind Alf was 'B', Back-up, whom Herbert called Bob.

On the other side of the street, more or less level with Alf, was the third, 'C' for Control – Charlie.

It was the work of a few seconds for Herbert to fix their respective statures and gaits in his mind; their faces he had memorised on the train. Bob was the tallest and Charlie the shortest; Alf looked like he might be the most athletic.

Herbert wondered whether their brief was simply to keep an eye on him, or to do him active harm. He supposed he would find out one way or the other before too long.

When the Minx and Wyvern had passed each other, Herbert crossed the road.

He took a quick look back up the hill just before he reached the other side, and tried very hard not to laugh. In a devotion to the rules that was positively slavish, Bob had come across with him. Charlie was now the one directly behind him – the 'eyeball' – with Bob still back-up and Alf acting as control.

Once he had put in a few more turns, Herbert thought, it would be like the old parlour game where a magician put a pea under one of three upturned cups and moved them round and round until the audience could no longer tell which was which.

Herbert turned into Cholmeley Park, and the order changed again. Charlie kept going across the entrance to Cholmeley Park, turning only when he was on the other side of the road from Herbert – in essence, regaining the control position. Bob quickened his pace and fell in behind Herbert as the new eyeball; while Alf, crossing from the far side of Archway Road, took up position behind Bob as back-up.

There was little either to commend or condemn any of the houses in the neighbourhood. They were all of a good size, relatively new – Twenties or Thirties, most of them, at a guess – and architecturally inoffensive. *The kind of place a bank manager would live*, Herbert thought, sounding like his mother.

His mother; he had to go and see her this afternoon. That in turn reminded him: it was his birthday. Thirty-five today – halfway to his Biblical allotment of three score and ten – and he had chosen to mark the occasion by wandering round Highgate with a trio of goons in tow.

It certainly ranked as an unusual way to celebrate.

Cholmeley Crescent was on the right-hand side of the road. As its name suggested, it looped back on itself, so if the next turning was the entrance, the one after that was the exit, and vice versa if one was coming from the other direction.

Would they know that Elkington was already here?

If they did, Herbert thought, there was nothing he could do about it. If not, there was no point in making it easy for them. Either way, he could not go directly to Stensness's house, that was evident; he had to lose his tail first.

So he kept on walking, though not without a quick, innocent look at the crescent as he went past. Most people glanced down side streets while they walked; keeping his gaze fixed straight ahead would have been as much of a giveaway as marching right up to the door of number 43.

Suddenly Herbert knew where he could lose the goons; he knew, too, a place which would offer a perfectly reasonable explanation for his having come up here at all.

Cholmeley Park turned into a small slope, the sizes of the houses increasing with the gradient. At the top, Herbert emerged on to the main drag of Highgate Hill, and stopped dead, all thought of evasion temporarily gone.

There before him was the city shrouded in mist, as though it were Avalon, an impossibly beautiful vista of soft clouds through which the odd rooftop poked like a periscope.

There was no telling, at this distance, that those tender billows reeked with clammy poison. From where he stood, the slanting rays of the sun gave the fog a coppery, rather handsome, appearance. It was only nearer at hand that it would appear yellow and ugly, a vast and unappetising sea of chicken soup.

Herbert stared in wonderment at the view for a few moments, then remembered that he had men on his tail. He turned left down Highgate Hill, almost immediately right on to Dartmouth Park Hill, and then right again into Waterlow Park.

London had more parks than virtually any other city in the world, and Herbert had always loved them – they were the city's lungs, and it had never needed to breathe more than it did now. By the standards of the great spaces in the middle of town, Waterlow was nothing special, but after almost twenty-four hours wading through fog, even the bare branches of winter trees seemed impossibly and refreshingly rustic.

Herbert stepped off the path and walked on the grass, for no other reason than that, unlike in Hyde Park, he could do so without getting hopelessly lost. He had never thought himself capable of rediscovering such childlike joy in nature.

He walked past a rubbish bin, counted five strides, and turned on his heel without warning, fishing the crossword out of his pocket as he headed back to the bin.

When one was performing surveillance, there were two things to avoid at all costs, and the first of these was sudden movement. Even when one's target did the unexpected, as Herbert had just done, one should keep behaving normally; better to lose sight of him for a moment than risk blowing the entire operation. Eyeball and, if necessary, back-up, should keep going past the subject, leaving control to keep watch while the other two rejoined the surveillance when they could.

The three comedians assigned to Herbert could hardly have behaved less normally if they had tried. They stopped dead and looked anywhere but at him: at each other, up to the sky, around the park, as if they were out for a nature walk.

It was said that ninja assassins were trained not to look at their targets, even if they found themselves directly behind them, for fear that some deep-rooted sixth sense would warn the subject that he was being watched. This, however, was ridiculous. Herbert was tempted to stop where he was; perhaps, had he done so, all four of them could have remained in petrified tableau for ever.

Instead, he put the crossword in the bin, turned

back round, and continued on his original course across Waterlow Park.

Behind him, he fancied he heard a communal sigh of relief.

In a strange way, their ineptitude was beginning to unnerve him. Professionals knew what they were doing, so there was less chance of things going wrong. Amateurs were unpredictable. If this lot could bungle the relatively simple task of keeping tabs on him without his noticing, he wondered what else they could mess up.

If, for instance, they had been ordered to bring him in unharmed, he would have put precious little money on the second part of that command necessarily following the first.

Herbert led them all the way through Waterlow Park, left out of the gate on to Swains Lane, and then immediately left again, into the eastern part of Highgate Cemetery. He took the main footway, tombstones dotting the pathside like signposts: Baird, Pocklington, Dalziel, Bruce, Hardman.

At the giant bust of Marx, near the north-eastern corner, the usual delegations of communist worshippers were paying homage. There would be a Watcher or two nearby, no doubt, taking pictures for the files back at Leconfield House; Herbert had done so himself on several occasions. That this was a largely pointless exercise had, naturally, seldom been an impediment to its implementation.

There was a brief moment, when he had walked past the flock of Marxist homage-payers but his trackers had still to get through, that Herbert was out of their sight. It was then that he moved.

Stepping quickly off the main path and on to one of the small, muddy passages which led to and between the serried ranks of gravestones, he dropped to a crouch, then to all fours, and scurried through the undergrowth, turning right and then left.

The vegetation around the less notable tombstones had been left to grow almost to waist height. Silently praising whoever was responsible for such neglect, Herbert crawled across graves, offering whispered apologies for any disrespect he was showing the dead, and eventually stopped in a particularly dense clump of bushes, invisible to anyone more than a couple of yards away.

Adjusting his position slowly, he found that he could see back to the main path.

Charlie was standing there, looking around frantically, his hands spread in bewildered supplication. Of Alf or Bob, no sign. Searching elsewhere, presumably.

Herbert caught his breath and considered his options.

The cemetery was not especially large, and there were not that many hiding places. More importantly, there was only the one entrance, which meant one exit.

If he stayed where he was, therefore, it would simply be a matter of time before they found him. Having given them the slip, it was better to keep moving, and press home the advantage that way.

He was on the far side of the cemetery, away from the main gate. They might not have put someone back at the entrance yet, but they soon would. Even these three could not be *that* incompetent.

Herbert stood up cautiously, brushing leaves and patches of mud from his clothes, and stepped smoothly but quickly through the tombstones until he found another wide gravelled path. This, he rapidly surmised, was the trail that led back to the entrance.

A group of six people were strolling a few yards ahead of him. He tagged himself unobtrusively on to one end. Ambling at such a slow pace was against all his instincts, but he reasoned that his pursuers were less likely to spot him in even a small crowd.

More tombstones, inscriptions to those who had died midway between fame and anonymity: Thomas, Barratt, Harrison, Wolf, Thornton, Shaw, Colnagi, Critchett.

Herbert was ten yards away from the main gate when he saw the goons, though of course he did not allow his disappointment to make him break stride. Someone in this whole farrago had to behave like a professional, after all.

Charlie and Alf were either side of the entrance – Charlie had moved fast for one with such short legs, Herbert thought – and Bob was approaching at speed from the path Herbert had originally taken, the one which led to Marx. Herbert had clearly underestimated them; or perhaps, by the simple law of averages, they were bound to have got some-thing right sooner or later.

Ten yards, and closing. Herbert had to make up his mind fast.

He realised suddenly that they might not be aware he was on to them. He had not behaved abnormally in any way; he had not even given a sign that he had registered their presence, benign or otherwise.

Herbert pictured himself as a tourist, come to visit the graves, as hundreds did every week; a man going about his business, with nothing to hide and nothing to justify another's suspicion. What would such a man do in this situation?

He walked right past them, across the road, and into the cemetery's western part.

Herbert felt as though he had entered another world.

Where the eastern portion of the cemetery had been relatively bright and airy, the western half was a fairytale forest, as dark and impenetrable in its own way as the fog which shrouded the city down the hill.

He moved down lines of oaks and hazels, sweet chestnuts and field maples, their bare branches bending to each other like lovers overhead.

Losing the trackers in here would be child's play.

Herbert took his time, pausing to admire the masonry on the graves. Men's tombs were adorned with symbols of their professions: whips and horse-shoes for mail-coach riders, painters with palettes, a general edged with miniature cannons. Columns were left broken when a life had been cut short; grieving women clutched wreaths or wrapped themselves round urns, all frozen forever in moments of stone.

He turned a corner and saw Egyptian Avenue, its entrance flanked by obelisks and columns of lotus flowers, and its roofed corridor leading through to the ring of vaults over which a vast Lebanese cedar towered. Even though the day was clear, the corridor was dank; as he walked through, water fell in steady, bulbous drops from a crack in the ceiling. He fancied the unsettling conditions as the result of an unquiet soul, brooding malevolently in one of the burial chambers that ran down either side.

He was nearly at the far end when he noticed that one of the iron doors to these chambers was open, though a ladder propped against the wall outside mitigated against supernatural explanation; even burial chambers required maintenance.

Before Herbert could consider what might be lurking inside – inside his imagination, if not inside the chamber – he had stepped through the door and flattened himself against the wall, out of sight from the corridor.

There was little enough light in here, but even so he kept his eyes shut. Too long in a room with only coffins for company could have sent the sanest man unstable, and he had in some ways less far to go than most.

Voices penetrated from outside, and it was pretty

clear that they belonged to his chasers. He had never heard any of them speak, of course, but what they were saying left little doubt as to their identity.

'He must have gone through there,' said one, in an accent tinged with Suffolk vowels.

'He could have gone right at the last junction.' A Geordie, this one. 'What's to have stopped him?'

'It's a circle up ahead.' The first man again. 'I'll go left, you go right. If he's there, we'll pincer him. Terry, you go back the way we came and follow the path up and round. There's a mausoleum at the top, I think. We'll meet you there.'

Any pretensions they might have had towards remaining unnoticed or keeping a recognised formation had well and truly vanished. They sounded rattled; presumably they would be in substantial strife if they lost him. To have done so once was bad enough, though at least they had rectified that. Herbert did not envy them the dressing-down they would receive when they returned empty-handed.

Their footsteps squelched slightly on the damp surface. Herbert counted backwards from sixty, making sure to separate each number with the word 'thousand' so he did not hurry the last twenty and break cover too soon.

When the minute was up, he stepped out of the chamber.

No one was around, which was just as well; anyone who had seen him might have run shrieking to the gatehouse to report that one of the dead had suddenly risen.

He walked back down Egyptian Avenue, checking that none of his pursuers were visible, and then continued with purpose but without haste back to the main entrance.

This time, there was no one waiting for him.

He turned left on to Swains Lane, zigzagged through the back streets until he was sure they had not somehow got on his tail again, and arrived at Cholmeley Crescent.

Number 43 was on the apex of the bend, pretty much equidistant from both entrances into Cholmeley Park. It was a two-storey semi-detached house, with a yellow front door on the left-hand side and bay windows on the right, on both ground and first floors.

It was an entirely unremarkable building. Herbert wondered how many similar façades across the city also hid dark secrets.

Herbert walked up to the door and rang the bell.

He waited several seconds, expecting to see Elkington's face appear at the window, or at least to hear him moving around inside; but there was nothing.

With intrigue blending subtly into alarm, Herbert rang the bell again; and again no answer came.

He walked away from the house, all the way down the road and out of sight, for the benefit of whoever may have been watching from inside.

He counted ten interminable minutes on his watch, and retraced his steps to the house.

Splaying the fingers of his right hand, he pressed lightly on the area round the lock. It gave slightly; on the latch, he surmised, rather than deadlocked.

He took a small steel card from his pocket, inserted it into the gap between door and jamb, and wiggled gently until it found the lock's tongue and pushed it back.

Ah yes; this was one of the many things they had been taught at Leconfield House. The trade referred to it as 'covert search'; most people would have called it 'breaking and entering', which was basically what it was. Five had long been bugging and burgling their way across London, while pompous bowler-hatted civil servants in Whitehall pretended to look the other way.

As far as Five was concerned, there was only one commandment – the eleventh: 'Thou shalt not get caught.' Some wag had once suggested amending the service motto from *regnum defendere*, 'defending the realm', to *rectum defendere*, 'cover your backside'.

They had all laughed uncomfortably, because it had rung very, very true.

Herbert was a police officer now, defender and enforcer of the law in a way he had never been at Five; but old habits died hard.

Herbert opened the door with painstaking slowness, waiting for a creak, but the hinges seemed well oiled, and he was inside without a sound. He examined the lock as he stepped through the now open door, and saw that it had not been forced.

He stood still for a few moments, listening for any noise.

Silence.

There was a kitchen straight ahead and a living-room to his right, which looked out on to the street through the lower of the two bay windows. He saw a couple of slightly threadbare sofas, a writing bureau, books crammed with hunched shoulders on to whitened shelves; and Elkington lying on the floor, his wrists bound behind his back with a necktie, his ankles strapped together with a belt, and a tea towel stuffed in his mouth.

When Herbert went closer, he smelt chloroform; but Elkington was moving, so the dose could not have been lethal.

Herbert squatted down by Elkington's face. Elkington looked at him with wide eyes, and then glanced up towards the ceiling.

One? Herbert mouthed.

Elkington nodded.

One attacker was upstairs. Herbert put his finger to his lips, to signal that Elkington should be quiet when Herbert untied him.

Elkington nodded again.

Herbert wriggled the makeshift gag free, allowing Elkington to gulp down lungfuls of breath. Then Herbert undid the tie round the wrists and the belt round the ankles, and helped Elkington to a sitting position.

'Rub them, get the circulation back,' Herbert whispered.

Elkington was all for getting to his feet and rushing upstairs, but Herbert stayed him; better to wait a few minutes and get his limbs working again.

The bottle of chloroform was on a table nearby.

'How do you feel?' Herbert asked.

'Pretty woozy.'

'How many times has he applied the chloroform?'

'Three or four; I can't remember.'

'Was he here when you arrived?'

'Must have been. Caught me clean by surprise.'

And that was a couple of hours ago, Herbert thought.

He looked around the room, and remembered what Rosalind had said about Stensness having housemates; it was hard to imagine the same person reading Thackeray, Wisden *and* raunchy Victorian threepenny pamphlets, though all appeared cheek-by-jowl in the bookcases, and the selection of prints on the walls – imitation Stubbses through *Punch* cartoons to luridly kitsch tigers prowling stylised jungles – also seemed extravagantly catholic.

Elkington pushed himself a trifle unsteadily to his feet. Herbert raised his eyebrows, and Elkington nodded; yes, he was all right.

They went upstairs, slow and silent, Herbert in the lead.

There were four doors on the first floor: one

straight ahead of them as he stood on the landing, two to their right, and one directly behind.

Herbert tried the one straight ahead first. It was spare to the point of spartan; a single bed, a wooden chair, and a tatty chest-of-drawers, on which was a copy of the *Evening News*. He recognised the headline as yesterday's.

Stensness had been dead since last night, and would hardly have had time to come back here between leaving the Festival Hall and going to the Long Water.

This was therefore not his room.

Next along was the bathroom, which would have benefited greatly from the services of a cleaner, and the room along from that belonged to Stensness, which Herbert surmised from several facts, all occurring to him more or less at once.

Firstly, the place looked like a bomb had gone off. Drawers had been overturned, the clothes inside spilling out as though from a burst suitcase. The mattress had been upended against the wall, down which it was now slowly sagging, kinked in the middle as if it were bowing to him. Oblongs of white on yellowing plaster blinked shyly, denuded of the pictures that had covered them.

Secondly, the person responsible for all this, and presumably for the attack on Elkington, was still in the room. He had his back to Herbert, but his head was turned slightly as he rummaged through a pile of papers, so half his face was visible – enough, at any rate, to see that he had a moustache.

Thirdly, he had not noticed Herbert yet.

By law, let alone anything else, Herbert should have identified himself as a police officer before proceeding, but to have done so would have cost him his chief advantage in this situation, which was the element of surprise.

Violence went against most instincts which Herbert possessed, but he knew it was the only way. He took a quick step forward and launched himself at the man's back.

The man must have sensed Herbert at that point, for at last he began to turn, but Herbert was already on top of him.

He knocked the man forward on to the bed. With the mattress gone, the man hit the solid base with enough force to smack the wind from his lungs. Herbert half rolled over the top of him, catching the man's head with his knee. The man lashed out with his right fist as Herbert went past.

The man had a decidedly un-English cast to his features. His face was doughy, like a soufflé improperly risen; the edges seemed slightly blurred, undefined. His moustache squatted beneath a nose pockmarked with archipelagos of burst blood vessels; his eyes were hooded, his forehead was extravagantly creased, and his dark hair was arranged into one of the most atrocious comb-overs Herbert had ever seen.

Still gasping for air, the man hit out at Herbert again.

Herbert grabbed one of the man's great slab-like

ears and cracked his head down on to the bed base. When he squirmed from Herbert's grasp, Herbert took hold of his jacket by the collar and pulled it sharply upwards, over his head. This brought the man's arms upwards too, which Herbert had hoped would disable him further, but in fact it was in this state that the man landed his first serious punch, a flailing roundhouse which caught Herbert halfway between neck and jaw.

Elkington now joined the fray; but the chloroform had clearly affected him more than he had thought, or at least more than he had wanted Herbert to think. The man caught Elkington across the temple with a kick as the young policeman came across the room with head lowered, and Elkington's legs crumpled beneath him as he sank to the floor.

Herbert clung on to his opponent's jacket, more through stubbornness than any great tactical imperative. It came so far over the man's head that he clearly reckoned divestment to be the best option.

With an ungainly wiggle of his shoulders, the man freed his arms, leaving Herbert clasping the jacket against his aching mandible like a security blanket.

The man muttered something Herbert could hardly hear, let alone understand. But it gave Herbert an idea. Attacked by a complete stranger, the man had not once cried for help, which suggested he was operating alone. If he could be tricked into thinking that Herbert had back-up . . .

Herbert stuck the index and middle fingers of his right hand into either side of his mouth, ignoring the flare of pain from his jaw, and whistled as loud as he could.

The man looked at him first in surprise and then in alarm. A quick glance out of the window, another to see whether Herbert was bluffing; and then, clearly unwilling to risk it, the man shot out of the door and down the stairs as if scalded.

Herbert heard the front door open and slam closed, and the house was silent again.

He sat back against the upended mattress and took deep breaths until he had returned to something approaching calm. His jaw was tender, but did not seem to be broken; he could still open and close it, though not without a click at about halfway. If he had ever played rugby, he would probably have found the sensation less novel than he did.

When he let the man's jacket slide to the floor, something fell out on to his leg, so obvious that he cursed himself for not having looked for it before. A wallet.

An identity card had brought Herbert to this house; now, it seemed, such a card would take him through the next stage as well. According to his press accreditation, Herbert's fellow pugilist was Alexander Kazantsev, London correspondent of the Soviet newspaper *Izvestia*.

* * *

Herbert called an ambulance for Elkington, and it arrived within ten minutes; the air was still clear up here, and so there were no traffic delays.

He felt guilty about what had happened to Elkington, of course he did; and the ambulanceman's snap diagnosis that any injury would be temporary provided only partial balm.

For his part, Elkington seemed most concerned at his evident failure to impress upon Herbert any sign of policing skills suitable for the Murder Squad. As they loaded the injured man into the back of the ambulance for the journey to the Royal Free Hospital in Hampstead, Herbert promised that he would call by later, or at the very least phone.

When they had gone, Herbert turned back to more immediate matters; specifically, what Kazantsev had been looking for.

Herbert could hardly fault Kazantsev for the thoroughness of his search. Now that he, too, had taken the time to root through the paraphernalia of Stensness's bedroom, he saw that Kazantsev had missed precious few possible hiding places.

The back of every picture had been slit, pillows and cushions sliced open (whatever knife he had been using for the purpose, Herbert counted himself lucky that Kazantsev had not been holding it during their struggle), floorboards ripped up and chunks torn out of skirting boards.

It was a shame that Kazantsev was Russian, Herbert thought; he would have fitted in just fine at Five.

Herbert took up where Kazantsev had left off, expanding his search beyond Stensness's bedroom to the rest of the house. It was not even lunchtime; the housemates would be at work for hours yet.

He felt round the inside of the oven, lifted every tin and jar in the larder, looked through the cupboards under the kitchen sink, rummaged through the soil in a window box now winter fallow, unscrewed the bases of lamps, pulled books from shelves to look behind them, felt behind paintings and mirrors, shook out curtains, went through overcoats and jackets with a pickpocket's nimbleness, and turfed clothes from cupboards in heaps whose untidiness spoke of his growing desperation; for, at the end of this gargantuan search, more than an hour in the execution, Herbert had found precisely what he reckoned Kazantsev had come across – to wit, nothing.

Stensness's life, or at least the part of it for which he had left evidence at home, seemed to have been as pedestrian as the vast majority of people's lives: bills paid and pending, a bucketload of cheap thrillers, and slim files of interdepartmental memoranda which could have cured even the most recidivist insomniac.

Breathless, though more from the adrenalin of thwarted progress than the rigour of the exercise, Herbert adjourned his hunt to go and answer a call of nature.

As he aimed at the porcelain, he looked around, trying to work out where *he* would have hidden something of vast importance. And then it came to him.

Forcing himself to finish peeing, he buttoned his fly, put the toilet seat down – see, he thought, he *would* have been a good husband – clambered on to the seat, and reached up towards the cistern.

Starting at the far right-hand corner, he walked his fingers slowly round the cistern's inside edge, fighting the natural inclination to keep his fingertips dry; toilet cistern water was no more or less clean than shower water, after all.

Halfway along the front side of the cistern, his fingertips brushed something rubber, and he almost jumped for joy.

He pulled hard enough to rip away the strip of adhesive tape he knew would be there, and away came his prize.

A condom.

Not just any old condom, however. This one held something inside, and it had been tied at the neck, like a balloon, to keep its contents dry.

The knot was so tight that undoing it with fingernails alone would have been virtually impossible. He tore it with his teeth, careful not to harm what was inside.

No one ever used condoms for the taste, Herbert thought, hawking from deep in his throat as he pulled the neck open and extracted the contents.

Whatever he had been expecting, it had certainly been more earth-shattering than what he found.

The condom contained an article from Wednesday's *Times* concerning revisions to the Queen's Coronation celebrations next June.

There was a map of the route: a circuit of central London, running almost straight past his flat, he noticed, which was nice of them.

Someone, presumably Stensness, had ringed many of the place names. That apart, nothing seemed out of the ordinary.

Herbert almost missed it. In the bottom right-hand corner, in tiny but legible writing, was a sequence of letters: *XXX CCD GVD RCC DPA XXX CDK S.*

They must have made some sense, he supposed, but damned if he could see what.

He read them again.

XXX CCD GVD RCC DPA XXX CDK S.

If anything, they seemed even more incomprehensible second time round.

Herbert consoled himself with the thought that, having had more than his fair share of excitement for one morning, he was hardly in the best shape for codebreaking.

He tucked the mysterious *Times* article into the inside pocket of his jacket, spent twenty further unproductive and increasingly half-hearted minutes looking through the rest of the house for anything vaguely relevant; and then, checking in advance that the coast was clear, he left 43 Cholmeley Crescent.

It was even money that at least one of the goons

was waiting for him at Highgate station, so instead of retracing his steps back there when he reached Archway Road, Herbert instead turned down the hill. Archway station was a good ten or fifteen minutes' walk, but it was time he could spare if it meant getting away undetected.

He passed under the high road bridge which every year contributed more than its fair share to the capital's grisly suicide tally, and remembered something Freud had said about human life being one long struggle against the death instinct.

Not for him, Herbert thought; not right now, at any rate. He could not remember the last time he had felt this . . . well, not necessarily happy, but certainly *alive*.

The ruck with Kazantsev must have done him good. There was nothing like being in danger to give a man vitality. Men who sought to protect the body at all costs died many times over; but those who risked the body to survive as men had a good chance to live on.

He had not enjoyed his birthday so much in years.

These thoughts must have distracted him, for before he knew it he was not only at Archway station but also virtually at the ticket barriers, and it was then that he saw the man he had christened Bob.

Bob was wearing a different coat, by which Herbert surmised that it was reversible and Bob had simply turned it inside out. Even if Herbert had not recognised Bob's face, however, he would have known him by his shoes. Whatever opportunity Watchers enjoyed to alter their clothes during surveillance, they rarely had the time or inclination to change their shoes. Bob was wearing the same shapeless, mildly unattractive brown lace-ups that Herbert had spotted on the tube journey up from Leicester Square.

There was another reason Herbert noticed him. After sudden movement, the second thing to avoid at all costs when carrying out surveillance was 'ballooning' – drifting round with no apparent purpose.

An experienced operative would always look as though he had a purpose, even if it was nothing more than waiting for someone. But Bob was making such a show – eyes darting, pacing back and forth, constantly checking his watch – that he would have looked odd even to . . . well, even to Hannah Mortimer, Herbert thought, even to a blind girl.

Bob was so busy looking around that he had not seen Herbert yet. Herbert turned his face away from him and went as quickly and unobtrusively as possible through the ticket barrier. Rather than standing on the escalator and letting it carry him down to the platform, Herbert walked down the left-hand side, the better to put distance between himself and Bob, not daring to turn back to see whether Bob was following.

Luck was on Herbert's side; a southbound train arrived on the platform at exactly the same time as he did. One usually had to endure a wait of several minutes. Judging by the tightly packed carriages, there must have been a long interval since the last train. The Northern Line had probably been hit by cancellations or delays caused by the fog, in town if not out here.

Herbert squeezed himself on board and burrowed through the crowd, the better to be out of sight if Bob had followed him down.

The doors stayed resolutely, obstinately open. Herbert supposed that, when it came to the underground, a quick exit as well as a smooth entrance was too much to ask.

Come on, he silently urged. Seeing Bob had been a shock; Herbert would not be able to relax until the train had resumed its journey without Bob.

Still the doors did not shut.

Herbert rained unspoken curses on whoever was responsible; idiots trying to drag outsize suitcases on board, or a driver who had hopped off to chat with a mate, or the signal controller keeping the light on red – or all of the above.

And there was Bob, running on to the platform. Since no one was still waiting, he knew he would find Herbert on the train or not at all.

Bob stood for a moment, seemingly unsure of what to do.

He could not have been certain that he had seen Herbert, or else he would have leapt into the nearest carriage – which happened to be Herbert's – and started looking the moment the train moved off, after which he would have had, perhaps literally, a captive audience.

No, he was hesitating because he knew that if he got on the train and Herbert was not there, he would have abandoned his post upstairs for no reason, and would therefore have been in for an even bigger carpeting than the other two stooges.

Close, Herbert willed the doors. *Close*.

Bob moved towards the train.

He was a few yards from the door through which Herbert had entered the carriage. If Bob got on now, he would surely see Herbert. Yes, there were people crammed in tight, but it was still hard to hide in such a confined space.

Herbert looked towards the far end of the carriage, and saw with dismay that even if he could force his way through the crowd before Bob got on board, it was still not nearly far enough.

Unbidden, a snatch of Watcher training floated to the surface.

Conventional wisdom ran that the average person would look for a follower at a distance of between ten and twenty yards, which was exactly the range at which most people preferred to follow.

One was therefore less likely to be spotted if one hung back further or, counter-intuitively, if one got closer.

If one got closer. Herbert was faster than his own thought. He was already moving back through the crowd, towards the door, as though Bob were an old friend whom he was going to embrace.

Herbert's haste made him tread on someone's foot and elbow another person in the kidneys, and with a flurry of muttered apologies he kept going.

Bob got on board at exactly the same moment Herbert reached the door.

It seemed inconceivable that he would not see Herbert, for he was right in his face, close enough for them to have been lovers. Herbert had to trust in the theory with blind, counter-intuitive faith.

Bob looked over Herbert's shoulder, literally over his shoulder, at the rest of the carriage, scanning their faces for any sign of the one closer to him than everyone else.

The doors hissed, in apparent preparation for closing, and Herbert choked back an absurd desire to laugh. Having spent so long, or at least what had seemed so long, wanting the doors to close, now he was desperate for them to remain open just a few more seconds – long enough for Bob to consider himself mistaken and step back on to the platform.

Miraculously, that is exactly what Bob did.

The train was too crowded, and Herbert was too shaken, to attempt to decipher the strange scrawl at the bottom of the Coronation map. He pulled the list of conference delegates from his pocket and, holding it in jittering hands, scanned it for Kazantsev's name.

Kazantsev was not listed. Nor was any other Russian, for that matter.

Herbert checked three times, on the last occasion

running his finger down the list name by name, and having to consciously stop himself mouthing the words as though in remedial class.

Definitely not. No Kazantsev, no Russian.

Hard as it was to credit, it seemed to Herbert that de Vere Green had been telling the truth: the conference was nothing to do with this case at all.

Instead, it seemed that the Coronation was somehow involved, and that could only be bad news; not least because it would elevate this case to levels far too stratospheric for one as lowly as he.

Well, if he had to give it up, he would do so only when he was forced, and not before. In the meantime, he needed more information; in particular, he wanted to find out as much as he could about Kazantsev, and there was only one place to go for that.

At Leicester Square, where Herbert changed trains, wisps of smog could now clearly be seen, even this far beneath ground.

He passed a bride and groom, the latter in his tailcoat and the former in her wedding dress, turned almost black by the grime. A phalanx of ushers and bridesmaids bobbed around them.

'We've already got married,' the groom was explaining to a passer-by, 'but this is the only way we can get to the reception. There are no taxis left on the streets, and even if there were, there's no way they could see where they're going.'

'Just look at my dress,' the bride said. 'It's ruined!'

'Well, it's not as if you'll be needing it again,' the groom replied.

'Cheeky!' she laughed, and slapped him softly, playfully.

Two happy faces, Herbert thought; there were not many others around, that was for sure. Certainly de Vere Green would not be looking too happy when he got wind of what Herbert was about to do.

When he returned to Leconfield House, Herbert asked not for de Vere Green but for Patricia Drummond-Francis, queen of the Registry.

'Herbert!' she cried, hurrying through the foyer to greet him before kissing him, hard and wet, on both cheeks. 'How's life in the force? Why is it you never come back and see your old friends any more? What are you doing here?'

The last, Herbert thought, was a question in which Patricia could justifiably have put the emphasis on any one of the five words involved.

'I need a peek at one of your files,' he said.

'You were snaffling around here this morning.'

'News travels.'

'Is this something to do with that?'

Herbert nodded, knowing that Patricia would understand his reluctance to go back to de Vere Green so soon. She shared Herbert's opinion of his former boss, and knew too that when dealing with a man like de Vere Green, the more information one had to hand before battle commenced, the better.

Patricia led Herbert back through the security gates and into Registry, where all the files were stored. The contents took up the entire ground floor, with its bricked-up windows and steel grilles; and rarely had anyone presided over a fiefdom with such benign firmness as Patricia did.

Her underlings were all daughters of high society or service families, straight out of Roedean or Swiss finishers, with a strictly tripartite vocabulary ('yah', 'really?', and 'nightmare', the latter elongated through several syllables) and little ambition beyond marrying as quickly and suitably as possible. 'If I'm going to be bored,' they would trill, 'I'd rather be bored by a Lord!' Patricia worked them like a head-mistress and read their minds as though telepathic.

Had she been a man, she would have been Director-General by now; had she been a man, and had she dressed the part too, that was. Patricia's default garb was old corduroys and patched jerseys dotted with the few clumps of earth that hadn't stuck beneath her fingernails.

Her true nature – ruddily outdoorsy, hunting and jolly hockey sticks – offset the way in which she carried her head tilted slightly back, a mannerism she had adopted not through any notions of perceived superiority but (and it had taken Herbert a long time to work this out) to disguise the incipience of her double chin.

'Oh,' she said, 'and happy birthday.'

'How on earth did you remember that?'

'I remember everything, Herbert,' Patricia said

with mock grandiloquence, holding the pause for a perfect second before laughing.

'You're a wonder.'

'One of the seven. Now, what's the name?'

'Alexander Kazantsev.'

'Write it down.' She pointed to the pile of request slips. She may have been on Herbert's side, but she still maintained a theatrical devotion to the rules.

He wrote, as requested, and signed an illegible signature. Patricia took the slip and perused it as though checking for obscenity.

'I'll be as quick as I can,' she said.

'Thank you so much.'

'You'll have to read it here.' Usual practice was to sign files out and take them back to one's own office, but this clearly could not apply to a visiting detective. 'There are a couple of desks round the back.' Patricia pointed through a forest of metal shelving.

Herbert smiled his heartfelt thanks; he knew she was running a considerable risk in helping him.

Patricia disappeared, her voluminous skirts giving her the appearance of a galleon under full sail beneath a helmet of hair that would have pleased a Valkyrie.

Herbert looked at the photographs on her desk; one each of her five sons, ranging from twenty-five through fifteen years of age, all immortalised in sepia at points various around her throne.

Patricia kept a small transistor radio on her desk, and Herbert listened to it while he counted back the minutes. The Automobile Association was being besieged with calls. The previous evening it had been motorists asking for advice on conditions, and this morning the same motorists were ringing back to moan that they had been misled. Thinking that the fog would last only a few hours, the AA had apparently suggested that people park in side streets under lampposts and leave their lights on to warn drivers of their presence. Now all those cars had flat batteries, and the AA vans could not find their way through the fog to give them a jumpstart.

Patricia came back in short order, plopping a small manila folder in front of Herbert and bustling onwards without interruption. A small queue of those wanting to take out or return files had already built up in her brief absence.

Herbert opened the file and began to read.

Kazantsev seemed to be a bona fide *Izvestia* journalist. He had arrived in London nine months ago, and had been placed under intense surveillance until the end of June, when surveillance had been discontinued 'due to lack of any espionage activity on the subject's part'.

During that period, he had visited the Soviet Embassy in Kensington Palace Gardens on only three occasions, all for simple administrative purposes pertaining to press accreditation or visa requirements.

This at least Herbert felt confident believing; there was probably no building in London which was watched with greater zeal than the Soviet Embassy.

Five's Watchers stationed themselves in cars parked outside (which were renumbered and repainted every few months) and in buildings opposite. They were constantly filming the comings and goings, and would inevitably requisition every new and improved listening microphone on which Five could get its grubby hands.

There was good reason for the endeavour. Of the entire Soviet Embassy staff – and, among adversarial countries, London was Moscow's second most important station, behind Washington – only about a third were genuine diplomats. Another third belonged to the MGB, Soviet civilian intelligence, and the final third were attached to the GRU, military intelligence.

Translations of several of Kazantsev's articles were attached to the file. One had been dismissed by an anonymous scribble in the margin as 'dreadful boring rubbish', but in fact the majority seemed to Herbert to be interesting and eminently readable.

That in itself meant nothing. If one could write well enough to pass oneself off as a journalist, then the espionage world was one's oyster. Unlike diplomats, reporters could go anywhere, from slums to palaces and all points in between, meeting people from every walk of life. It was a rare journalist who could keep secrets like a spy, but that did not mean such people did not exist.

Perhaps if Kazantsev had been posted to London in the days when Herbert was a Watcher, he would have been tailed more efficiently and Five might have been less inclined to dismiss him as a bog-standard correspondent. No reporter Herbert had ever met would have searched the house in Cholmeley Crescent the way Kazantsev had. Floorboards and skirting boards were the mark of a professional, someone who'd learned their craft in MGB school, not on the news desk at *Pravda* or *Tass*.

Whatever the Five files did or did not say, Kazantsev was a spy, of that Herbert was certain; and foreign espionage was the one thing that the police would always leave alone. Robbers, rapists, even murderers were ten-a-penny, but international intrigue meant politics, and the police liked to stay as far away from politics as possible.

This was Herbert's dilemma; the one he had been facing, in one form or another, since the moment he had learned of de Vere Green's involvement.

On the one hand, this was clearly an espionage case, even if Herbert did not know exactly how. The sensible thing to do, therefore, would be to hand it over to Five and be done with it.

On the other hand, a murder had been committed; and Five, whatever else they might or might not do, would be neither especially concerned with bringing the killer to justice, nor particularly qualified to do so.

And this was not even to mention Herbert's own personal interest. He was tired of being the outsider fobbed off with the nothing cases. This was his chance to do something special, to use his experience and contacts; and to show Tyce that his support, as welcome as it had been unexpected, had not been misplaced.

Herbert was turning all this over in his head when his thoughts were interrupted by voices from next door. There was only a thin partition wall between the desk where he was sitting and de Vere Green's office. And de Vere Green was angry; angry enough for his voice to carry through the partition with some ease.

'What do you mean, lost him?' he was saying.

'He gave us the slip in the cemetery, sir,' came the reply, from the man with the Suffolk accent whom Herbert had heard on Egyptian Avenue in Highgate Cemetery, when he had been hiding in the burial chamber.

Herbert stopped breathing. It was de Vere Green who had ordered him followed.

'And that was the last time you saw him?' de Vere Green asked.

'Yes, sir.'

If the other two goons were also in there, they did not dissent. When it came to the incident at Archway station, Herbert thought, Bob must have decided that discretion was the better part of valour. His sense of self-preservation was evidently better than his aptitude for surveillance.

It was serious enough, Herbert thought, that the goons had come here in the first place. The Watchers did not operate out of Leconfield House for fear that they would be too identifiable to the Soviets. Instead, they were based in an unmarked four-storey

Georgian house on Clarence Terrace, on the south-west side of Regent's Park. Herbert knew that building as well as he did his own flat. In his capacity as a senior Watcher, Herbert had come to Leconfield House more often than most; the majority of Watchers would visit Leconfield House once a year, if that.

'So where is he now?' de Vere Green barked. No *dear boys* here.

Herbert could not resist. He stood up, walked round the corner and into de Vere Green's office, where he amused himself for a brief moment by trying to work out which of the four men looked most astonished by his appearance.

'Right here,' Herbert said.

The argument raged for fifteen minutes, going first back and forth, and then nowhere.

De Vere Green, scattering *dear boys* around like confetti, assured Herbert that the decision to send the Watchers – long since banished from the room – to follow him was nothing personal. He simply wanted to know where Herbert went and what he found. In fact he was rather hoping, gentleman to gentleman, that Herbert would be so kind as to share such information with him.

No, Herbert said; this was a murder investigation, plain and simple. If de Vere Green had anything to contribute, he should say so; if not, he should leave well alone. De Vere Green was clearly hiding something, Herbert added; why else would he have had him trailed? And how was Kazantsev, whom Herbert had found in Stensness's house, involved?

De Vere Green would not, of course, presume to speak for Kazantsev, but the correspondent's very presence indicated that this was way out of a detective inspector's league. Herbert should simply turn it over to Five and be done with it.

This was not a request; that much was clear.

Herbert thought of what Tyce had said, about loyalties, and jurisdiction, and he made the decision almost without realising. If de Vere Green had nothing concrete to show that Five merited control of this case, then Herbert would not hand it over.

After a stretch of mutual, glowering silence, de Vere Green tried another tactic.

He feared, he said, that Stensness's murder was a matter of national security. Not necessarily in and of itself, but perhaps as part of wider ramifications. He would tell Herbert what he knew, if Herbert in turn told him what he had managed to find. They could help each other.

A tacit admission, Herbert said, that de Vere Green had been economical with the truth in the first place.

An occupational hazard of their mutual trades, de Vere Green replied. Deal?

You first.

'I, er, I . . .' De Vere Green steepled his hands, which was as penitent as Herbert had ever seen him. 'I misled you, dear boy. Earlier.'

Herbert said nothing, ushering de Vere Green to fill the silence, which he did.

'I told you that when I saw Stensness at the conference, he said he didn't have anything new for me. That was not, in fact, true . . .' De Vere Green paused, his inner thespian never far from the surface. 'He told me he had something that would change the world.'

'Change the world?'

'Change the world.'

'Meaning what?'

'Dear boy, if I knew *that*, we wouldn't be in this fix.'

'What did he propose to do about this something?'

'He didn't say. Just that he would contact me shortly.'

'Shortly? Not last night?'

'That is correct.'

'He didn't give a time or place?'

'No.'

'And that was it?'

'That, dear boy, was very much it.' De Vere Green smiled wryly. 'Quid pro quo.'

So de Vere Green had lied earlier. What else had Herbert really expected, knowing what he did about the man? At any rate, de Vere Green was proving more co-operative now, and there was much he knew that Herbert wanted to know too.

So if Herbert really wanted to find out who killed Max Stensness, and why, he needed all the help he could get.

Herbert pulled the map of the Coronation route

from his pocket and handed it to de Vere Green. 'I found this taped to the inside of the toilet cistern,' he said.

De Vere Green winced momentarily, presumably at the unspeakably plebeian nature of the word *toilet*.

'I've no idea what it signifies,' Herbert added. 'But I'm sure it must be involved somehow, if only for the lengths that Stensness had gone to in order to hide it. Had he simply left it out in the open, one unobtrusive paper among many, I doubt I'd have noticed it.'

De Vere Green studied the paper. Some place names had been ringed; ten or twelve at a quick count, among them the Houses of Parliament, Marlborough House, and Piccadilly Circus.

They could, Herbert thought, have passed for doodles, the kind of patterns a man would make while waiting on the phone or bored in a meeting; but when the same patterns were hidden in a condom in a toilet cistern, that was a different matter entirely. The mundane became instantly suspicious.

'God help us,' de Vere Green said. 'God help us all.' He looked up at Herbert. 'You realise what this means?'

'What?'

'That the communists want to assassinate the monarch.'

'That is the most ridiculous thing I have ever heard,' Herbert said, more as reflex than anything

127

else, for he knew that the Coronation map must mean *something*, and de Vere Green's theory was as good as anything he could come up with.

'Dear boy, what else do you think the marked points are? Locations for sandwich stalls? If you work here long enough, you end up believing six impossible things before breakfast. Why is it so ridiculous? The Americans are paranoid about communist attempts to kill their President, aren't they?'

'The Americans are in thrall to that lunatic McCarthy,' Herbert said. 'It'll be a tragic day if we ever follow suit.'

'And by extension,' de Vere Green continued, as though he hadn't heard, 'the British worry that our Prime Minister is also at risk, especially after the way he and Roosevelt diddled Stalin at Yalta. Stalin hasn't forgotten, you know. Uncle Joe will remember slights against him till the end of time. But, unlike the President, Mr Churchill is not head of state, is he?'

'The monarch's role is largely ceremonial.'

'Perhaps, but the importance of this Queen to Britain goes far beyond her official role. She's young and glamorous; people are looking to her to help this country finally slough off the lethargy of war and restore Britain to its rightful position at the top table of world affairs.'

Spoken like a true patriot, Herbert thought. 'It still makes no sense,' he said.

'On the contrary, dear boy. You have no idea

how well you have done to obtain this information. There have long been rumblings of some large underground movement planning what I believe they refer to as a "spectacular". This must be it. What, indeed, could be more spectacular?'

'But *how*? And *why*?'

'If you keep thinking in such narrow-minded, conventional patterns, dear boy, we'll never solve this.' *We*, Herbert noted; not *you*, but then again not *I* either. 'Any act of fanaticism makes sense if one is sufficiently warped to see the logic. The Cold War is chillier and more intense than ever before. Remember what happened a couple of months ago? On that godforsaken archipelago off Australia?'

Herbert nodded; the British had successfully exploded an atomic bomb, making them the third country in the world to have nuclear weapons.

'There you are,' de Vere Green said. 'That makes it two against one. Poor odds for Stalin, who is, according to every piece of intelligence coming out of Moscow, increasingly paranoid and unpredictable, even by his own legendary standards. He has legions of men obedient and resourceful enough to do something like this.'

'But *why*?'

'Imagine the disruption, my dear old thing. Imagine the blow to capitalism and the deeply un-Marxist doctrine of hereditary monarchy. Remember Franz Ferdinand and Gavrilo Princip, and grenades and guns and processions, and what happened afterwards? Remember, and shudder.' De Vere Green sat back in his chair. 'Well, it would certainly change the world, we have to give him that.'

De Vere Green, entirely predictably, demanded that Five take over the case, now that it was demonstrably a matter of national security.

Herbert stood firm. He reminded de Vere Green what had happened the last time he had let him ride roughshod, and said that, if he was to hand over control, he would do so only after it had been agreed on both sides.

Then he rang Tyce and apprised him both of what they had found and what de Vere Green wanted. Tyce said that he would be right over. First, however, given the evident gravity of the discovery, he would need to alert the Commissioner, Sir Harold Scott.

If the Commissioner was coming, then so too should Sillitoe, the head man at Five; but he was out of town, and would not be back until Sunday.

In the Director-General's absence, de Vere Green, though clearly unhappy at being outnumbered, deemed himself of suitable rank to represent Five.

At least the urgency and short notice spared both sides the usual welter of bobs and nabobs at such events. Herbert already had experience of Five's myriad stagnant layers, and things were no better in Scotland Yard; beneath Scott were rafts of Deputy Commissioners, Assistant Commissioners, Deputy Assistant Commissioners, and Commanders.

So Herbert and de Vere Green sat for half an hour in a silence that only the charitable could have described as companionable, waiting for the arrival of the Met's finest. De Vere Green's efforts at conversation were dashed on the rocks of Herbert's impassivity, as Herbert's thoughts tumbled lazily over themselves through eddying currents of connection.

August 1914, Sarajevo. Archduke Franz Ferdinand, travelling in a motorcade along streets lined with heavy crowds, is attacked twice by Serbian nationalists; with grenades, which he survives, and with a gun, which he does not.

In 1917 the Royal Family changes its name from Saxe-Coburg-Gotha to Windsor, because a German name is deemed unpatriotic in wartime. Its personnel and lines of descent remain unchanged, however.

July 1918, Yekaterinburg. Tsar Nicholas, Tsarina Alexandra and the rest of Russia's last Imperial Family are shot and bayoneted by a detachment of Bolsheviks.

June 1941. Hitler invades the Soviet Union. Four years later, with millions killed on the Eastern Front, the Third Reich is no more and hatred for Germany is branded on the Soviet psyche.

Add to the mix the fact that communism was by definition godless, whereas monarchies were founded on a divine right to rule; then sprinkle all the points de Vere Green had mentioned – McCarthy's witch hunts, Stalin's paranoia, Britain's new-found nuclear capability – and Herbert no longer thought the assassination theory absurd. There *was* a logic there; a logic, and therefore a threat.

*　　*　　*

'Show me what you have,' Scott said, once he and Tyce were installed and coffee had been brought.

Herbert had not been unproductive during the wait. He had made notes on the possibilities raised by Stensness's map; now he consulted these notes while he spoke.

The Coronation was to take place on 2nd June next year, he said. The route had been decided as follows. The Queen would leave Buckingham Palace at 10.26 a.m., the last of five separate processions involving everybody from colonial rulers through prime ministers and princes to the Queen Mother. She would proceed in a horse-drawn carriage along The Mall, Northumberland Avenue and the Embankment, arriving at Westminster Abbey at 11.00 on the dot.

The service would then take place, lasting five minutes short of four hours. It would be televised, though the processions before and afterwards would not.

At 2.55, the Queen would leave the Abbey, proceeding up Parliament Street to Whitehall and Trafalgar Square, where she would arrive at 3.07. From there, she would go along, in order, Pall Mall, St James' Street, Piccadilly (3.19), Hyde Park Corner, Park Lane, Marble Arch (3.46), Oxford Street, Oxford Circus (4.00), Regent Street, Piccadilly Circus (4.10), Haymarket and Trafalgar Square (4.18), before returning up The Mall to Buckingham Palace at 4.31.

Even assuming that no attack could take place

inside the Abbey itself, where access would be strictly controlled and security tighter than a drum, that still left two hours of what Herbert, in his military days, would have termed 'major exposure'; the monarch on the open roads, in full view of her people.

Yes, troops and police would line the route, but even if every soldier and constable in the country stood side by side, they could not be absolutely sure of covering every member of a throng which would surely be several millions strong.

As Sir Harold could see, Stensness had circled twelve locations on the map, some of them abbreviated to save on space. In order of their appearance on the procession route, they were: Northumberland Avenue; Victoria Embankment; Parliament Street; Trafalgar Square; Marlborough House; St James's Palace; St James's Street; Hyde Park Corner; Oxford Street; Regent Street; St James's Park; and Piccadilly Circus.

Herbert had gone through them one by one, trying at each turn to put himself in the shoes of a would-be assassin. If *he* wanted to kill the Queen, and make *his* getaway, where would *he* choose to strike?

He had divided the locations into three categories: Likely; Possible; and Unlikely.

It depended, he supposed, on what the weapon of choice was.

In such circumstances, it was hard to look beyond either a sniper's bullet, or a bomb thrown from the crowd.

A sniper would want a tall building with uninterrupted views down to the procession, and in particular the royal coach. Government buildings would, or at least should, be harder to access than commercial buildings – unless the plotters had someone on the inside, and with fifty thousand members and thirty MPs at least partially beholden to them, the CPGB must have fingers in many official pies.

Northumberland Avenue had its fair share of tall buildings, as did Parliament Street, St James's Street, Oxford Street and Regent Street. These five Herbert had classified as 'Likely'.

Next came the 'Possibles': Victoria Embankment, Trafalgar Square, Marlborough House, St James's Palace and Piccadilly Circus.

Hyde Park Corner and St James's Park he considered 'Unlikely'.

A bomber, on the other hand, had an entirely different set of requirements. He had to be close enough to throw his device at the coach, and yet have at least one escape route within easy reach.

In this scenario, Hyde Park Corner and St James' Park suddenly became much more attractive propositions; a sufficiently adept, and lucky, bomber would have at least a chance of escaping through the parks themselves.

Herbert had put them in the 'Likely' column for the bombers, along with Oxford Street and Regent Street, both of which sprouted warrens of side streets along their length.

In contrast, anyone attempting a bombing at St

James's Palace, or on Parliament Street, or by Marlborough House, would find themselves hemmed in by the buildings behind them. These three Herbert had therefore classified as 'Unlikely'.

This left the remaining five – Northumberland Avenue, Victoria Embankment, Trafalgar Square, St James's Street and Piccadilly Circus – as 'Possibles'.

'Well,' Scott said, 'it certainly sounds grave enough. I suppose it's lucky that we've seven months to put a stop to it.'

'By "we", I presume you mean "us",' de Vere Green said. 'As in "Five". I have never seen an investigation that falls more clearly under our remit.'

'Detective Inspector Smith would be more than happy to help, I'm sure,' Scott said. 'He is uniquely placed to liaise between us and you, after all.'

They all recognised the admission for what it was: the renunciation of the Met's claim to this case, or at least to operational responsibility, which as far as Herbert was concerned amounted to the same thing.

Scott was no policeman, Herbert remembered; he looked every inch the civil servant that he was. A civil servant running the police force, a policeman running the spy service – no wonder the country was in bad shape. At least Scott was not ex-military; the list of his predecessors was littered with Brigadier-Generals, Generals, Colonels and Lieutenant-Colonels. He had been Commissioner since the end of the war, and rumour had it not only that he was up for replacement soon, but also that his successor would, for the first time, be a serving police officer.

135

Tyce, for one, would clearly welcome that. He spoke up now.

'I'm sorry, sir, but I can't accept that.' Give Tyce credit, Herbert thought; one always knew where one was with him. 'All this is very interesting, and alarming too, but we've no proof that it's actually linked to the murder.'

'That's not true,' de Vere Green said.

'No, that *is* true. We have a plot, which is still conjecture, and we have a murder, which is fact. I'm not saying the two are not connected, just that we don't know for sure. And until we do, this case is still ours.'

'Mr Tyce, you have no idea what you're dealing with.'

'No; I have every idea. My job starts and ends with one belief: you can't go round killing people on British soil and get away with it, no matter who you are – spies included. Dead-letter drops, surveillance, invisible ink, all that clobber, yes, fine with me. Murder, no. Not murder. Every civilised society draws the line there.'

Herbert had never had Tyce down as an orator, but his words had saved the day. Scott had first agreed and then pulled rank, informing de Vere Green that while Five were welcome to assist, the case was both legally and morally still the Met's.

It was a turf war, simple as that, as atavistic and ineradicable as all conflict. The turf caused the war, and there would always be turf; therefore there would always be war.

Not that Herbert was complaining. This time yesterday, he had been an habitué of procedural backwaters; now, as the one man whose career had straddled both Leconfield House and New Scotland Yard, he seemed all but indispensable.

He wondered whether – hoped that – he was up to it, and reminded himself that things could change back just as quickly.

De Vere Green had a raft of meetings scheduled – for which, Herbert thought, read an afternoon of intriguing; how nice it must be, to have a job which was also one's hobby – and therefore, with some apparent reluctance, left Herbert to his own devices, asking only to be informed of progress on a regular basis.

Tyce and Scott, having made identical requests, returned to Scotland Yard.

So, Herbert thought; where next?

The simplest option would have been to go round to the *Izvestia* offices and arrest Kazantsev. A charge of burglary would do, let alone suspicion of murder.

Herbert, however, thought that such a course of action might be counterproductive. He had already seen how Kazantsev, when cornered, would lash out. A repeat performance, followed by the inevitable hardening of respective positions, would suit Herbert not at all. He needed answers, not simply the fleeting satisfaction of a criminal charge.

Besides, weren't the Russians supposed to be devious? Softly, softly, catchee monkey, and all that.

Herbert picked up the early editions of all three evening papers – the *Evening News*, the *Evening Standard*, and the *Star* – from a vendor on Curzon Street whose extravagant cries of '*News, Star, Standard!*' were acting as a sort of aural lighthouse in the fog.

There was nothing in any of the papers about a body in the Long Water, which left him both relieved, for this was a case which in no way needed publicity, and irrationally angry, for Max Stensness had clearly been too small and unimportant for the papers' news desks – the same news desks who had chosen to give half a page to the statue of Eros at Piccadilly Circus being taken down for cleaning.

It was a minute's walk from Leconfield House to Herbert's flat. He put more coal on the fire, aware that he was doing his bit to make the smog worse but knowing that the alternative was freezing away his various appendages, made a cup of coffee, picked up the phone and rang the *Izvestia* office.

A man answered almost immediately.

'I'm looking for Alexander Kazantsev,' Herbert said.

'Who's calling?'

It was Kazantsev himself; Herbert knew it was.

'I've got your jacket,' Herbert said. And your wallet, he thought, and your press card, and everything you need to move freely around. A Soviet national without papers in London was a man in big trouble. This was the Cold War, after all. Stripped of his documentation, Kazantsev could face expulsion, and that would just be the start of it. Whatever the British could do to him would be merely an appetiser for what awaited him in Moscow.

'Ah,' Kazantsev said wistfully, as though recalling a long-lost love, 'that is my favourite jacket. I would be most grateful if you would return it.'

His accent was strong and unmistakably Russian, but there was little wrong with the quality of his English. Herbert decided to play along with him.

'And I would be most pleased to do so. You understand, though, that you attacked a police officer – two, in fact – and that we tend to take a dim view of that.'

'I understand entirely. The view would be much dimmer in my country, I can assure you.'

'So, I would like a little . . . a little chat with you first.'

Herbert might have wanted answers, but Kazantsev wanted his stuff back, and also to avoid being arrested for what had happened in Cholmeley Crescent; so Kazantsev needed Herbert just as much as Herbert needed him, maybe more.

'Of course.' Kazantsev seemed mildly surprised that Herbert had even felt the need to ask. 'You have something I want, I have something you want. The very essence of communism, no?' He laughed so briefly that Herbert almost missed it, and then was serious again. 'I'm free from six thirty onwards. Where shall we meet?'

Herbert thought quickly. The *Izvestia* offices would not offer much privacy, and he knew that the MGB did not like to use rendezvous points in central London, as they felt there were too many police there. Dead drops were one thing – Herbert had in the past spent fruitless days watching the lamppost outside 2 Audley Square, an exercise so futile it had made him seriously question the point not only of his job but of existence itself – but they involved by their nature no human contact, so the risk was deemed permissible.

When it came to actual meetings, though, the MGB preferred slightly more remote locations: Wimbledon post office, the bandstand in Hendon public park, Chelsea Town Hall, the ABC café opposite Ealing Broadway underground station.

The answer came to Herbert in a flash.

'Do you know the Peter Pan statue in Kensington Gardens?' he asked, and the swift, slight inhalation on the other end of the line told him two things: first, that Kazantsev did indeed know it, and second, that he knew too why Herbert was asking.

Fog did not mean a day off for the lamplighters, that curious vampiric breed whose working day began at dusk. In fact, their services were even more important than usual. Visible only from directly beneath, the amber lights mounted halfway down what were now invisible lamp standards seemed to hang unsupported in the air. Even the pigeons, denied their usual landmarks, were on foot.

Herbert had been on the go since early morning, and yet he felt no fatigue. Perhaps this was what happened to all men who had experienced war; they tried, usually without realising, to recreate those memories, seeking out jobs which involved long hours of tedium interspersed with brief snatches of action.

He thought of all the times he had sat at his desk meandering through paperwork, resolve and energy seeming to ebb away like oil from a holed sump, and wondered whether what he had was not so much a disease of despond as one of extremes, where he could starve or binge, stay awake for days or sleep for a week, walk in wet cement or run on a hamster wheel.

He had a couple of hours before he met Kazantsev, and there was little real progress he could make until he had spoken to the Russian; so, having rung the Royal Free and ascertained that the damage to Elkington amounted largely to a splitting headache, he set off for Guy's Hospital to see his mother.

The journey was a tortuous one, involving three separate trains however one cut it. At Embankment, Herbert watched a man stand close to the edge as the train approached, and knew the man was wondering how much he would be missed if he simply stepped off the platform a moment ahead of the arriving engine's silver snout and let the grim laws of physics do the rest.

Herbert's mother had a long list of things she abhorred, and suicides were right at the top. One could not kill oneself, she said, because one's life was not one's own. One was the steward of one's life and body, but they were not one's to destroy. Only weaklings committed suicide, she said, and there was no greater damnation in her eyes than being a weakling.

She and Herbert had discussed the issue of suicides on many occasions, and in the end they had simply agreed to disagree.

At London Bridge, Herbert fought against the commuter tide, instinctively looked left and right along the tramlines as he crossed the road, even though London's last tram had been decommissioned five months before, and followed the labyrinthine trail through the hospital corridors until he found his mother's ward.

Mary was sufficiently ravaged by age and illness for no amount of make-up to be truly effective, though God knew she had given it a go. Lipstick firmly in place, foundation and mascara just so, her hair perfectly brushed. Still Herbert's eyes were drawn to the way her translucent skin hung from her bones, and to the liver spots which dotted her neck.

He stood and looked at Mary for a good few seconds before she noticed him.

'Herbert! I didn't see you there.' She glanced at the watch which hung loosely from a twig-thin wrist. 'What time do you call this?'

'I'm late. Sorry. A man was drowned in the Long Water last night.'

Mary held up an admonishing hand. 'Stop, Herbert. You always try to tell me what you're up to, when you know full well I hate hearing about all that palaver. As far as I'm concerned, the sooner you find a new job, the better. If you never have to deal with another dead body again, it'll be too soon.'

'I'm a murder detective, Mama. Dead bodies pretty much come with the job.'

'Enough! Murders mean murderers, and murderers are dangerous. One day the dead body will be you, God forbid, and where will I be left then? But you never think about that, do you? Ah, enough of that. Come give your old mother a kiss.'

She clung on to him a beat too long for comfort, and then pushed him away with unexpected sharpness.

'Good grief!' she said. 'You smell as if you've been down a coal mine all day.'

'It's the fog, I suppose.'

'Huh! More rubbish to wreck my poor old lungs.'

There were four other beds in the ward, all currently empty but all clearly in general use; their sheets were rumpled, and magazines rode up the pillows like tidemarks. Mary was in a nightdress and dressing-gown, sitting at a table next to her bed. Three pillows were piled on the table and she was leaning forward on to them so that they supported her chest. Her forearms rested on her thighs.

'Some damn fool breathing exercise they're making me do,' she explained. 'Complete waste of time.'

The rattle in her throat as she inhaled told a different story, as did the ochre nicotine lagoons on her fingertips. For Mary, asthma and bronchitis came together, squeezing her airways and filling her lungs as though they were toilet cisterns. Advanced cases came in two categories: over-weight blue bloaters and underweight pink puffers. Mary was definitely one of the latter.

'It would help if you didn't smoke, you know,' Herbert said. If one smoked when one had a chest disease, he thought, one was either mad or tired of life; and his mother was not mad.

Mary's eyes blazed defiance. 'Hogwash! Smoking's good for me. It relaxes me, so I'm less likely to get an anxiety attack. Anxiety attacks are deadly if you've got what I've got. Aren't they? Herbert?'

It took Herbert a moment or two to realise that she was talking to him. His attention had been far away, turning over various permutations of Stensness, de Vere Green and Kazantsev.

'Absolutely,' he said.

'That's right. Absolutely.'

A nurse came bustling in. She was mid-forties, seemingly five foot cubed, with a red face beneath ginger hair fading in places to grey.

'This is my son Herbert,' Mary said.

'Nice to meet you,' the nurse said. Her accent was Irish. 'I'm Angela.'

'He's a detective at Scotland Yard, you know,' Mary added. '*Very* important job, but dreadful hours. He hardly ever visits, and he never brings anyone round. How's he ever going to meet a nice girl when he works all the hours God sends?'

'I *am* here, you know,' said Herbert.

'Sounds like you have an interesting job,' Angela said.

Herbert opened his mouth to reply, but Mary was in there first. 'Don't waste your time asking, Angela. He's never allowed to talk about his cases. Very hush-hush. Top secret. Now, that clipboard looks ominous.'

Angela brandished said clipboard in Mary's general direction. 'Foods for Mary Smith to avoid,' she read. 'Dairy produce, pork, sausages, ham, bacon, tomatoes, malt vinegar, red wine, white sugar, chocolate and common salt.'

'What?' shrieked Mary, torn between genuine horror at this prescription and gusto at the prospect of a good-natured haggle towards compromise. 'Are you trying to starve me to death, or bore me there? Was the National Health founded for this?'

'Five small meals a day rather than three large ones. That way you'll avoid that awful gassy feeling. The distension in your abdomen presses up against your diaphragm, compressing the space available for your lungs and making your breathlessness worse.'

'If you're going to put me on that kind of rabbit food, you can at least give me a room of my own.'

Like all bullies, Herbert thought, Mary pushed forward when the going was soft, and pulled back the moment she encountered serious resistance.

Angela turned to Herbert. 'They all say that when they arrive. Give her a day or two, and she'll be best friends with everyone here.'

'Rubbish!' shouted Mary.

'Forty-eight hours till you're playing bridge, or my old ma's a Dutchman.'

'Never!'

Herbert saw the relish of this sparring on both their faces, and felt briefly and shamefully envious. This nurse had known Mary less than thirty-six hours and already they had established a joking, careless rapport which he could never hope to emulate.

The bonds between mother and son – between this mother and this son, at any rate – were too tangled and entwined for Herbert ever to feel truly comfortable. It was just the two of them; his father had died at Passchendaele before he was born, and he had no siblings. So they swirled around in an endless *pas de deux*, caught between responsibility for and watchfulness of each other.

It was not until Herbert left the hospital that he realised: his mother, preoccupied as ever with herself to the exclusion of all else, had forgotten his birthday.

Seeing his mother often left Herbert feeling suffocated and needing air, even air by now noticeably brumal, so he walked across London Bridge and reflected that the fog was good for at least one thing; it hid some of London's unlovelier vistas.

Seven years after the war, vast tracts of the city were still little more than rubble; broken walls slid into bomb craters, exposed rooms blinked in surprise, and darkened gaps between buildings were so many entrances to hell. Ruined areas became patches of jungle; cracked houses leant heavily on sagging wooden buttresses.

The faces which loomed from the murk were sallowed by years of privation. For most, meat and two veg meant beige mutton and two forms of overcooked potato. It was no wonder he felt down; the whole city must have felt down.

Herbert arrived at the Peter Pan statue twenty minutes early. He had wanted to be there with half an hour to spare, but the fog forced him to walk slowly, for fear that he would bump into something or someone he had not seen until it was too late, and once he had taken a wrong turning and had to retrace his steps.

Kazantsev came out of the fog like a wraith, absent one moment, present the next, with seemingly no transition between the two. The shock made Herbert catch his breath. The Russian was bigger than he remembered.

'You have my jacket?' Kazantsev asked.

'If you have the answers.'

'Give me your questions, and I'll see whether I've got your answers.'

His English was impeccable, Herbert thought. But then again, MGB agents attended Moscow's School of Foreign Languages, so it would be. The Soviets were many things, but amateurs rarely.

Herbert took his police badge from his pocket and flipped it in front of Kazantsev's face. 'Remember who you're dealing with,' he said. 'Detective Inspector Herbert Smith, New Scotland Yard. You attacked me.'

'No, Inspector. You attacked me.'

That much was true, Herbert conceded silently. 'You chloroformed my colleague.'

Kazantsev's eyes darted to a spot over Herbert's left shoulder, and in a trice Herbert knew, and was moving; round Kazantsev's back, one arm encircling the Soviet's neck and the other emerging from his pocket with a small kitchen knife, which he had taken the precaution of bringing from his flat.

Whatever Kazantsev was involved with, it must be important, Herbert thought. The Soviets were not usually so brazen as to take on the police with such directness.

'How many?' Herbert hissed.

'Three.' Kazantsev knew what he meant: *How many men waiting?*

'Where?'

Kazantsev motioned with his head. There was one at the point where he had looked earlier; one on the path south between where they were standing and the bridge; and one the other way, north towards the Bayswater Road.

148

Herbert turned Kazantsev to face north. 'How far?' he asked.

'Twenty, thirty metres.'

'Walk,' Herbert said. 'The moment we clear the hedges on the left-hand side, we take to the grass. We go exactly where I say. And if you make a sound, this knife goes all the way through your coat. It's easily sharp enough.'

Kazantsev's people may have been out of sight, but they were not out of earshot. One shout from Kazantsev and they would come running.

Herbert and Kazantsev stepped on to the grass and walked in an arc across it, easily wide enough to bypass Kazantsev's colleague, who was presumably still standing on the path, oblivious to anything happening beyond five feet of his nose.

Without the comfort of stone beneath his feet, and the knowledge that stone meant path meant destination, Herbert felt a touch panicky.

After a few strides, he could no longer tell where they were going, and in such fog he trusted his own sense of direction not a jot.

He kept his breathing neutral, so as not to transmit his worry to Kazantsev, and consoled himself with the fact that, even if they were not heading directly towards the Bayswater Road, they would at least be putting distance between themselves and Kazantsev's reinforcements.

After what could have been twenty yards or three miles, for all Herbert knew, he decided that fortune favoured the bold, and that they had taken a sufficient detour.

He steered Kazantsev a little to the right.

And there they were, back on the path again, right by the Marlborough Gate.

More luck than judgement on Herbert's part; but, as Napoleon had said, a lucky general beat a good one any day.

Herbert and Kazantsev passed through the gate and on to the pavement which ran adjacent to the Bayswater Road. Herbert thought for a moment, and then remembered trailing a Czechoslovak dissident to a place round the corner from they were standing.

Most people remembered pubs because they had been there with friends; Herbert remembered them because they were natural sites for the voyeurism which, since he had been trained and paid a salary for it, he had chosen to call surveillance.

He turned to Kazantsev. 'Care for a drink?'

The Archery Tavern was dark and smelly, conditions exacerbated respectively by the fog and the nearby presence of riding stables. The windows were tight shut against the cold and the pollutants, but the rich scents of manure and tack wormed their way undeterred through invisible gaps in the brickwork.

There was a smattering of drinkers inside, but they were all either too drunk, too bored or too short-sighted to give the two interlopers more than a casual glance.

Kazantsev ordered a whisky, Herbert a pint of bitter. The barman gave Herbert the price; Herbert gave him the money.

'No, please; let me,' Kazantsev said.

'You have,' Herbert replied. 'That money comes from your wallet.'

Kazantsev seemed oddly pleased at this.

They found a table in the corner and sat down. Herbert manoeuvred Kazantsev against the wall in case he tried to make a run for it, though that seemed unlikely. The Russian appeared quite content to stay where he was.

'I need hardly explain to you the severity of the situation,' Herbert began, and winced inwardly at how pompous he sounded. 'Assaulting a police officer is a grave offence. You probably reported the case of Bentley and Craig, the two who killed a police officer last month, no? So you know how seriously we take that kind of thing.'

'The chloroform, your colleague – I'm sorry. I'd taken it along in case I was disturbed. I heard him come in, I snuck up on him from round the corner and surprised him. By the time I saw his uniform, it was too late; he was already out cold.'

'And then you tied him up, and reapplied the chloroform, again and again.'

Kazantsev spread his hands, conceding the point. 'I did. But what else could I have done? The initial mistake is always the worst. Everything else just compounds that.' He paused. 'Is he all right? Your colleague.'

Herbert tried to work out whether appealing to Kazantsev's compassion would work, and decided that on balance it would not. 'His head's hurt, and his pride too. Other than that, he'll be OK.'

'Good.'

Kazantsev seemed to mean it.

The easy thing to have done, perhaps the sensible one too, would have been simply to arrest Kazantsev; but Herbert wanted the bigger picture, and he reasoned that the less formal he kept things, the better. He would remind Kazantsev of the leverage he had over him, and look for dividends that way.

'Assault aside, I've got your wallet and your identification, without which you're in big trouble, especially if I tell those higher up the food chain how I came across it. You're registered as a newspaper correspondent but not as a diplomat, so you have no official protection from either international law or the Soviet government. I've also got a dead man, who –'

'Dead? Who?'

Herbert doubted he could have looked more shocked if he had tried. Whatever he had been expecting Kazantsev to say, it was not this.

If Kazantsev was bluffing, Herbert thought, he should have been in line for an Academy Award; he seemed quite genuine in his surprise.

'Max Stensness, of course,' he replied.

'When? How?'

Herbert was beginning to recover. 'I'm sure you know as well as I do.'

'You suspect me?' Kazantsev spread his hands. 'I'm a journalist, not an actor.'

'You're a spy.'

'I'm not an actor.'

'All spies are actors.'

'If I'd known the first thing about this, trust me, you would have been able to tell.'

'You really didn't know?' Herbert realised too late that this was an incredibly stupid thing to say. Never ask a question to which one would only get one answer; it was a waste of everybody's time. 'All right,' he continued. 'Stensness drowned in the Long Water, right by where we just met, sometime last night.'

Kazantsev took a sip of his whisky; neat, no ice. Like all good Russians, he regarded diluting spirits as sacrilege. His eyebrows lifted a fraction: *Go on*.

'You met Stensness there last night,' Herbert said.

Kazantsev paused for a moment, no doubt wondering how much to tell Herbert, and how much he already knew; then shook his head.

'No,' he said.

'No?'

'No. I didn't meet him there last night.'

'That's a lie.'

'It's not.'

'Then why did you break into his house this morning?'

'I was *supposed* to meet him by the statue at six thirty. But he never showed up.'

'How long had you known him?'

'About two hours.'

Two hours, Herbert thought. 'Where did you meet him?'

'At the Biochemical Conference.' The only answer he could have given.

'Your name's not on the list of delegates.'

'I wasn't a delegate. I'm press.'

'*Izvestia* wanted a story about the conference?'

'*Izvestia* want stories about everything.'

'How did you meet him?'

'He approached me and suggested an appointment.'

'Professional, or personal?'

'Professional, of course. He told me he had something for me.'

'He didn't tell you what it was?'

'No.'

'But if you made the rendezvous, he would give it to you?'

'That was the implication, yes.'

'You'd never met this man before, and he gave you a meeting point in the park, in the fog, and you went along without question?'

'Of course. Why not?'

'What if it had been a hoax?'

'What if it had? What would I have lost, apart from an hour of my life?'

'How did you know his name?'

'He had it on his conference badge.'

'And his address?'

'Everyone's badge had their name and institution. I rang King's this morning after he had failed to show up, and asked for his home address. Then I went up there.'

'And broke in.'

'The door was unlocked.'

'Prove it.'

'Prove that it wasn't.'

The lock had not been forced; Herbert remembered that; he'd checked when he'd picked the lock. But of course if Kazantsev was a Soviet agent, he too could pick locks – certainly bog-standard domestic locks – in his sleep. No chance of proving it either way.

'It's still trespass, locked or not.' Kazantsev shrugged; Herbert continued. 'Why did you go up there?'

'I was looking for what Stensness might have wanted to talk to me about.'

'You go to such lengths on all your assignments?'

'Not at all.'

'Then Stensness must have made whatever he was offering sound very tempting.'

'He did.'

'What did he say?' Herbert asked, already knowing and fearing the answer.

'He said it was something which would change the world.'

*   *   *

155

Herbert spent another hour questioning Kazantsev, and in that time he managed to break him down not an iota.

Of course Kazantsev's story sounded ludicrous, and of course every instinct of Herbert's cried out that Kazantsev was a spy; but, knowing what he knew, and more precisely what he did not know, there was no way Herbert could prove that Kazantsev was lying.

Herbert took his questioning round in circles, asking Kazantsev the same thing several times to see whether he slipped up. He came at the problem from different angles, sometimes ruminating for minutes as his thoughts meandered, sometimes jabbing with a quick surprise thrust. Every time Kazantsev answered firmly, concisely and, most importantly, without contradiction.

Stensness had approached him at the conference and arranged the rendezvous, presumably because Kazantsev's badge had identified him as an *Izvestia* correspondent.

Kazantsev had gone along to the statue at the agreed time, six thirty.

Stensness had not shown up.

Kazantsev usually waited no more than fifteen minutes at an appointment. If someone had not shown up by then, he left. Because of the fog, he had given Stensness an extra five minutes before leaving.

This morning Kazantsev had rung King's and obtained the Highgate address – the English were so trusting, unlike the Soviets, who did not even have phone directories – and that was where Herbert had run into him.

Herbert did not mention the Coronation; better not to let Kazantsev know what he knew, or at least what he suspected. Besides, what would he get apart from a denial?

Herbert felt as though he were in a maze; everyone could see what was happening bar him, blundering around like a blind fool.

Outside the pub, Herbert gave Kazantsev back his wallet – a man needed money, after all, even one born and raised in the workers' paradise – but kept his accreditation, partly to retain some leverage over him and partly to be bloody-minded. He also kept open the possibility of charging Kazantsev with trespass and assault on a police officer.

The accreditation would be returned and the charges dropped, he said, if Kazantsev could remember anything further which might help Herbert with his enquiries.

'If I could help you, Inspector, believe me, I would,' Kazantsev replied.

'Really?'

'Of course. I am a serious admirer of England and the English. In my short time here, I have come to love your country. London impresses me with its gravity and variety. London is wise; London always comes with a subtext. I love Marks and Spencer, a cheap, democratic shop, not charging the earth like Harrods. Perhaps Mr Marks was really spelt with an "x", yes? I love Berry Brothers, the best wine shop in London, where the prices are lower than in Moscow, and so is the water content in the bottles. I love going to the cinema and seeing the screen gradually disappear in the smoke from all the briar pipes, especially during the last sitting, after which retired colonels from the colonies leap from their seats and bellow "God Save the Queen". All these things I love. So of course I would help you. Of course.'

Herbert didn't have enough time to go home *and* make it to Hannah's on time, so he headed straight for Soho. It should have been a quick hop east on the Central Line, but the fog was causing havoc. Herbert jumped train after spending ten minutes stationary at Oxford Circus with no word as to what was happening, and resolved to walk the rest of the way, but he got his bearings wrong on leaving the station, and before he knew it he was at Piccadilly Circus.

Piccadilly was lined with girls too young and pretty to be tarts, but tarts they were, their mothers lying in wait beneath darkened porches behind. Swarthy men glided from girl to girl with more menace than charm; the foot soldiers of the Messina brothers, Maltesers who ruled the West End prostitution racket with razors.

The fog was making even London's most colourful areas seem monochrome. Light from the vast neon billboards of Piccadilly Circus groped weakly through the gloom, embers from a blazing riot of brand-names: Guinness, Bovril, Vortix Vermouth, Ever-Ready, Swallow Raincoats.

Beneath the lights flashing baleful welcomes to the lonely and bored, rent boys negotiated prices with men in kerbside cars, engines still running and exhausts thickening the fog yet further. One young man clambered into a Paramount 10 Roadster; another shook his head and walked away from a Citroën Light 15.

There was a police phone box on the Circus itself; a large blue kiosk topped by an electric light, which in this particular instance was flashing to indicate that the officers on patrol should make contact with their station.

Herbert opened the door and stepped inside. The interior was as spartan as he had expected: a stool, a table with a telephone, a brush and a duster, and an electric fire which looked far too small and inadequate ever to require the services of the extinguisher beside it.

The telephone was linked directly to the local subdivisional police station; in this case, the one at Savile Row. Herbert picked up the receiver, waited until the connection was made, identified himself, and asked to be transferred to New Scotland Yard, Murder Squad.

'Murder Squad.' It was Veal's voice.

'Veal, it's Smith.'

'Hello! I hear you're the sunshine boy.' There was no trace of sarcasm in Veal's voice, as there would have been in some of the others'. Veal was the most sanguine and cheery of all Herbert's colleagues, the one best at putting people at their ease and, not coincidentally, the one who could always be relied on to winkle information out of a suspect.

'For the moment,' Herbert said.

'Enjoy it while it lasts. What have you got?'

Herbert recounted the salient points of his conversation with Kazantsev.

'Tyce will want to know why you didn't arrest him,' Veal said, when Herbert had finished.

'It's lucky Tulloch's not in charge, then. For attacking two police officers, he'd want him hung, drawn and quartered.'

Veal chuckled laconically. 'And the rest.'

'I didn't arrest him because I'll get more out of him this way.'

'You're sure?'

'I'm never sure. But that's what I believe, yes.'

'Then that's what I'll tell Tyce.'

'Thanks.'

Herbert hung up, stepped out of the police box, spent a few seconds ensuring that he had orientated himself correctly this time, and then set off down Shaftesbury Avenue.

Frith Street loomed at him from the gloom, a left turn into another bank of grey. Number 14 had doorbells but no intercom. Herbert rang three times before he heard from inside the sounds of feet descending the stairs.

'Herbert?' Hannah asked from behind the door.

'Yes.'

She fumbled with locks and latches, and opened the door.

'You found it,' she said, smiling a searchlight-bright display of teeth and presenting her cheek for a kiss. 'Come in.'

Hannah lived on the top floor, in a small flat made smaller by the number of people there. Herbert counted at least ten, all young, mostly male, and all conversing in a strange, slightly guttural language that he was unable to place but which he fancied came from Eastern Europe – a conjecture reinforced by their Slavic features, and of course by Hannah's own accent too.

There were questioning cries in the guttural language. Hannah replied in the same tongue, presumably explaining who Herbert was, for when she had finished the others turned and smiled their welcome at him.

The air in the flat was as thick as the fog outside, a blend of cigarette smoke and rich smells from the kitchen. Herbert felt a curious mixture of self-consciousness and relief; the former because he was so obviously the outsider in this group, and the latter because at least now he wouldn't be left alone with Hannah, groping for conversation.

'It's Shabbat,' Hannah said.

'You're Jewish?'

'No, I just want to party on a Friday night.' She laughed, but without cruelty, and the sarcasm in

161

her voice was instantly diffused. 'Of course I'm Jewish. You never meet a Jew before?'

'Of course I have.' Herbert did not like to say where.

'Well, then. Now it's Shabbat. Oh!' Hannah opened a drawer, brought out two candles, set them in candlesticks already on the table, and lit them. For a moment, Herbert was surprised by her dexterity, and then realised that perhaps it was not so difficult on home turf; he could probably have found most things in his flat blindfolded too.

Herbert opened his mouth to enquire about the candles, and Hannah answered his unasked question. 'For the start of Shabbat. Sunset, so I should have done it hours ago. You light them only when you can see three star in the sky, but people say the fog is bad, so we might have one week without Shabbat because we cannot see three star. For me, I *never* see three star. Or two star, or one star.' She laughed again, quite the happiest person he had met all day.

'You joke about being blind?' Herbert said.

Hannah looked at him as though he were the stupidest man on earth. 'Of course. I joke, or I go mad. Being blind is better than being mad, no?'

Herbert thought back to the grim resolve that Hannah had shown in the Long Water that morning – that morning, was that all it was? It seemed he'd known her much longer – and realised that her jokes about blindness were a veneer, genuine but thin, plastered over the deep

162

vein of cripple's anger within. She might laugh about her sightlessness to stop herself going mad, but laughter did not equal resignation. On the contrary, she channelled her rage, fuelling the determination of her independence.

'You have a nice day?' she asked, lengthening the indefinite article slightly, so that it sounded more like *aw*.

'Oh, you know. Got chased round Highgate by three guys. Hid in a cemetery. Had a fight with a Russian. The usual things you do on your birthday.'

It had slipped out, as though made word against his will. He hadn't meant to tell her.

'Is your birthday?'

'Yes.'

'How many years?'

'Thirty-five.'

'Thirty-five is good age. Enough experience, enough energy.'

Herbert doubted both, sometimes.

He expected her to ask whether he had nothing better to do than dine with a stranger on his birthday, but instead she said simply, 'All this, you do for the dead man, yes?'

'Yes.'

Hannah put her hands on the back of a chair and sat gracefully.

'What language are you speaking with those men?' Herbert asked, also sitting – though, he could not help feeling, with slightly less poise than she had exhibited.

'Hungarian.'

A plate of food appeared in front of him, smelling more delicious than anything he could remember eating. 'You're from Hungary?'

'Yes.'

'Your English is very good.'

'You lie, but thank you.'

'It's not a lie.'

'My English is OK. I understand you, you understand me. I listen to language more than others perhaps, than people with sight. I hear vocabulary, grammar, accents. But I speak Hungarian translated to English, not English. You understand?'

Herbert nodded, a motion which for Hannah his silence gave away.

'Imagine me like radio,' she laughed. 'On radio, you can't see. So is no help, to nod or shake head.'

'Yes,' Herbert said, knowing, or at least hoping, that Hannah was laughing *with* him rather than *at* him. 'I understand.'

Someone put a plate in front of her. Without a trace of self-consciousness, Hannah bent her face to the table and sniffed around the entire circumference, seeing – discovering, more accurately – what was where. Whoever had served her knew her needs, Herbert saw; the food was arranged as though on a clock-face.

He looked at his own plate. There were mushroom pancakes, liver with figs, wild rice and mashed potatoes, apricot chicken and cabbage nut salad. To procure all this, with rationing still in force, Hannah, or her fellow Hungarians, must have been even more resourceful than he had thought.

'Let's eat,' Hannah said. 'For Shabbat dinner, everything can wait.'

That she was Hungarian was in itself unremarkable enough, Herbert thought. Britain had been a repository for refugees since the war. Poles, Czechs, Greek Cypriots and Spaniards had all made their way there to escape persecution and worse, and now were being joined by the first waves from the colonies of which Britain was divesting itself with some haste.

Not everyone approved, of course. No boarding-house seemed complete without a sign on the door proclaiming: *No Blacks, No Irish, No Dogs*.

Herbert wondered how many of Hannah's friends he had watched, questioned or otherwise checked up on during his years in Five. The service as a whole had interviewed almost a quarter of a million Eastern European refugees in the past couple of years, of which three thousand were earmarked for immediate internment should there be war with the Soviet Union.

Perhaps some of them were working with MI6, too. It was an open secret in the intelligence community that Six were spiriting Hungarian dissidents across the border into the British zone of Austria, where they were giving them resistance training in preparation for a future uprising against the Soviet occupation.

'You ever have matzo?' Hannah asked.

'Never.'

'Here.' She handed Herbert a piece of what looked like rough biscuit. 'The first time I ever have it, a rabbi on a park bench give it to me. You know what I ask him? "Who write this rubbish?"'

She laughed again, loud and infectious. If Herbert could have bottled even a fraction of her *joie de vivre*, he felt, he could have cured half the capital's ailments in a stroke.

It took him a moment to get the joke, and then he was laughing with her.

He wondered, too, whether this type of joke against her blindness was, in addition to what he had noticed before, some sort of defence mechanism against unwanted sympathy, or perhaps Hannah's way of testing people out and seeing what they were made of when it came to sensibilities and sensitivities.

Herbert ate fast, ravenous for such amazing food and unable to follow the conversation which babbled around him. Hannah, in contrast, lingered over each mouthful, smelling it on her fork, holding it in her mouth, chewing copiously before swallowing.

'Hannah Mortimer isn't a very Jewish name,' Herbert said when she had finished.

'Is not my birth name. I was born Hannah Moses.'

'Why did you change?'

'Why does anyone change their name? To seem less foreign.' She rolled the *r* slightly at the back of her tongue. 'To change their luck, if the old name brings bad chance. Jews always change their names.'

'They do?'

166

'Always. Asher becomes Archer; David Davies; Jacob Jackson; Levi Lewis . . .'

Herbert had stopped listening, because he was still thinking of what she had said a couple of sentences before, about the destiny of misfortune.

With a leap of muscular induction, he knew – at least, he could make a good guess – when she had come to Britain, and why. If he was right, he knew what she must have been through in her life.

'I was at Belsen,' he said.

The British soldiers arrived in Belsen on 15th April 1945, a date Herbert could no more forget than his own birthday. If they had ever doubted the justness of the cause against Nazism, then with one look at Belsen, they doubted no more.

They had expected to hear shouting from a mile off: 'The Allies are coming! The Allies are coming!' – but when they drove through the gates, it was in complete silence. And at funeral pace, too. They had to keep stopping, because the inmates were too weak to get out of the way of their tanks.

There had been no food or water for the five days before their entry. Outside the huts was an almost unbroken carpet of shit, filth and corpses. Some of the bodies had been dismembered and the flesh ripped from their bones; yet there were no animals which could have done this.

Everywhere was typhus and starvation, the dead and the dying indistinguishable. People collapsed as they walked; upright one moment, then dead before they hit the ground. Or they crawled to the sunshine to die there.

The British doctors marked red crosses on the foreheads of those they thought had a chance of making it. They were never in danger of running out of ink.

Everything Herbert had known about suffering was turned on its head. He and his fellow soldiers had spent months existing on army rations and whatever food they had found during the German retreat. They were filthy with sweat and diarrhoea and the general stink of war. But compared to the inmates of Belsen, they looked as though they had been holed up at the Ritz.

Their khaki uniforms, mixed and matched from inadequate equipment stores, could have been regal robes when set next to the rags of the deportees. Even with their various ailments, the British soldiers were the picture of ruddy-cheeked, well-fed health among the tenuous, skeletal silhouettes who tried to touch and finger them, as if the eddies of their passing were the waters of life itself.

When the soldiers ran to answer a command, or climbed a ladder, they would sometimes stop dead not knowing where to look, for in the inmates' wide-eyed gazes they saw an unpalatable knowledge: that such movements, so natural and easy for the soldiers, would have killed the inmates as surely as a bullet in the temple.

How did Herbert know this? Because they *did* kill some of them, that was how.

The soldiers gave away their rations – dried milk powder, oatmeal, sugar, salt and tinned meat – and within hours hundreds of those who had eaten were dead, the food too rich for systems starved partway to death.

How in the name of God could oatmeal and tinned meat be too rich?

The initial admission, that he had been at Belsen, had come out of Herbert's mouth without thinking, and as he told his story, his guts lurched with the possibility that he had spoken out of turn; that at best he was wrong, or that if he had been right then the reminder would be unwelcome, and she would ask him, perhaps politely, perhaps with anger ablaze, to leave, to trudge back through the fog to a flat even emptier and colder than before. For before there had been neither Hannah, nor the chatter of her friends – which was no less comforting for its incomprehensibility – nor the textures of her food.

Reactions flitted across Hannah's face like clouds in front of the moon. Her mouth dropped slightly; surprise more than dismay, Herbert hoped. He saw the slight quiver of her cheeks as she battled the silt of dormant memories suddenly stirred.

Finally, as she resolved the manner in which she would handle this, she narrowed her eyes and turned to him.

'Then you understand,' she said.

* * *

I come from Pécs, a small town several hour from Budapest in the car. My mother was a teacher, my father worked for Ford. American cars were popular in Hungary before the war.

In 1944, springtime, the Germans arrive, and suddenly comes order after order: wear a Star of David, yellow; obey curfew; prohibit to travel; searching the homes; people in prison; seize stores and businesses.

And then they take us to Auschwitz.

It is May. I remember barbed wire between pylons, green tar-paper covering the barracks. Striped clothes for prisoners. Everything before is now gone.

When I think of Pécs, it is like life on another planet.

Auschwitz was . . . No need to tell you, you can guess. I was there until beginning 1945. The Red Army is almost at the gates when the guards evacuate us. We march through the snow; frostbite and exhaustion. People lose fingers, toes, arms, legs. Dancers don't dance any more, pianists don't play.

You stop, they shoot you. We drag those who don't walk.

I am fifteen. I should be in school, kissing boys behind classrooms and quarrelling with my mama. Instead, I march through snow without seeing. Twenty thousand of us left Auschwitz; less than ten thousand reached Wandsbeck, the labour camp in Hamburg. Only two thousand arrive in Belsen.

Belsen was the terminal, in every way. Never before is reflected so purely man's darkness, his sadism and brutality. I try to describe with words what I remember from it, but there is no language on earth to express such horror, even to imagine it.

It is so horrible because no longer the Germans are in charge. The guards have nothing to do – Death does everything for them. Death keeps us so hungry and so crowded that we cannot move, not even when our lives depend on it. Death stands guard on the walls, Death keeps all the food and water for itself. Death makes sure we have no work, no order. Death leaves us on a giant heap of rubbish.

I arrived in Belsen on 7th March, so I spend five week there. The rest of my life, whether I die tomorrow or in next century, will never be as long as those five week. Difference is this: in Auschwitz, we do things, we work, we have reasons. In Belsen, we exist. No more.

One day, I ask a guard: 'Warum?' *'Why?'*

And he reply: 'Hier ist kein warum.' *'Here, there is no why.'*

After first few days, I never think of death. Death all round, so why think of it? Like to thinking why grass is green or sky blue. Neither I think of the Germans very much. Yes, I like to defy. Just to be alive is enough. My hatred against them increases my desire to live; it keeps me alive in actuality, perhaps.

Truth is this: you think too much of what happens, you go crazy. After few day, I decide to think of my hair only. I think of when I can wash it, or way to comb it with my finger, or way to tie it on my head, off my face. I think of how to stop guards cutting all my hair, and how to stay away from lice. Lice everywhere in camp.

I think of my hair, nothing else. It fills my mind and

closes me from actuality. I have a focus, something for me to control.

And that is how I survive Belsen. In that way, and also because I cannot see any more. For first time – for the only time – I give thanks to be blind.

And then we are free. Allied soldiers give us uniforms to wear and food from their kitchen, putting us at the head of the queue. On the trains, we ride without paying if we show the conductor our camp tattoo. We stay in monasteries, where my friends say the sheets are the most white in their lives. I cross Europe, and eventually, at the end of summer, I take a boat and come to England.

The others were still there, of course, hived off into small groups – Herbert supposed that was typical of dinner parties, that the conversations would splinter once the food was eaten and therefore no longer the communal focus, though since he had been to so few dinner parties in recent years it was hard for him to claim much authority on the matter – but every fibre of his attention was on Hannah.

He wondered how many other people Hannah had talked to about this. Not that many, he supposed. The luminosity in her expression suggested that this had been some form of catharsis, no matter how small and temporary.

'Now you know,' she said.

Actually, he thought, he knew very little. 'No more than you know about me.'

'I know you are lonely.'

'Really?'

172

'Yes. Very, very lonely.'

It was a statement, not a question; stark in its bluntness, yet delivered with neither judgement nor care that it would cause offence.

Above all, it was true. Why else would he have gone, on his birthday, to dinner with someone he had barely met, knowing even at the start of the day that he would have no better offers by night-fall?

Herbert supposed that he should have been cautious, as they were moving into areas he had barely explored himself, let alone shared with anybody else; but Hannah's unerring accuracy re-assured rather than concerned him, and if they had only known each other a few hours, then so what?

He had known his own mother all his life, and yet still he felt a sense of estrangement from her.

So Herbert told Hannah, and told her everything.

Yes, he was lonely; an intense isolation which nothing seemed to quench. Every day, he looked around and saw the ways in which others seemed to be happy with the most superficial relationships.

They passed the time of day, but never talked about what really mattered. They made noises and thought they were communicating; pulled faces and thought they understood.

He was looking for something more, something which was at the very least empathetic, perhaps veering towards telepathic, to the point where his emotions began to merge with another person's.

He found it very difficult when someone did not instinctively know what he was feeling, because then he had to explain himself to them, which he hated doing.

Conversely, of course, finding someone like Hannah who *did* seem to read his mind was in itself unnerving.

At times when Herbert was speaking, some of the Hungarians would approach them, check that he and Hannah had all the food and drink they needed, and then drift away again.

Herbert saw one man squeeze Hannah's shoulder as he walked past the back of her chair; another bent to whisper something which made her smile.

Herbert wondered whether these men were, or had ever been, Hannah's lovers, and had to bite back a swift swell of jealousy.

If they were, then it was nothing to do with him; though equally Hannah seemed too untrammelled to be any one person's sole property.

So he kept talking, ushered forward by the ease of her manner, by the lack of eye contact, and perhaps by his assumption that, as a foreigner and a Jew, her cultural norms were slightly different from his.

He was an only child, with all that the unwanted status involved; a certain melancholy, tendencies towards introversion. When, as a child, he stayed apart from his schoolmates, they accused him of being aloof; but when he tried to make friends, he tried too hard, came on too strong, and they turned against him just the same.

Most people seemed to understand instinctively the balance between communality and self-sufficiency. Not Herbert. He felt like a novice pilot, constantly over-correcting as he tried to steer a steady course.

He had a teddy bear with one eye, to whom he would talk for hours. In place of real friends, he had imaginary ones, loyal and inspiring.

He even had an invented him, one who was braver, cleverer, more lovable, more daring – more of all the things in which he was less. Herbert wanted to follow and imitate this hero, who took the paths he had eschewed and told him about them, just as Herbert told him what he had done, sharing the good and the bad as equally as the thrilling and the banal.

The invented him lived Herbert's life the way he would have chosen, if only Herbert had possessed the gumption; for one became the person one chose to be, didn't one? He was a second chance, a confidant, a mirror image, a mentor, a guardian angel, a counsellor, a guide.

He was everything. And of course he never existed.

Then Herbert had won a scholarship to Cambridge, where he felt like a fraud from start to finish, neither one thing nor the other; too posh for the children at home, too common for the Etonians and Harrovians.

There was a coal miner there, Jimmy Lees. He told Burgess, 'You'll get a First, because your energies aren't exhausted by life, because of the class prejudice of the examiners, and because you got here easily and aren't frightened by it all. I don't have the brilliance of ignorance. I'll do ten times as much work as you, and get a good Second.'

And that's exactly how it happened, for Herbert as much as for Jimmy.

One could interest oneself in truth or brilliance, one could write essays or epigrams. Herbert chose the former.

No. He *did* the former, because he could not do the latter. He had no choice.

Then came the war, and then came Belsen. There were plenty of soldiers there with him, the happy-go-lucky ones, who managed to put away the horror and get on with their lives. Perhaps Herbert had less far to go than them; because, for him, Belsen took a world already negative and skewed it into darkness, a murk he had to face alone.

There was no one he could talk to. Those who hadn't been there wouldn't understand; those who had been there simply wanted to forget about it.

Belsen showed him that life delivered little but bad news: disaster, disease, disorder, distress, disgrace, divorce, and of course death, inescapable and inevitable, because even if nothing else went wrong, one was still going to die.

What Herbert already had inside him, Belsen had exacerbated, and then Maclean and de Vere Green took it still further, till he could hardly tell where cause began and effect finished, or vice versa.

In Belsen, Hannah, you said you had existed, no more.

That's what Herbert feared above all: being absent from his work, from other people, even from himself. In such circumstances, nothing would matter, neither humour nor love, sadness nor anger, let alone pain. And surely there could be nothing worse than feeling so desolate that even the tears would not come.

'Well,' Hannah said, 'no one say that life is a bowl of cherries.'

No, Herbert agreed; they did not.

'You play piano?' she asked.

'A little.'

'You ever hear "Life's a Bowl of Cherries" in 5/4 time?'

'It's in 4/4 time, isn't it?'

Hannah put on a flawless Cockney accent. 'Life's/a bowl/of fuckin'/cherries,' she sang, and in spite of himself Herbert burst out laughing.

There was an upsurge of chatter at Hannah's singing, which he understood to be calls for her to play the piano. She demurred, at first through concern for Herbert, and then with mocking half-heartedness after he assured her he was fine, and that he had monopolised her enough for one evening.

When she stood, everyone cheered, and cleared

a path to a piano in the corner which he had not even noticed. Usually it took him a couple of seconds at most to fix the layout and furniture of a room in his head.

Must be slipping, Herbert thought.

He had never heard the tunes Hannah was playing – they must have been Hungarian folk songs, judging by the enthusiasm with which the others started singing – but it hardly mattered. Her playing was exquisite. She could surely have been a concert pianist, if she had put her mind to it.

Diver, cook, musician; Herbert wondered if there was anything she could not do.

He looked at his wristwatch for the first time since arriving in Frith Street, and was amazed to find that it had gone midnight.

Now that the spell between Hannah and him had been broken, Herbert felt somewhat flayed. He had never exposed so much of himself.

Once more at the edge of a group, once more on the outside looking in, he slipped quietly through the door and out into the fog.

The stillness was so complete as to be incredible. A disaster could have taken place, leaving Herbert the last man on earth, and he would not have known the difference.

Every city, especially one as big as London, has its own hum, its own cadence, even in the small hours, because cities never truly sleep.

But that night, there was absolutely nothing.

No people, no traffic, no distant shouts, no industrial whirring. The fog concealed anything which Herbert would otherwise have seen, and silenced everything he would otherwise have heard.

When he held out his hand in front of him, he lost sight of his own fingers, and wondered if his own body was disappearing. Even the streetlights had been reduced to the faintest of glows.

One step into the hanging mist, and perhaps the fog would swallow him whole, spitting him out only in another dimension of space and time.

It did not, of course; but it might as well have done. Seconds later, Herbert was lost. From Hannah's flat to his was no distance – less than a mile, even going the long way via Shaftesbury Avenue and Piccadilly – but from the very first turning he took, he had absolutely no idea where he was, or even which way he was going.

Every pace looked the same, for he could see nothing: no landmarks, no street signs. When he paused at a street corner to get his bearings, he could no longer remember from which direction he had come.

It was akin to being buried in an avalanche, when one was so disorientated that one had no idea which way was up. At least in such situations one could use gravity to find out; clear a space round one's mouth and let saliva flow. But he had no such resources here.

He kept walking, knowing that he was as likely to be making things worse as better, but having no idea what else to do. And he had to keep warm, too; to stop was to freeze, and to freeze was to die. He could have been right outside his front door without knowing it, or he could have been halfway to Bethnal Green. He would have stopped a passer-by or flagged down a car to ask them where he was, but he saw neither. At times he fancied he recognised a patch of pavement or the particular orientation of a corner, but in the very next stride everything seemed alien again.

The air around him was thick and resistant, as though full of mushed-up bread. It seemed to be setting like glue into a strange, viscous stiffness. Fear snatched at him, a mild gnawing below his diaphragm which quickly escalated into a swarming, crawling beast.

Herbert thought of the moment when one slipped and the earth rushed up to meet one, and realised that that was how he felt, but a sensation that usually lasted a fraction of a second persisted interminably, as if he were anticipating a terror beyond dread but never receiving the release of actually experiencing it.

He tried to run, but within moments his lungs were burning from all the filth in the air, and he had all but turned his ankle on a sharp piece of kerb.

He stopped. It was below zero, and he was sweating heavily.

At that very moment, Hannah's voice came to him softly through the fog, calling in a lilting song as though he were a sailor and she a Siren.

Herbert marvelled at the power of his imagination.

Then, with a start, he realised that the voice was becoming louder.

She was coming towards him. No; he was walking towards her.

And there she was, standing by her front door, her hand outstretched for his and her lips fluttering in a smile.

'I knew you would come back,' she said.

He had walked, unknowingly, in a vast circle. It was what people did when they were lost, Hannah said; something to do with gyroscopy and homing instinct. When the Hungarians had left – they didn't live there, after all, did they? – they had told her how thick the fog was, and so she had waited for his return.

'But how did you know it was me?' Herbert asked.

'Your scent. And your footsteps.'

'My *scent*? I'm not an animal.'

'Everyone smell different.'

'Well, I can't smell anything through all the chemicals in the air, and I certainly couldn't hear anything. You must have amazing senses.'

'Not at all. I use them more than you, I believe. Blind people hear better? It's just a myth. Many myth concerning blind people.'

'What are the others?'

'A hundred myth. Let's see . . . Oh, yes. Blind

people, their spirit is more pure. Blindness makes us saints.' Hannah laughed. 'Complete lie.'

She found Herbert blankets and a pillow, and he lay down on the sofa. When she went through into her bedroom, she left the door ajar. But before Herbert could decide what, if anything, she had meant by that, he heard the unmistakable sounds of someone going to sleep: a rustling of bed linen as she found a comfortable position, a couple of rapid snorts, and then a long, lazy rhythm of slow breathing.

Hannah was asleep in minutes. Herbert lay awake in the darkness for hours.

6TH DECEMBER 1952

SATURDAY

The radio was already on when Herbert woke, giving him the fleeting sensation of being at home. The sight of Hannah preparing coffee more than erased the slight dislocation he felt when he remembered where he was. Even in this prosaic, workaday aspect of her being, hair dishevelled and with the sleeves of her dressing-gown rolled up as she did last night's dishes, she almost frightened him with her beauty.

He watched her until to have continued doing so would have felt uncomfortable.

Every football match in London had been cancelled, the newscaster said. The BBC schedule itself was having to be revised because artists and presenters were unable to get to the studios.

Shipping in the Thames was at a standstill for a second day; quarter of a million tons of cargo sitting idle, and the owners paying by the hour in terms of maintenance, wages and loss of earnings.

The airports at Heathrow, Northolt and Bovington had also suspended operations.

Trains were running late, ones from the West Country by as much as two hours.

'Sleep good?' Hannah said, handing Herbert a cup of coffee.

'Yes,' he lied, feeling the steam from the cup tickle his lips. He felt absurdly, post-coitally awkward; doubly so because there had, of course, been no coitus in the first place. How did one behave when one woke up in the flat of a woman of whose existence one had been ignorant just twenty-four hours before?

'Could I take a bath, please?' Herbert said. The fog seemed to have settled on him during the night; when he blew his nose, the mucus came out black.

'Of course. Just let me finish there first.'

She left the door open as she cleaned her teeth, putting the top of her toothpaste tube carefully down on the flat part of the basin so that it would not roll away. When she applied lipstick, she did so with her left index finger directly above the middle of her upper lip. She parted her hair by running the same finger up from the bridge of her nose to her crown, so she knew where centre was.

She did all this fast and with flawless accuracy.

'All yours,' she said.

It was only when Herbert was in the bath, the taps spitting a mixture of scalding and freezing water around his legs, that he saw there was no soap.

He stepped out of the shower and looked for a bar on the basin, then in the drawers of the bathroom cabinet. He could find none.

Wrapping a towel round his waist – some vague sense of propriety stopped him from leaving the bathroom naked – he opened the door.

Hannah was not in the bedroom.

Herbert saw that her clothes drawers were arranged with meticulous care. Some were labelled in Braille and others had embroidered knots hanging from the handles, so that she would know which type of garments they were.

He found her squatting by the fireplace, feeling with now blackened hands round the pile of coal in there. Her touch was sufficiently lingering to ensure that the stack was secure, but fleeting enough to avoid getting burnt by the residual heat.

'I can't find the soap,' Herbert said.

Hannah paused before answering. 'No surprise. I have none.'

If he had been more awake, the tone of her voice would probably have warned him off; but it was early and he was slow. 'Why ever not?'

Hannah turned towards Herbert and looked at him in abject, wordless despair; at last without an answer, bereft of the words in her language or anyone else's.

Herbert could hardly get out of Hannah's flat fast enough after that, and with every fumbling attempt to fasten his trousers or knot his tie, he cursed his tactless stupidity.

In a single, unconsidered sentence, he had surely undone every special thing that had happened last night. He had wanted to hold those hours for ever, Hannah and him, a little bubbleskin outside of time.

A burst balloon, more like.

It was quarter past seven, and even at this time on a Saturday morning, in a fog so thick as to more than halfway resemble the pea soup of renown, Soho was fairly thrumming with life.

Two gentle old ladies busied themselves with the Welsh dairy at the bottom of Frith Street; a Frenchman was buying croissants from Madame Valerie's; soon the dirty bookshops would be wrapping customers' purchases in plain brown paper. Italians shouted over thick sludges of black coffee at Café Torino's on the corner where Dean Street met Old Compton; and at Richard's on Brewer Street, blocks of ice kept Mediterranean squid and sardines fresh.

It was the spirit of the Blitz reincarnated, Herbert thought. Londoners would not let something as mundane as a fog get them down, and for a moment he felt inordinately proud to be a resident of this city which he could love and hate pretty much in the same moment.

Herbert found his way home as much by luck as by judgement, and ran into Stella outside his front door.

'The wanderer returns, eh?' she laughed.

'I've been taking your advice, Stella,' he said.

'Have you? Have you, now? Good lad.' She clapped him on the shoulder, and he smelt the sweetness of fermenting alcohol on her breath. 'Anything to tell me about?'

'Maybe later.'

She made a *moue* that, though exaggerated, was only half in jest. 'Holding out on Auntie Stella?'

'Not at all. I just haven't got far enough to have anything specific to report.'

It sounded clumsy, but maybe that was what convinced her of its veracity. 'Good for you,' she said, with a throaty cackle. 'Goodnight, Herbert. I'm off to bed.'

He wondered whether she had been waiting up for him. If she had, it would not have been from the purest of motives, that was for sure. Stella's heart was by no means gold, and Herbert liked her all the more for it. She had seen too much of life's seedier side to be a saint. Her determination was altogether simpler; to make the best of her situation, and retain a shred of decency while doing it.

Inside his flat, Herbert had a bath deep enough to wash away not only the smog but also the detritus that mornings could bring; things often seemed worse first thing, and the more he thought about how unique and unexpected last night had been, the longer the fall became.

Hannah had gone out of her way to find Stensness's overcoat, *and* to feed Herbert, *and* to let him confide in her. And what had he done for her in return? Put his foot in it about the soap, that was what; gone and reminded her of the darkest time of her life.

He had seen with his own eyes, while in Belsen, the *commodities* made in the extermination camps – the lampshades and book bindings, and the more prosaic too.

Brilliant, Herbert. Sheer genius.

When he was out of the bath, dry and dressed, he rang the Yard. This time, it was Connolly who answered the phone.

'What a dreadful day, Smith,' Connolly said, when Herbert had identified himself. 'I wonder whether this fog isn't the wrath of God, or something like that.'

'Any messages for me?' Herbert asked, as much to cut Connolly off as anything else. Connolly could tumble into melancholy at the drop of a hat, and was too deep a thinker for a member of the Murder Squad.

Herbert saw a lot of himself in Connolly, truth be told.

'Tyce left something for you,' Connolly said. 'He tried to ring you at home last night, but you weren't there.'

'No, I wasn't,' Herbert said, sidestepping the implicit question. 'What did Tyce say?'

'Hold on.' Herbert heard rustling as Connolly hunted through papers. 'Here we are. He said if you haven't got anything out of the Russian by tonight, you're to bring him in, and that's an order.'

'Anything else?'

'No. But he means it.'

'I'm sure he does.'

Herbert hung up, and then, since he was thinking about the case – when had he not, apart from the time he had spent with Hannah? – he took out the *Times* article about the Coronation, and puzzled once more over the handwritten code.

XXX CCD GVD RCC DPA XXX CDK S.

He had been thinking in crossword clues, where every answer was a trick of the language, a clever piece of wordplay.

But what if this code had little or nothing to do with English?

He looked at it again, without trying to impose words over the top.

Still nothing.

He was stumbling over the threefold divisions, he realised.

So he took them out.

XXXCCDGVDRCCDPAXXXCDKS

Too many *X*s running together. They made the whole thing seem lopsided.

More to keep his brain turning over than anything more purposeful, he reversed the whole lot.

SKDCXXXAPDCCRDVGDCCXXX.

And just like that, the answer hit him.

Well, one part hit him, anyway; four letters near the end. *RDVG.*

Richard de Vere Green.

It was too unlikely to be a coincidence.

If there was a Richard de Vere Green, there might be an AK, Alexander Kazantsev.

No AK. But an SK, at the end.

Russians were forever shortening names, Herbert remembered; nine out of ten men were known to their friends by their diminutive. What was Alexander shortened to?

Sasha.

SK: Sasha Kazantsev.

Herbert put in his own spaces now. *SKDCXXX. APDCC. RDVGDCCXXX.*

Grammar school had given him a classical education, so he had no problem recognising what the strings of letters after the initials meant. Roman numerals.

SK, 630. AP, 700. RDVG, 730.

Herbert remembered that Kazantsev's rendezvous with Stensness had been scheduled for six thirty. The first of three, Herbert now saw, with AP, whoever he was, slotted in at seven. And de Vere Green at seven thirty.

De Vere Green had told Herbert that Stensness and he had arranged no meeting. De Vere Green had lied; here was the evidence, in black and white.

It had been prearranged, that was for sure. Stensness could not have had time to return home between leaving the conference and going on to Kensington Gardens, which meant that the latest he could have placed this in the Cholmeley Crescent cistern was on Thursday morning, before he left home for the conference, which in turn meant either that he had organised the meetings by then – in which case Kazantsev was lying about only having met him at the conference – or, at the very least, that he had known he would see the three men involved at the conference to inform them of their appointments.

Which meant that AP would almost certainly have been at the conference too.

Herbert opened the list of delegates, scanned rapidly through, and there he was, the only AP on the list – Ambrose Papworth, Embassy of the United States of America.

Or more precisely, as Herbert knew from his days at Five, a ranking CIA officer under embassy cover.

Papworth had a tanned, well-fed face bursting with vitality, eyes of cornflower blue, teeth which flashed white when he spoke, and a thatch of blond hair. If Herbert had not known better, he would have wagered the house on Papworth not having been in London long; but Papworth had been in London for three or four years, of that Herbert was sure.

'Been away?' Herbert asked.

'California,' Papworth replied, with a smile that spoke volumes for the charms of the Golden State.

The metal inserts on the heels of Papworth's shoes clicked loudly as he led Herbert through the marbled corridors of the Embassy, an elegant townhouse on the north side of Grosvenor Square. Not just shoes, Herbert saw; Church brogues, immaculate, the best a man could buy. Papworth was evidently one of those foreigners who, in certain areas, liked to be more British than the British.

'Man, you Brits sure know how to put on a fog,'

Papworth said. 'That's a serious goddamn mist you got out there. Could hardly find my way in this morning, so I guess it's lucky you caught me here. Place is normally deserted weekends. That's why I like to come in; too damn cramped in the week. Can't wait till we move.'

A vast site on the west side of the square had been earmarked for a new embassy, Herbert remembered. It would be many times the size of the existing one, and doubtless as ugly as it was large.

Papworth ushered Herbert into a drawing-room, all buttoned leather sofas and open fires. 'Can I have someone get you something?' he asked. 'Coffee? Tea?'

Herbert shook his head. 'Thank you, no.'

Have someone get you something, Papworth had said; he had not offered himself, as most people would have, even if someone more menial had actually been doing the bringing.

Elkington had rung just as Herbert was leaving the house, having persuaded New Scotland Yard to disclose Herbert's home number, and had begged to be part of whatever Herbert was doing today.

Herbert had refused. The disappointment in Elkington's voice had cut him unexpectedly deep, but he knew it was the right thing to do. The waters of the case were becoming murkier, and the last thing he wanted was to have to watch out for someone else. Elkington had demurred, and Herbert had cut him off.

Now Herbert sat, and Papworth spread his hands wide; the gesture, Herbert thought, of a man keen to show he had nothing to hide. 'Shoot.'

'A man named Max Stensness was drowned in the Long Water on Thursday.'

Papworth furrowed his brow. 'Max Stensness?' He pulled the name into a sing-song. 'Max Stensness?' And then: 'Gee, I remember. I met him at a conference on – Thursday, you said? Yeah, on that very day.'

At last, Herbert thought; someone who was up front about where they had been and who they had met, someone who wasn't going to play silly buggers.

'That's terrible,' Papworth added.

'That would have been the biochemical conference at the Festival Hall?'

'That's right.'

'What were you doing there?'

'Looking after Professor Pauling.'

It took Herbert a moment to place the name; L. C. Pauling, on the front of the pamphlet Rosalind had given him.

'The honorary chairman?'

'And the keynote speaker. Except he didn't speak, in the end. He contracted food poisoning the night before and was laid flat out for a day and a half. Probably some divine retribution for his pinko leanings.'

Like many things said half in jest, the last line gave away more of Papworth's feelings than he might have wanted.

'You don't approve of Pauling's politics?' Herbert asked.

Papworth sighed. 'Herbert, I'll level with you. When I say that I'm here to look after Professor Pauling, that's a slight euphemism. The job is more like baby-sitting: keeping an eye on him, making sure he doesn't get into trouble, or attract the wrong sort of attention. That's why I had to go to California – to collect him. He's a professor at Caltech, the California Institute of Technology. When it's over I'm going to deliver him all the way home, too. How much do you know about him?'

'Not much.'

'OK. As a person, he's perfectly pleasant, though he can be a bit awkward – comes with the territory, absent-minded scientist, mind on higher things, all that. As a scientist, he's awesome. *Awesome*. Totally focused. He was once shown a picture of a beautiful woman, completely naked, standing on a large rock in the middle of a rushing mountain stream. Pauling peers intently at the photograph for a few seconds and then exclaims: "Basalt!"'

Herbert must have looked blank, because Papworth swallowed his own laugh. 'Basalt,' he said again. 'The woman was standing on a basalt rock, but no one else had noticed, because . . . Anyway. He's won just about every award going, bar a Nobel Prize. Few years back, he got the Army & Navy Medal of Merit – the highest military award a civilian can get – for his work with explosives, his oxygen meter and his invention of a synthetic blood plasma.'

'You seem to know a lot about him.'

'It's my job to know a lot about him. So – he was the government's golden boy. Then the love affair began to cool. He started to criticise the nuclear weapons programme, and from someone like him, no ordinary Joe, that can mean something. He claims he worked out the amount of plutonium in the atom bomb all by himself, with no inside information. Personally, I think that's hooey, but anyway. People start paying attention. Pauling slams Washington for this and that, and soon questions are being asked, including the most obvious one.'

'Whether he's a fellow traveller?'

'Exactly. So he's asked the question – *Are you or have you ever been a member of the Communist Party?* – and he refuses to answer, claiming he believes that no citizen should be required to announce his political beliefs. Ducking the question, if you ask me. That's basically pleading the Fifth, and we all know what *that* means, whatever the law says. Anyway, earlier this year he applied for a passport, and the application was rejected under the terms of the McCarran Act. You know the McCarran Act?'

Herbert not only knew it, he remembered the wording verbatim; another legacy of his days in Leconfield House. 'It's intended to restrict the foreign travel of any Americans with suspect political sympathies on the grounds that secrets might be passed to enemy agents abroad.'

197

'Damn straight it is. So there's this big hoo-hah about the whole thing, people coming out the woodwork in support of Pauling. Einstein himself spoke up. So eventually Pauling's given a limited-duration passport, good only for specific trips. One of which is this.'

'And have any enemy agents tried to get in touch with him?'

Papworth shrugged. 'You get too paranoid, you see them round every corner.'

'Any you know of?'

'None that I can be sure are agents, but if I could they wouldn't be very good agents, would they? This one guy, reporter for some Russian paper, *Izvestia* or something –' Herbert's heart seemed to miss a beat, though his face remained unruffled – 'keeps ringing up asking for an interview with Pauling. Now, I'm as keen on freedom of speech as the next man, but not when it comes to those goddamn commies, you understand? It's an evil system, my friend, godless and evil, and if I can do anything to keep them from getting their claws into America, then that's just what I'll damn well do. I helped take the Rosenbergs down, and I'd do it again, and again, and again. We fought the Nazis to a standstill; the Reds are just as dangerous, mark my words.' Papworth took a deep breath, and laughed sheepishly. 'I'm sorry; it gets me worked up, that's all. My wife's eyes have taken to glazing over whenever I start on this. Where were we?'

'You and Stensness – how did you get talking?'

'Oh, you know, social chit-chat, the way people do at these things.'

'Did you see him after the conference ended?'

'No.'

'Were you supposed to?'

'Sure was.'

Papworth's answer was smooth and instant. A man incredibly adept at calculating scenarios, Herbert thought, or perhaps more simply a man with nothing to hide.

Papworth smiled complicitly at Herbert, a tacit admission: he knew that Herbert knew, or could at least guess, who he really was. Putting spies under embassy cover was pretty much a game. If one suspected every embassy official of espionage, one would never be caught out.

'Can you tell me where and when?'

'The Peter Pan statue, seven o'clock.'

'And Stensness didn't turn up?'

'Never showed.'

'How long did you wait?'

'Fifteen minutes.'

The same as Kazantsev, Herbert thought; or at least, the same leeway Kazantsev had said he gave people when waiting for them. Spies were spies, the world over. You were too late, they were gone.

'That's not long to give someone, especially in the fog.'

Papworth shrugged. 'In that cold, fifteen minutes was plenty enough. Besides, where I come from, punctuality equals professionalism.'

'Do you know what he was going to offer you?'

'Not exactly.'

'But he intimated something?'

'Yes, he did.'

'Something that would change the world?'

Papworth nodded. 'There's no use me asking how you know that?'

Stensness had tried it on with an American, a Brit and a Russian; the same hook each time. An amateur dealing with professionals, and one of them must have killed him.

'How long had you known Stensness?'

Papworth shrugged. 'Year or so.'

Herbert swooped. 'But you just told me you only met him at the conference.'

'I did. But I'd – forgive me, my phrasing was bad. I hadn't actually known him before. I'd known *of* him.'

'How come?'

Papworth smiled. 'The special relationship. Information sharing.' He frowned briefly. 'That . . . you said your name was Herbert Smith, right?'

Herbert nodded, knowing where this was going.

'The one who used to work for Five?' Papworth said. Taking Herbert's silence for assent, he leant back in his chair and whistled. 'Boy, have I wanted to meet *you*.'

One could hardly blame him, Herbert supposed. Burgess and Maclean had both spent time in Washington, and the CIA still wondered, not without reason, exactly what kind of American secrets they had taken to Moscow. And whether they were the only rotten apples in the Whitehall orchard.

The special relationship had been a little rocky ever since.

When it came to British intelligence, there were two schools of American thought.

There was the official one, which held that the British were the most sagacious, experienced and successful spies in history, and therefore the transatlantic alliance should be nurtured with care.

Then there was the unofficial one, which cast the British as supercilious snobs worthy only of the disdain they themselves showed.

Or perhaps it was a mixture of both: *Our liaison with the British is one of our greatest assets; don't tell the bastards anything important.*

The Agency, Herbert knew, were playing for high stakes.

Eisenhower had won the American election by a landslide the previous month, and was due to be inaugurated next month, when he would face the question which would surely dog not only him but every future president at the start of their administration. Was he running the CIA – or were the CIA running him?

In the past four years, the Agency had multiplied their overseas stations sevenfold, their staff by ten, and their budget by a factor of seventeen. It was unlikely they would be willing to slow down now.

'Did Five give you access to my testimony to the Maclean inquiry?' Herbert asked.

'Of course.' Papworth sounded insulted, as though even the implication that his reach did not access all areas was mortally offensive.

'Then you know that I was stitched up.'

'You were in charge of watching him, you lost him. Pretty clear, in my book.'

'De Vere Green did for me.'

Papworth made a *moue*. 'Richard and I go back a long way.'

Herbert was conscious that he had let the conversation drift away from Stensness's murder, but he also had the feeling that he was still making progress, albeit in a more oblique manner. 'How long?'

'Six years. Los Alamos.'

'Counter-espionage?'

'You got it.'

That made sense, Herbert thought. Los Alamos, in the high New Mexican sierra, had been the location for the Manhattan Project: the atom bomb. A joint Anglo-American enterprise, perhaps the most clandestine ever to be managed on such a large scale, and therefore packed with almost as many spooks as scientists. De Vere Green, and clearly Papworth too, had been among those tasked with ensuring that no atomic secrets had found their way to Moscow.

'And since then?'

'In and around DC after the war, then moved here, to London, in '48. Ran into Richard again when we interrogated Fuchs a couple of years back, and then last year we started working on a joint committee. The bosses are paranoid that secrets are still going to Moscow, so it's –'

'What kind of secrets?'

'Science secrets. The MGB have recently ramped up Line X, and –'

'Line X?'

'Informal name for the MGB's Directorate T: Science and Technical.'

'And what have you found?'

'That I can't tell you.' Papworth looked genuinely regretful, Herbert thought; brotherhood of spooks, and all that. Spies were no different from everyone else. They preferred to be among their own kind.

'Why not?'

'Because it's classified.'

'It may be relevant to this inquiry.'

'Trust me; it's not.' De Vere Green had said much the same thing, Herbert remembered. 'Now listen, Herbie –' Herbert bit back his natural response, that no one ever called him Herbie. He was not a Herbie – 'we're the good guys, right? We're all on the same side. I'm doing all I can to help you here, but I can't go opening up files just on the off-chance that you might find something in there that'll help you. You ask me what you like, I'll tell you all I know.'

That was fair enough, Herbert conceded, and as much as he could have reasonably expected to get. In any case, Burgess and Maclean or not, Papworth was being more helpful than de Vere Green had ever been. Perhaps it was the American commitment to the concept of freedom of information.

203

'What did you know about Stensness?'

'He gave Five information now and then.'

'What kind of information?'

'Stuff concerning his work. What other kind would there have been?'

Papworth clearly did not know about Stensness' informing on the CPGB.

'Can you remember what kind of stuff?'

'Crystallography – X-rays, that sort of thing. I'm sorry if that sounds vague, but I get so much of that across my desk every day that I lose track of any but the most important stuff – which I guess also tells you that his information was pretty mundane.'

'Then why keep using him?'

'Ask Five. He was their asset, not ours. But I guess they kept on using him for the normal reasons: you never know when someone will turn up gold, and better too much data than too little.'

'Was Stensness under suspicion for passing secrets to Moscow?'

'Not as far as I know. But maybe he should have been.'

'Why do you say that?'

'He made a rendezvous with me at the conference. I wasn't the only one, I guess. How else would you have known what he said to me, unless he was pitching it to others too, and unless you've talked to them? Either way, he was a scientist. And he was killed. You do the math.'

You do the math indeed, Herbert thought.

De Vere Green had lied to him about his

rendezvous, or lack of it, with Stensness. Now, it seemed at least possible that he had also lied about what he thought Stensness might have had to offer him.

Kazantsev and Papworth both had no doubt that the material in question was in some way scientific. If they were right, the Coronation was a blind, a code, or simply a mistake on Herbert's part, because he had been too keen to see connections where there were none. And because de Vere Green, eager to send Herbert off chasing wild geese, had spun seven leagues of yarn about terrorist plots and the like.

Herbert was just working out what next to ask Papworth when there was a knock on the door, and two men walked in. They were both in their forties.

One had a high forehead and a hairline which receded sharply on the right side of his crown, as though it had been burnt away.

The other's head was like a cat's, wide at the temple. Dark brown hair slicked back from a widow's peak, and his eyebrows described a circumflex accent. Herbert saw a mark on his left ear, a flat round disc on the cartilage, and a triangular cleft between his upper front teeth.

Papworth was on his feet, every East Coast inch the genial host. 'Linus! We were just talking about you.' He made the introductions: the man with the high forehead was Linus Pauling, the cat's head Fritz Fischer, a colleague of Pauling's from Caltech.

'Police?' Pauling said, when Papworth explained who Herbert was.

'Purely routine,' Papworth said soothingly. 'We pride ourselves on maintaining good relations with local law enforcement, of course.'

Pauling had a slight squint, his right eye veering to the outside. He turned to Herbert. 'You have a beautiful city; what I saw of it before the fog came down, at any rate,' he said.

'Thank you. How long are you staying for?'

Pauling shrugged eloquently, a man undone by nature's vicissitudes. 'How long is a piece of string?'

'There's a scientist's question for you!' Papworth exclaimed.

'We –' Pauling indicated Fischer – 'my colleague and I were supposed to have flown home this morning. But of course all flights out of London are cancelled. PanAm and TransWorld have been completely grounded. So we go when we go.'

'And in the meantime, I'm trying to keep them amused,' said Papworth. 'We're off to have a look at the Tower; show them where they'll end up if they get on the wrong side of the Metropolitan Police, huh?' He laughed. 'Then this evening, we've got tickets to *The Mousetrap*.'

'The new play at the Ambassadors? I've heard good things about it,' Herbert said.

'Me too. And I promise not to tell you who did it.'

Herbert laughed. 'Assuming it's not cancelled,

206

like everything else seems to be in this fog. Right, I must be getting on. You've been most helpful.'

'Any time.' Papworth shook Herbert's hand in both of his. 'I mean it. Our business shouldn't mean that we forget basic humanity, you know.'

The doorman at Leconfield House greeted Herbert like an old friend. Hardly surprising, Herbert thought, given that this was his third visit here in just over twenty-four hours. Any more of this, and they would be giving him his old pass card back.

De Vere Green wasn't there, the receptionist said. Herbert was just wondering how best to get to whichever vast country estate was that weekend playing host to de Vere Green, when the receptionist added: 'I think he's gone to a funeral.'

Herbert asked to see Patricia, who proved, as usual, the fount of all knowledge.

'What funeral?' she said. 'The poor chap who drowned the other night.'

'What?'

Herbert grabbed Patricia's phone and dialled the Murder Squad.

'Tyce.'

'It's Smith. What the hell's going on? Max Stensness is being buried, and no one told me?'

'I only found out myself an hour ago. If I'd known where you were, I'd have called you.'

'Who authorised this?'

'Scott.'

'Scott?'

'Old man Stensness called in some favours, put pressure on the right people . . . you know how these things work, Smith.'

Herbert sighed; he knew all too well.

'It's the old school tie, and I don't like it any more than you do. Look; if you really need to, we can always exhume him afterwards.'

'Is that supposed to make me feel better?'

'Don't take it out on me, Smith. I had nothing to do with this.'

'I know, I know. I'm sorry.' Herbert thought for a second. 'You don't happen to know where the funeral's taking place, do you?'

'Highgate Cemetery.'

Of course.

Herbert stood at the edge of the cemetery and watched, finding the role of observer to be unexpectedly satisfying, like shrugging on an old, favourite coat and feeling it settle just so on one's shoulders.

There was a score of people huddled by the graveside, shrouded in lung-shaped plumes of breath as they followed the order of service. De Vere Green was right in the middle, as though he had somehow been a major part of Stensness's life. Perhaps he had, Herbert thought, chiding himself for his lack of charity, for there did not seem to be many people of Stensness's own age there, not many who looked like friends.

Herbert wondered what the clientele at his own funeral would be like.

He let his gaze roam over the mourners. Sir James was there, of course, with his arm round Lady Clarissa, and she looked every bit as bad as he had intimated to Herbert; her features were sunken and bird-like, markers of the terminally ill.

Max had been an only child, so there were no siblings.

Herbert spotted Wilkins and Rosalind, she looking rather magnificently severe in black. Next to them were others whom Herbert pegged as fellow scientists: a man with a strong jaw, features as sharp as they were open, and the merry, knowing eyes of the super-bright; another with wispy hair and protruding eyes who kept looking around with the horizontal scanning gaze of radar, and seemed to have dressed not only in a hurry but also in a darkened room, as his garb was a scruff of mismatched clothes and trailing laces.

The scientists were all men, apart from Rosalind. In the sidelong glances they gave her, even in such circumstances, Herbert saw their suspicion of her. There was something slightly off-kilter about a woman who would choose a field of research so demanding, where absolute dedication was a given. Dedication in a man suggested a priestlike quality, a willingness to selflessly serve a higher cause; but in a woman, it smacked of failure – failure to marry, failure to reproduce, failure to fit comfortably into the boxes society decreed.

Marie Curie apart, Herbert could not call to mind a single woman scientist, and he guessed that the same held true for most people. Science seemed such a *male* profession, in the most British sense of the word; not simply masculine but a specific type of man – upper middle class, a product of one of the older, provincial universities.

The service, short as it was, finished, and Stensness's coffin was lowered jerkily into the ground.

Sir James clearly had clout, Herbert thought; not only to have a body removed from police custody without the knowledge of the investigating officer, but also to secure a plot in Highgate Cemetery.

The mourners broke ranks and began to file away from the graveside. De Vere Green moved smoothly among them; a word for the scruffy Martian string-bean with bug eyes, a hand on the shoulder of Stensness's father, and a peck of sympathy for the mother – this, by some distance, the most human, humanitarian and humane gesture Herbert had ever seen de Vere Green make.

And then de Vere Green had run out of people to console. The moment he was left all alone, he wiped away a tear from halfway down his cheek.

It was not the tear that made Herbert start; it was the look that came after it, a thousand-yard stare of utter devastation, the kind of expression found only on the face of a man whose world has crumbled and who knows not what to do. The mask had dropped.

Herbert saw all this, and he knew. He *knew*.

*   *   *

There was a wake being held in one of the pubs nearby. Herbert fell into step beside de Vere Green as the mourners wended their disjointed way there.

'I always find wakes pretty mawkish, to be honest,' Herbert said.

'I have to say, I tend to agree with you.'

'Shall we go somewhere else?'

De Vere Green looked puzzled at Herbert's apparent solicitousness, but not suspicious; and that in itself showed how deeply Stensness's death had cut him, because de Vere Green was suspicious of the man who sold him his newspaper and the man who shined his shoes.

'If you like,' he said.

They walked back through Waterlow Park, and Herbert felt a sharp jab of guilt at hitting a man when he was down as low as de Vere Green was – even after all de Vere Green had done to him.

But he went ahead and did it anyway; not for vengeance, but simply because he needed answers. The pragmatist in him knew that this was as good a time as any, and probably better than most, to get them.

'How long had you and Max been lovers?' Herbert asked.

De Vere Green tried to bluff his way out of it; he was too much of an old hand not to.

What an absurd suggestion! Had Herbert lost his mind?

You get that upset at the death of all your informers?

All my informers are alive, Max apart.

No; this was different. Herbert knew what he had seen.

Herbert was mistaken.

No, Herbert was not. And here was something else. Whatever Stensness had offered de Vere Green, he had offered to Washington and Moscow too.

Impossible.

Ambrose Papworth, Sasha Kazantsev – Herbert had spoken to them both.

Well, if they were involved, then it was definitely Five's case.

Perhaps; but it was now Saturday, and Five being Five, nothing would be done until Monday morning, by which time anything could have happened. De Vere Green had lost Burgess and Maclean over a weekend; who knew what he might lose this time?

Clumsy, dear boy. And somewhat beneath you, if truth be told.

It made sense now; why de Vere Green had been so keen to propagate the Coronation theory, because that would let him take control of the investigation, which would in turn allow him to bury his own involvement in the whole farrago.

Ridiculous. But said with notably less conviction than before.

Here was what was going to happen. De Vere Green could tell Herbert the truth, in which case Herbert promised to spare him as much as he possibly could; or de Vere Green could continue to hold out, in which case Herbert would regard him as fair game, at least as much as anybody else he might be investigating, and probably more, and he would not hold back for a moment if – *when* – he found something damaging.

Five minutes to think about it?

Of course.

'You always were a good Watcher, Herbert,' de Vere Green said. 'You always saw things very well.'

With most people, the confession would have come in four stages; first haltingly, then with the jittery beginnings of confidence, thirdly in an uncontrollable gush, and finally with the dwindling eddies of the almost spent.

De Vere Green was too much of a professional for that. He told Herbert the story in clear, measured tones, pace and cadence never varying, as though he had been waiting a long time to unburden himself.

Maybe he had.

There were no wooden boxes, metal grilles or murmuring priests in Waterlow Park, but as a confessional it was more than adequate.

De Vere Green had been entranced by Stensness from the moment he'd met him, of course he had. There had been something of the Ganymede about Stensness, with his blond hair, which he would push back from his forehead every few moments, and the unlined quality of his skin, as though he had sprung into the world fully formed and life's vicissitudes had simply washed off him.

This was eighteen months ago – yes, round about the time of the Burgess and Maclean business. Stensness and de Vere Green had met at some party or other, a ghastly boring official drinks thing. De Vere Green had sounded him out there and then: help your country, pass over some scientific data, get a bit of pocket money, that kind of stuff.

Stensness had turned him down flat. He didn't think much of the government, or the country in general, and the only cause he wanted to help was that of science itself.

Young, idealistic, naïve, hot-headed – and, for de Vere Green, utterly irresistible.

De Vere Green had scribbled down his phone number and asked Stensness to call if ever he changed his mind. Fat chance of that, Stensness had said; but he'd pocketed the number in any case. If anything was to hook Stensness, de Vere Green had seen, it would be the secrecy of the whole thing.

For months, de Vere Green had wondered if Stensness would call. Wondered, desired, waited, like a teenager with a crush. He had wanted, he knew, nothing more than an excuse to see Stensness again.

Months turned into a year, and in that time de Vere Green had forgotten about him, more or less; even lonesome bachelors couldn't maintain crushes indefinitely, not without a little oxygen of encouragement.

Herbert reflected that he had always thought of de Vere Green as curiously asexual; as likely as not to be found at his club in St James' on any given night, happy in the company of men who were as shy of their emotions as he was of his own, untroubled by the trials and tribulations of anything so base as sexuality. Clearly he had been wrong.

And then, out of the blue, a few months back, Stensness had called.

He had wanted to meet up. More, he had wanted to take de Vere Green up on his offer.

On his offers, plural, come to that: the spoken one, and the unspoken one.

They had become lovers that night.

De Vere Green had not been so cockstruck that he had failed to enquire about Stensness's change of heart. Stensness said that he had been to Moscow in the summer – a piece of information that it had taken de Vere Green no more than a minute to confirm – on some sort of cultural exchange programme.

Herbert knew the type of thing: fatuous exercises in which each set of visitors saw exactly what their hosts wanted them to, no more and no less.

But Stensness said that he had seen enough to realise that the Soviet Union was not all it advertised itself to be, and few men were as disillusioned as idealists who had suddenly lost their heroes. He had maintained his membership of the CPGB, but only in order to funnel information to de Vere Green. To this he had added whatever snippets of scientific discovery he thought might be interesting or useful.

They had seen each other perhaps once a week, always discreetly, always in de Vere Green's bachelor apartment. De Vere Green had asked Stensness to move in – ostensibly, and for form's sake, as a lodger – but Stensness had refused. He wanted to keep his own life. De Vere Green had understood, and he had respected Stensness for it, but of course he had wanted it otherwise.

This was de Vere Green in the raw, Herbert knew; an ageing man, head over heels in love with a beautiful youth he knew would never be his.

Stensness had loved what he had seen as the glamour of de Vere Green's job. For Stensness, as de Vere Green had surmised long before, the whole thing had been a game, replete with secret codes and furtive meetings, and the thrill of this would have palled for him much quicker than de Vere Green could ever have tired of Stensness' looks and enthusiasm.

Stensness had been the one thing in his life that de Vere Green had not shared, he said. Nothing in the files, and nothing with the Americans.

So Herbert had met Papworth? A good man, Papworth, and on the side of the angels. But if de Vere Green was to lick a man's backside, then he would at least like to be given the choice, rather than find himself shanghaied into it by the dictates of international politics.

Herbert asked; what about Stensness' parents?

216

Good question. As far as de Vere Green knew, Sir James had been aware of Max's communist leanings, but had treated it very much as a passing phase.

Like homosexuality?

Quite so. That was the only way Sir James could have dealt with it; otherwise he would have had to face the possibility that his son might have ended up like, in his own words, those damn mountebanks Burgess and Maclean.

Lady Clarissa?

Not a clue. Sir James had kept it all to himself. In Lady Clarissa's eyes, Max had remained unsullied, perfect, like all sons were to their mothers.

Herbert could have begged to differ, but anyway. What about Max's informing? Had they known about that?

Absolutely not.

Sure?

Positive.

All right. Back to the topic in hand; the conference, and the rendezvous.

In the fog and the cold, de Vere Green had seen his lover's body floating by the shore of the Long Water, already lifeless. To have been found there would have exposed him to all sorts of questions, both professional and personal, which he would rather not have answered.

What else could he have done, other than what he actually did: go home, stare numbly at the wall in shock all night, go to work the next morning as though nothing had happened and, the consummate actor, feign ignorance when Herbert had appeared in Leconfield House a few hours later?

It was not hard, showing the outside world what it wanted to see. De Vere Green could have kept that up pretty much indefinitely. Had he known that Herbert was watching back at the cemetery, he would never have let his guard slip like that, not even for a second.

No; what was hard was when the door shut on him at night and it was just him, in his musty rooms with the dark red wallpaper and the hunting prints, without the laughter and arguments of children and the gentle nagging of a wife. Most of all, without the mundane, delicious normality of being a man who had nothing to hide.

Back in town, people – ordinary citizens, acting out of public spirit – were using flares to guide motorists, and only the men who sold torches were happy; they were charging five shillings for a tinny-looking thing five inches long and with a wax face an inch across.

'It's daylight robbery,' one man protested as Herbert walked past.

'Ain't no daylight round here, squire,' said the torch seller.

Herbert felt an inestimable sadness. At last he had seen de Vere Green brought low before him, a reversal of fortune he had imagined would afford him the coldest, purest of triumphs.

Now it had happened, however, his emotions were quite the opposite. De Vere Green had appeared to him like the Wizard in Oz: behind the bluster and the façade was a man for whom there was nothing beyond love but an endless, reaching void. Herbert saw too much of himself in that to do anything other than shy from it.

Be careful what you wish for, Stella had said, and Herbert himself had supplied the kicker; *It might just happen*.

Of course, there were still practicalities to consider, and chief among them was that Herbert had de Vere Green over a barrel.

Notwithstanding what he had said about going easy on de Vere Green, Herbert knew full well that he retained the whip hand. If at any time in the future de Vere Green failed to co-operate, Herbert could threaten him with exposure. It was a threat he had to be careful not to overdo, for then it would lose its bite, but equally it was a threat he had ultimately to be prepared to carry out, if it was to serve its purpose, and with a timing that he would have to judge with discretion; for once he exposed de Vere Green, he would of course have lost all the leverage that the threat had given him in the first place.

Judgements and margin calls; these were the parameters of Herbert's life.

The *Izvestia* offices – address kindly supplied on Kazantsev's press card, which Herbert still held – seemed to be, as far as Herbert could tell through the murk, housed in a down-at-heel mews in a down-at-heel area behind Victoria Station.

Privacy be damned; Herbert had been lied to.

Kazantsev wore a soft smile that crinkled the ends of his moustache.

'Inspector,' he said. 'I wondered when you'd be back. How are you?'

'Fine. You?'

'Not so good.'

Herbert liked the way the Russians took the question literally, not as a social pleasantry. There was something refreshingly honest in it, in contrast to the British – *mustn't grumble, mustn't grumble*, knowing life was crappy but pretending it was not – and the Americans – *fine, fine*, determined to be in ruder health than the next man.

He reminded himself why he was there.

'You weren't straight with me last time,' Herbert said. Kazantsev shrugged as if to say, *What did you expect*? This was no less a negotiation than the haggling in a bazaar, and should therefore be treated as such. 'This time, you'll tell me the truth, or I'll have you turfed out of here by Monday morning.'

'Have you eaten?' Kazantsev asked.

The question was so random that Herbert felt himself answering almost without realising. 'Now you come to mention it, no.'

'Neither have I. And a man needs to fuel himself during the cold.'

They went to a greasy-spoon café on the main road which ran from the station down to Vauxhall

Bridge, and ordered two full English breakfasts; Kazantsev's with tea, Herbert's with coffee.

It was past lunchtime, but the breakfasts were available all day, and there was something about the fog which so dislocated time that eating breakfast mid-afternoon seemed entirely appropriate.

Herbert took a table by the window, exits and entrances within his sightlines. Once a spy, always a spy.

'Before we start, Inspector,' Kazantsev said, 'I want you to clear something up for me – the biggest mystery I have encountered in this country.'

'I'll try.'

'I cannot for the life of me fathom this. How is it, despite all the crowds that trample and lie on it, the grass of England always springs up freshly and so green; while at home in Russia, where walking on the grass is strictly forbidden at all times, is it always so crushed and muddy?'

Despite himself, Herbert laughed.

If circumstances had been different, Herbert thought, perhaps he and Kazantsev could have been friends.

'I know who Stensness was supposed to meet that night,' Herbert said. 'And knowing what I know about that person, or those people, I think it's safe to say that if you are merely an *Izvestia* correspondent, and have no connection whatsoever with Soviet intelligence, then I'm a Dutchman.'

Kazantsev was encouraging Herbert as he talked, interjecting little phrases – 'I see', 'I understand' – leaning forward, enough to show interest but not so much so as to be threatening.

Herbert continued. 'I want to know what your relationship with Stensness was – the whole lot, chapter and verse, start to finish. I don't care about anything else. I'm not interested in your operational details or exposing your agents or anything like that. A man has been murdered and I want to know who killed him. Simple as that.'

The food arrived. Kazantsev took three mouthfuls, one after the other at a fearsome pace, and began to talk only when immediate hunger had been satisfied.

'Max was an informer,' Kazantsev said at length. 'No, not an informer, that's the wrong word. That implies the information he was giving me came from sources who didn't know and wouldn't have wanted it. Max was a *liaison*, that's better. He was my link to the Communist Party of Great Britain. He would tell me what was going on, pass over documents and stuff. In return, I would hand over instructions from Moscow. The CPGB knew he was doing this, of course. The top brass encouraged it. But they liked to let people like Max do the dirty work, for obvious reasons.'

'Anything scientific?'

'Sometimes. Low-level stuff. Crystallography, mainly. Nothing we weren't getting from other sources. Nothing that a thousand scientists in Soviet academies weren't finding out for themselves every day, come to think of it.'

'Was he ever approached by other intelligence agencies?'

'Five had a go at him once, about the time of Burgess and Maclean. He told me about it. I calmed him down and told him not to worry. This kind of provocation is pretty routine.'

Herbert saw then why Kazantsev would have been a good agent runner. He gave sufficient confidences for one to want to return the favour, and he was as happy talking as listening.

The problem, said Kazantsev, was that he had never been entirely convinced of Stensness' communist credentials. On one occasion Stensness had started banging on about what Marx said in *Das Kapital*, and Kazantsev had interrupted him.

'You have read *Kapital*?' Kazantsev had asked.

'Of course,' Stensness had replied.

'All ten volumes?'

'Of course.'

'Then you have accomplished the impossible. There are only three.'

That was Stensness in a nutshell, Kazantsev said: a blowhard, a bullshitter. A nice enough man, sure, but one for whom the romance and secrecy of what he did were just as important as the content. No; they were *more* important than the content. His commitment was not to international socialism as such, but to snatched meetings in darkened pubs, to dead drops and tradecraft and the thrill of being clandestine.

Just as de Vere Green had said.

Kazantsev had pondered the issue long and hard, and was convinced that if a man was homosexual, as he knew Stensness was – come on, the MGB weren't amateurs – then perhaps that kind of subterfuge was second nature.

Maybe Stensness *had* believed, once. But it had all gone wrong in the summer, when he had gone to Moscow.

There, he had met someone.

His Intourist guide, in fact; also young, also handsome, also homosexual. Misha someone – Kazantsev could not remember the family name.

Misha and Max had started an affair.

It had not been a honey trap, a deliberate provocation, but no matter; the MGB were not ones to look gift horses in the mouth.

They had recorded the last night of international passion on hidden cameras and sent the tapes to Kazantsev, in case he ever needed them.

Then they had taken Misha away and shot him.

Herbert gasped. Kazantsev shrugged: *What did you expect?*

In the Soviet Union, homosexuality was not only illegal, it was also a mental illness, for it was a deviance from general social norms. It was anti-social, in the purest sense of the word. An act of dissidence, a statement of rebellion, and there were only two sentences for that: a decade in the labour camps, maybe two, or a bullet in the back of the head.

Herbert shook his head in disbelief; not that

Misha had been killed, he could believe that all too easily, but that any society with pretensions towards civilisation could possibly think that this kind of behaviour was anything other than savage.

Yes, Kazantsev admitted. It did, on reflection, seem a bit harsh. Perhaps there had been some kind of administrative misunderstanding, and Misha was supposed simply to have gone east for a few years, but somewhere along the line, wires had been crossed.

These things happened all the time. The Soviet Union was a country sadly accustomed to death. No one worried too much about one more here and there.

Had this romance just been a holiday affair, then Stensness would have remained none the wiser as to Misha's fate. But he seemed to have taken a genuine shine to this young man. He had written long letters full of frankly adolescent long-ings, and had become increasingly agitated when he received no answer.

His angst was such that he had begun to miss his appointments with Kazantsev. His information had become sporadic and unreliable.

Yes, of course the MGB had other points of contact within the CPGB, but this had been Kazantsev's job on the line; it was he who would have been in trouble had Stensness failed to deliver. So, in order to snap Stensness out of his lethargy, he had told him the truth about Misha.

Well, it certainly did *that*, Kazantsev said wryly.

Stensness had gone berserk. He had tried to attack Kazantsev, and had then cracked a couple of knuckles punching the wall.

After that, he had started demanding money for his reports.

Kazantsev had shown him the footage from the hidden cameras and pointed out that he was in no position to be making bargains. Reluctantly accepting the truth of this, Stensness had continued to work for Kazantsev, though with ill grace.

Kazantsev had spoken to Moscow about cutting ties with Stensness and finding another source. There were four reasons why people became informers, and, as Herbert knew, they could be summarised in the acronym MICE: Money, Ideology, Compromise, and Ego.

Stensness was unusual in that all four of these applied to him in some way or another. But Kazantsev knew, as any agent handler did, that the ideologically motivated agent was the only one worth running in the long term. All the other motivations could eventually make an informer greedy, lazy or resentful, and once that happened, they were as good as lost.

Yes, Moscow had said, sever contact.

And Kazantsev had been about to break the news to him, at the conference, when Stensness had said he had something so huge, so important, that it would change the world, and he was going to sell it to the highest bidder, Kazantsev and his black-mailing be damned. This information was so precious that whoever got it would protect him as a matter of course.

Of course Kazantsev had been tempted to dismiss this as fantasy, Stensness' imagination run even more riot than usual. Perhaps Stensness had got an inkling of his impending dismissal and was throwing caution to the wind in a last-ditch attempt to save the arrangement.

But there was always that nagging doubt. What if it were true? What if Kazantsev turned down the chance of a lifetime? Worse, what if someone else grabbed it?

It would have been bad enough in the West: dismissal, disgrace, menial jobs until the end of time. At least Western agents would still have been alive. Kazantsev would not even have been offered the Siberian option.

Stensness had not spelled it out, but Kazantsev had known that there would be at least three interested parties: the MGB, the CIA, and Five.

Nothing personal, Kazantsev said to Herbert, but the MGB's biggest concern was the Americans; they were now the GP, the *glavny protvinik*, the main enemy.

Before the war, sure, the British had been Moscow's premier adversaries, but times had changed. Now, the average Englishman was apolitical and indifferent. He did not care who was governing him, where the country was going, whether the Common Market was good or bad.

If he had a job, and a salary, and the wife was happy, that was enough for him.

The Americans, on the other hand, *believed*. They believed in democracy and freedom and the American way, and that made them dangerous.

So Kazantsev and Stensness had arranged to meet at the Peter Pan statue.

But Stensness had not shown, and nor had he made contact to explain why, or to reschedule. Given his insistence on the intergalactic significance of the whole thing, this had seemed strange.

So Kazantsev had gone to Stensness's home address, only to find that he had moved out recently without telling him. Perhaps the omission was deliberate, perhaps not.

King's had given Kazantsev the right address – on the Thursday evening, however, not the Friday morning, contrary to what he had said last time – but Stensness had not been at home. Kazantsev had posed as one of his colleagues from King's, and Stensness's housemates said that they had not seen him.

Worse, the housemates had then stayed in all evening. Kazantsev had watched from the car until midnight and then slept there, wrapped in five layers and freezing as though it were Murmansk in January.

Eventually, sometime after breakfast on Friday, the housemates had left, and Kazantsev had broken into the empty house to see if he could find anything of interest. Midway through the search, Elkington had arrived. The rest Herbert knew.

Herbert thought fast. Kazantsev had been first on Stensness's list, at six thirty. If he was to be believed, Stensness had not shown, but still his body had been found in the Long Water. Maybe Stensness had been intercepted en route to his meeting with Kazantsev.

'You never saw Stensness after he left the Royal Festival Hall?'

'Never.'

'Sure?'

'Sure.'

'Absolutely positive?'

'You can ask it any way you like, Inspector, but the answer's still the same.'

Kazantsev had nearly finished his food. Though he had done most of the talking, he had somehow managed to eat at a fearsome pace too. 'Now, Inspector . . .' The Russian speared his final piece of sausage with his fork and waved it at Herbert. 'You want to know why the British preserve the monarchy? To distract the masses from the path of socialism, that's why. The Bolsheviks had only been secure in their revolution once they had killed the Romanovs. For every Englishman a Soviet spy manages to recruit, there are fifty they miss. How will you ever have a revolution in a country where the milk is delivered to the door every morning at eight?'

'If I have you sent back to Moscow, what will happen to you?'

'If I'm lucky, they'll relocate me. Vienna would be nice. Murmansk is more likely.'

'They won't dismiss you?'

'There are only two ways you leave the MGB, Herbert: in handcuffs, or feet first.' He smiled. 'Ach, the hell with it. If you send me back, I have bigger problems.'

'Such as?'

'What to do with my cat, for a start. Would you like him?'

Herbert laughed. 'I'm not much of a cat man.'

'That's because you're a cop, not a spy. All spies love cats; their devious feline mentality appeals to us more than the stupid sincerity of dogs. What about my jazz 78s? They're quite brittle, but let me tell you, back in Moscow, we'd listen to homemade copies scratched on used film taken from hospital X-ray departments. Jazz on bones, we called it.'

'I'm not much of a jazz man, either.'

They could, Herbert thought, have been lovers killing time while one of them waited for a train.

Herbert's next notion was in every aspect absurd, but still it nagged at him. Kazantsev, more than de Vere Green, more than Papworth, was the one man in this whole affair who could help him, *really* help him, if he was allowed to do so.

But that would never happen. Kazantsev was a Soviet spy. Co-operating with him might not have technically been treason, as Britain was not

230

officially at war with the Soviet Union, but it would surely be seen as such.

Herbert remembered something John Harington had said. 'Treason doth never prosper, what's the reason? For if it prosper, none dare call it treason.'

In other words, the end justified the means. That was certainly something a good Marxist like Kazantsev would understand.

Inevitably, perhaps, Herbert thought back to Burgess and Maclean. Whatever one's opinion of them – and everyone had one – there was no denying that they were both intelligent and gifted men. Perhaps their dilemma had also been that of an entire generation caught in the contradictions and confusions of post-war Britain, where every-thing – the country's role in the world, the health of its economy, the state of its colonies – seemed muddled and without philosophic purpose.

True, there was an understanding on both sides of the political fence that a return to pre-war levels of unemployment and poverty could not and would not be tolerated. The British were better fed, better educated, better doctored than ever before.

But how superficial was this success?

Houses were being built, but homelessness remained.

Health care was being improved, but no new hospitals were appearing.

People were being employed in their droves, but neither production nor investment were up much.

Who would not be bewildered, in such a place?

Why should loyalty to the Crown be the highest loyalty? Who had not betrayed something, or someone, more important than a country? Did governments have a monopoly on what was right and sensible?

Actions could be noble, even – or especially – when they were illegal. Look at Alan Nunn May, who had passed atomic secrets to Moscow, and in doing so helped them develop their own bomb, a decade ahead of Western intelligence's best estimates. Was he a traitor, or a saviour?

Perhaps his actions would, in time, help foster and preserve détente by levelling the playing field and, in ensuring the mutuality of any nuclear destruction, provide a more effective deterrent than a thousand North Atlantic treaties.

'Tell me a bit about yourself, Alexander,' Herbert said.

'Please, call me Sasha. We are friends now, no?' Kazantsev smiled. 'Tell you about myself . . . well, I'm a normal fellow, I guess, with normal hobbies. I'm married, with two daughters. I collect old locks and the wise thoughts of my friends. I'm interested in numismatics and the poetry of the Silver Age. Out of choice, I drink Moskovskaya vodka and smoke Camel cigarettes.'

'What about your parents?'

'Ah-ha! I am the true son of proletarians.' He said it with a slight flourish, as if to let Herbert know that he was not taking all this rigid communist doctrine too seriously. 'My father, Sergei Grigoreyevich, was a factory accounts clerk; my mother, Elizabetha Stanislavovna, used to sew costumes for the Bolshoi. Both have passed away now, sadly. But they and their forebears left me with the best legacy a man can have in Soviet Russia.'

'What's that?'

'Not a drop of Jewish blood in our family, not for at least three generations! Ridiculous, of course. But then all governments are, in the end. And it's not just the Jews Moscow has a problem with. Balts and Caucasians are allowed abroad just as rarely. Whatever we say about internationalism, in the end we prefer to rely on Russians.'

'Do you enjoy what you do?'

Kazantsev puffed out his cheeks 'I don't think enjoyment is any kind of criterion, to be honest. Sometimes I think the whole thing's a joke. I studied at the MGB college out in the woods at Balashikha. On the wooden perimeter fence someone had scrawled in chalk: *School for spies*. So much for secrecy!

'Since you're asking me seriously, though, I'll say this: spying is as necessary and as disagreeable as cleaning toilets. It widens one's understanding of human nature, that's for sure. But at the same time it coarsens you. Could any decent person peep through keyholes and gather, crumb by crumb, information that his neighbour would rather keep to himself?'

Kazantsev could have been bluffing, Herbert thought, playing the mildly rebellious cynic in

233

order to impress him. Besides, there was nothing a Russian liked more than a good bit of maudlin philosophy.

But at some stage, Herbert supposed, one had to trust.

The Russian went on: 'Perhaps the worst is that, sooner or later, no matter how much you fight it, you come to see man, with all his joys and sorrows, all his merits and shortcomings, as nothing more than an object for recruitment. You sniff and lick at him, you ensnare and seduce, and finally you hook him . . .' He paused. 'At least whores have the decency to demand money.'

Outside the café, Herbert returned Kazantsev's wallet to him, press pass and all.

Kazantsev said something in Russian.

'What was that?' Herbert asked.

'I said "thank you" – but using the informal version of the second person, *ty*. We communists use *ty* to each other. *Vy* is for waiters and class enemies.'

Herbert could see more through his shirt when he pulled it over his head of a morning than he could outside.

The fog was three-ply, double-milled and thick-weave. Ambulancemen and women had forsaken their days off and returned to work, if only to walk in front of those vehicles ferrying the sick around – a group which they might shortly be joining, to judge from their streaming eyes and bloody feet. Passengers staggered ahead of cabs carrying their suitcases.

Herbert should have rung in to New Scotland Yard and let them know what he had ascertained over the past few hours on his trawl round the representatives of three espionage services; but he was still angry at being deceived over the funeral, even though he knew full well that, had it not been for what he had seen at the graveside, he would never have worked out the truth about de Vere Green.

Besides, what exactly would he tell Tyce? Herbert seemed at first glance to have discovered an awful lot, but when he put it all together, he didn't feel any closer to the truth.

So he went back to Hannah's flat in Soho, both to take his mind off the case, and to apologise for having offended her earlier, albeit unwittingly.

She was in, which pleased him, and happy to see him, which pleased him more.

'Happy birthday,' she said, kissing him on the cheek and pressing something into his hand. It was a present, beautifully wrapped in bright paper and tied with a bow.

'Can I open it?' he asked.

'Don't be silly. Of course.'

It was a little black enamel box, about six inches by three, the lid painted in exquisite swirls of red and green. 'It's beautiful,' Herbert said, and meant it.

'You like it? That please me. It's for your cufflinks and collar studs.'

'I don't have any.'

'Then you buy some,' she laughed. 'A man should look smart.'

'Is it from Hungary?' Herbert said.

She cocked her head. 'Yes. Hungarians make lovely things.'

She had the radio on, and Herbert listened for the news.

Visibility at Kew and Kingsway was still officially nil; wind was one knot at Kew, zero at Kingsway. The high-pressure anticyclone remained immovable; the centre was straight above the Thames Valley, and the thermal inversion was intact. The weather forecast talked of widespread fog and frost.

It did not mention that London was completely sealed in, its inhabitants forced to breathe choking fumes from chimneys and power stations all working full tilt to provide heat, light, and poisoned air to those below.

It did not mention smog, or people dying.

It did not say that hospitals were busier than at any time since the Blitz.

The BBC prided itself on being the best news organisation in the world, so this omission could only have been deliberate. The Soviets weren't the only ones who knew how to control public information, Herbert thought.

'We should go out,' Hannah said.

'Why?'

'My friends come back later. There is big party nearby, so they use flat to meet.'

'Won't they want you to be there?'

Hannah shrugged. 'There is key, with owner of café next door. They can get in.'

They went down the stairs, Hannah moving ahead of Herbert with what seemed to him extraordinary assurance. Then he realised that the staircase had a handrail, the steps were all the same height, and objects were unlikely to be left where they shouldn't have been. In other words, it was predictable.

Outside, he took her firmly by the upper part of her right arm. She stopped dead.

'Listen,' she said. 'If I want help, I ask.'

'I was only trying to –'

'I know. And thank you. But you do the opposite. You grab my arm, I lose my balance – bad, when you try to direct me. I hold on to you, is better. Here –' She clasped Herbert's arm, just above the elbow. 'Ah, wool. My favourite colour.'

It took Herbert a moment to realise that this was a joke.

Then they started walking, with him wondering whether Hannah's strange mixture of sunny delight and blazing defiance would somehow physically light their way through the gloom.

It was strange, Herbert thought; every time he went out into the fog, it seemed as dense as it could possibly get without solidifying into concrete. Yet still it seemed to thicken, hour by hour. It was like walking through semolina. He felt blind; Hannah was surely the one for whom these conditions were normal.

She scoffed when he put this to her.

'Oh, Herbert. You're like all people with sight – you think only with your eyes. Stop a moment. Listen.'

He did so. It was eerily quiet.

'What can you hear?' she asked.

'Nothing.'

'Exactly. Me neither. Can't see, can't hear, the both of us. My favourite weather – what you think it is?'

'I've no idea.'

'Guess.'

'Sunshine?'

She laughed. 'You are predictable. You say "sunshine" because it's *your* favourite. You think everyone think like you. No, don't argue, is true. OK, try another way; which weather you hate most? Apart from this fog, obviously.'

'Rain. Everyone hates the rain.'

'Not me. I love rain.'

'You do?'

'Of course. Rain makes me see. Every surface it hit, it sound different; roofs sound different to walls, shrubs to lawns, fences to pavements. It splash in puddles, run in gutters, it hiss when car makes spray. Rain is orchestra, and orchestra where I know every instrument. For me, unless I can touch, world is invisible. But rain makes everything have . . . have, how you say . . . ?' She paused, searching for the right word.

'Contours?' Herbert suggested.

'Exactly. Edges. It is blanket of colour over what was invisible. It make whole something before in pieces. It take me from isolation and bring me to world, in manner you take for granted. When you say "nice day" to people, for me, is horrible day. For me, nice day is what you hate: wind in face, thunder like roof over my head. Those are things I love, Herbert. Without them, nothing.'

Herbert watched her face as she said all this. He had never felt so desperate to be consumed, and yet so conscious of his solitude.

'Oh,' she said suddenly. 'I think we lost. Is your fault, make me talk so much.'

'My fault? I . . .'

She laughed. 'I joke, Herbert.'

They were next to a large block of stone. A plinth, it seemed. When Herbert looked up he saw a long, grooved column disappearing into the fog above their heads, as though this were an Indian rope trick.

'We're in Trafalgar Square,' he said. 'Nelson's somewhere in the clouds.'

'Trafalgar Square? We have come wrong way, no mistake.'

Herbert remembered that Nelson's Column sat atop a bunker, supposedly to shelter the government in the event of a nuclear strike. There were others beneath High Holborn, Judd Street in

Bloomsbury and Maple Street in Fitzrovia. The fear of a pre-emptive Soviet strike was very real.

As they walked, Herbert tried in his head to sort out what he now knew.

Stensness had fixed three meetings for Thursday evening by the Peter Pan statue: Kazantsev at six thirty, Papworth at seven, and de Vere Green at seven thirty.

All three men maintained that they had gone to the statue as instructed, and that Stensness had not shown up for any of them.

Yet Stensness must have been in Kensington Gardens around that time, as de Vere Green had found him dead there sometime between seven thirty and ten to eight, when Elkington had discovered the body.

Unless, of course, someone had killed Stensness elsewhere and then dragged him to the Long Water.

No. That was unlikely, especially in a rapidly thickening fog. Herbert knew he had to be wary of over-complication. If it waddled and quacked, it was probably a duck.

So what were the possibilities?

The first was that Kazantsev was lying, and Stensness *had* made their meeting. Then either Kazantsev had killed him, or someone else had done so after Kazantsev had gone.

Second, that Papworth was lying, and Stensness had made *their* meeting. After that, the same as with Kazantsev: either Papworth had killed Stensness, or someone else had done so after Papworth had gone.

240

Third, that de Vere Green was lying, and Stensness had made *their* meeting.

Things were slightly different here, for two reasons: de Vere Green said he had found the body (which did not of course exclude him from being the killer); and, as Stensness's lover, de Vere Green perhaps had more reason, certainly more *visceral* reason, to have drowned Stensness, in a temper after a lovers' tiff, say.

And if de Vere Green was the killer, then that brought with it a whole raft of problems.

Firstly, his history with Herbert, which hardly helped any claim Herbert might have had as to impartiality.

Next, the question of de Vere Green's quiescence. As things stood, de Vere Green was being co-operative for one of two reasons. If he was innocent, because he wanted to keep his own crime of homosexuality quiet; and if he was guilty, because he hoped that Herbert would never find enough evidence to be sure of his guilt.

If Herbert ever did find such evidence, though, de Vere Green would have nothing left to lose, and then Herbert's leverage over him would be finished.

There was a fourth possibility: that they were all telling the truth, and Stensness had been killed by a fourth party, who would be not so much a known unknown – that is, something Herbert knew he did not know – as an unknown unknown, one that he did not even know that he did not know, for this would be introducing an entire other level to the affair of which he was ignorant.

This last prospect so depressed him that he gave up thinking for a while.

'It's too much,' Herbert said to Hannah. 'Say something. Take my mind off it.'

'I remember pea-souper of 1948. I remember how Londoners are accepting of such fogs, they don't worry about them. Like it is earthquake, or volcano. More, there is pride, weird pride in this. We live in splendid city, so maybe fog now and then is price to pay. In old days they call fog the "London particular", no? Is pride in that term. People now talk of money and, is this right word, "muck"?'

'Muck is money.'

'Exactly. Like dirty air is good thing, as it come from industry, and industry mean jobs and profit. But where is government?' She was angry now. 'Why they not protect people from this? Why industry not make own cleanings? Everyone do nothing until tragedy happens, and by then is too late.'

An outsider's perspicacity and an underdog's anger; the mixture had felled greater men than Herbert, that was for sure.

In Herbert's flat, Hannah asked him to take her to a chair and place her hand on the back of it. The rest she did herself. When she was seated, she asked him to describe the room to her.

'Oh, you know.'

'No, Herbert, I don't know. So I ask you.'

242

'Yes. Sorry.' Looking round, Herbert realised how much he disliked this place. It stank of, if not failure, then certainly inertia. He ran quickly through what was where: writing desk, armchairs and sofa, coffee table, radio, television set.

'What about the pictures on the walls?'

Blimey, Herbert thought. He had not looked at some of them in years.

There were a couple of landscapes; a picture of Nelson dying below decks at Trafalgar; a large photograph of Pennsylvania miners that he could not for the life of him remember getting; and a painting he had found in Portobello Market of a man banging his fist against a mirror in frustration because there was no reflection in it.

Hannah nodded when he told her all this, and said nothing.

Herbert put more coal on the fire, and then went into the kitchen, poured two glasses of wine, and came back into the sitting-room.

When he handed Hannah's glass to her, he saw that there was a red blister on her hand, at the point where her index finger met her palm.

'How did you get this?' he said.

'How I get what?'

'This blister, here on your palm.'

'Herbert,' Hannah said, her eyes suddenly sheened. 'You really want to know?'

'If it's important, then yes, of course.'

She laughed. 'Oh, it's important. That, I promise you.'

The silence leached around them as she composed herself.

Herbert had no idea what he could have stirred up, and as with this morning, wanted nothing more than to be able to retract it; but how was he to have known that a little blister was the portal to so much?

'Esther burnt her hand on the stove,' she said.

'Esther? Who's Esther?'

'She burnt her other hand, her left, at exactly the same spot; and at same second that blister appear on me, but on my right hand. I never touch the stove.'

'Hannah – who's Esther?'

'Esther was my twin.'

We were mirror twin, identical in every way, except that everything was in reverse. Our hair curled in opposite directions; our fingerprint was perfect reflection; I was right-handed and Esther was left-handed, so I never sit at her left in meal or in classroom, and she never sit to my right, as then our arm hit and we start fighting, is impossible for us to do anything.

When you are twin, your relationship begin before you're born – is so difficult to understand that. You know the other twin is there, even though you don't know that you know. Most people come into world after nine month of solitude, but for twin, isolation and everything alone – being individual, being independent, being sufficient in self – is completely alien.

People always ask: 'What is it like to be twin?' For twin, question is this: 'What is it like not to be twin?'

Because from very moment you born, you are 'twin': one unit no one can divide, a little world which only you share and no one can enter from outside.

To be identical twin is complete privilege, because you carry the other one with you wherever you go. Never are you truly alone. When the outside world becomes difficult, or unkind, uncertain, you retreat, and then everything is safe and bright and without effort.

As baby, Esther and I suck the other's finger and toe, it look like we don't know where one ends and other begins. We look so comfortable together, like we are with each other for whole life after lifetime. We behave as one creature, working together. And with much serious, like young babies are.

When we are three day old, our mother holds Esther, and suddenly Esther begins to scream and have shakings. No reason for this, it looks; one moment she fine, the next she screams to wake dead people.

And then my mother see me on sofa, face to the cushions.

I suffocate, and she saves me.

The doctor not believe. Not believe I still alive, not believe how Esther save me.

This kind of thing happens all time, though not again with such drama.

Someone hits one of us, and the other screams. When we sleep, we move same limb at same time. We have same dream. One sings tune the other think of, one answers question no one ask yet.

But, but . . . to be twin is enormous contradiction. Twins are unique because they are two, but being two means you not unique. You look in mirror; is that you, or twin? How to find out? Bite your sister, and see the reflection which cry.

Now I am blind, I cannot look in mirror and see Esther looking at me, even for one second, before I remember it me not her.

People see twin as two half of same person, so as follows, they see twin as half a person. All the time, one mistake for the other, and vice versa, like you can be changed one to the other, like you leave no mark of your own. Our headmistress asks Esther one day where is the other half. Esther shout at her: 'I am not half, I am one, and Hannah too!'

But of course, always one big difference between twins, and can never be escaped: who is first? Being twin is race, and I won. I am first, I have more age, and Esther never forgive that. Me, I not care, which make her more angry.

With learning the potty, our mother teaches me, so Esther follows. She follow, sure thing; she make the potty empty, all over my head.

Every Passover, Esther must tell the Four Questions, because she is youngest child, and that is Jewish tradition. Always she try not to do it, because it make her know too much that she second.

In some part of Africa, the younger twin is thought more important. People they think he make his twin go out first to certify that the world is ready for him. Esther like that story very much. Always she ask when we move to Africa.

Of course, the good is more than the bad, always.

The good is this: amazing relationship, affection, support, doing things together, encouraging, stimulate, sympathy. Always someone for playing games, and to help in house with boring jobs. Always someone who understands you, someone with total honesty for you. You have soul mate.

Then the bad. Which one dominate, which one depend? Help the other, or compete against them? Sometimes, being close like this feels bad. No distance make you unhappy. Always you interfere, them too.

We are older. More difference now. We are more different, we want to be more different than that, even. People put us in box; this the good girl, this the bad. We like the box, we make it be true. Esther is loud one, me the quiet; she is bad and always make rebellion, I am good and obey; she plays the sports, I make the studies. Only difference from here is swimming; she not good swimmer, so I make myself best swimmer in school, of course.

When we walk to school, I want to go in line with other children, proper line, organise; she want to run, jump, hide, make trouble.

When teachers separate us in class, it pleases me. When Esther not with me, no one make me responsible for things she does.

I am scholar, she must do exam once and again, not because she is stupid, but because she do a million thing in one time. Always she look for adventure.

I am cardboard imitation of her. I have no passion, am not wild; she is.

You look for killer in fog, Herbert; if she alive, she

come to help you. Not me. I make the horror and sit by fire with a book I like.

And then came Auschwitz.

Jewish stories make tales of the Malach Hamavet, the Angel of Death. He disguises as doctor, brilliant doctor. Come to earth in white doctor coat, and he destroys everything, but he charms and seduces all the time.

The Malach Hamavet waits for us at Auschwitz, on the ramp as the trains arrive.

He is handsome devil: hair dark, skin like olive. He look like Gable, or Valentino. He has gold flower in lapel, his boots polished and bright, his shirt cornflower blue.

Like a host who greets his guests, he ask how our journey is, looks horrified to the discomfort we have suffered. He makes the dictation for postcards, us to send home, telling people the Nazis treat us well.

He whistle with his mouth the 'Blue Danube' waltz, and says that children to call him Vater, Vaterchen, Onkel – *Father, Daddy, Uncle.*

When he speak to women, they try to impress him. They pat their hair and smile, they imagine the rags of their clothes as white gowns, and their feet which swell as ballet shoes. Some break bricks and put red dust into their cheeks, like rouge.

The Angel divide us into two groups.

To the left go old, sick, women with children under fourteen.

Everyone else go to right.

He say nothing to worry about, a simple division:

248

those who can work and those who can not. Necessary for the bureaucrats, that is all.

He rolls eyes. Bureaucrats, *he say, and we laugh, he is with us against bureaucrats, everyone hate the bureaucrat.*

His finger go left, right, left, right. He shout that families to find unity again after administration finished.

His hand soft, his decision quick; he is like conductor of orchestra.

Group on the left go to gas chamber.

In one hour, they are dead, mothers with their children. No mother will work if child is dead. Some children scream, they know what will happen. Adults believe in reason, they not see what comes.

The Angel squat down, his face at level with yelling child, and he say with voice of honey that there nothing to worry about. To make them feel better, he make a little game called 'on the way to the chimney' – that is chimney there, that b-i-i-i-g tall one, to make warm all people working in that building. He can play game with the child. The child like that?

Of course, the child like that.

Group on right go to work, and to every horror in Auschwitz. They bleed from thousand sore. Hunger makes belly into strange shapes. Eye bad, making moans and screams like mad people. Even lice in camp leave them alone at end, because nothing left in their bodies for food for lice. Most dead in four month.

Often, I think that better, to be in first group.

The Angel knows. He makes choice like directing waltz, and he makes them sober. Other doctors in camp,

Koenig and Rohde, make to be drunk before. Angel never drunk.

His name was Josef Mengele.

His name was Josef Mengele, and he was God. We discover that very fast.

An old Jewish prayer tells story of the flock which pass beneath the rod of the shepherd, the Lord, who decides who will live and who will not. On Yom Kippur, the Day of Atonement, Mengele make a board at certain height above ground, and make us all walk below it. You must reach board with head to live. People put stones in shoe or stand on tiptoes to succeed.

What is the point to this? There is no point. That is the point.

Mengele takes pleasure in power of life and death; he wants to control everything, every person, every behaviour.

Always with him is aura of dreadful, dreadful menace. I cannot tell you what it was like, not in proper terms. Be happy you never experience it. Never do I feel such thing before; if ever it come to me again, I think I die of fright, simple as that.

Mengele's charm is real, but also it is only half of him. He is friendly man on the outside; but on inside he is vicious, and it explodes for no reason, without warning.

He make rabbis dance, and then he send them to gas chamber.

He rip gold teeth from corpses and send them to his family home in Günzburg.

He hit a man over the head with an iron bar until

eye and ear disappear under blood, and head is simply red ball on body.

He throws youngest baby on to stove, other baby on to pile of corpses, because no one tell him that their mothers are pregnant.

He shoots people for stopping on street without permission.

He has whole kindergarten, three hundred children, burnt alive in open fire. Children try to escape, and he hit them with sticks until they die.

One time, he find us cooking stolen potatoes, and he fly into huge rage. 'Yes,' he shouts, 'yes; this is how I imagine a Jewish hospital. You dirty whores, you unspeakable Jewish swine.'

And then someone shows him a jar with a foetus in one piece – this is very rare – and he calms down instantly, all smiles and appreciation.

Oh, we discuss his psychology; everywhere were rumours about Mengele, and you know Jews: we'll gossip as long as we've got tongues in our mouths.

Mengele's mother Walburga was huge woman, one moment warm and maternal, next moment a raging bull. Josef – Beppo, she call him – was her favourite son; the only one who can get her to smile.

In return, he very loyal to her, always takes her side.

His father Karl was at the family factory all the time; the Mengeles were the biggest employers in Günzburg. Karl wanted Josef to follow him into the business, but Josef had aims for higher things.

A mother who wanted that he be austere and chaste

251

when he likes luxury and to indulge, and a father whose place he must take through achieving more.

No wonder that Josef becomes the Janus Man; one moment affectionate, the next cruel. Maybe he is man of two part, one made at Auschwitz, the other in place long before. The Auschwitz self let him operate in extermination camp; the other let him keep pieces of decency.

You see, Herbert, my thinkings towards him are also split.

Yes, I hate him, for everything he did. He sent my mother to the gas chamber on our first day there. He make it that my father works to death.

As for me and Esther, well, you see soon enough.

But also I remember his kindnesses, and I know too that without him I would be dead now.

Because Esther and I were twin, and twins were privileged in Auschwitz – a stupid word to use, 'privilege', in there, but it feels like that.

Mengele is interested – no, to call spade a spade, he is obsessed – with twins. In his evil heart, he has soft spot, small core of good, especially for twins.

And so they keep us apart and away, separate from all the shit.

We get best food – chocolates, white bread, milk with lukchen, *mixture like macaroni – in camp this is very special.*

For us the smartest clothes; white pantaloons for boys, silk dresses for girls.

Also, and the best, we keep our own hair, so at least we look human.

We don't have to be at roll call.

They slap our wrists for offences which usually have death penalty.

They let us play under skies which crematorium flames make red like blood.

We are chosen ones, darlings always spoiled, and all because of Mengele. For his being two – angel and monster, gentle doctor and the sadistic killer – no better symbol than twin.

They put us in Barrack 14 of camp F in Birkenau, sister camp to Auschwitz. All kinds of twin there, like the Ark: big Hungarian soccer players, old Austrian gentlemen, gypsy dwarves. Mengele himself tattoos us with numbers, all beginning with letters 'ZW' for zwillinge: twins.

'You're a little girl,' he said. 'You will grow, and some day you say that Dr Josef Mengele himself give you your number. You'll be famous. But important not to scratch it. Do this for your Uncle Pepi, no? Be more brave than Uncle Pepi, you know? Here is secret. They want to make number mark for Uncle Pepi, under his armpit, but he refused.'

Hygiene in the twins' barrack was perfect; Mengele insisted that no infection is allowed.

Infection. You begin to see where this goes, yes?

We were like horses, a stud farm for him.

He wants twins because he thinks we give to him the secrets of life, show the parts of humanity nature is controlling, and also the parts which are from environment. If we share things, he think them from the gene; when things differ, must be from environment and experience.

They put us in baths and clean us. Then they take us to the laboratory on trucks with Red Cross; must be stolen, maybe just fakes.

Laboratory is smart, no different to laboratory you find in a large German city; marble tables with channels on sides for the drainage, porcelain sinks against the wall, rooms with armchairs, microscopes and bookshelves, all the latest scientific publications.

First he weighs us, then he measures and compares, every part of our bodies – every part.

Esther and I always sit together, always nude.

We sit for hours together, and they measure her, and then me, and then me again and then her: how wide our ears and nose and mouth, the structure of our bones. Everything in detail, they want to know.

They talk of Jewish-Bolshevik commissars and sub-humans, prototypes, repulsive, characteristic; all hard to understand, all sounding bad.

We are scared, of course, but never at the same time. When I shake, Esther holds me until I stop, or she cries while I hold her hand. We know that one of us has to remain strong at all times. The moment we give in together, we never recover.

We forget our differences the moment we arrive in Auschwitz. Every day, we are closer than ever, because we have to. It is that, or death.

Now the endless probes: needles to take fluids from our backs, immersion in steel vats full with cold water, pulleys holding us head to floor to measure speed of blood draining from our stomachs.

Awful, no?

I tell you, you compare to the others, and Esther and I are the lucky ones.

Mengele injects twins with typhus and tuberculosis.

He sterilises women, he castrates men.

When twins are brother and sister, he makes them have sex with each other.

He takes a girl, seven year old, and tries to connect her urine tract to her colon.

He sews two gypsy twins back to back. He wants to connect their blood vessels with their organs. For three days, the twins scream and cry, all the time. Then they die of gangrene.

I know all these medical terms in English, because every day I think of them.

Then Mengele decides that in vivo *tests are no good. Results much better from corpse than from living person. In normal life, twins die at same time not often; now, he can kill them at once, and make dissections to see results.*

He takes needles and fills them with Evipal or chloroform. Five cubic centimetre of Evipal into the right arm, the victim sleeps, then ten cubic centimetre into the left ventricle of the heart, and instant death. Perhaps a little humane.

But sometimes, when not much stocks, maybe a day when he wants to be sadist, he fills the needles with petrol instead.

These experiments don't work, of course. He tries to take from twins secrets we just don't have, it's insane.

Always he tells us that it's a sin, a crime, not to use the possibilities which Auschwitz has for twin research, as never will another chance come along like this.

Maybe he looks for the secret of multiple birth so he can help repopulate the German nation. Perhaps he thinks he creates a new super-race, like breeding horses. After us, maybe the Poles; then maybe someone else.

And all so, so ironic, you know? Two ironies, both vile.

First, Mengele is fixated on purity of race, but this not something applying to he himself. Somewhere among his ancestors is doubt about paternity, and so he has no place in the Sippenbuch, *the Kinship Book, for those who can prove that their families are pure Aryan for at least two hundred year. Himmler sent silver spoons to every family which has borne a 'pure' child. For Mengele, no spoon; not for his own birth, not for his son.*

Secondly, I don't know if the experiments on twins have scientific meaning, but if there is, Mengele is not the man to find it. He is no genius. Dedicated and fanatic, yes, but at heart an assistant, not a leader. An efficient assistant. For him, he takes theories of genetics and race like he puts on white gloves and hat. He does whatever pleases him; he does experiments and ignores the result, blood all over his clothes, his hands examining like a possessed man. The mania of a collector; typical Germanic characteristic, gone wild.

You know what we are? A private zoo.

If twins are the lucky ones – and we are, even with all this – then Esther and I are the most fortunate of all, almost up to the end.

Maybe Mengele likes us more than the rest. Maybe his hated bureaucrats keep us safe, more in what they miss than what they do.

One day, early 1945, our luck runs out.

It is bitterly cold. I remember tongues of fire and smoke from the crematorium stacks, the air full with stench of burning bodies, the walls bouncing with screams of the damned, everywhere the rat-tat of machine guns fired point blank.

The fires were so big; Allied aircraft must have seen them.

Why didn't they bomb? Why didn't they come and blow us all to bits?

Mengele comes rushing in, gone berserk.

'The Bolsheviks are coming!' he screams. 'The Bolsheviks are coming! All this will fall into their hands. Well, I won't have that. Not in a thousand year.'

He starts putting everything in his trunk: papers, stationery, instruments. Pack, pack, pack, all very fast, not another word spoken to us, his face distorted in frenzy.

And then he stop, eyes blazing. Shouts he could still make great scientific discovery that will save the Reich.

He has insane ideas, many, many, almost all; but the most lunatic, if you ask me, is that he can make blond hair and blue eyes. Genetic engineering, he calls it.

He looks round the room, and he stops on Esther and me, because we are the most dark there: black hair, brown eyes.

If he can make it work on us, he can make it work on anybody.

He takes us into a small room. Every nurse, he tells them to come, hold us down.

I start to scream. I know what he is going to do.

Mengele works at a table. He takes huge needle and

fills it with vile chemical. I think, as I watch, that it spits like a snake.

The dose must be stronger than ever before, he says. Previous experiments did not work because dosage too weak. He is almost shouting.

The nurses hold me down and clamp my eyes open with pincers.

Mengele advances on me. The needle looks as big as the Eiffel Tower.

I look away, to the wall.

There, pinned up like butterflies, are hundreds of human eye, rows and rows, all labelled neatly with numbers and letters, and in half the colours of the rainbow: brilliant blue, yellow, violet, green, red, grey.

Eye without body and without sight, all watching me without blinking.

It is the last thing I ever see.

You ask me how it feels to be blind, sudden and without warning.

Well, to be honest, it is only one of my problems; because Esther is right next to me, and when she sees what Mengele has done, she starts screaming, louder than I ever hear anyone.

They hit her, I hear her fall, people shout in German; and still she screams.

Then there is a gunshot, no louder than Esther's cries, and she is silent.

Of the next few days, I don't remember much.

I said nothing and had no real thoughts, just sensations; confusion, bafflement.

258

My first real memory is when they push us out of the camp, and we start on the death march. These things, the savage cold and perfect agony, these are the only ones which can stop me being numb.

I was alone, but I still had so much to say to Esther and share with her. Everything she and I had ever done was now without meaning. The biggest tragedy of my life, and who else would I seek but her for help?

But she is gone.

Dreadful, dreadful, that the disaster takes from me the only person I needed.

As though half of me is ripped out.

People who lose limb say they still get phantom pains, years later. That is how I feel; a part of me was missing, a physical part.

I am without balance, lopsided, bleak, hollow. The world is distant. I watch, I do not take part. I am an observer.

An observer who cannot see.

There were thousands of us on that march, but I walked alone. My soul pirouetted silently through life, joined with her shadow. We had arrived together, Esther and I; why would we not leave together too?

Without Esther, I could not imagine myself. Worse, I could not imagine life itself. I had ceased to exist.

Why hadn't Mengele shot me too? I begged him to. But no; he wanted me alive. He had injected a super dose of methylene blue into my eye, and he wanted to see if it had worked.

You're married and your spouse dies, so you change; you go from wife to widow, husband to widower. But when your twin dies, you're still twin. I played with words. I was twin. I had twin. I am twin. They all mean nothing.

For everyone else, they lose someone close, and is awful, but they still have memories of life without that person: husbands before they met their wives, parents before they had their children.

Not for a minute did I know how it was, not to have a twin. You can marry again, even have another child; but you can never have another twin. You are still the person you were, except when you're a twin; then you are half, and that's it.

What did I do? I did what any twin would do. I take on Esther's characteristics. Her mannerisms, her laugh, even her voice sometimes.

Like she borrowed me for a moment.

I had been quiet; now I was a chatterbox, like I had swallowed a gramophone needle. Before, I avoided danger. Now I looked for it, and being blind helped, because if I could not see it, it could not hurt me.

In any case, I knew already the worst pain possible. What else could there be?

Now, years later, I know the truth: I felt guilty for still being alive, and thought that, if I could die, that guilt would go.

For Esther, I was Cain: I had taken her place, her life.

Would I have changed positions, given my life for hers? In the beat of a heart.

I had no one else; all my family had died in Auschwitz.

Why was I the only one to live? For one person, one single person, to come out with me; someone else to share my responsibility, someone else who failed to save our family.

I was angry, and at everyone. Angry at myself, more lucky than my twin and my parents. Angry at the good fortune of those who had survived with their own families, more or less.

I felt an impostor. I was no saint; why was I so lucky?

Guilt, humiliation and shame. How to beat them? How to take back dignity?

Over time, I found the answer. The same way to live life itself: day by day.

I realised that things happen, and not necessarily for a reason, but still they happen. Someone must survive, after all. Someone must bear witness.

Oh yes, Herbert, that is big part of being Jewish, bearing witness. You want to find what happened to Max Stensness, I try to help you, because he was killed, and that must be made better.

I stopped thinking: 'Why me?' I started to think 'Why not me?' Maybe I was chosen, maybe not. I was still here, because, maybe I don't know it, but because I struggle, I have strength, I make the best of what I have.

I want to give Esther a gift, and now I see what that gift is. I must not let go of this life and be with her. Instead, I stay alive for as long as I can. I live my life for her as well as for me; I am her window on the world, and all the joys and sadnesses in my life are for her as well.

We had shared life before birth; we share it after death too.

Being a twin doesn't stop when there's only one of you, because there's never really only one of you. We who have been are one another for ever.

Suddenly I was afraid to die because, if I died, then

so would she. With her alive, I would not be so lonely. But at the same time, I would forever have been half a person, always existing against her, compared to her, opposed to her. We had been one soul in two body; now we were one soul in one body. The skin was around us, not me.

In Nigeria, solo twins from Yoruba tribe carry round their necks a wooden image which represents their dead twin. This way, the dead twin's spirit has a refuge, and the survivor has company. For me, no such souvenir, but nonetheless I carry Esther with me wherever I go.

So the me I knew before was gone, and instead came discovery, rebirth, excitement. And that's why I forgive Mengele.

You're surprised? Don't be. I forgive him because that is only way to sanity.

I don't know what he does now. He escaped the Allies, they had him at a camp and he escaped. He's probably in Brazil, or Paraguay, or Argentina, getting fat and molesting the local girls. I don't know, and I don't care.

I don't absolve him, no, never; but he left me with life, and so with a choice: what to do with that life.

So I make my choice, and my choice is to forgive.

I forgive, and he has no hold over me any more. For some survivors, everything is always Auschwitz; they're more at home with their memories than in the real world, and that's all they can think and talk about.

Not me. This is first time I tell anyone this, Herbert. No one else knows, because until now no one could understand; but you I think are different, and I hope you are worthy of it.

I have many friends, but no one for such confiding.
I have many lovers, but no one who I give my heart to.
How could I? How will I ever have with someone
what I had with Esther?
I already have a soul mate; I don't need another.

'Can I touch your face?' Hannah said. 'I want to see if you smile or not.'

Perhaps when she found out she would let him know, Herbert thought; after hearing all that, he was not sure he could tell.

He *did* understand, or at least hoped he did; because while anyone could have comprehended it, in purely intellectual terms, he had actually *felt* it.

The wrenches, the fury, the gaping wounds of loss had flowed from her as she spoke, or maybe they had been in him all along, and she had brought them to bloom.

As for whether he was worthy of this knowledge, well, he hoped so, for it seemed more important than anything he had ever encountered.

Hannah traced the fingers of her right hand over his mouth, forcing his lips slightly apart. Then she moved her fingers up to his cheek, fluttering them along the ragged sproutings of his late-night stubble, while her left hand flowed and undulated through the lines on his forehead.

'Hmm,' she said. 'A smile, a frown; hard to tell.' She paused. 'Say something.'

He could not speak, for what could he say that

could possibly do justice to the things Hannah had been through?

The words had not yet been invented that would have sounded adequate, and it was fear of being thought otherwise – of proving, through some ham-fisted platitude, that he was not the man she had taken him to be – that held him silent.

That, and the sudden vertigo-inducing thought that he had never felt closer to any human being.

'Oh, Herbert,' she laughed. 'You know why I like you? Because you're different.'

'Different? In what way?'

'Most men, they get you alone in a room, and they want sex, sex, right now.' Her tone suggested that this had not, on occasions, been entirely unwelcome. 'Not you. We sit here till the end of time and still you do nothing, no?'

His gut churned. 'I'm not much to look at, Hannah.'

'Well, you find the right person, then.' She laughed again, her delight a golden firework which fell on him and lit him up. 'Herbert, Herbert, even if I see you, I don't care what you look like.'

She moved her lips to his, and he was destroyed.

7TH DECEMBER 1952

SUNDAY

Herbert woke with a start, already thrashing at the python which had wrapped itself round his body as he slept. Then he realised, with shamed surprise, that it was Hannah, her legs curled round his and her arms clasped across the back of his neck, as though she were a koala clinging to the trunk of a eucalyptus.

Spot the man unaccustomed to waking up with a woman, he thought.

Hannah stirred but did not wake. Herbert dropped his head back on to the pillow and dared a small smile as he thought about the previous night.

Now, granted, he did not have much experience in these matters, but even if he had been Casanova, he would still have thought that Hannah was, as lovers went, incredibly skilled.

Her fingertips were calloused, rough against his skin; from Braille, no doubt.

She had told him, as her hands had traced intricate patterns across his skin, that some Indonesian masseurs were blinded in childhood to increase their sense of touch. Feeling the exquisite way in which her own fingers had known exactly where to apply pressure, and to what extent, he had easily believed it.

Hannah had taken the lead, of course, extraordinarily confident both in her own desires and in the instructions she had given him, which made him think of all the practice she must have had to become that adept, and therefore of how many men had been with her before he had, and of how most of them would inevitably have measured up better than him.

He blinked twice to rid himself of the thought.

What did it matter? He seemed to have given Hannah some pleasure too, unless she was a much, much better actress than he had given her credit for. And now she lay there, snuffling contentedly against his neck, and he was happy.

So what did it matter, indeed, who had come before him?

It mattered much more, he thought, that there be no one after him.

The radio said that it was freezing at Kensington Palace, and colder still at London airport. Northolt had 90 flights scheduled in and out, and none were moving; of London's 107, only 6 were still running.

Herbert saw in the dim dawn light that the fog had crept into the edges of the room where they lay, grey streaks which would hang there until the fire had warmed enough to disperse them.

The fog had settled for less than three days, but already there was a thick black film on everything inside Herbert's flat. The curtains looked as though a chimney-sweep had towelled himself down with them, and the metal surface of the draining-board was dusted in a fine layer of sooty grime.

Putting more coal in the grate would hardly make the place cleaner, but the fire had gone out, and the room was appreciably colder than it had been when they had retired.

Faced with the choice of freezing or choking, Herbert decided that warmth was the *sine qua non*. He scooped a pile of black nuggets from the scuttle next to the fireplace.

He watched Hannah as she dressed. In some inexplicable way, this seemed even more intimate and invasive than making love with her a few hours before had done.

Only when she had finished did Herbert remember that he still had a killer to find.

He had been lost in Hannah for hours, a blissful time out of time; he would have stayed there for ever, but she would not have let him, and for that he loved her more than ever.

The knock at the door was loud and sudden enough to startle them both.

Herbert jumped slightly in his chair, sloshing coffee over the side of his mug. Hannah, who was standing, took a step backwards, and turned her foot slightly on something. She bent down to pick it up, and Herbert saw as she ran her fingers over it that it was his makeshift paperweight; a model car, about six inches long with one wheel missing, an old childhood toy. It must have fallen from the desk.

Strange, he thought, that she should jump so. For her, all sounds must in some way be sudden, and therefore the unexpected must have gradually become the norm.

Herbert got up and went to the door, tensing himself.

'Who is it?' he called out.

'Me. De Vere Green.'

Herbert looked at Hannah, who raised her eyebrows in surprise.

'Are you alone?' Herbert asked.

'Of course.'

Herbert opened the door.

De Vere Green looked terrible. A week's groceries would hardly have filled the bags under his eyes, his hair rose and fell in spiky clumps, and his knuckles were white where he gripped a manila folder whose edges sprouted paper sheets.

Herbert half-ushered, half-dragged de Vere Green inside and steered him to the kitchen table, kicking the front door shut behind him as he did so.

'Coffee?' Herbert asked.

'Please.' De Vere Green's voice was hoarse. He

looked around the room, his eyes seeming to focus only intermittently. When he finally realised that Hannah was there, he stared at her for several seconds before shaking his head, though Herbert could not tell whether this was disapproval or disbelief.

De Vere Green had been drinking, that was clear from the mosaic of burst blood vessels on his nose and in his eyes – not to mention the sweet, slightly high odour which leached from his pores. Herbert wondered whether he was also on drugs. It seemed unlikely, but then de Vere Green had turned enough suppositions on their head in the past twenty-four hours; nothing about him would surprise Herbert any more.

When the coffee came, de Vere Green warmed his hands on the mug, visibly collected himself, and began his spiel.

'You have the whip hand here, dear boy. You know my secrets, you could destroy me just like that –' he clicked his fingers – 'if you wanted, and heaven alone knows I'd deserve it, after the way I've treated you. I could appeal to your kindness, but men like me don't understand such concepts, not really. So forgive me if I address you in my language: that of the deal, an arrangement of mutual benefit . . .'

Herbert did not really know what de Vere Green was talking about, but he nodded anyway: *Go on*.

'I have something here which may be – no,

let's be honest, which I think *is* most definitely – germane to your case. It's something which in the normal course of events you should never see, but under the circumstances I feel it only proper to make an exception. Before I show it to you, however, *you* must in turn give *me* an undertaking: that you will never reveal my secret, that indeed you must take it to the grave, if God forbid you reach that dreadful gate before me.'

It was strange, Herbert thought, and perhaps telling too, that though de Vere Green knew full well that Hannah was there, he seemed not in the slightest bothered by her presence. Perhaps he thought she was deaf as well as blind; or perhaps he was so dismissive of women that he considered her a trifle.

Herbert remembered the calculations he had made about his leverage over de Vere Green; in particular, about when best to use it.

'How do I know that what you have is worth my silence?' Herbert asked.

'You have to trust me.'

After everything that had happened between them, it sounded absurd. 'You have to trust me,' de Vere Green repeated, audibly more desperate than before. 'It'll be worth your while, I promise you.'

It was pitiable, to see a man reduced to this; and Herbert was less comfortable with pity than he was with hatred, that was the uncomfortable truth he knew too well.

But there was another truth, equally apparent: he wanted to solve this case. If de Vere Green had the means to help him do so, then it would be the most ridiculous act of self-spiting to reject the offer of aid simply because of its provenance.

And besides, what was to stop Herbert giving de Vere Green the assurance and then, if need be, going back on it?

Information could not be unlearnt, after all. The hold he had on de Vere Green expired when he made the truth public, not when he agreed not to do so.

He was becoming harder; he was becoming more pragmatic.

He did not know which.

'You have my word,' Herbert said.

With a smile of such pathetic gratitude that Herbert almost rescinded the agreement on the spot, de Vere Green opened the manila folder he had brought.

Inside were sheets of typewritten paper in various sizes, some foolscap, some little more than scraps, most somewhere in between. De Vere Green fanned them out on the kitchen table like playing cards.

'You told me yesterday that Papworth knew about Max,' he said.

Herbert nodded. 'That's right.'

'And I told you that no one knew about Max; he was my secret.'

'You did.'

'So how can they both be true?'

'One of you is wrong.' Lying or mistaken, it did not matter which; one more falsehood in this investigation could hardly be detected, let alone considered.

De Vere Green shook his head. 'No. We're both right.'

Herbert shrugged. 'Then how?'

'Because Papworth is a Soviet agent.'

Impossible, Herbert said. He had met Papworth, and the man had taken virtually every opportunity to launch into a tirade against the mortal evil that was communism.

Come on, said de Vere Green. You leave Five, and instantly forget everything you know about reading people's motives? Of course Papworth would say that, if he was a Soviet agent, of course he would. He'd lambast them at every turn, to make you think exactly what you're thinking now, that there's no way he could be anything other than America's finest.

Prove it, Herbert said.

These papers are decrypts from the Venona programme, de Vere Green said. Yes, the very programme that had first alerted London to Maclean's treachery. Venona covered only the war and the few years afterwards, but there was such an enormous backlog that most of the transmissions were only now being decoded.

That was by the by. The point was this: double

agents did not simply stop. Once they were in, they were in, and they were terminated only by death or discovery.

Venona was implicating hundreds of people, mainly in Washington and New York. There were informants in the State Department, and Agriculture, and Justice, and the Treasury, not to mention the Office of Strategic Studies, the Army Signal Corps, the Office of National Intelligence, and that was before you got to General Electric, Standard Oil, and US Rubber.

The West was crawling with closet Reds, in other words.

But the decrypts which de Vere Green had brought were more scientifically-orientated than most, and concerned a Soviet agent known only as Achilles.

They had been sent to him under the auspices of the counter-intelligence committee on which he sat with Papworth, and spanned a period of four years, on and off, 1944 through 1948, and various branches of science: non-ferrous metals, three types of engineering (aeronautical, chemical and manufacturing), crystallography, physics, biochemistry – and, of course, atomic energy.

The rub was this: Papworth had been involved with all of these.

Times, places, areas of expertise; they all matched. Here were transmissions made from Los Alamos during the Manhattan Project; there were outgoings from London just after Papworth had arrived. Each different decrypt in itself could have applied to several people, sometimes even scores. But take them together, and one by one the possibilities were whittled down until only Papworth was left.

It had taken de Vere Green a while to be sure, and even then he had shied from it. He was a patriot, and he liked Papworth, so both in terms of friendship and ideology, he did not want to believe that the truth was the truth, as it were.

'You're sure?' Herbert asked.

'Positive.'

'There's no doubt?'

'Papworth is the only man who fits all the decrypts. The only one.'

'And you think he was somehow running Stensness too?'

'I don't know. But if he was there, and he is who he is, then . . .'

'Well, there's only one thing for it.'

'What's that?'

'We must go and talk to Papworth.'

De Vere Green sighed. 'I knew you'd say that.'

'You don't seem thrilled by the prospect.'

'I'm . . . well, it's not as simple as all that.'

'Why not?'

'Because all these decrypts I get, Papworth receives them too.'

The fog was black and gauzy, like a widow's funeral veil. It hung in cold, clammy sheets, scummy and tight. It wanted to suffocate, that was obvious enough. It was no longer simply a meteorological phenomenon; it was a sentient, malevolent being.

Hannah had demanded to come too. De Vere Green had refused – she had already heard too much – but when he and Herbert went out of the flat, they could see so little that for long moments they did nothing but stand still and try to orientate themselves, clinging on to the doorframe as a child would clutch the side of a swimming pool.

So Hannah had come too. Besides, Herbert felt that she might be useful as more than a guide; if she was half as perspicacious about the case as she had been about him, perhaps she would uncover some piece of evidence, or make some connection, which had hitherto eluded him.

Herbert had no doubt that he was breaking the rules in bringing her along, but if the best the Met could offer him from their own resources was Elkington, then perhaps the rules needed fracturing in the first place.

Hannah walked with extraordinary assurance, much faster and more confidently than anyone else shuffling along uncertainly in the mist; the only person for whom the fog was not debilitating. Hannah alone, handicapped in everyday conditions, could now bestride this strange world without pause or worry.

She gripped her cane with thumb and three outer fingers, index pointing down the shaft towards her feet, and swept the stick before her like an antenna or the beam on a radar screen, low across her front and to each side, touching the ground every stride in front of the foot that was about to come forward.

Arm, hand and cane: lines of protection.

At first, it almost scared Herbert to keep up, convinced as he was that at any moment they would run headlong into someone coming the other way, or perhaps an object even more unyielding, such as a lamppost or a wall. Then he pulled himself together; if a small, blind girl could go at that pace, then so could he.

The only time they missed a beat was when Herbert tried to speak. Hannah stopped, muttered something which he took to be a reminder of where they were, and turned to him.

'Please,' she said. 'Blind people walk with their heads as well as their feet.'

'I'm sorry?'

'A draught of air which change mean to be a revolving door. Sudden smell of exhaust is passing car. Leather in the air, a shop for shoe repairs is nearby. I know route we take, but I must concentrate hard. So, I cannot listen to you. Every second, I must remember how far we are gone, and so how far is still left for us. I know, from A to B, it take me certain minutes. I can't do it quicker. I try to do it slower, I get lost. So always maintain same speed.'

They walked on in silence after that.

They were almost at the door of the American Embassy when Papworth came out.

He was no more than two or three yards from them, but still he did not see them, partly because of the fog, and partly because he was intent on where he was going. He turned left out of the door and set off.

When De Vere Green made as if to call out, Herbert clamped a hand across his mouth. Better to follow Papworth, he whispered, and see what he was up to, than beard him here and now.

Papworth walked with a strange mix of purpose and slowness, the urgency in the set of his body undone by the restrictions of progressing through such gloom.

It was Herbert rather than Hannah who now led the chase, making constant, minute adjustments to their pace. They had to be close enough to Papworth to keep him in sight, but far enough away to remain undetected.

With any other quarry, pursuit would have been well nigh impossible; but the metallic clacking of Papworth's heel inserts helped them track his progress as surely as a homing beacon.

Papworth headed right at the first corner, so that he was going down the east side of Grosvenor Square; all the way down, across an intersection, and into Carlos Place.

He stopped without warning.

Herbert flung out his arms to stop de Vere Green and Hannah in their tracks.

This was what it must feel like to be Hannah, he thought; doing everything by sound alone.

Papworth began to turn slowly.

Herbert took a couple of steps backwards, forcing the others into reverse too, and grabbing at Hannah when, startled, she began to stumble.

Papworth was still turning; and then Herbert lost sight of him, obscured by a particularly thick finger of fog which floated across the pavement.

Footsteps sounded muffled in Herbert's ears: Papworth, coming back to check.

If he found them, he would know they had been following him. It was hardly the weather for a Sunday-morning stroll, after all.

Herbert took another pace backwards, willing them to melt into the fog.

The footsteps stopped, and then started again, this time receding.

Perhaps Papworth had just thought himself lost, and had retraced his steps to check. Or perhaps he had heard something suspicious, and after a moment dismissed it as paranoia. Following someone through this fog was no task for the faint-hearted.

Herbert hurried forward again, concerned that they shouldn't lose Papworth.

It occurred to him as he did so that, if the situation had been reversed and he had wanted to flush out a follower, this was exactly what he would have done: stopped, resumed, and then waited for the trackers to come careering out of the mist so as not to lose their quarry.

No; Papworth was still walking, several paces ahead.

He passed through a pair of gates beyond which the fog seemed even blacker than elsewhere. It took Herbert a moment to realise that it was the outline of a building.

More precisely, according to the sign, the Church of the Immaculate Conception, Farm Street, Mayfair.

It was neither much warmer nor much clearer inside the church than it was outside. Matins would be sparsely attended, Herbert thought, when it began in an hour or so. Today was a morning where communing with God would best be done from home.

Papworth entered at the altar end, and immediately turned right, into a small alcove where three statues clustered. Herbert saw Our Lady Montserrat, with a golden ball in one hand and a child in her lap; a group at Calvary; and St Francis Xavier, rather magnificent in flowing robes.

Further along the side, just at the edge of the mist, Ignatius Loyola loomed in black, one hand raised and the other clutching a Bible. A Jesuit church.

There was nothing Jesuit, however, about the man waiting for Papworth in the alcove. It was Kazantsev.

Herbert and de Vere Green looked at each other, and de Vere Green must have made some sound of surprise or disgust, because Kazantsev raised his head with the languid vigilance of a zebra who had just heard a lion rustling in the bush.

Papworth looked round, first at Herbert, then at de Vere Green, then back at Herbert again, and then finally at Kazantsev.

'Go,' he said simply.

With unhurried pace, Kazantsev slipped through the door and out into the fog before either Herbert or de Vere Green could react.

'Who's she?' Papworth asked, looking at Hannah.

'Why don't you ask her?' Herbert said.

Papworth turned to Hannah. 'Who-are-you?' he said slowly, as though she didn't speak English, or was a child, or a retard, or all three.

Hannah did not answer, dignity restraining her fury.

'She's with me,' Herbert said.

Papworth flipped a hand in dismissal, as if to say that if she was blind, she was clearly of no consequence.

'I've got nothing to hide,' he said.

Then he sighed, the exasperation of a man whose plans had been undone by well-meaning but limited drones who could not possibly understand the grandness of his vision and talents.

'I told you,' de Vere Green said.

'Told you what?' Papworth said.

Herbert stared at him.

'That you're a Soviet agent,' Herbert said at length.

Papworth snorted. 'Don't be so ridiculous, Herbie.'

Herbert gestured to the space where Kazantsev

282

had been, as if to say: *Well then, if you're not a Soviet agent, how do you explain that?*

Papworth's eyes widened in recognition of Herbert's implication, and he laughed.

'You guys.' He shook his head in amusement. 'You couldn't find your own assholes with a mirror, could you?'

'That was a clandestine meeting with an MGB agent,' de Vere Green said.

'Of course it was,' Papworth said.

'Of course?' said Herbert.

'Of course,' Papworth reiterated. '*He's* working for *me*.'

Things got ugly after that.

'You stupid, stupid bastards,' Papworth hissed, making de Vere Green flinch at the use of profanity in a church. 'You think we'll keep running both sides of the fence now? I tell you, if I've lost him as an asset, I'm going to make your lives a misery, I swear to God.'

A priest came over. 'Is everything all right here, gentlemen?'

Papworth, getting angrier by the second, only just refrained from telling a man of God, in the house of God, to do something which was not only biologically impossible but also surely in breach of every religious stricture going.

The priest went away again.

'What the hell were you doing following me in the first place?' Papworth asked.

'The decrypts,' Herbert said. 'Material from Venona – it all points to you as a Soviet agent, code-name Achilles. Times and places all match.'

'Let me guess,' Papworth said, and turned to de Vere Green. 'This is your doing, yes? Why am I not surprised? Well, let *me* tell *you* something. I get the decrypts too, and it's funny that de Vere Green should suspect me. You know why? Because the more *I* read, the more *I'm* starting to think that maybe de Vere Green is Achilles.'

'Impossible,' de Vere Green said.

'Far from it. Check the times, check the places. Everywhere those decrypts refer to, if I've been there, so have you. We were at Los Alamos together. We've been in London together for four years. Hell, you even spent nine months in Washington just after the war.'

'This is absurd,' de Vere Green said.

'You find me a single Achilles decrypt which you could categorically not have been involved with, and I'll retract it all. Until then, you're in the frame as much as I am. More, in fact.'

'More?' Herbert asked.

'Of course. What better disinformation than trying to blame someone else for your own treachery?'

'That applies to both of you.'

'All right, then. Take a look at our careers. I've helped bring down the Rosenbergs, I helped winkle out Klaus Fuchs. I've also worked with Senator McCarthy, on the Malmedy massacre trial. De Vere

Green, on the other hand, told you not to worry when Maclean waved from the platform at Charing Cross. In effect – and you must have thought of this before, Herbert – *he* was the one who let Burgess and Maclean escape. And then, *and then*, he blamed it on you. He let you take the fall for something you didn't do. See any parallels yet?'

De Vere Green's mouth was working, but no sounds were coming out. A thin trail of saliva spanned a corner where his lips met. He looked as though he might keel over at any moment.

Papworth's flow was unabated. 'Not to mention the fact that he spends half his time in Cambridge, where Burgess and Maclean were, and which, let's face it, is hardly known for eschewing communists in the ranks. It's all there, Herbert, if only you'd look; more precisely, if only you'd *see*.'

Red and pink, Five had taught Herbert, red and pink: sodomy equalled heresy, and heresy equalled treachery.

'That's not true,' de Vere Green managed to splutter.

'Which particular bit is not true, Richard?' Papworth asked. 'Name me *one*.'

De Vere Green could not.

No wonder de Vere Green had been diffident about coming to see Papworth. Trying to pin it on the Agency's man had been his last throw; it had also backfired, as he must have known it could.

285

If de Vere Green had looked bad at the funeral yesterday, and worse when he had barged into Herbert's flat a few hours before, those occasions suddenly seemed pictures of gaiety and vitality compared to his appearance now.

Like Kazantsev – appropriately enough, Herbert thought, under the circumstances – de Vere Green left the church; though, unlike Kazantsev, he did it with a stumbling panic that bordered on hysteria.

Papworth was breathing hard, more through anger than anything else.

Herbert, hoping to defuse the tension, said the first thing he could think of.

'What was *The Mousetrap* like?'

Papworth stared at him, trying to make the mental leap back to this most banal of questions; and then, rather unexpectedly, he smiled.

'It was horseshit. It'll close down before New Year. You see if I'm not right.'

The fog squatted before, behind and around them. Herbert could not remember a thicker one, and certainly none dirtier. The sulphurous yellow tinge was becoming ever more pronounced. Hannah may not have been able to see it, but she could certainly smell and taste it.

There was a police box on Berkeley Square, right around the corner from the church. Herbert sat on the stool for a few moments, working out how best to proceed; and Hannah, understanding the need for silence, gave him the quiet in which to think.

Eventually, he picked up the phone, went through the same rigmarole as before in getting the local station to patch him through to New Scotland Yard, and explained to Tyce what had happened.

Tyce understood immediately. Much as he wanted to keep jurisdiction of this case, treason put control of de Vere Green out of police hands. Tyce would take it instantly to Scott, who would doubtless pass it to Sillitoe; all at the highest level, as was proper for an accusation of this magnitude against an official of de Vere Green's status.

Not that Herbert was out of the loop, however. The murder investigation was still very much alive, as it were; he had every right to continue his enquiries both into Stensness' death and the extent of de Vere Green's involvement in it. De Vere Green may have been a traitor but not a murderer; he may have been a murderer but not a traitor; he may have been both; he may even have been neither.

In effect, there were now two investigations, nominally separate, more probably connected. So Five could ask their questions, and Herbert his; and if he had anything to do with it, Tyce said, he'd make sure that Herbert got first dibs, for he, Tyce, no longer doubted which side Herbert was on.

But Five had to be the ones to find de Vere

Green, unless Herbert had absolutely concrete evidence linking him to the murder.

No, Herbert said; nothing concrete.

Then they had to wait for Five. The complexion of the case had changed drastically since Tyce had fought his corner with de Vere Green on Friday. It was cumbersome, infuriating, and perhaps even illogical, but that was the way things worked.

Herbert said he would ring in again when he next found a phone. He wanted to thank Tyce, but Tyce did not go long on expressions of gratitude, whether given or received.

'You think he is guilty?' Hannah asked, when Herbert had hung up.

'Who? De Vere Green?'

'The man who came to flat this morning? Him?'

'Yes, that's de Vere Green. And yes, he's guilty. There's no doubt.'

'Herbert, always there is doubt, in life.'

'You didn't see him when Papworth turned on him, Hannah. He looked . . . gone.'

'No, I not see him, but I listen. Is harder to hide tones of voice than expressions of the face, or gestures. Voice gets more tight, higher. Little muscles in throat, resonance in head and chest. Voice reveals anger, fear, people who lie. People know you watch them, they change the language of their body; but they forget to change the voice.'

Herbert was staring at her. 'And?'

Hannah shrugged. 'I don't know. When de Vere Green come to flat, I think he tell the truth. He in bad way, but he no sound like man who lie. Then here, Papworth say that de Vere Green lie.'

'And Papworth's voice?'

'That's the thing. Papworth sound the truth. He has positive voice. So I think, they both sound like they tell the truth. But only one can be doing so.'

Only one, indeed. And de Vere Green's reaction had surely proved which one.

'Where now?' he said, more to himself than her.

'You go to laboratory already?' she asked.

'Of course. Straight after you found the coat in the Long Water, actually.'

'Yes, but you search it then?'

'No.'

'So. You find clue at his home; why not at office?'

Why not, indeed?

He should, Herbert reflected, probably have searched Stensness' laboratory before; but when had he had the time, until now?

Or, for that matter, pending the arrest of de Vere Green, so few alternatives?

The underground was still running, so they took a tube from Green Park; not that they had much choice. They would have been more likely to find a taxi in the Sahara.

Sunday service was much slower and less frequent than weekdays, and they had to wait ten minutes for a train. Herbert took his mind off the wait by reading the platform advertisements, and almost laughed at one for tobacco which read simply: *When you find that things go wrong, fill your pipe and smoke Tom Long.*

He wondered whether Tom Long would make him a company director.

In the train, Herbert looked at his distorted reflection in the window. He listened to the wheels on the tracks, and to the creaking of the carriages as they swayed. He smelt printed newspapers, cigar smoke, and sweat, and thought how often he had failed to notice all these sounds and odours.

Hannah was right. Sighted people thought with their eyes, and little else.

'Kazantsev was there too, you know,' Herbert said.

'I know. I smell him.'

'You *smelt* him? How? You've never met him before. How do you know what he smells like?'

'He smells like Russian.'

'Which is?'

'Shit. Russians are all scum.'

Herbert laughed, and Hannah cut him off, genuinely angry now. 'You come to my country, Herbert. You come to Budapest, see what the Soviets do there. Stalin, he try to finish what Hitler started. They as bad as each other. Four years' time, you wait, bad thing happen.'

'Four years? Why four years?'

'Every twelve years, Russians do bad things.'

'Really?'

'You think I joke? In 1920, civil war finally ends; 1932, collectivisation; 1944, deporting Chechens, entire country, all the way to Kazakh Republic – they still there, thousands kilometres from home. So 1956, something bad is due; and Hungary's turn then, I'm sure. You come to my country; then you no laugh no more.'

The rest of the journey passed in strained silence, Herbert once more cursing his insensitivity and giving silent thanks for the distraction of an investigation.

At Temple station, they got out. King's was literally next door, so even in the murk they found it first time.

The laboratory was silent; no bubbling beakers or demented scientists brewing up lethal chemicals. Perhaps Herbert had watched too many second-rate movies.

He had not looked around too closely on Friday morning, when he had been interviewing Rosalind and Wilkins.

Now he saw that the laboratory was clearly for two people only, which must have meant Stensness and Rosalind; there were only two chairs, after all, each tucked under a different section of the workbench.

They effectively had a wall's length of work space each; about three times as much space as Herbert enjoyed at Scotland Yard, but then he did

291

not need a panoply of instruments and apparatus as these people did.

Rosalind's was the nearer of the two desks. A red Chinese silk evening gown was hanging from a hook nearby, and pinned to the wall above the bench was a typewritten card. Herbert leant in closer to read it.

> A scientist makes science the pivot of his emotional life, in order to find this way the peace and security which he cannot find in the narrow whirlpool of personal experience. His research is akin to that of the religious worshipper or the lover; the daily effort comes from no deliberate intention or programme, but straight from the heart.
>
> Albert Einstein

There were machines and equipment whose purpose Herbert could not have guessed in an aeon, strange contraptions of dull steel and fraying rubber. How would he find anything in here? He might not have known what he was looking for in Stensness's house, but at least there the possessions had been items which Herbert recognised. Here, he thought, he might stumble past some vital clue a thousand times and be none the wiser.

The average Joe could have a good crack at naming at least half of England's monarchs, but science really was an alien discipline; either one spoke the language or one did not, and Herbert knew on which side of the fence he sat.

The first thing he saw on Stensness's desk was, at least, something with which he was familiar: a typewriter, dark green metal and pretty cumbersome in appearance. Herbert poked around it, more in hope than expectation, and found nothing out of the ordinary. No secret compartments, no incriminating documents still wound round the roller, not even a trace of typescript on the ribbon.

That last brought him up short.

Typing any kind of text left indentations on the ribbon, no matter how faint. If one was skilful and patient enough, one could decipher pretty much anything typed within the past few weeks.

The only way a ribbon could be as clear as this was if it was new – and it certainly did not look new, for the material was beginning to wear at the edges, and it had lost the glinting sheen of one straight out of the box – or if it had been boiled. Boiling ribbons eradicated the typescript.

Boiling ribbons meant that Stensness must have had something to hide.

Herbert felt his ears twitch, as though he were a terrier.

Maybe there was something here after all.

There were more machines on Stensness's desk, and more still in the storeroom on the far side.

Herbert looked through all of them, and again came up blank. One small piece, presumably a spare part, looked as though it could have been familiar, but he could not place it, and eventually he conceded that his imagination was playing tricks.

It would have been helpful if the machines had been labelled, he thought; but why should they have been, when the only people using them would know perfectly well what they were for?

He went back to Stensness's desk, a little deflated.

Apparatus apart, there was nothing there which he would not have expected: two adjoining piles of books, about the same height, all with scientific titles; a long wooden ruler half-hidden under a manila folder; and an old metal mug from which an assortment of pens bristled.

Herbert opened the books one by one and flicked through them, hoping to find something pressed between the pages.

When he found nothing, he held each book horizontally by the spine and shook hard; perhaps he had missed something first time round.

Ten books; ten blanks.

He put the books back in their piles, picked up the metal mug, tipped the pens out and looked inside the mug, to see if Stensness had hidden anything there, perhaps taped to the sides or the bottom.

Nothing.

Nothing on the base, either, when Herbert turned it over. He scooped up the pens and began to stuff them angrily back into the mug; and he stopped.

One of the pens was much heavier than the others.

He took the lid off and pressed the nib against the back of his hand. It left a mark of blue ink. So it worked. That in itself proved nothing, he knew; and with a swirling of exhilaration, Herbert knew what he was going to find.

He unscrewed the nib from the main barrel of the pen.

There was a small ink sac within the nib itself; but it was what was in the barrel itself that excited him. He shook it gently, and into his palm popped a small metal cylinder, no more than a couple of inches in length.

He turned this cylinder vertical, and almost yelled for joy. The ends, as he had expected, were not solid metal, but glass: small lenses.

'What is it?' Hannah said, as attuned to emotions as a shaman.

Herbert looked at the desk, at the books, and the ruler, and then again towards the storeroom, where most of the apparatus was stored. The answers came tumbling through his mind with the speed and mechanical accuracy of hand-crafted cogs.

He pulled the ruler from underneath the manila folder, and saw that it had a small hole drilled through the middle, perhaps half an inch in diameter.

In four quick strides he was back in the storeroom, hunting for the piece of metal he had thought familiar.

There it was, a tiny knurled cylinder; half as long as the one in the pen, but twice as wide, and instantly recognisable the moment he knew what he was looking for.

Herbert went back to Stensness's desk, where it took him scant seconds to arrange everything in the correct place.

The books he kept in their piles but moved nine inches apart.

The ruler he placed across the top of the stacks, so that it served as a bridge.

Then, adjusting things slightly, he took the uppermost book from each pile and placed them on top of the ruler, one on each side, to hold it in place.

The knurled cylinder from the storeroom fitted exactly into the hole in the ruler.

'Herbert, what the hell you do?' Hannah asked again.

'Microdots,' he said. 'Stensness was making microdots here.'

'Microdots? What is that?'

'Ways of hiding lots of information in a very small space.'

He took her hand and placed it on the left-hand pile of books. 'Go up until you get to the ruler,' he said. 'Then feel along the top of the ruler. When you get to a metal cylinder, that's halfway. There's another pile of books on the other side.'

She ran her hand up, right and down, as he had instructed.

'The metal cylinder is a microdot camera,' Herbert said. 'The top opens to allow the film to be inserted. Then, working downwards, there's a spiral spring, a disc to hold the film in place, the film itself, a container for all the lens stuff, and a cap which doubles as a shutter; we're talking long exposures here, up to several minutes sometimes. The ruler holds the camera at precisely the right height above the table; there's no adjustable focus on these things, they're far too small for mechanisms like that. He puts the documents on the table, between the books, directly below the camera, makes sure the whole thing is well-lit, and takes the photographs. And with this –' Herbert passed Hannah the second cylinder, the one he had found in the fountain pen – 'he can view the microdots to make sure they came out OK.'

'But where are the microdots themselves?' she asked.

'Oh, they're the size of a full stop, you can conceal them in any document you like . . .' And already he was pulling the *Times* article from his pocket.

Herbert turned on Stensness's anglepoise lamp and held the paper beneath it, tilting it this way and that to find the gleam where the microdot film caught the light.

There was none, at least not that he could see, but the method was not foolproof; some types of film were matted, making them harder to discern under illumination.

297

He put the Coronation map down on the desk and studied it again.

He was looking for a full stop, perhaps more than one, but there were hundreds on the page. It would take hours to study them all.

The place names which Stensness had circled, he thought. Perhaps that was it.

Crude, sure; but if Stensness had been in a hurry, he might have taken the chance.

Herbert looked at the circled place names, and the first he saw was Regent Street. The word *Street* had been abbreviated to *St.*

St., with a full stop.

He put the viewer to his eye and zoomed in on that stop.

Nothing; just a tiny circle of finest *Times* ink.

And now he saw the pattern; every place name Stensness had circled had at least one dot somewhere in it. *St. James's St.; St. James's Park; St. James's Palace; Victoria Embt.; Trafalgar Sq.; Piccadilly Cir.; Marlboro. Ho.; Northd. Av.; Parlt. St.; Hyde Park Crnr.; Oxford St.; and Regent St.*

He scanned them all, one after the other, and each time nothing, nothing, nothing.

Damn Stensness, Herbert thought. Damn him and his ridiculous schoolboy obsession with tradecraft, damn him for playing at these games which had killed him. Damn Stensness, most of all, for dangling the prize just out of Herbert's reach, beckoning him so far and no further, as though Herbert were Tantalus in the underworld, destined forever to be given that most cruel of commodities; unfulfilled hope.

Herbert cursed loudly. Hannah put her hand on his shoulder.

'What is it?' she asked.

He told her, as calmly as he could, what he had – or, more precisely, had not – found; and she laughed.

'I'm glad you think it's funny,' he said.

'Herbert, don't be like that. What did I tell you yesterday?'

'You told me lots of things.'

'No; well, yes, but I mean, what did I tell you about way you think?'

'You said I think only with my eyes, like all sighted people.'

'And now, you do that, exactly.'

'How?'

'Because you *see* something – here, circles – and for you they are answer, because your eye go to them. But they are not answer. So he give you wrong direction. What you do now, is you turn your eye off. What your eye say, you think opposite. No; don't look at the paper again' – how was she always ahead of him? – 'that is point I make. Shut your eye. *Think*.'

Herbert could have done without the lecture, but he knew Hannah was right.

Stensness had hidden something in that article, he was sure. And he had drawn circles around various places, knowing they would be taken as indicators, whereas in fact they were nothing of the sort.

If the microdots were not where the circles were, therefore, they were where the circles *were not*.

Only now did Herbert turn back to the map, knowing what he was looking for: a place name which had a dot, but no circle round it.

Herbert found it more or less instantly, checked to see that there were no others, and then put the viewer to his eye and homed in, this time on London's most famous Gothic edifice: the Houses of Parliament – or, as written here, Ho. of Parlt.

And they were there, two little microdots, clear as day through the tiny lenses.

Herbert did not know how long they could count on remaining alone in the laboratory, and he did not want to have to explain himself to any wandering biophysicists, so they made their way back to Hannah's flat. Herbert checked behind them every so often but saw no one. The air was clearer below knee level, strangely, and once or twice he squatted down to peer through this unexpected corridor of clarity; but Hannah hurried him along, for she was cold and wanted to get home, so he could not fully assuage his paranoia.

Besides, the contents of the microdots were sufficiently baffling to require further study, perhaps hours' worth – time he wanted away from de Vere Green, or Papworth, or Kazantsev, or anyone else who might have found out where he lived.

The moment they were inside Hannah's flat, Herbert put the radio on; his constant companion for so long, it seemed, maybe even some kind of security blanket, an unfailing voice through the quiet in his life.

All bus and train services bar three had been withdrawn, it said.

The AA were now appealing to people to leave their cars at home, as conditions were the worst they had ever known. *Tell me about it*, Herbert thought, having just seen how abandoned vehicles were littering the streets as though London were a metallic battlefield. They'd had several near misses and two actual hits: Herbert barked his shin on a Sunbeam Talbot, Hannah smacked her hand on a wing mirror.

The emergency services were becoming more stretched by the hour; police rushing to crime scenes hidden by the fog, ambulances trying to save those whom the pollutants were killing, fire engines struggling to quench blazes inadvertently started by people desperate to keep warm.

The newsreader reeled off a litany of burglaries, assaults and robberies: a cinema manager robbed of the day's takings on the Edgware Road; a Post Office safe blown open in Isleworth; thieves had smashed the window of a jeweller's in Brixton and made off with the display; and in Great

Windmill Street, the offices of boxing promoter Jack Solomon were lighter to the tune of twelve boxes of cigars, a case of whisky, a camera, two fight films, and £50 in cash.

Herbert listened to all this as he sat at Hannah's kitchen table. Then he phoned Tyce again.

No word on de Vere Green as yet, Tyce said. He had spoken to Scott, who had pledged to contact Sillitoe immediately. There was nothing now they could do but wait.

Herbert told Tyce what he had found in the lab, and gave him Hannah's number; he would be here until further notice.

When the call had finished, Herbert looked through the viewer at the microdots.

The first one, after the *o* of *Ho*, appeared at first glance to be one of those ink-blot tests that psychiatrists gave patients to assess their state of mind. It was in black and white, and it was a circle, divided roughly into an inner and an outer ring.

The outer ring was more or less uniformly dark, all the way round.

In the inner ring, which was lighter, four horizontally-striped lines radiated out from the centre in an X-shape.

The lines were not quite at right angles to each other, so the X appeared to have been squashed slightly from either side; it was taller than it was wide.

There were therefore four lighter areas, almost

diamond-shaped, in the spaces between the limbs of the X.

At the centre was a small circle, brilliantly white.

It could have been anything, Herbert thought; absolutely anything.

The other microdot, after the *t* of *Parlt*, was another piece of code; much longer than the scrap written in the corner of the map, and therefore many times as baffling.

MGX Q-KGHDXI DHMMXJZ TK ITAAJHLMT-
BZHWWR LGHJHLMXJTKMTL BA H
GXWTLHW KMJNLMNJX. MGX ITHYBZI
KMJNLMNJX KXJOXK MPB ANZLMTBZK.
ATJKM, TM TZITLHMXK MGHM MGX
DHMMXJZ JXDXHMK HEBOX HZI EXWBP
MGX LXZMJHW Q-KGHDX, KTCZHWWTZC
MGX LBZMTZNHMTBZ BA MGX GXWTQ.
KXLBZI, TM HJTKXK AJBY H JXCNWHJ
KXJTXK, HWBZC MGX YBWXLNWHJ HQTK,
BA MGX KNCHJ DGBKDGHMX CJBNDK
MGHM ABJY MGX YBWXLNWX'K
EHLVEBZX. MGX KRYYXMJTLHW
DHMMXJZK BA MGX GBJTSBZMHW
KYXHJK BZ MGX HJYK HZI WXCK BA MGX
'Q' IXYBZKMJHMX MGHM MGX GXWTQ
YHVXK H MPTKM HM JXCNWHJ
TZMXJOHWK. MGX ABNJMG WHRXJ-WTZX
BZ XHLG WTYE TK YTKKTZC; MGTK YHR
GTZM HM H IBNEWX GXWTQ, PTMG MGX
YTKKTZC WHRXJ-WTZX JXDJXKXZMTZC

303

MGX DBTZM HM PGTLG MGX MPB
KMJHZIK LJBKK XHLG BMGXJ.

Herbert felt a begrudging admiration for Stensness; whatever his secret was, he was not giving it up easily.

Codes and ciphers had been part of Five training, at least to a level somewhere between elementary and intermediate. Although Herbert had taken the course several years before, and was therefore bound to have forgotten much, his crossword habit had surely kept his brain in some kind of requisite shape.

Hannah came back into the living-room with a pot of coffee and two cups. She crooked the top joint of her finger over their rims so she knew when to stop pouring.

Herbert told her that this would take some time; several hours, perhaps.

She said that was fine, she was happy reading.

He watched her run her hands along the spines of the books on her shelves, up and down, up and down, feeling for their titles.

She found the one she was looking for, took it from the shelf, sat down, opened it and began to read, eyes fluttering as her fingers danced across the pages.

Herbert found it hard to reconcile the knowledge that she was reading with the visual evidence that she did not once look at the book in front of her; but in the context of everything that had

304

happened these past few days, it was just about the most reassuringly normal thing he could remember.

He smiled at Hannah, took a few quick breaths to make himself alert, and turned back to the microdot.

Peering through the viewer hour after hour would give him the mother of all headaches, so the first thing he had to do was transcribe the text on to a piece of paper. As he wrote, he could also keep a tally of the frequency with which each letter appeared, without which he would have no hope of solving Stensness's code.

He was already making several assumptions, but he figured that they were sensible and therefore likely to be true.

The text was clearly laid out as it had been originally written; word lengths, spaces and punctuation were all unchanged. This suggested that Stensness had used a mono-alphabetic cipher; substituting each letter with another, all the way from A to Z, according to a system Herbert had yet to work out.

Usual practice in such ciphers was that each letter had a unique proxy; that was, the cipher did not use any given letter to replace more than one letter in the original.

It sounded simple, and in essence it was, but the permutations were horrific. Herbert had forgotten what the actual figures were, concerning the number of ways in which twenty-six letters could be rearranged, but he remembered there being something in the region of twenty or thirty zeros tacked on to the end.

However, codes tended to use systems, and mono-alphabetic ciphers were usually based on a starting key: a word or phrase which filled the first few places of the cipher alphabet (minus duplicate letters and spaces, naturally), followed by the continuation of the original alphabet from the last letter in the key through to Z, and then by whichever letters had not yet been used, still in original alphabetical order.

This way, the decoder needed only to know the key to decipher the message.

Herbert, of course, had no key, so he had to try it another way: frequency analysis.

In normal English, some letters appeared much more often than others. Herbert knew what these were; every cruciverbalist did.

By finding out which letters appeared most frequently in the coded text, he could match them to their originals.

So he drew a grid down one side of the paper, with a little box for each letter from A to Z, and as he transcribed Stensness's code, letter by letter, he put a stroke next to each relevant box in the grid: four vertical strokes and one diagonal for the fifth, just as they had been taught in schoolboy mathematics.

It was not especially difficult work, but it was slow and painstaking.

He was especially concerned not to make mistakes

at this stage, as an error now could skew his results and send him chasing up blind alleys all day.

Thus it took him almost an hour, including two full check-throughs at the end, before he had finished.

Only three letters had appeared more than fifty times: *M* and *X*, both with sixty-seven, and *H*, on fifty-one. Herbert decided to focus his attention here first.

It was fairly safe to assume that the three commonest letters in the cipher text probably represented the three commonest letters in the language proper – *e*, *t* and *a* respectively – but in such a small sample, perhaps not in the same order.

In other words; he was sure that *M*, X and *H* between them signified *e*, *t* and *a*, but he could not be certain which was which.

He had more counting to do.

E and *a* were vowels, and as such tended to be found next to pretty much most other letters, both before and after them.

But *t* was a consonant, and was therefore pickier about the company it kept. For instance, one rarely saw *t* next to *b*, *d*, *g*, *j*, *k*, *m*, *q* or *v*.

And so it proved here.

In the cipher text, *H* and *X* were sociable to a fault, spreading themselves throughout sentences with the ease of an ambassador at a cocktail party.

M, on the other hand, was something of a recluse, lurking around only a few letters and avoiding many others outright.

Herbert had his first breakthrough.

M represented the letter *t*. He wrote as such next to its box with the sixty-seven strokes.

H and *X* therefore stood for *e* and *a*, but which one for which one? Did *H = a* and *X = e*, or vice versa?

He looked back through the text again.

Only two English words consisted of a single letter: *a* and *I*.

There were four single-letter words in the text, all of them a simple *H*.

Whereas texts without the first person singular were common, those without the indefinite article were rather rare.

So Herbert surmised that *H* stood for *a*, and therefore *X* for *e*.

Since the word *MGX* appeared seventeen times, and Herbert knew the identity of the first and third letters, he figured that this combination must stand for the word 'the', which therefore meant that he could swap an *h* for the *G*.

With these four in mind, he amended the text to reflect what he knew.

He placed in lower case the four letters he had already deciphered, while the ones he had yet to work out remained in capitals; for obviously, though he knew that *X*, *M* and *H* stood for *e*, *t* and *a*, he did not yet know what *E*, *T* and *A* stood for.

The text now read:

*the Q-KhaDeI DatteJZ TK ITAAJaLtTBZaWWR
LhaJaLteJTKtTL BA a heWTLaW KtJNLtNJe.
the ITaYBZI KtJNLtNJe KeJOeK tPB
ANZLtTBZK. ATJKt, Tt TZITLateK that the
DatteJZ JeDeatK aEBOe aZI EeWBP the
LeZtJaW Q-KhaDe, KTCZaWWTZC the
LBZtTZNatTBZ BA the heWTQ. KeLBZI, Tt
aJTKeK AJBY a JeCNWaJ KeJTeK, aWBZC the
YBWeLNWaJ aQTK, BA the KNCaJ
DhBKDhate CJBNDK that ABJY the
YBWeLNWe'K EaLVEBZe. the KRYYetJTLaW
DatteJZK BA the hBJTSBZtaW KYeaJK BZ the
aJYK aZI WeCK BA the 'Q' IeYBZKKtJate that
the heWTQ YaVeK a tPTKt at JeCNWaJ
TZteJOaWK. the ABNJth WaReJ-WTZe BZ
eaLh WTYE TK YTKKTZC; thTK YaR hTZt at
a IBNEWe heWTQ, PTth the YTKKTZC WaReJ-
WTZe JeDJeKeZtTZC the DBTZt at PhTLh the
tPB KtJaZIK LJBKK eaLh BtheJ.*

Herbert looked through the text again, and his
eye fell on the word *YBWeLNWe'K*.

An apostrophe tended to precede only two
letters – *t*, as in 'wouldn't', and *s*, as in 'someone's'.

But he already had *t* accounted for. He knew
too that *s* appeared at the end of many words,
mainly third person verbs and plural nouns.

When he searched the text for the letter *K*, he
found it on the end of nineteen words, which was
proof enough for him.

This in turn gave him several instances of the

words *Tt* and *Ts*, which would be either 'it' and 'is' or 'at' and 'as'; but he already had his *a*, so *T* became *i*.

By now he had a word *aJises*, so *J* became *r* – there was no other alternative. This in turn left him with a *Bther*, and *B* became *o*.

He remembered something from the cryptographic exercises Five had set them; that there came a time when deductive progress stopped being linear and began to become exponential, a point where the decipherer felt solid ground beneath his feet, as it were, when one clue led so rapidly to another and another and another that they appeared faster than they could be followed up.

It was like the initiation of a chain reaction in atomic physics; once the critical threshold was passed, the reaction propagated itself.

Herbert had been at it for more than two hours now, and by rights he should have been exhausted, for, without human or mechanical assistance, it was a mentally wearing process; but the sight of the finish line infused him with a zeal that felt for a moment superhuman.

He knew already that he wanted to be worthy of Hannah. In a strange way, he realised, he wanted to be worthy of Stensness too.

He looked again at the paper.

the Q-shaDeI DatterZ is IiAAraLtioZaWWR
LharaLteristiL oA a heWiLaW strNLtNre. the

310

*IiaYoZI strNLtNre serOes tPo ANZLtioZs. Airst,
it IZIiLates that the DatterZ reDeats aEoOe aZI
EeWoP the LeZtraW Q-shaDe, siCZaWWIZC the
LoZtiZNatioZ oA the heWiQ. SeLoZI, it arises
AroY a reCNWar series, aWoZC the
YoWeLNWar aQis, oA the sNCar DhosDhate
CroNDs that AorY the YoWeLNWe's EaLVEoZe.
the sRYYetriLaW DatterZs oA the horiSoZtaW
sYears oZ the arYs aZI WeCs oA the 'Q'
IeYoZstrate that the heWiQ YaVes a tPist at
reCNWar iZterOaWs. the AoNrth WaRer-WiZe
oZ eaLh WiYE is YissiZC; this YaR hiZt at a
IoNEWe heWiQ, Pith the YissiZC WaRer-WiZe
reDreseZtiZC the DoiZt at PhiLh the tPo straZIs
Lross eaLh other.*

Pieces were coming thick and fast now, clambering on top of one another in their haste to be discovered, and Herbert no longer cared about progressing in the most efficient way, for there were so many paths he could take.

Lross gave him his *c*. *SecoZI* and *aZI* coughed up *n* and *d*. From *centraW* came *l*; *diaYond* was clear even to a moron, as were, in rapid succession, *Dattern*, *strNctNre*, *siCnallinC*, *douEle*, *interOals*, *aQis*, *Aourth*, *sRmmetrical*, *Phich*, *bacVbone* and finally, joyfully, *horiSontal*.

He wrote the whole text out again, with capitals in the right places, and sighed in a mixture of satisfaction, amusement and resignation; because, though it plainly made sense, it would be meaningful only to someone far more scientifically versed than Herbert was.

> *The X-shaped pattern is diffractionally characteristic of a helical structure. The diamond structure serves two functions. First, it indicates that the pattern repeats above and below the central X-shape, signalling the continuation of the helix. Second, it arises from a regular series, along the molecular axis, of the sugar phosphate groups that form the molecule's backbone. The symmetrical patterns of the horizontal smears on the arms and legs of the 'X' demonstrate that the helix makes a twist at regular intervals. The fourth layer-line on each limb is missing; this may hint at a double helix, with the missing layer-line representing the point at which the two strands cross each other.*

He went through it several times, unable to shake the sensation that, the more he read it, the less he understood.

Then he took the viewer and looked at the first microdot again.

It was clear that the text referred to the image. Stensness had mentioned an X-shaped pattern, a diamond structure and horizontal smears, all of which were visible even to a duffer layman like Herbert.

He looked at his two sets of alphabets; the cipher one in order from A to Z, and their clear text counterparts, necessarily jumbled.

He took a new piece of paper and reversed the process, writing the original alphabet out in order, and then matching it to its cipher. This way, he could see the code Stensness had used.

It came out like this:

Plain	A	B	C	D	E	F	G	H	I	J	K	L	M	N	O	P	Q	R	S	T	U	V	W	X	Y	Z
Cipher	H	E	L	I	X	A	C	G	T	U	V	W	Y	Z	B	D	F	J	K	M	N	O	P	Q	R	S

So H E L I X A C G T was the key.

H E L I X was 'helix', the proposed structure of whatever the X-shaped object represented, that was obvious enough.

As for A C G T, Herbert thought, with some aptness, that he hadn't the foggiest.

He had been so engrossed in the decryption that he had been oblivious to everything else, even Hannah's presence.

He looked over at her with a quick flush of anxiety, wondering if she would think him impossibly rude.

He need not have worried. She was asleep on the sofa, the Braille book lolling open on her lap.

Slumber had made her serene, softening the spiky edges of her feral energy. He could have watched her like that for hours, but when she woke up Herbert knew she would have been angry that he had not immediately shared his discovery with her.

So he nudged her shoulder, stroked her hair

313

with trembling hands while she slowly kicked her way up from under the surface of sleep, and told her what he had found.

He described the image to her, read her the text, pointed out where one fit the other, and explained the key Stensness had used.

She had no better ideas than he did, which made him feel that perhaps he was not being that stupid after all.

'Your cane,' Herbert said to Hannah. 'Is it solid?'

'No. Is hollow.'

'And is there a top to it, or something?'

'Yes. The end come off.'

He took the Coronation article, rolled it tight, took Hannah's cane, unscrewed the top, wedged the article inside the tube, replaced the top, and returned the cane to Hannah. It was a token gesture, no more, but he felt safer that way. If this thing was sufficiently valuable for men to have killed each other, then it was sufficiently valuable to merit a hiding-place, no matter how inadequate.

It could be argued, of course, that he was putting Hannah in potential danger, but Herbert knew her well enough by now to know that she would never have entertained such a notion.

And nor did she; she simply nodded and said, 'Good thinking.'

The tube again, where there would usually have been a smattering of people in their Sunday best, on their way to or from church, but the fog was clearly keeping almost everyone at home.

One couple who had braved the conditions were in the same carriage as Herbert and Hannah, and the woman of the pair was not impressed.

'Did you count how many people there were there today, Jerry?' she said. 'I'll tell you. Twenty-six. *Twenty-six!* They usually get a thousand, you know. It'll have played havoc with the collection, that's for sure.'

Herbert had rung Tyce before leaving Hannah's flat, to let him know where he was going. There was still no word about de Vere Green.

He had not told Tyce that Hannah was with him, nor that without her he wouldn't have discovered the microdots in the first place. He was aware that others might not be as convinced of the case for her involvement as he was, and thought it best to leave this supposition untested.

Hannah and Herbert disembarked at Gloucester Road, where Sherlock Holmes had once wandered the tracks in search of the Bruce-Partington plans, and found their way slowly and cautiously to Drayton Gardens; more specifically, to Donovan Court, where Rosalind Franklin lived.

She had given Herbert her address on the Friday morning, several lifetimes before, when he had first told her about Stensness. If he needed more information, she had said, all he had to do was ask.

He needed more information now, that was for sure.

Drayton Gardens was a not unpleasant tree-lined street, and Donovan Court was a not unpleasant Thirties block on the east side. Not that Herbert could see much of either, of course. He rang the bell to number 22.

It would be just his luck if Franklin was not in, he thought.

Yes, there were others who could explain what all the palaver with helices and diamond structures was about, but something atavistic in Herbert had warmed to the outsider in Rosalind, and it was her with whom he wanted to speak.

Minutes passed. The fog eased tendrils of clammy cold around them.

Herbert stamped his feet and muttered billowing plumes of nonsense, before stabbing at the bell again in irritated, disbelieving desperation; and suddenly the block's main door opened, and there she was.

'Inspector Smith,' she said. 'Have you found the killer?'

'Yes. I mean, I think so.'

Hannah raised a sardonic eyebrow, and Herbert remembered; actually, he hadn't.

He had found various layers of truth about de Vere Green, and Papworth, and Kazantsev, but he had yet to prove conclusively which one had killed Stensness.

'Excellent. Come in, come in. You must be freezing.'

Rosalind ushered them through the door,

appraised Hannah quickly up and down, and introduced herself to her. Rosalind did not offer Hannah any more help than that, Herbert noticed – indeed, she had not batted an eyelid at anything to do with Hannah's blindness – and he thought with quick unease of his own gaucheness when he had first met Hannah, and the ways in which he had attempted to aid her progress.

Rosalind Franklin clearly understood an awful lot about pride, Herbert thought.

Rosalind led them up the stairs; she did not seem the kind of person to have taken a lift, whether there was one available or not.

Herbert wondered briefly who this reminded him of, and realised that it was Hannah herself.

Number 22 was a four-room flat, and it was clear that Rosalind lived alone. The décor and possessions were too consistent in theme and appearance to have belonged to more than one person, though the effect did not feel contrived. The flat, while neat, was not obsessively so.

Rosalind went into the kitchen and came back with tea for three; a peculiarly British reaction, Herbert thought. There were few ills in the British world that could not at least be alleviated by a good old cuppa.

'Well,' Rosalind said, when she had poured, 'what can I do for you?'

Herbert told her briefly of what he had found at her laboratory earlier.

Then he took Hannah's cane, unscrewed the

top, tipped the contents into his hand, and laid them out on the table in front of Rosalind, explaining what was what, where the microdots were, how she could see them, and what he had deciphered.

He had thought that Rosalind would start with the decipher, but she went instead for the microdot viewer, and he saw the scientist's logic: begin at the beginning.

It took her a moment to get comfortable with the viewer and find the right place on the map. She homed in on the first dot and looked at it for no more than half a second before speaking.

'Goodness me,' she said. 'That's DNA.'

'What's DNA?' Herbert asked.

Rosalind lowered the viewer, looked squarely at Herbert, and allowed herself a single moment of melodrama.

'DNA, Mr Smith, is the meaning of life.'

Rosalind explained, in concise but comprehensive terms.

The quest for the structure of DNA – deoxyribonucleic acid – was the Holy Grail of genetics, and therefore of all contemporary science. Whereas lightning, plague, famine, or even the atomic bomb affected some people some of the time, heredity was something that affected all people all of the time.

It was mankind's destiny; intimate, inborn, inescapable, but thus far inexplicable.

DNA held the very key to the nature of living things. There were ten trillion cells in the human body, and DNA was in the nucleus of every single one.

It orchestrated the incredibly complex world of the cell, and stored hereditary information which was passed from one generation to the next.

DNA distinguished man from all other species on the planet; it was what made man the creative, conscious, dominant, and destructive creature that he was.

In short, DNA was the human instruction book, previously known only to God himself. It was the Rosetta Stone of life.

The problem, however, was this.

Even though the molecule had been discovered two-thirds of the way through the last century, when it had been isolated from pus in the bandages of wounded soldiers, still no one knew for sure what its structure was.

And without the structure, everything else was irrelevant, for the structure held within itself the methods of reproduction and organisation.

It would be like trying to drive from London to Edinburgh without the slightest idea of which direction one should be heading in, let alone anything as precise as a map; no guide whatsoever beyond the knowledge that there was a place called Edinburgh.

DNA was the secret of life, four billion years old and being unpicked every day.

It was already known that the DNA molecule consisted of multiple copies of a single basic unit, the nucleotide, which came in four forms: adenine, guanine, cytosine and thymine.

Adenine and guanine were purines, bicyclic compounds.

Cytosine and thymine were pyrimidines, heterocyclic compounds.

Adenine and thymine were found in identical quantities within DNA, as were guanine and cytosine.

That was, in essence, all that was beyond doubt.

The rest was guesswork, and there was a lot of *that* around, because of all the people trying to find the structure.

Pauling was the most famous of them, and the topic was to have formed his keynote speech at the conference, before he had been taken ill and forced to cancel.

'A Proposed Structure for the Nucleic Acids', it had been titled, and would have been Pauling's public shot at immortality, the greatest chemist in the world taking on the most golden of all molecules.

Pauling and his colleagues at Caltech aside, the hunt was centred around two other institutions: Rosalind's own King's College, and Cambridge University.

Herbert saw the pattern at once.

King's was a notorious communist hotspot, even more so than Cambridge, where de Vere Green went on a regular basis, and which had supplied the bulk of Britain's spies for a generation.

A neater correlation of institution and intelligence service – the MGB at King's, Five at Cambridge, and the CIA at Caltech – would have been hard to imagine.

De Vere Green, Kazantsev and Papworth; they must all have known exactly what Stensness had been offering. Perhaps Stensness's boast of something that would change the world had been a sort of password as well as a promise.

But by God, he had been right. This thing *would* change the world, in every way and for ever.

'Is it a race?' Herbert asked.

'It's valuable,' Rosalind replied. 'But racing's vulgar.'

'Only if you lose,' Hannah said.

Rosalind smiled to concede the point. 'Most scientists spend their careers contributing to the long, slow accumulation of dates and ideas,' she said. 'To be involved in a dramatic victory is a rare privilege.'

But it *was* a race; Herbert could see that full well. The structure of DNA remained unknown, Everest was yet to be climbed, the four-minute mile was yet to be run, the moon was yet to be walked on. History would remember only those who were first. Scientists who had theories named after them – Darwin, Newton, Einstein – were not just geniuses; they were pioneers.

If Beethoven had not written his Ninth

321

Symphony, no one else would have done so. But if Pauling did not discover the structure of DNA, then someone else would, and sooner rather than later.

Herbert remembered the Einstein quote above Rosalind's desk, and thought that she had no idea of the magnitude of what she was working on – politically, that was, not scientifically. No matter her brilliance as a scientist, it simply would not have occurred to her that governments would kill for the secret.

For Rosalind and her ilk, knowledge was key, its application to be aimed at the greater good, irrespective of nation or creed. Science was science, they believed; it was no one's property.

The world would be a better place with more Rosalind Franklins, Herbert thought.

He handed Rosalind his transcription of the deciphered code, and she read it with annoyance. 'Unsound . . . premature . . . conjecture . . . *wrong*,' she said, half to herself, and then looked up. 'This is what Max was killed for?' she said.

'Yes.'

'What an *idiot*,' she snapped. 'Stupid, stupid fool. What a waste.'

'What is that, anyway?' he said.

'The X-shape?'

'Yes.'

'It's photo 51, a photograph I took last May.' Herbert must have looked surprised, for Rosalind smiled. 'Not a photograph as the layman understands

322

it; an X-ray photograph. What you see on the microdot was originally about three or four inches in diameter. Wait, I'll show you.'

She left the room again, and came back a minute or so later holding a metal contraption and a stoppered glass bottle with some white fibres sitting at the bottom.

'This is a Phillips microcamera,' Rosalind said, setting the metal apparatus down on the table in front of Herbert.

It looked like something from a science fiction movie; a more or less flat circle with a knurled edge, a pipe sticking diagonally out of its shoulder, and a lens in the middle, all supported vertically above a base plinth.

'I use it for recording X-ray diffraction patterns,' Rosalind added.

'*What* kind of patterns?'

'Diffraction patterns. Imagine an object that's invisible in every way. You can't see it, smell it, hear it, touch it or taste it. The only way to study this object is to shine light through it, or reflect light off it. By observing the patterns formed by the light, and matching them up with what you know of patterns caused by different kinds of diffraction gratings, you can get a great deal of information about the object's structure.'

She held up the glass bottle. 'This is DNA, from a calf's thymus. It's dry now, but it photographs much better when it's wet; it's longer, thinner and easier to see. As far as I know, we at King's were the only ones to have realised this.'

'Which means Max was selling the others something he knew they didn't have.'

No wonder Stensness had been trying to sell photo 51 when he had. The conference had brought together all the main players on each of the three teams hunting for the molecular structure. It was one of the few occasions – perhaps the only one for many moons – when everyone involved in the race would be in one place.

Rosalind dropped her gaze, and Herbert realised that, for her, Max's treachery bit deep. 'Yes. Of course, the clearer the photograph, the easier it should be to discern the molecular structure. So . . . Dry DNA, crystalline, we call the "A" form; hydrated is the "B" form, paracrystalline.

'We smear some "B" into fibres, like those in a spider's web. We insert it in the camera here –' she indicated the rear – 'in front of a piece of film. The X-rays come in through the pinhole here –' tapping the small lens – 'and the pipe at the top right is to allow humidified gas to be passed through the camera to control the water content of the fibre. We concentrate on one strand of fibre, about a tenth of a millimetre across.'

'And the X-rays bounce off that strand?'

'They bounce off the *atoms* in that strand, because their own wavelengths are so short; and they leave a pattern on the film as they do so. The marks on the photographic plate are not those of the atoms themselves, therefore, but of the spots that the X-rays make when they're scattered after hitting the atoms. Because the X-rays reinforce each other in some directions and cancel each other out, the spots vary in intensity. From this intensity and positioning, the atomic structure can be guessed at; that is, you can turn two-dimensional patterns into three-dimensional molecular structures. Clear so far?'

'Just about.'

'So you should be. I've already explained that bit to you twice.'

She said it without malice, and Herbert realised that there could be few things more frustrating for a scientist than having to describe things to a layman, having to fill in the kind of background knowledge that a professional would take for granted, and at the same time simplify problems and procedures enough to make sense.

He picked up the transcript of the decipher and read it again to refresh his memory.

The X-shaped pattern is diffractionally character-istic of a helical structure. The diamond structure serves two functions. First, it indicates that the pattern repeats above and below the central X-shape, signalling the continuation of the helix. Second, it arises from a regular series, along the molecular axis, of the sugar phosphate groups that form the molecule's backbone. The symmetrical patterns of the horizontal smears on the arms and

325

*legs of the 'X' demonstrate that the helix makes a
twist at regular intervals. The fourth layer-line on
each limb is missing; this may hint at a double
helix, with the missing layer-line representing the
point at which the two strands cross each other.*

Rosalind had said the only thing known beyond
doubt about the structure of DNA was the presence and relative quantities of the four nucleotides;
yet here was Stensness strongly suggesting that
DNA was not only a helix, but a double one at
that.

'You don't think it's a helix?' Herbert asked.

'No,' Rosalind said. 'The "A" form is certainly
not a helix. I proved that back in the summer.'

She handed Herbert a three-by-six index card
with a hand-drawn black border; it was half invitation, half death notice. He read it.

It is with great regret that we have to announce the death,

on Friday, 18th July 1952, of D.N.A. Helix (crystalline).

Death followed a protracted illness which an intensive course

of Bessel injections had failed to relieve. A memorial service

will be held next Monday or Tuesday. It is hoped that

Dr M.H.F. Wilkins will speak in memory of the late helix.

'You wrote this?' Herbert asked.

'Yes.'

Herbert remembered the argument in the laboratory, and the hostility by the grave.

'And Dr Wilkins didn't find it amusing?'

'He might have done, if it hadn't come from me.'

'That bad?'

'Why do you think I've got these machines at home? Sometimes I find Maurice so intolerable that I literally can't bear to be in his company, so I have to come back here to work. I'm leaving for Birkbeck in March, almost exclusively to get away from him. We're at loggerheads on – oh, just about everything, if you must know.'

'Including the issue of whether DNA is a helix or not?'

'*Especially* that. He accepted, with some reluctance, that the "A" form was antihelical, but he's absolutely adamant that the "B" form is different.'

'And Stensness shared his views?'

Rosalind sighed. When she spoke, Herbert heard the slightest catch in her voice. 'I *had* thought that Max agreed with *me*.' She flapped a hand towards the Coronation map. 'Evidently not.'

Herbert had assumed that science, besides being a male preserve, was also carried out in a vacuum, by people whose brilliant minds allowed them no scintilla of doubt, error or human frailty, and that progress was consequently linear and inexorable.

Now he saw that the opposite was true. Behind

327

the baffling terminology, scientists were largely the same as the rest of humanity. They argued, they loved and hated, they were pliable and stubborn, and their flaws and follies informed their work just as much as the flaws and follies of laymen informed theirs.

And it was such disputes that had prompted Max Stensness to see, or to think he saw, something in an X-ray photograph that his colleague Rosalind Franklin did not or would not or could not see.

'Why do you think Max was wrong?' he asked.

'It's not so much that I think he was wrong; more that his conclusions were woefully premature. He's inferred far too much from the data available. Listen to the words he used: "indicates", "demonstrates", "arises". But the evidence he quotes does nothing of the sort.'

Rosalind put the viewer to her eye and looked at the microdot again. 'For instance, I see double orientation here, which would refute his assumption of radial symmetry. The reflection is more intense in the left-hand quadrant than the right. That is asymmetrical, and a helix is symmetrical; therefore, this can't be a helix.'

'How can two of you see such different things in the same picture?'

'We all see what we want to see, don't we? Look, I've taken nearly a hundred of these photos; some have been atrocious, some all right, some pretty good. This one, photo 51, is just about the best of the bunch, but it's still not perfect. If it *were* perfect, the answer would be clear and we wouldn't be arguing about it. It's like the photo that makes you look more handsome than you are, because by a fluke it's caught your features arranged more attractively than usual. It might show you at your best, but it doesn't show you right.'

Herbert nodded; he knew that feeling all too well.

Rosalind continued. 'Maybe the equipment's slightly faulty, maybe I got the viewing angle slightly wrong. Maybe, maybe. They're small things, yes, but we're dealing with molecules here, so even a small thing can distort your results. Every scientist knows the position, because we've all been there. Sometimes there are several observations jostling for your attention, all apparently contradictory or discordant, and you don't know which ones are the vital clues and which ones are irrelevant.

'What I'm saying is that I need to do more experiments before I can be sure, one way or the other. Each successful experiment takes you closer to the truth, not just for what it proves but also for what it disproves, for the possibilities it eliminates. That's the only way to do things.'

'But others don't think so?'

'No. Some of them think I'm too . . . hidebound.'

'Who thinks that?'

'Watson and Crick, up in Cambridge. They think I need a collaborator, someone to break up the pattern of my thinking. They argue over everything, pushing their collaboration, and their friendship, to the limits, but they justify it by saying that they make each other *think*.'

'And?'

'Look what they've discovered. *Nothing*. They build models out of rods and metal plates and wires and plastic balls – childish, Tinkertoy stuff – then they test them, trying to make the facts fit the theory. Science isn't a game. I set up my experiments carefully, and only when I'm happy that the results are sound do I move forward.'

'And they think you plod away with your experiments?'

'I do not *plod*. It takes imagination and intellect to know what experiments to do, to prepare the specimens and observe the results . . .' She paused, and laughed at herself, so quick to rise to slights. 'But yes, you're right, they *do* think that. Crick told me the other day that Nelson won the Battle of Copenhagen by putting the telescope to his blind eye so he didn't see the order to stop fighting. He thinks scientists should adopt the same principle: let the experimental evidence go hang and allow our minds to wander.'

Something Rosalind had said jarred in Herbert's head, but he could not be sure what. He tried to catch it for a few moments, but it was no good;

answers like that only came when one was least expecting them.

It was past two o'clock, and Rosalind had not yet had lunch. Would Herbert and Hannah, she asked, like to eat with her?

Herbert called Tyce for what seemed like the umpteenth time that day, feeling like a persistent suitor. Still no word about de Vere Green, and Herbert shouldn't hold his breath. The fog was causing intermittent havoc, so even the most straightforward tasks were taking much longer than usual.

In that case, Herbert thought, he might as well eat now; not least because, if and when they found de Vere Green, the interrogation might go on for hours, and in that eventuality, who knew when his next meal would be?

Rosalind was an excellent cook, which Herbert supposed was not surprising, since in many ways cooking was a branch of chemistry. Like Hannah, Rosalind used ingredients which seemed exotic in dreary old England – olive oil, garlic, parmesan and basil. She and Hannah discussed with earnest animation the best way to cook pigeon, rabbit, and artichokes. They swapped techniques and short cuts. Hannah said that the way to test the readiness of Camembert was to put one finger to the cheese and the other to a closed eyelid; if the consistency matched, the cheese was ready.

New potatoes tasted better cooked without

water, Rosalind replied. Put them in butter in a heavy pan, cover it, and let them cook in their own juices. She admitted putting garlic in everything, especially roast beef for her father, who always claimed that he hated garlic and who equally never noticed it in his own food.

Hannah howled with laughter at this.

When at last they drew breath, Herbert remarked on the preponderance of photographs of Paris in the flat. For a moment Rosalind's eyes seemed to cloud over, as though at the memory of a lost love.

'Oh, Paris,' she said, and her earthy practicality danced away. 'I could have stayed in Paris for ever. I *should* have stayed there for ever. London is a man's city, a place of furled umbrellas and bowler hats and gentlemen with their clubs and tailors. Paris is a woman. She does not tolerate stupid vacant faces and childish complacency. Why did I ever come back? To change the banks of the Seine for a cellar in the Strand seems more insane with every day.'

'Insane.' Herbert laughed. 'In Seine.'

'Unintended, I assure you,' she said, and was on to the next sentence before Herbert could feel too gauche. 'Paris was perfect for me. The French like intellectuals and women; the English can deal with neither. When I argued with my colleagues there, they weren't taken aback, because that's the way they do things. Here, I can hardly open my mouth without being shouted down. I always revel in the company of the French. The standard of conversation is vastly superior to that of any English gathering I've ever been in. The French are so much more quick-witted and alive.'

Herbert had been right and wrong. There was a lost love in Paris, but it was the city herself; nothing so prosaic and corporeal as a man.

After lunch, Rosalind brewed coffee in a laboratory flask and served it in evaporating dishes – one of the many legacies, she explained, of her time in Paris.

She and Hannah began to discuss things: their mutual distrust of America's materialism and prosperity; what it meant to be a Jew; the merits of Zionism. Hannah was pro-Israel, Rosalind was sceptical.

'If you feel that strongly about it, why don't you go and live there?' Rosalind said, once more with bluntness, once more without the slightest spleen.

'Because in Belsen, British soldiers save my life,' Hannah replied simply.

Rosalind asked what it was like to be blind, and Hannah replied with her curiously elegant form of halting English that once she had gone through the usual stages of reaction – shock, despair, anger and acceptance – even her memories of the visual world had begun to become faint and fossilised, vanishing behind her as she advanced through the tunnel. There was no light at the end of this tunnel, no hope of emerging.

At some point, so gradual that she had not consciously noticed it, she had reached a place where she could no longer summon up memories of faces or places, where she could not even remember whether letters faced left or right. This was the bend in the tunnel; beyond that was the deep, endless night of total blindness.

Mengele had made her totally sightless. She could no longer tell day from night, or ascertain even the slightest flicker of sunshine. Not only had she no idea what people looked like, but she could not even begin to imagine. For her, people's faces were the sources of their voices, nothing more. She looked in that direction when they were talking, but purely to show that she was listening. With most people, she would have been better off looking at their backsides; that was their chosen orifice of speech.

Herbert was happy to sit in silence, watching and listening. He had never been in the company of someone like Rosalind, at least not for a sustained period, and to be honest he found the force of her intellect somewhat intimidating.

Hannah, however, showed no such fear; she was, as ever, forcefully herself.

Some people – Herbert wondered how often he had been guilty of this – changed with the situations they found themselves in, and could all too easily become reflections of those to whom they were talking.

Hannah was the antithesis. She threw her personality down to Rosalind as a gauntlet, daring

Rosalind to like her, in which case Hannah would have been pleased, or to find her too difficult, in which case Hannah would offer a sincere thanks for lunch and be on her way.

Hannah might have been less obviously cerebral than Rosalind, but she compensated with native intelligence and an unutterable belief in her right to an opinion. Perhaps, too, she knew instinctively that she was dealing with a kindred spirit, though Herbert felt it would have mattered little either way.

Hannah and Rosalind were now discussing science, with even more animation than before. Rosalind was pointing out the ways in which popular consciousness was already moving away from tradition and church to secular rationalism; perhaps, she said, the fog would clear on to a new world, as the Flood had.

'It's dangerous,' Hannah said.

'What is?'

'To let science free like that, with no check on it. You know, I had a twin.'

Rosalind made the same calculations as Herbert had done on Friday night, and came to the same conclusions, though hers were inevitably more specific.

'Mengele?'

'Yes.'

'I'm sorry.'

Gentiles would never understand, Herbert thought, not really; not viscerally.

'Thank you,' Hannah said. 'But now you see why I think how I do. It gets out, no putting back; it like Pandora Box, never go in. If you discover the structure of DNA, then in the future, don't know when, you have the tools for genetic engineering, maybe crude but still present, and then is no more than a tiny step to eugenics, and presto! Back come the Nazis, with their lives unworthy of life. Is all – ah, horrific.'

'But Hannah, you can't let the prospect of evil, no matter how dreadful, deter you from trying to do good, otherwise the world would just grind to a halt. There will be laws to stop things like eugenics and cloning.'

'There are laws to stop murder, too, Rosalind. People still do it.'

'You think we should leave things to nature?'

'Of course. Who know where it end? You make the test, so only elite, genetic elite, have power? You create race above all others, super-race? For humanity, evolution is millions of years, and now you want to change all that in one generation, two perhaps? We change nature, maybe we change the human race. Maybe something else come along in our place.'

'But we reshape nature all the time. We divert waterways, combine crops, cross-breed animals.'

'Yes. And in most times, those are done very badly.'

'Exactly. But now we have a chance to integrate ethics with progress, right from the very start.

It's the difference between the sledgehammer of traditional agriculture and the tweezers of biochemistry. If you took your argument to extremes, there would be no medicine, no clothes, no shaving or haircuts. Is the world a worse place for their existence? Of course not. Science's highest moral obligation is to use what is known for the greatest benefit of mankind. Knowledge is nothing without its purposeful application. And nothing will benefit mankind more than what comes from this discovery, because the discovery *is* mankind.'

'The answers are not with science, Rosalind, not all of them. Science is only as good as methods it uses, as people who use them. No, is only as good as the worst of them, the weakest link. Because even the best can't see where things will end up. Alfred Nobel, he invent nitroglycerine to end wars, and now it makes them longer. Science and technology produce ship that cannot sink, and it called the *Titanic*. The Manhattan Project is designed for peace: it killed hundreds of thousands. Now, the atom bomb is biggest threat in world, and to world.'

'But whose fault was that? The politicians', or the scientists'? Perhaps when we uncover the secrets of DNA, we will find that the capacity to love is inscribed there; that all of us have within us the impulse which has permitted our survival and success on this planet, and which will safeguard our future.'

'You think that? Really?'

'Absolutely. Yes, we're disposed to competition, but we're also profoundly social. We understand that collective action is, in evolutionary terms, extremely desirable. Maybe you don't see life this way, Hannah – I'd hardly blame you if you didn't, after what's happened to you – but I really believe in it. We've the opportunity to enhance love at the expense of hatred and violence. We've the opportunity to put right what chance has put wrong, because nature *doesn't* know best, there's not a scientist on earth who believes that it does, and if they do they're in the wrong job. We're learning the language with which God created life, and with it, we're on the verge of having immense power to do good, to heal. It's almost too awesome to comprehend.'

Rosalind Franklin, Herbert thought, asexual, and the biggest romantic of them all.

The phone rang. Rosalind picked up, listened for a moment, and handed the receiver to Herbert without a word.

'Smith.'

'Five have found de Vere Green,' Tyce said.

'About time. Where is he?'

'He's dead.'

De Vere Green had had rooms in Piccadilly – well, Herbert thought, he would have had, wouldn't he?

The stench hit Herbert the moment he started up the stairs, long before he reached the flat itself.

338

Smell was the sense most intimately connected to memory, and he recalled immediately where he had last encountered that sweet, high odour of rotting carrion, though on a much greater scale: in Belsen, when they had arrived to liberate the dead. And this despite the fact that the windows had all been thrown open, ushering fog and cold into the room in equal quantities. When Herbert exhaled, he could see his breath mesh with the murk.

The place was small – three hundred square feet at most – and packed with death's inevitable attendants; in this case, several men whom Herbert recognised as eminences in Leconfield House and, bristling with the pugnacious belligerence of the outnumbered, Tyce. Herbert waded through the scrum towards him.

'Bloody circus,' Tyce shouted. 'Lucky it's suicide – we won't find any evidence once these clowns have finished their trampling.'

'Suicide?'

Tyce pointed to the open windows. 'Carbon monoxide; you could hardly breathe.' He indicated de Vere Green's corpse, slumped forward from his chair on to the writing bureau; then he squatted down by the gas fire, ran his finger along the influx pipe, and tapped the valve. 'This was wide open. Leaking gas like it was going out of fashion. The windows were closed, the doors too. He'd have been breathing in pure fumes; killed him stone dead. Easy way to top yourself.'

Herbert nodded. He was already looking back at the desk; in particular, at a neatly written sheet of foolscap half-pinned under de Vere Green's right hand.

Tyce followed his gaze.

'He left a note.'

Herbert walked over, picked it up, and read it.

I no longer wish to live this life; or rather, I no longer wish to live these lives, all of which have been dragged from their bushels these past days and thrust into the open.

Those who have trusted me – my country, my colleagues, my friends, and my lover – I took their confidence and trampled it underfoot. I have deceived and betrayed them all.

Whatever anguish they experience at this is but a fraction of my own. Being mendacious and treacherous is bad enough. Far, far worse, I am, in the final judgement, a murderer too.

I took Max's life from him, because he would not give me what I wanted. Perhaps, somewhere in the next world, he will forgive me.

Do not mourn me. I am not worthy of it.

It was unquestionably de Vere Green's handwriting, and equally unmistakably his voice, Herbert thought; florid to the end, tinged with desperation, as though his flamboyance was pot-pourri to sweeten the stench of his self-loathing.

Carbon monoxide was colourless and odourless;

a fitting exit for a spy, perhaps, creeping up almost undetected on one.

De Vere Green would not have suffered too much. He would at first have had a slight headache and experienced some shortness of breath – symptoms, in other words, indistinguishable from the run-of-the-mill fog malaise.

These would gradually have worsened, giving way to nausea and chest pain before unconsciousness had kicked in. All in all, there were worse ways to go.

Herbert looked at his watch. It was past five; more than six hours since de Vere Green had run from the church in Farm Street. The carbon monoxide would have taken some time to have full effect, which meant that, even if de Vere Green had returned straight home from the church, written the note and turned the gas on, he could still have been saved, had bureaucracy been bypassed.

Herbert looked around him. It was as bachelor a flat as one could have imagined. Where Rosalind's flat had been devoid of male presence, so de Vere Green's seemed almost surgically bleached of any influences feminine.

Despite his differences with de Vere Green, Herbert was sad that things had ended this way. He remembered his belief that only the brave committed suicide; and he thought that, in his own fashion, and in more ways than one, de Vere Green had probably been as brave as the next man.

Herbert suddenly, badly wanted to be elsewhere; it didn't really matter where.

It was less than three minutes' walk to Shepherd Market, even in the fog. All this time de Vere Green had exercised such a pull on the course of Herbert's life, yet he had never known that they lived so near to each other. It seemed to Herbert as sad as it was fitting.

From his flat, Herbert rang the American Embassy. The receptionist said that Papworth would be dining that night at Wheeler's in Soho. Herbert knew the place well. Sheltering behind a green façade, Wheeler's was luxury at a time when British food was at its dreariest. It served sole and lobster in thirty-two separate ways, but offered no vegetables bar salad and boiled potatoes.

Herbert had felt it best not to bring Hannah to de Vere Green's flat. Now, she was the only person he wanted to see.

He picked his way through the mist to Frith Street, and when he got there she did nothing but hold him, listening as he recounted in a meandering jumble what de Vere Green had done.

By the time he had unburdened himself, it was almost dinner time. Time to go and find Papworth.

It might have been Sunday night, but there was no sense of winding down in Soho, which was, as ever, a world apart.

Herbert and Hannah passed a group of musicians outside their union on Archer Street, arms draped lazily over their violin cases as though they were a gathering of gangsters. The queues for Humph's jazz club were already stretching all the way round the corner, a line of worshippers at a New Orleans temple of warm sex.

On Dean Street, since they were slightly early, Herbert and Hannah stopped for a drink in the York Minster pub, known universally as 'the French' after the Resistance had used it as a hideout during the war.

The landlord, a Frenchman with a moustache to which the word 'flamboyant' would have done scarce justice, greeted Hannah like a long-lost daughter.

'*Chérie*,' he cried, and kissed her hand. 'I thought you'd left us for ever.'

Hannah introduced Herbert – 'Gaston,' said the landlord, '*enchanté*' – and bought drinks over Herbert's protestations that he should pay.

There was no draught beer; Herbert had wine.

'Let her pay, Herbert,' Gaston said, with ersatz conspiratorialness. 'It's been so long since she was last here that I'm surprised she's not using sovereigns.'

And Herbert saw that Gaston, too, was captivated by Hannah's luminosity, this little blind girl whom everyone wanted to protect, but who needed nothing from anybody. Humanity had yet to find a more alluring combination.

'He is nice man, but don't let him fool you,' Hannah said as they sat down. 'He has no beer because Pernod and wine make more money for him.'

As if to prove Hannah's point that he was no saint, Gaston immediately started quarrelling with a drunk. 'One of the two of us will have to go,' Gaston shouted, 'and I'm afraid it's not going to be me!'

And it was not.

Herbert was too on edge to taste the wine, let alone enjoy it.

He wanted to find Papworth and tell him that de Vere Green was dead, and no, it was not Papworth's fault, any more than it had been Herbert's; but they had helped de Vere Green get there, and for that they bore some responsibility, logic be damned.

Hannah may have moved easily among the flotsam of Soho, but they were not Herbert's type. With every person that came up and chatted to her about some inconsequence or other, he felt the fuse of his patience fizzle away a touch further. He had neither the time nor the inclination to watch, for instance, bleach-blonde tarts in rabbit fur complain to Hannah that people were trying to pick them up.

A drunk staggered up to them, virtually collapsed into Herbert's lap, and gasped: 'The price of a drink! The kiss of life!'

Herbert pushed him off and stood up.

'Come on, Hannah. Let's go.'

When she started to demur, he added: 'please', and she understood.

No, Herbert thought as they walked the streets again, Soho was not so much a world apart as another country, a Bohemian exclusion zone where the only sin was to be boring, and where there was no such thing as post-war depression.

In this reverse world, people cried in public, travelled in taxis, cashed cheques everywhere but the bank, did not know what day it was, thought nothing of missing an appointment if they were having a good time, and had been barred from at least one establishment.

But the drinking and bitchiness and sex obscured one fundamental: this was a place of great innocence. Every day brought manuscripts to be finished, trips to be made, masterpieces to be painted, dreams to be fulfilled. Whatever commodities were in short supply, hope was not among them, and never would be.

Maybe, Herbert thought, maybe, one day, he could sneak in at the edges.

They walked into Wheeler's past a long counter where a waiter in a white apron was opening oysters at lightning speed. Another waiter intercepted them. Herbert told him who they were looking for, and the waiter indicated a plain wooden table without tablecloth in the far corner.

Papworth was there with Fischer; Pauling was nowhere to be seen.

'Herbie!' Papworth staggered to his feet – he was already quite drunk – and embraced Herbert woozily. 'Join us, old bean – isn't that what the British say, "old bean"? We were just celebrating. The radio says the fog's going to lift tomorrow, so Fritz here and Linus can head back to the good ol' US of A.'

Papworth gestured to a bottle of champagne on the table. 'Champagne for your real friends, real pain for your sham friends!'

He laughed loudly, and Fischer with him.

'De Vere Green's dead,' Herbert said.

It seemed to take a moment for the news to filter through to Papworth's brain, and another moment for it to sober him up.

He took half a step back, squinted his eyes in a manner that might in different circumstances have been comic, peered at Herbert, and said 'Dead?'

'Dead. Carbon monoxide poisoning.'

'Where?'

'In his flat.'

'Suicide?'

'Yes.'

'Jesus.' Papworth puffed his cheeks out and wiped his forehead. 'Jesus.'

He gestured to the table. There was room for four, would they not sit down?

'You want to eat?' Herbert asked Hannah.

She shook her head.

'I don't have hunger,' she said. 'Maybe I go.'

'Are you all right?'

She nodded jerkily. 'Fine. Am tired, is all. Not feeling so good. Maybe the fog. You come see me later, yes?'

'Yes.'

'Promise?'

'Promise.'

'Good.'

She kissed him on the mouth, unashamed, turned and walked out, tapping her cane in front of her; stubbornly, magnificently independent.

Herbert watched her go, and then sat down. He hadn't intended to eat, but Papworth called for a menu and insisted. He seemed suitably shaken by the news about de Vere Green, so Herbert considered it politic to keep him company.

'You didn't really meet properly last time,' Papworth said, indicating Fischer. 'Herbert Smith; Fritz Fischer.'

Herbert shook Fischer's hand.

'Did de Vere Green find it?' Papworth said.

'Find what?'

'What Stensness was offering.'

Herbert pondered how to answer.

Technically, the answer was 'no'; the only people aware of what Stensness had been trying to sell were Herbert himself, Hannah and Rosalind.

But de Vere Green had known, in general terms, as had Papworth, and Kazantsev too; of that Herbert was sure. Why else would they have been at the conference?

Herbert was suddenly very, very tired of all this.

'You know exactly what he was offering,' he said.

Papworth started to protest, and Herbert stared him down with the unblinking weariness of a basilisk until Papworth quietened.

'You know what he was offering,' Herbert repeated. 'You all did, or else you wouldn't have gone to meet him. He said he'd found something in the DNA structure that no one else had. Yes?'

Papworth said nothing.

'Yes?' Herbert pressed.

Papworth nodded. Herbert continued. 'Well, I've seen what he was offering, and I've shown it to someone in a position to know, and I tell you now, you were wasting your time. What Stensness was trying to sell was research that didn't stand up. He was a huckster, no more.'

'You're sure?' Papworth said.

'Positive.'

'Maybe you'd let me have a look, just to confirm this?'

Herbert shook his head. 'You think I was born yesterday? This whole thing has done more than enough damage as it is. You send Professor Pauling and Mr Fischer –'

'*Dr* Fischer,' said Fischer.

'– home tomorrow, and let them continue working on the structure, like the scientists at Cambridge will, and King's. Let the best team win, and let the discovery be made available to the whole world.'

'You understand nothing,' Fischer said.

Papworth raised a hand. Herbert couldn't tell

whether he was trying to stop Fischer or admonish him. Either way, Fischer ignored it.

'The structure of DNA will be the greatest scientific achievement of this century,' Fischer said. 'Upon this discovery rests much of the determination of the shape of the future. When we know what our DNA looks like, we will know why some of us are rich and some poor, some healthy and some sick, some powerful and some weak. The intellectual journey that began with Copernicus displacing us from the centre of the universe, and continued with Darwin's insistence that we are merely modified monkeys, has finally focused in on the very essence of life itself.'

His speech was accented with traces of German which flickered like a radio dial, stronger on some words than others, but there was nothing wrong with his English.

'The vistas which this discovery will open up are extraordinary,' Fischer continued. 'We will at last come to grips with all the great killers – cancer, heart disease, diabetes – because they all have a genetic component. We will be able to compare healthy genes with disordered ones, and replace one with the other, thus rooting out diseases at the most basic level, removing the imperfections at source. Pills and treatments will become things of the past, for healthy organisms need no correction.

'Science puts a sword in the hand of those fighting disease. It will enable us to go beyond

Tiresias, the seer of Thebes whom Athena struck blind after he had seen her bathing. Afterwards, she repented and gave him the gift of prophecy, but he found this to be worse even than his blindness; to be able to see the future, but not to change it. With DNA, we will not have to choose; we will be able to see, *and* to change.'

Despite himself, Herbert was transfixed. It was not just Fischer's words, though they would have been compelling even if spoken by an automaton; it was the way his voice rose and fell, it was the visionary's animation in his eyes, it was the angle at which he held himself hunched forward at the table, taking his weight on his arms like a sprinter on his marks.

'The discovery of DNA will revolutionise criminal justice. The genetic code runs through every cell in a human body. Hair, saliva, blood, sweat, semen, mucus and skin – all imprinted with the unique DNA of their owner, which is distinctive not only from everyone else alive but everyone who has *ever* been alive.

'No longer will lawyers have to rely on the unreliable testimony of eyewitnesses or the too-vague discipline of fingerprinting. DNA will identify the guilty and exonerate the innocent.'

The wonder was not that the intelligence services of three countries had been so keen to get their hands on the secret of DNA, Herbert thought; the wonder was that *only* three were involved, and that they had not gone further in their quest.

The Soviets had got the bomb three years ago, a decade before the West thought they would. No one underestimated the importance of science any longer; paranoia ensured that every threat was a mortal one, every belch a breach of national security.

He realised, too, the irony in Stensness's murder. DNA – the very thing he'd been killed for – would be the key to solving crimes like the one perpetrated on him.

Fischer continued: 'DNA will also allow us to profoundly revise our opinions about human origins, about who we are and where we came from. Our ancestors' genes are a treasure trove of information, but until now we have not known how to read them. In agriculture, too, we will be able to improve important species with an effectiveness we have previously only dreamed of.

'And these are merely the applications that present themselves to us at this stage. With each new development, each new piece of research, a myriad of other opportunities will open up, things that none of us will possibly be able to foretell.

'This is where the next war will be fought, of that I am convinced. From the moment the first of our ancestors fashioned a stick into a spear, the results of conflicts have been dictated by technology. World War One was the chemists' war, because mustard gas and chlorine were deployed for the first time. World War Two was the physicists' war, the war of the atom bomb. Why shouldn't World War Three be the biologists' war?

'The biggest challenge we face is from our own aggressive instincts. In caveman times, these gave definite survival advantages, and were imprinted on our genetic code by natural selection. But now we have nuclear weapons, such instincts threaten our destruction. And since we don't have time for evolution to remove our aggression, we'll have to use genetic engineering.'

Fischer gave a small, almost shy smile, entirely at odds with the thunderous images he had been conjuring. 'We will not live to see much of this, of course; nor will our children, nor even their children. Vesalius worked out the anatomy of the heart more than four hundred years ago, and we've still yet to transplant a heart from one human to another. But progress will come, because progress is like time; it moves only one way.'

He curled the fingers of his right hand around his water glass, no doubt needing a drink after such a monologue.

And then Herbert saw it.

On Fischer's little finger was an indentation, a fraction of an inch in depth and circling the skin.

The mark of a ring. A ring like the one Herbert had found by the Peter Pan statue.

Herbert gestured towards Fischer's finger. 'Wedding ring?'

Fischer clicked his tongue in his throat. 'Ach. Took it off in the bath.'

It might have been, probably was, almost certainly would turn out to be, nothing; but Herbert's curiosity was an itch that would not be scratched.

'Where's the bath?'

'What?' Fischer looked puzzled, as well he might. It must have seemed an extraordinary question.

'Which bath did you take it off in?'

'My bath.'

'Here, in London?'

'Yes, I suppose so.'

'Where?'

'At the Embassy, where I'm staying.'

Space was tight at the Embassy, Papworth had said; but nonetheless Fischer was staying there, probably Pauling too.

Not so much the lap of luxury, Herbert thought, as a gilded cage.

'So if we went to that bathroom right now, the ring would be there?'

'Where else would it be?'

'You tell me.'

'What the hell is this all about?' Papworth demanded.

'I found a ring by the Peter Pan statue, where I believe Stensness had been struggling with his assailant,' Herbert said. 'Kind of a coincidence, don't you think?'

'If you're implying that Dr Fischer had something to do with Stensness' death,' Papworth said, 'then yes; a coincidence is exactly what I think it is.'

Herbert turned to Papworth. 'When you were waiting for Stensness that night, were you alone?'

'Of course.'

'Then how do you know where Dr Fischer was?'

'He was with Professor Pauling.'

'Who isn't here to confirm that.'

'The fog's got to him. He's feeling poorly again. But we can go and ask him.'

'I think I'd like to ask Dr Fischer some more questions.'

'I must protest.'

'You can protest all you like. Dr Fischer isn't a diplomat. He has no protection in the eyes of the law.'

'I'd prefer to stay with him.'

'And I'd prefer that you don't.'

'Are you arresting him?'

'If I was arresting him, I'd have said so. And if you keep on at me, I *will* arrest him, and then we'll be doing this the hard way.'

'This is ludicrous.'

'Go back to the Embassy. *When* I've finished with him, and *if* I'm satisfied with his answers, I'll return him to you there.'

'This case is done and dusted, Herbie. You know that damn well. De Vere Green's dead, by his own

354

hand, all loose ends tied up. What more do you want?'

Herbert shrugged. 'I'll tell you when I find it. Now; *go.*'

'I wasn't there,' Fischer said, when Papworth had left. 'I wasn't in the park.'

'Did you know about Stensness's offer beforehand?'

'No.'

'Even though you're working on exactly the same quest that he was?'

'Mr Papworth is looking after me during my stay here. I'm a scientist. He works for the Embassy. I'm no fool, I know as well as you do what his real job is, but that's his business. I am a scientist, no more.'

'How long have you known him?'

'Mr Papworth?'

'Yes.'

'Only these past few days.'

'Not before?'

'No.'

'You never met him on, say, the Manhattan Project?'

'I'm a biologist, Mr Smith, not a physicist. My science is that of life, not of death.'

'How long have you worked at Caltech?'

'Six years.'

'And before that?'

Fischer paused. 'Before that, I was in Germany.'

The maths were inescapable. Herbert saw the connection instantly.

'You were a Nazi?'

'No.' Fischer almost spat out the denial. 'I was *not* a Nazi.'

'You were not a member of the Nazi party?'

'Yes, I was a member, of course.'

'Then you were a Nazi.'

'Not in the way you mean. I was a member because I had to be one; without that, I would never have secured an academic posting of any repute.'

'And did you have good postings?'

'Yes.'

'Where?'

'The Institute of Biological Research at Berlin-Dahlen, and the Frankfurt Institute for Hereditary Biology.'

'You have a tattoo under your armpit?'

'No. I told you: I was a member because I had to be. I did the very minimum I could. Only the SS had such tattoos.'

Herbert remembered the SS, with their oak leaves and their motto of their honour being loyalty. 'Show me.'

This irritated Fischer, though Herbert suspected that was more for the inconvenience of pulling his shirt open than anything else. Fischer undid sufficient buttons to slide his shirt off his shoulder, and exposed his armpit to Herbert. Diners on neighbouring tables looked at them curiously.

Herbert rummaged through the hairs in Fischer's armpit, feeling like a monkey rooting for ticks, until he was satisfied that there was indeed no tattoo there.

Herbert withdrew his hand and wiped his fingers on his trouser leg.

'If you were a member of the Nazi party, how did you get to America?' he asked.

'What do you mean?'

'American law explicitly prohibits any convicted or even suspected Nazi officials from emigrating to the United States.'

'I don't know anything about that.'

'Truman brought it in. You went to America when Truman was president. You must have known.'

'As I said –'

'Dr Fischer, right now, we're having a chat in a restaurant. We can easily take ourselves somewhere less convivial; somewhere where I can be sure of making you miss your plane back to America tomorrow, even assuming that the fog lifts.'

'But this is nothing to do with the boy in the park.'

'I don't know that.'

Fischer was silent for a few moments, evidently weighing up his options.

'Have you ever heard of Operation Paperclip?' he asked eventually.

* * *

Operation Paperclip sounded like a bad spy novel, but was gospel truth, sickening or pragmatic, depending on which side of the fence one sat.

What did Herbert think had happened to all the Nazi scientists? Did he think that the Americans had let them stay in Germany to help rebuild the country? Or, God forbid, skip the border and go to work for the Russians?

Of course not. That would have presented a far greater security threat than any former Nazi affiliations which they may have had, or even any Nazi sympathies they might continue to maintain.

So the Americans had taken the scientists. In fact, they had gone after the scientists with at least as much zeal as they had the war criminals.

Not that the two were necessarily mutually exclusive, Herbert said.

Fischer clicked his tongue and chose to ignore this last comment.

To get round Truman's ban on Nazis entering or working in America, the CIA had found ways to whitewash their war records:

Investigation of the subject is not feasible due to the fact that his former place of residence is now in the Soviet zone, where investigations by US personnel are not possible.

No derogatory information is available on the subject except NSDAP records which indicate that he was a member of the Party and also a major in the SS, which appears to have been an honorary commission.

The extent of his Party participation cannot be determined in this theatre. Like the majority of members, he may have been a mere opportunist.

Based on available records, there is no indication that the subject is either a war criminal or an ardent Nazi.

In my opinion, he is not likely to become a security threat to the US.

Operation Paperclip, because the relevant files were marked with a paperclip; nothing more than that, all very low-key. It had originally been sold to the American people as a temporary measure, six months only. Like many such 'temporary measures', it had never been rescinded or superseded.

Were the Germans willing to comply?

Of course. Not only would they escape punishment, but they were as ardent an enemy of communism as the Americans were.

America and the Soviet Union against the Germans; America and Germany against the Soviet Union. One day, the Reds and the Boche would gang up on the Yanks, and the circle would be complete.

It was like *1984*, Herbert reflected, where Eastasia, Eurasia and Oceania were always at war, two against one, but the alliances were always shifting, and the past was always being rewritten. There was no such thing as history.

And if that was the case, Herbert thought, then what the hell had he and the millions of others been fighting for in the war?

He remembered what he had told Hannah the first night he met her; that if he had ever doubted the justness of the cause against Nazism, then with one look at Belsen, he doubted no more.

And now that struggle counted for nothing, because everyone needed scientists, no matter where they had come from and what they had done.

It did not altogether surprise Herbert that governments continued to place expediency above ideology, but he was gratified to find that it still had the power to revolt him.

He turned his attention back to Fischer.

Had people protested? Of course. But what good had that done? The public was tired of atrocity stories. It was long ago, and they wanted to forget all about such unspeakable happenings.

Or rather, Herbert thought, the public reckoned that what had been done was so horrific that there was no punishment on earth suitable; so when the law was violated and justice perverted, they just shrugged and said, ah well, told you so.

Herbert did not add the rider: America's war had been primarily in the Pacific, and so what the Nazis had done resonated less, at least on an emotional level, with them than with the Europeans.

But surely, Herbert asked, surely the scientists

screened by the US to prove that they were untainted must also have been screened in Germany to prove their loyalty to Hitler?

Of course, said Fischer.

Then the whole thing was a farce.

Of course. Fischer called it Persil*schein*. Bogus certificates could wash off even the brownest stains.

Despite himself, Herbert laughed.

Herbert took Fischer back to the Embassy, again going the long way round via the main thorough-fares – Shaftesbury Avenue, Regent Street, Oxford Street – rather than risk getting lost in the back streets.

Papworth looked relieved to have his charge back. Herbert imagined that losing Fischer to the Metropolitan Police, if only for a night, would probably not have done the CIA man's career prospects much good.

Herbert wondered how much Papworth knew of Fischer and Operation Paperclip.

Probably most, if not all of it. Papworth seemed the kind of man keen to equalise quantities of pies and fingers.

'Where's the bathroom?' Herbert asked.

'Down the hall, first right,' Papworth said. Herbert had already taken a step when he realised his mistake.

'Sorry; I meant the *bathroom*. As in the English definition. With a bath. And Dr Fischer's ring.'

Papworth laughed. 'Two nations divided by a common language, huh? Upstairs. I'll show you.'

He led the way, Herbert following, Fischer bringing up the rear.

The ring was on the side of the bath. It was silver, it was engraved in willowy swirls, and it fitted Fischer's little finger perfectly.

8TH DECEMBER 1952

MONDAY

'You hear that?' Hannah whispered.

Herbert was so deeply asleep that Hannah had to repeat herself twice, shaking him from side to side, before he realised that her voice was not part of his dream.

'Hear what?' he said, struggling awake.

'That.' She paused. 'There.'

'I can't hear a thing.'

'Footsteps.'

'You're imagining it.'

'I know every sound in this building, Herbert. I know noise of plumbing, windows opening, people downstairs, all. And that is not sound that should be here.'

'How do you know?'

'They footsteps. The stairs wooden. Footsteps quiet. Means that someone walk with much care.'

Herbert understood now. 'Which means they don't want to be heard.'

He got out of bed, rubbed his eyes, and walked

365

out of the bedroom. The light switch for the living-room was by the front door; he would turn it on and investigate.

He never got there.

A quick, expert clicking of the locks from outside, and the door was open.

In an imperfectly darkened flat – the dull orange glow of the fading fire gave glimmers of ambient light – a man loomed from the shadows.

He dived at Herbert.

It was like a rugby tackle, shoulder slamming into Herbert's midriff, head tight against Herbert's hip and arms wrapped round the backs of Herbert's thighs. Herbert went down hard on to his back-side, the impact zagging stingers up his spine.

'Herbert?' Hannah shouted. 'What happen?'

'Where's Stensness's stuff?' the man whispered.

His voice was too low for Herbert to identify – was it Papworth, was it Kazantsev, was it Fischer? – and, since his head was pressed up close against Herbert's, Herbert could feel from the rough scratch of wool against his cheek that the man was wearing a balaclava.

'I've no idea,' Herbert said, more calmly than he felt.

The punch came out of nowhere – at least, out of the darkness, which equated to more or less the same thing.

With no time to anticipate, prepare himself, flinch or try to duck the blow, Herbert was left only with an explosion of light behind his eyes and, after a second, a wave of pain radiating out from the bridge of his nose.

'Herbert!' Hannah's voice was louder this time, more urgent.

Herbert heard her get out of bed; and the man did too.

He hit Herbert again, more to keep him quiet than anything else; then he pushed himself to his feet and ran over to the fireplace, too fast for Herbert to tell whether his gait was recognisable.

Hannah's fire tools were laid out in neat rows, the easier for her to find them: a poker, a shovel, and a pair of bellows.

The man picked up the poker, turned round, and saw Hannah advancing blindly across the room towards him, her screams edged hard with the righteous outrage of one who has suffered more than her share of violations.

Herbert saw what was going to happen, and was already shouting, but to no avail.

The intruder swung the poker in a wide arc, from far behind his shoulders to maximise the speed, and then flatstick through the air.

Hannah must have felt the wind as the poker came towards her, for she tried to turn away at the last minute, but too late.

The poker reached the end of its considerable and rapid travel pretty much dead centre on her forehead. She collapsed as though someone had cut her strings.

The man did not wait to see her hit the ground. He turned back towards Herbert.

'Where?' he hissed, again too low for Herbert to identify his voice.

Herbert shook his head.

Someone else, in his shoes at this moment, might have simply capitulated, but Herbert had come too far just to give in, even at the risk of further stoking the rage which pulsed from behind the balaclava.

The intruder shifted his grip on the poker, and placed the end into the pile of coal still burning gently in the fireplace.

He left it there for a few moments, twirling it from one side to the other as though participating in an elaborate glass-blowing process.

When he took it out, the end shimmered orange.

He advanced towards Herbert again, shrugging his shoulders. What did Herbert expect, the gesture intimated, if he wouldn't be reasonable and give up the secret?

Herbert tried to get up, but he was still groggy from the punches.

The man put his foot on Herbert's breastbone, pushed him back prone, stepped on to his chest. Then, placing his feet apart the better to balance himself and keep Herbert flat, he held the poker so that the end was hovering a few inches from Herbert's right eye.

Blind, Herbert thought, *blind*. This man would

blind him, just as Mengele had blinded Hannah in Auschwitz.

Herbert's mind simply would not compute the terror.

He wanted to answer, but he could not; it seemed that he had lost not only the power of speech, but the very memory of what speech was.

The poker came nearer; close enough for Herbert to feel the heat on his cheek.

Would one eye be enough, or would the intruder want both?

'Hannah? Are you all right?'

It took Herbert a second or two to work out that the voice had come not from within himself, or indeed from the man standing over him with a poker, but from the direction of the front door.

'I heard shouting through my ceiling; it woke me up. Is everything all right?'

It must be the downstairs neighbour, Herbert thought; and at that moment the neighbour turned the overhead light on, summed up the situation in short order, and launched himself at the man with the poker, knocking him off Herbert and back against the low wooden table by the sofa. Herbert heard a sharp crack as one, maybe more, of the table legs gave way.

The neighbour was quick, but not quite quick enough. Though he had taken the poker man off balance, he had not managed to pin his arms.

The intruder shook his head, smiled beneath the balaclava as though he were an uncle ragging with his eager nephews, and then swung the poker twice.

The first blow knocked the wind from the neighbour, the second jerked his head upwards as he fell to the floor.

The intruder's eyes never blinked; not once, not even at the moments of impact.

Lights on, one neighbour already alerted; both Herbert and the intruder were making very much the same calculations.

Herbert saw the final swing of the poker, but he was too groggy to do anything about it.

His arm was still coming up to block a blow that would surely have broken his hand had he got there in time; but he was half a second too slow, and the impact of metal on the side of his head was enough.

Oblivion.

Herbert came round with several sensations competing for his attention: a pain at the front of his head which suggested that someone was sledgehammering a drill bit into his skull; shrieks in a voice which he identified as Hannah's; a warmth on his cheek that graduated to an uncomfortable heat even in the few moments he lay still trying to work out what it was; and a tart choking in his throat that was harsher than anything the smog had managed to cause.

He processed all these disparate pieces of information through the sludge of his poker-battered mind, and came to a conclusion that a fully sentient human would have reached long before: the flat was on fire.

It was Hannah's screams that had Herbert opening his eyes and pushing himself upright. Her howls were yelps of terror, atavistic and visceral, and he understood why.

For a blind person, there could surely be few fears greater than that of fire. But for a blind woman who had also, as a teenager, played in the lee of the Auschwitz crematorium as it spewed tongues of flame through spiralling smoke and turned the air leaden with the crisp stench of burning bodies . . . well, one could imagine.

For all Hannah's stubborn independence, Herbert sometimes had to remind himself that she, barely out of her teens, had already been through several lifetimes' worth of grief and trauma.

Herbert looked round the room.

Furniture was everywhere, sofas overturned and tables upended. Hannah was in the far corner, pressed hard up against the wall. The neighbour was lying by the splintered remains of the low table, and now he too was stirring groggily.

The flat was on fire, and they had to get out.

Fire was a living thing, and Herbert knew that it hunted. Never content to burn itself out, it was forever seeking its next target, its next source of fuel and new life.

It had already climbed high enough on the curtains to leap like an acrobat across to a picture frame, and from there to a bookshelf; and from every beach-head it had made came two more, until it was propagating itself like the code Herbert had deciphered the day before, burning too fast and wide and furious to contain.

Herbert got to his feet, staggered slightly as his head swam in protest, went over to Hannah, and pulled her upright.

'Herbert thank God you alive I no find you help get me out of here,' she yelled.

Her face was smeared in blood, and her breath came in scraping rasps.

She had come round earlier than they had and had pushed herself upright, both of which had led to her inhaling substantial amounts of smoke. Herbert and the neighbour, prone unconscious on the floor, had remained beneath the worst of the fumes.

The neighbour was up too now, hurrying over to them.

'My cane!' Hannah cried. 'My cane!'

There was a loud crash to their left as the curtain rail burnt free from its stanchions and dropped in swirls of orange to the floor. Smoke as thick and black as that from a power plant chimney was already rolling in billows across the room, obscuring the ceiling and walls.

'I'll get it,' Herbert yelled. 'Go! You two go!'

The neighbour, bless him, did not demur. He laced Hannah's fingers firmly in his and set off across the living-room towards the door. Left and right and right and left they went through pockets of fire, quick sidesteps past tongues of flame lunging with malicious desperation at them.

This was what it had been like under fire in the war, Herbert remembered. Never think, never think, the first to think died, keep moving and don't look back if you wanted to stay alive.

He had missed that feeling, and he embraced its return with relish.

Herbert took a deep breath and immediately choked it out again; superheated air singeing the inside of his throat, acrid smoke pulverising his lungs.

He crouched down close to the floor, blinked hard to get some water on to his eyeballs, and ran as if the hounds of hell were at his heels.

The fire had worked its way through the door into Hannah's bedroom, and for a second Herbert thought all was lost. Then the smoke shifted sufficiently for him to see that the bed was as yet untouched, and Hannah's cane was still there.

Herbert grabbed it, winced slightly at how warm it was already to the touch, turned round – and there was the fire again, right in his face, even bigger and more impenetrable than before, draping a sheet of flame across the doorway.

He was trapped.

Funny how the mind worked.

Herbert was trapped, minutes at most from

certain death unless he could find a way out of his predicament; and yet he felt no fear.

A sense of urgency, yes, but no more. He had honestly been more vexed while cracking Stensness's cipher.

What he faced was, quite simply, a puzzle.

The only way out was the way he had come in: through the door and down the stairs. He had to get out. As things stood, he could not.

There was the window, of course.

Thirty feet or so down to the pavement, though he could lop a quarter off that distance by hanging at full stretch from the window sill before letting go.

Even so, on to concrete, he would inevitably break one leg, perhaps both, and who knew what else?

Ambulances were as unreliable in the fog as fire engines, so he would face an indeterminate delay, unable to move and very possibly suffering serious internal bleeding to boot.

He would have to be very desperate to jump, he decided.

Then there was the bathroom, which adjoined Hannah's bedroom, and which the fire had not yet reached.

Herbert ran into the bathroom and shut the door behind him.

There were two towels hanging on the rail, both grimy from the fog, but that was the least of his worries.

He grabbed both, hurled them into the bathtub and turned the taps on full blast. The water darkened the towels and pooled in their folds, soaking them through in a few seconds.

Herbert climbed into the tub and placed his own body under the taps, constantly shifting position to get as much of himself wet as possible.

It might not make the slightest bit of difference in the end, he thought; but it was pretty much all he had going for him.

He remembered the mountaineer's old adage, that the summit was not the end but only halfway, because once there one had to get down again.

The water splashed in and around his mouth, but he could not taste it.

He got out of the bath, wrapped one of the towels like an Arab headscarf around his face and head, leaving only a thin strip free around his eyes, and tied the other towel tight on the cane.

His arms and legs he kept free for speed and balance. He couldn't afford to have them wrapped inside a towel, notwithstanding the extra protection that would give.

If Herbert had stopped for a second and considered the magnitude of what he was attempting, and the mortal danger he was in, he would have frozen, simply stood and waited for the fire to come, hoping that the smoke got to him before the flames.

But then that went for everything in his life over the previous few days. To cease, even to pause, was to die, whether slowly or fast.

The fire was merely another enemy, the latest in the collection he had recently been amassing.

So this, perhaps the gravest predicament he could remember being in, seemed nothing out of the ordinary; and that was the most extraordinary thing of all.

Besides, there was something very pure about the situation. It was a question of survival; either he would, or he would not.

Nothing else mattered. Not his mother, not Stensness nor Papworth nor Kazantsev nor Fischer nor de Vere Green, not even Hannah; not one of the thousands of strands which formed the matrix of a life.

He reached for the handle of the bathroom door, and took his hand away even before he touched it; the metal knob was virtually glowing with the heat coming through from the other side.

He pulled the wet sleeve of his jacket over his hand, twisted the knob and opened the door, holding himself flat behind the door, against the wall, in case there was an inrush of flame.

There was not, but there might as well have been.

The bedroom was ablaze, a frenzied dance of reds and yellows which tore at the wood panelling and devoured the bed with swift mouthfuls.

He could just about see the doorway back into the living-room, but little beyond that. No matter; there was no point in waiting.

Herbert remembered a mock Confucius motto: *Coward man keep safe bones.*

Once more hunched low to the ground, hearing the angry sizzle as his towels and clothes spat back marauding flames, he ran through the bedroom, through the doorway into the living-room, and felt his stomach lurch as his footing partially gave way. A floorboard gone, he realised, thankful that he had been carrying sufficient momentum to bridge the gap; a twisted ankle would have been lethal, no question.

Hannah's flat was the face of Mount Etna, the court of Vulcan; it was Stromboli.

He could no longer feel the cane in his hand, but when he looked, he was holding on to it as though it were life itself.

Time crawled; each step seemed an eternity.

It was the carbon monoxide, he knew, depriving him of oxygen and slowing him down; just as it had killed de Vere Green.

Herbert battered through flames and upturned furniture alike, the towel-wrapped cane alternately talisman and protection, the water on the towels evaporating fast, but he would be at the front door any moment, out and down and free.

Something hard hit him in the face, and idiotically Herbert wondered whether the intruder was still there, having been lying in wait all along.

Then he realised that his assailant was a wall, and from what little he could see, there was no door there.

He had lost his way.

A normal-size living-room now felt as vast as Yellowstone.

Which way was out? Which way was out, damn it?

Fire and smoke all around him, and yet he could no longer smell them.

There was a moment of paralysing shock as Herbert saw how far and fast the fire had spread. It was now a snarling, roaring monster which reared up at him, daring him to find a way through the searing maze.

Panic started to come on him like a shroud; paralysing, whitening panic, the surest killer of all. He had only a few seconds left before it engulfed him completely.

Then he heard Hannah's voice, and with three senses already gone, he wondered whether he was hallucinating.

She could not have come back up here. She could not have.

There it was again, faint but definite.

She must have been by the front door, he thought; and therefore she was safety.

Through the fire again, up and down over chairs and upholstery, stumbling, calling for Hannah with breath he no longer possessed, and now getting no answer back.

Herbert reached the door, but there was no sign of her.

The flames were diving down the stairway, but

he could see far enough through them to know she was not there. She must have been somewhere in the flat.

Perhaps he really had imagined it; conjured her up as a guardian angel.

He took two paces to the side to get a better view back into the flat, and inadvertently stood on something.

Hannah's arm.

She was lying on the floor, flames circling her like angry wolves.

There was no time to wonder how she had got there.

Herbert picked her up, slung her over his shoulder, and ran down the stairs, timbers cracking round him, one hand on the cane and the other holding Hannah's legs tight.

A crowd had gathered on the pavement. Herbert heard a communal gasp as he came out of the door and laid Hannah on the pavement.

The neighbour ran up and began hitting at Herbert's right side, and Herbert was about to turn round and clock him one when he realised that the man was patting down small eruptions of flame which had clung to Herbert during his descent.

Herbert looked up.

There was only the faintest orange glow through the mist, even though the fire was just a couple of storeys above them. He wondered how thick this fog could get before it officially shifted from gas to viscous, or even directly to solid.

Hannah was in a bad way. Burnt patches of skin on her face wept raw and peeling. Her nostrils were caked in soot and swollen almost shut. Her eyebrows and eyelashes had been singed brittle. It seemed as though every blood vessel in her eyes had burst; the whites were now reds.

She spoke in a hoarse voice through sharp breaths. 'Gone . . . so long . . . Thought you'd . . . died . . . Came . . . get you.'

'I tried to stop her,' the neighbour said. 'No chance.'

Herbert stroked Hannah's forehead, and she screamed at the touch of his hand on sizzled skin.

He looked up at the faces around them. He had never seen such a bovine bunch.

'Get an ambulance!' he yelled. 'Quick! And the fire brigade!'

The neighbour and another man ran off, and Herbert turned back to Hannah.

He wondered how long she had been waiting by the door. He had been in the flat much longer than she had, but had only been exposed to the worst of the fire for a relatively short period, and half of that had been while dripping wet and breathing through a sodden towel.

It would not have taken much more than a few seconds for Hannah, blind and unprotected, to have found herself on the wrong end of savage burns and serious smoke inhalation.

Stupid, stupid girl to have come back for him,

through the fire, through her own crippling fear. Stupid girl.

Amazing girl.

Herbert enlisted three of the men standing round them, and together they moved Hannah as gently as possible into the hall of the Welsh dairy, a few doors down.

The old ladies there – dairies started their days when the rest of the world was usually asleep – brought blankets and made Hannah as comfortable as possible; which was not very comfortable at all, given that she was alternating between screaming in pain from the burns and coughing so hard that Herbert thought she would bring her own lungs up.

The neighbour appeared. 'The ambulance is on its way,' he said.

'How long?' Herbert snapped.

'Well,' the neighbour said, with evident reluctance, 'they said it might be some time.'

'How long?'

'What with all the fog, and all the calls they're getting –'

'*How long*?'

'A couple of hours, maybe.'

'A couple of hours' turned out to be a conservative estimate.

It was more than three hours before the ambulance arrived; three of the longest, slowest, most agonisingly helpless hours Herbert had ever sat through.

Hannah was a trouper. She understood the situation. The fog was making a mockery of emergency response times. The Middlesex was the nearest hospital, just the other side of Goodge Street, ten minutes' walk on a normal day, but in these conditions, and with her suffering the torments of the damned, trying to take her there would almost certainly have done more harm than good.

Not that there were not several occasions on which Herbert thought about it; the occasions when Hannah screamed like a mother in labour, so loud and hard that she vomited from the effort, which in turn left her short of breath, which in turn made her hack violently, and so the whole cycle would start again.

At other times she would close her eyes and either sleep or simply pass out – Herbert could hardly tell the difference – and he would think that they could stay like that for a long time, ambulance or not.

When she opened her eyes again, she would try and do the deep breathing exercises she used in diving, and sob tears of frustration when she found that she could not, so clogged were her lungs. It was all she could do to sip at the water that the dairy ladies brought.

People wrapped Herbert in blankets, took his sodden clothes away, and returned with them bone dry and smelling of coal smoke.

The fire brigade arrived after an hour and a

half, by which time the entire block of flats was ablaze.

It was something of a miracle, Herbert thought, that the fire had not yet spread to the adjacent buildings.

Finally the ambulance turned up, a woman walking ahead of it with a flare to light the way. Two ambulancemen hopped down from the cab and walked over to where Hannah was lying.

Herbert should not have shouted at them, for they were only trying to do their job in the most trying circumstances imaginable; but equally he was by now past caring.

'You take three hours, and you walk?' he screamed. 'Run, damn you!'

The older of the men looked at Herbert, and Herbert saw that he was just as close to exhaustion as Herbert was, maybe more so. His eyes were almost as red as Hannah's, and his skin sagged from his face in great, tired, canine folds.

He was too dignified to reply.

He and his mate, equally shot, picked Hannah up with as much care as they could.

When Herbert accompanied them round to the back of the ambulance, he could see why they were so enervated.

There were four other patients already in there, all the far side of sixty: two women, one of them flat out on a stretcher, the other crying softly into the collar of her dressing-gown; and two men, slumped against the sides.

'We don't have no radio, you see, guv'nor,' the ambulanceman said. 'So we're out of contact from the moment we leave until the moment we get back, unless we can find a phone. You were last on our route. I'm sorry, but that's the way it is.'

'Didn't they tell you it was serious?'

'Everyone says theirs is serious, sir.'

They found a space for Hannah along one side. Herbert climbed in next to her, earning himself a reproachful tut from one of the old men already in there, and made himself as comfortable as possible, still clasping Hannah's cane.

'Rodney, you want to drive?' said the ambulanceman. 'I'm all in.'

'Sure thing, Derek.'

Derek joined them in the back and closed the doors on them.

Herbert heard the engine start and they set off, so slowly that it was several minutes before he was sure they were moving at all.

Derek checked on the prone old woman, asked everyone else how they were doing in a tone that suggested that he could do little about any answer they chose to give him, and let out a sigh that spoke eloquently of the kind of day he'd had.

'Do you have any oxygen?' Herbert asked.

He shook his head and gestured towards empty compartments above the stretcher.

'All gone, sir. No oxygen, no dressings, no morphine, no blood. We're out of everything except the petrol to keep this thing running.'

'Are we going back to the hospital?' Herbert said, and, when Derek nodded, added: 'How long will it take?'

'It'll take as long as it takes.'

'That's not very helpful.'

'Maybe not, sir, but it's the truth.'

The journey that followed made the hours spent watching over Hannah on the floor of the Welsh dairy seem like the most idyllic of summer afternoons. Every few minutes, the ambulance would brake without warning, presumably to avoid an obstacle, real or imagined, which had loomed suddenly through the fog.

Only the prone woman seemed oblivious to this. The rest of them would crack their heads against the metal walls with moans, curses, sobs, screams, or silent eye rolls. Each time, too, Rodney would get going again with a bunny hop and a revving of the engine that sent exhaust fumes scudding into the rear compartment.

Herbert's poker-induced headache had gone during the race through the fire and the ministering to Hannah, or maybe he had simply forgotten about it.

Now, however, it was back with a vengeance. With each new sudden emergency stop, and every belch of carbon monoxide, he felt another dart being wheedled with expert sadism into his skull.

He would have preferred a session of trepanning, he really would.

He had no idea where they were, or which

385

direction they were heading. He wondered whether the trains to Auschwitz had been this hellish, and on balance decided that this was not the time to ask Hannah.

The next time Rodney piled on the anchors, the old man next to Herbert toppled on to his shoulder; but this time he did not groan or cry out.

Nor did he move when the ambulance started again.

Scarcely believing what he thought had just happened, Herbert raised his hand and placed the back of it against the old man's mouth, counting out the seconds: five, ten, twenty, and still nothing, not the slightest breath.

'Derek,' Herbert said.

The ambulanceman looked at Herbert with scant interest. 'Yes, sir?'

'This man's dead.'

'I dare say he is.'

It seemed that Derek and Herbert were destined to be at loggerheads on just about everything. 'That's all you can say?' Herbert asked with incredulity, spacing out his words in flabbergasted sarcasm. 'You *dare-say-he-is?*'

Derek sighed again; the short, sharp exhalation of the misunderstood. 'Sir, I've been on duty for more than twenty-four hours without a break. If this man is dead, and I'll grant you it looks like he is, then he's the fifth person to pass away in the back of this ambulance in that time. There's not a lot I can do about it. Nor you neither.'

'But we must do *something*.'

'Like what, sir?'

Derek was not being facetious, Herbert could tell that in his voice. He was merely pointing out, with extreme reasonableness, that extraordinary circumstances made a mockery of ordinary norms.

'What will you do with the body?' Herbert asked.

'Drop him off at the mortuary, sir. Same as all the others.'

What had things come to, Herbert thought, when an ambulance made the mortuary as regular a stop as the hospital?

'He wasn't the first, sir, and he won't be the last,' Derek added.

Ten minutes later, as if to prove Derek right, the old woman on the stretcher ceased what sporadic movements she had been making.

No fuss, no agonised death cry; simply there one minute and gone the next.

Hannah had been silent for quite some time, drifting in and out of consciousness. Now, suddenly, she vomited copiously on to the floor, and then began to foam at the mouth, looking at Herbert with wild eyes which were no less frightening for being sightless. She lashed out, first with one arm, then with both, and finally with her legs as well, and even Derek and Herbert together could hardly subdue her.

'What's going on?' Herbert yelled.

'Seizures are quite common with smoke inhalation,' Derek shouted back.

Somehow, knowing that offered Herbert no comfort whatsoever.

Still holding on to Hannah with one arm, and checking that Herbert was not about to relinquish his grip, Derek unstrapped the old woman's body from the stretcher and rolled it as gently as he could on to the floor; gently for the sensibilities of the other two patients, who were watching this turn of events with a sort of resigned horror.

Derek and Herbert manoeuvred Hannah on to the stretcher and managed to get her limbs tucked under the straps; not that these would hold her if she was really determined, but it was better than nothing.

She thrashed around a little more, and then stopped as abruptly as she had begun.

For a dreadful moment Herbert feared the worst, but then he heard her breathing and realised that she had passed out once more.

'What else?' he gabbled at Derek. 'Coma? Death? We can't stop it here, can we?'

Derek shook his head. 'Only when we get to the hospital, sir.'

The ambulance came to yet another sudden stop, and even as the thought of what Herbert was going to do came to him, he was already opening the rear door, notion and action fused into one. He ran round to the front of the vehicle, yanked open the driver's door and climbed in.

'Derek, I . . .' Rodney began, and then saw Herbert. 'What the hell are you doing?'

Herbert shunted him hard along the bench seat. 'Where are we, Rodney?'

'You're mad. Get out of here.'

'There are two people dead back there, Rodney, and that might not be the end of it. So tell me where the hell we are.'

A blob of light in front of them shrank and died; the warning flare extinguished.

A few seconds later, the flare woman appeared at the window, as blackened and grimy as the rest of them.

'Bloody typical,' she began, too exhausted, as Rodney had been, to instantly register the presence of a stranger. 'Right in the middle of Blackfriars Bridge' – *Blackfriars Bridge*? Herbert thought. Blackfriars Bridge! They were miles from Soho. The fog was not so much causing havoc as flipping the world upside down – 'and that's the last of my flares gone.'

That was the last Herbert saw of the flare woman too; her eyes wide and her mouth drooping in surprise as he accelerated away with a sight more smoothness and vigour than Rodney had ever managed.

It was Hannah who had given Herbert the idea. Well, not her as such, but the way in which she negotiated the streets through a combination of fierce concentration and memory. Herbert knew

389

London at least as well as she did, after years of tailing all sorts of undesirables round the city. Until this fog, however, he had never had cause to test his ability to negotiate it blindfold.

He could get to Guy's pretty much on main roads: straight over what was left of Blackfriars Bridge, and then east on Southwark Street, all the way to London Bridge station. There would be precious few cars on the road, if any. None that were moving, at any rate.

The flotilla of abandoned vehicles was another matter, but at least most of them would be empty.

A risk? Definitely. A calculated one? If one was charitable, yes.

As for those in the ambulance; well, two of them were dead already, and Herbert had no idea how close Hannah was to joining them.

The only thing he did know for sure was that he would never, could never, forgive himself if he simply sat there and watched her die. Better to do something about it and know that he had tried.

No, he thought, even that would not be enough. He could not conceive of how he would feel if she breathed her last right then. It would finish him.

And so, as in the fire, he went forward because it was the only option.

He set off at a speed which would have been normal in everyday conditions, but which in a whiteout seemed positively suicidal.

Rodney yelled at Herbert that he was insane, he was going to get them all killed.

Then Rodney lunged across Herbert and grabbed at the wheel, but Herbert batted him on the side of the head with a half-closed fist, and Rodney realised that attacking him was simply going to make things worse.

A set of traffic lights appeared suddenly, and Herbert turned the wheel hard left.

The ambulance took the corner with a shriek of tyres and doubtless a cacophony of similar sounds from the rear compartment, but Herbert was concentrating too hard to pay them any mind.

There was a slight echo as they passed under the railway bridge which carried the tracks out of Blackfriars mainline station to the north of the river, and Herbert tried to remember how long this road – Southwark Street – was, and which way it curved.

At a rational level, he knew that this was crazy. Visibility was far too poor to avoid objects by braking, not at the speed he was driving. He had to swerve this way and that, as though the ambulance were a dodgem, bracing himself against the metallic whines as he scraped the side of a parked Vauxhall Velox, and ignoring Rodney's muttered imprecations as a pedestrian scampered to safety inches from their bumper.

Herbert's first serious mistake would be their last. If he crashed into something front-on, Rodney and he would both go through the windscreen. If he swerved too violently, he would flip the ambulance on to its roof. Either could be fatal.

Would Herbert have killed the others in the ambulance to save Hannah? He could not know. But yes, he was prepared to risk their lives to do so; his too.

It was, by any reasonable standards, a horrendously, arrogantly irresponsible thing to do; but Herbert defied any man who had ever loved to tell him that he would not have done the same.

They weaved between more traffic lights and more parked cars, reliant only on the hope that they were alone and that a higher force was watching over them.

Another booming echo as another bridge came and went overhead; a railway bridge again, he remembered, this one leading to London Bridge and Cannon Street.

He knew that the road veered slightly to the left after this bridge, and so he turned the wheel in that direction; not a moment too soon, either, for just as he did so he caught a glimpse of solid stone wall skimming his window.

My window, he thought; he had gone all the way over to the wrong side of the road without realising.

Rodney was looking at Herbert as though he had taken complete leave of his senses.

Herbert could hardly blame him, but he felt very still and empty, like the eye of a tornado; hullabaloo all around him, and yet he was moving along with dull serenity.

Potholes threw themselves beneath the wheels,

sending juddering crashes through the ambulance and bouncing Rodney and Herbert on their seats, but Herbert was not going to stop for anything now, not even a flat tyre; they were as good as there.

Herbert looked for the last set of traffic lights, at which he wanted to turn right; but they did not come, and still did not come.

When they went under a third bridge Herbert knew that they had come too far, for this bridge was the final approach to London Bridge station, and they wanted to be on the near side of it.

Herbert yanked the ambulance round in a violent, squealing arc, squinted through the gloom for a turning on the left, could not see one, and decided to trust in fate.

Hard left again, up on to the pavement, ready to dodge any onrushing walls . . . but no, somehow he had judged it correctly, and they were on what he was sure was St Thomas' Street, which meant that Guy's was on their right.

Which meant that they had done it.

He pulled up outside the nearest building and was out of the door almost before the ambulance had stopped moving. Derek was already on the pavement, pulling Hannah with him. Derek motioned for Rodney to take the other end of the stretcher, and together they ran into the hospital, carrying Hannah like a sack of cement.

Herbert glanced quickly inside the rear of the ambulance, and felt a surge of relief to see that both surviving patients were, not to put too fine a point on it, still alive.

They stared at him.

'You're a bloody disgrace,' the man said.

'You must really love her,' the woman said.

Herbert should have stayed to help them out of the ambulance and into the main building, but, God help him, he wanted to be with Hannah.

He took her cane from inside, gave the woman a weak smile, and hurried in the direction that Derek and Rodney had taken, slightly salving his conscience by telling the first orderly he found that there were two patients in an ambulance outside who needed urgent attention.

'We're out of stretchers,' he shouted at Herbert's disappearing back, and at any other time Herbert would have found the irony amusing; half the railings in London were made from old stretchers, the ends slightly curved to act as legs and the metal mesh between each side still intact. There had been a shortage of building materials after the war. Perhaps now, when there was a shortage of medical equipment, the process would be reversed.

Guy's was even fuller than it had been on Friday, when Herbert had come to see his mother. There were signs on the walls declaring that the Emergency Bed Service had issued a white warning, signifying that hospital admissions were less than eighty-five per cent of applications for beds. People were being turned away in their scores.

But somehow they found a bed, and a doctor, for Hannah. A curtain was pulled round her bed, a pair of nurses circling like buzzards.

Herbert sat in the corridor, staring alternately at the wall, the ceiling and the floor.

He prayed to his God, and hers, and every God he had ever heard of, to let her be all right.

Time ticked past, and with each minute gone he wanted to run into the ward and pull back the curtain, to see what abominations they were committing on her.

Every time the door opened, he would start forward and slightly upwards, before subsiding, a little sheepish, as nurses and visitors and doctors all bustled past without the slightest glance in his direction.

Herbert twirled Hannah's cane around his wrist, flicked it from hand to hand, and worried his fingers up and down it. Still no one came to tell him what was going on.

Hospitals were considered a great leveller, Herbert thought; but he wondered whether there was any place on earth where people were so wrapped up in their own problems, to the exclusion of everyone else's. Not the staff, of course, but the patients and their families. For instance, Herbert was here for Hannah alone, and her health was all he cared about, not that of the many others who might quite possibly be substantially more ill than she was.

No, he thought, he was not here for Hannah

alone; he suddenly realised how near he was to his mother's ward, and thought that he should perhaps go and see her, if only to do something and therefore take his mind off Hannah's condition.

He went via the toilets, which was a good thing, for he was filthy, and his mother would not accept something as banal as escape from a fire as a decent excuse for sloppiness in his appearance.

He cleaned himself up as best he could, scrubbing his face three times until the dirt was gone, and hoped that she would not notice the tidemarks on his clothes.

Herbert approached the swing doors which opened on to his mother's ward, and peered through the circular windows which were set in the doors at face height and which always put him in mind of the viewfinders on submarine periscopes.

She was there, her face as long as a horse.

His mother was rarely less than jovial, but she could snap without warning, and on the odd occasions when her mood was bad, like the girl with the curl in the middle of her forehead in Longfellow's poem, she was horrid.

Herbert sighed and went in.

'The prodigal son,' Mary snarled. 'You come and see your old mother . . .'

She had been speaking rapidly, but now she stopped dead.

'No, I . . .' Herbert began.

'. . . only when you feel like it?' she finished with a rush, and Herbert realised why she had been talking so fast and why she had ceased so suddenly. The first to get through the sentence before she ran out of breath, and the second because it had not worked and she'd had to wait for the air to return, rather like the refilling of a toilet cistern. 'And don't interrupt me,' she added.

Herbert looked closer. Her eyes were rimmed in crimson; she had been crying.

'I'm sorry I didn't come and see you over the weekend,' Herbert said.

'Too busy running around after murderers?'

'Yes.'

'Why don't you pay more attention to the living than to the dead?'

Herbert shrugged; there was no answer he felt appropriate.

'And what are you doing here so early?'

'I was in a fire. They've brought Hannah here.'

'You only came because you were here anyway?' She looked as though he had caused her mortal offence. 'Good Christ, Herbert, that makes it even worse.' She paused. 'Who's Hannah?'

'She's a friend.'

'A lady friend?'

'A friend who's a lady, yes.'

'You know what I mean, Herbert.'

'I do indeed, Mama.'

Herbert had no desire to wind her up, but equally he felt that she had no right to pry.

Mary opened her mouth to continue, and then began to wheeze again. This time, Herbert knew better than to reply.

The wheeze grew louder, which momentarily alarmed him until he realised that it was the rush of air from her breathing more freely.

She coughed hard, hawking up a gobbet of phlegm which she caught in her hand and wiped discreetly on the sheets, decorous to the last.

There were several other people in the ward, all long past their best, if indeed they had ever had one. They stared into space or chatted in low voices. All were far too discreet, far too polite, far too British to step between a mother and her son.

'Perhaps we should take a holiday, Mama,' Herbert said.

'Where to? Somewhere with a better climate than here, I should hope.'

'Egypt?' Herbert had served some time during the war in North Africa, and now felt a sudden desire to be back in the desert, where the air was blistering hot, dry and clear. 'We could take a boat across the Channel, cross France by train, take another boat over to Egypt. Amble through the Cairo souks, go sightseeing in the Valley of the Kings. What do you say?'

'Will you be bringing Hannah?'

'For heaven's sake, Mama.'

'That's not an answer.'

Angela came in at her usual bustle.

'The prodigal son,' she said. The same words Mary had used, which was unnerving, but at this time spoken with jocular merriment. 'Hope you haven't been letting your mother bully you.'

'You're the only bully round here, Angela,' said Mary. 'Why won't you let me out of here? For an hour or two? Why can't you give an old woman some pleasure, ask the Lord?'

'Don't be ridiculous, Mrs S,' Angela said. 'You'll only make things worse, you know you will. Come on, let's get you into position.'

She arranged Mary into a posture designed to help her breathe: turned on to her side, her head propped up on a couple of pillows, another pillow underneath her flank, knees bent. Mary put up resistance which started as half-hearted and quickly subsided to token. Bullies always knew when they were beaten.

Just as with Rosalind Franklin, Herbert couldn't help thinking that the world needed more Angelas in it; endlessly forgiving of her patients' foibles, but absolutely intolerant of serious nonsense.

Maybe the sick were like children: they would try to get away with anything if you let them, but deep down they welcomed boundaries, they wanted parameters, and they knew that laying down the law did not equate to a lack of love.

Angela knew how to handle Herbert's mother, which was more than he did.

'That's better, isn't it?' Angela said, when she had finished.

'Giving me a cigarette would be better,' Mary replied.

'Loathsome to the eye, hateful to the nose, harmful to the brain, dangerous to the lungs, and in the black stinking fume thereof, nearest resembling the horrible Stygian smoke of the pit that is bottomless,' Angela said.

Herbert and Mary stared at her in surprise.

'James the Sixth,' Angela continued. 'A man who knew what was what, I can tell you. Now, I'd love to spend all day chatting, but as you can imagine, the place is bedlam right now, and I've got hundreds more patients to check on.'

'Hundreds?' Mary said. 'Absurd.'

'Not absurd, Mrs S, and kindly don't take that tone with me. It's true. Literally hundreds. We haven't been this busy since the Blitz. Bronchial spasms, pneumonia, corpulmonale, myocardial degeneration; all made worse by this wretched fog. Senior citizens like yourself, Mrs Smith, and young children too. It's terrible. So, if you'll excuse me . . .'

'You can go too, Herbert.' Mary flapped a weak hand towards the door. She looked like she was going to start crying again. 'Go on. Get out.'

He did not even consider protesting. What good would it have done?

In the corridor outside, Angela took his arm.

'Maybe it isn't my place to say this, Herbert,

but I believe in telling things like they are, so . . . I see the way your mother is to you, all smiles most of the time and then sometimes like she is today, and I don't fully understand why. I know she loves you and worries about you; she might not show it the best sometimes, but rest assured you're not the first son I've seen who finds his mother difficult, and you surely won't be the last. When all's done and dusted, she's your mother and she's here for a reason – and she's not going to be around much longer, not if this fog continues the way it is.'

How did one react, when one was told that?

'Are you sure?' Herbert said. 'I mean . . . how long? Days? Weeks? Months?'

'Only the Good Lord can answer that one, Herbert. I'm a nurse, not a soothsayer. But for you to let her drive you away, it would be wrong. No matter how badly she behaves. You do realise that, don't you?'

'Yes, I do.'

'And I don't know you from Adam, but I see things in you, so if you'd let me give you a piece of advice, I'd be very grateful.'

Herbert nodded.

'The more you absolutely must not have or feel something,' Angela said, 'the more certainly you'll have or feel it. Make room for the darkness, when it comes. Open up a space for it, invite it to stay a while. My nephew used to have nightmares about monsters, you know. He would get them night after night; screamed his little head off. No one knew how to make it better.

'Then I told him that the reason the monsters were there was that they had nowhere else to go, so what he should do was keep a small box under his bed where they could stay. That's all they wanted, I said; a little place of their own. I found him an old wooden box and we wrote "MONSTERS" in red letters on the lid, and under his bed it went. He never had the nightmare again, would you believe? He had his space and the monsters had theirs. That's all it's about.' She touched Herbert on the shoulder. 'See you next time, Herbert.'

He hurried back through the corridors to where Hannah was being kept.

When he got there the doctor was waiting, looking round to see where he had gone.

'Mr Smith? I've examined your friend, and I'm pleased to say I think she'll be all right, though perhaps not immediately. She's suffered second-degree burns to her face, and we've applied ointment and dressings to those. The chest X-ray shows that her lungs have some quite serious smoke damage, and there's also some internal burning in her airways. But her red blood count is good, as is her lung capacity; she's young and fit, and I don't see any long-term problems there.'

'Doctor, she had a seizure in the ambulance.'

'As the ambulanceman told you, this is not uncommon as a reaction to the unusual number of foreign bodies in the respiratory system. There seems to be no history of such fits otherwise, so I wouldn't worry too much about a repeat. Just to be on the safe side, I've given her some medication for that, as well as some ephedrine tablets with adrenalin solution for her inhalation. Now, these have some side-effects – they can raise both blood pressure and pulse rates, they might make her head thump and her pupils constrict and, since they're diuretic, they'll probably affect her bladder too – but they're perfectly safe.'

'She . . . er, she hit her head quite hard.'

'I know. An emperor-sized lump; lucky she's got such long hair, to hide it.'

'No fracture?'

'No, no.'

'Do you need to keep her in overnight?'

'Very much so. Again, largely as a precaution, but precautions tend to stop dramas becoming crises. You can see her now, if you wish, but I would ask that you don't stay too long. She's very tired, and she needs some rest.'

Herbert pushed open the door and went over to Hannah's bed. She had dressings on both cheeks and a bandage across her forehead.

Hannah pointed to the dressing on her right cheek. 'You know what happen here?'

'What?'

'I am ironing, and the phone rings. It happen all the whole time.'

'And the other cheek?'

'They call back.'

First laughing, then crying, then laughing again, Herbert held her for as long as the nurses would let him; saying nothing, and feeling everything.

By the time Herbert got on to the tube, it was already packed with the first phalanxes of grim-faced office drones, en route to another day of repetitive monotony, another eight hours of their lives gone without excitement, without any reward beyond their salaries; more of their precious allotments ticked off without protest.

He supposed it said something for the average Londoner's tenacity, or perhaps his lack of imagination, that he was still determined to make it into work in such conditions. The country would hardly fall apart if a day's filing was missed, after all.

He read the classifieds on the front page of *The Times*.

'Look, sir! Hounds!'

Boys at Kestrel's Preparatory School, East Anstey, North Devon, not infrequently have such experiences and views from the form rooms. Rather nice. A breath of England while wrestling with Latin Primers.

When this was over, he might retreat to a remote bucolic paradise like Kestrel's.

Back at his flat, he soaked so long in the bath that he had to refill it twice. By the time he got out, his skin was wrinkled like that of a washerwoman. The radio said that the fog would start to clear by mid-morning, and that the temperature would rise from freezing to around forty-five degrees.

He began to reach for the phone to ring New Scotland Yard, to tell them what had happened, and perhaps ask for protection into the bargain. As if in anticipation of his movement, the phone began to ring. He unhooked the receiver.

'Hello?'

'Detective Inspector Smith?'

'Speaking.'

'Rathbone here.'

It took Herbert half a moment to place the name; Rathbone, the pathologist who had conducted Stensness' autopsy.

'Mr Rathbone,' Herbert said, remembering that he could not have used Rathbone's Christian name even if he had wanted to; Rathbone had never volunteered such information. 'What can I do for you?'

'I've got some . . . well, some news, I don't know whether it's bad or good . . .'

'Go on.'

'I've just finished the autopsy on Mr de Vere Green – I know he died yesterday, but we've got quite a backlog in this fog, as you can imagine, and suicides aren't given high priority, yes?' On the slab as at the altar, Herbert thought. 'Anyway, we got to him in the end, and . . . well, to cut a long story short, his suicide, it, er, it wasn't suicide.'

Herbert was half out of his chair. *'What?'*

'Oh, it was carbon monoxide poisoning all right. We found all the usual traces: microscopic haemorrhages in the eyes, congestion and swelling of the brain, liver, spleen and kidneys, and a distinctive cherry red colour to the blood, yes? But the autopsy also revealed chloroform.'

Chloroform. Kazantsev. Elkington. Cholmeley Crescent.

'You're sure?'

'Oh yes. For a start, I could smell it, very faint, and only when I was right up close to the cadaver, but unmistakable. Then there was blistering on the skin around the mouth, where the liquid must have come in contact. Also burning inside the mouth, and down in the oesophagus, yes?'

'Could he have administered it himself? Trying to knock himself out beforehand?'

Rathbone shrugged. 'It's possible, technically, but unlikely.'

'Why?'

'The degree of burning is consistent with the chloroform being applied with considerable force, which is unlikely when self-administered. And anyway, why would one, er, knock oneself out when the carbon monoxide would have the same effect eventually?'

Herbert's head reeled.

Not suicide. But with a note and chloroform, not an accident either.

It would have been the easiest thing in the world, he supposed, to open the valve on the gas fire in a small, stuffy room, and leave an unconscious man to take that final, small step into the next world.

What was Herbert sure of?

That the suicide note had been in de Vere Green's handwriting. And, as much to the point, in his tone, style and voice too.

Also, that he had had every motivation to kill himself.

So in order to kill de Vere Green in this manner, and then make it look like suicide, one would have needed two things.

First was the capacity to force him to write the suicide note, which anyone with a knife or gun could have done; and then to knock him out, which meant anybody with a working knowledge of chloroform.

Second was sufficient knowledge of de Vere Green, his history, and his idiosyncrasies to ensure that the note contained no false chords to arouse suspicion.

And that was something very few people could have done. Not Kazantsev, for a start, unless he and de Vere Green had a connection that Herbert knew nothing about.

In fact, Herbert could think of only one person who fitted the bill: Papworth.

A process of elimination was one thing, concrete evidence quite another. If accusing de Vere Green of treason had been serious enough, then levelling a murder charge at a member of the CIA was just as grave. Herbert could not confront Papworth without being absolutely sure. And to be sure, he needed proof.

If he was to find such proof anywhere, he felt, then de Vere Green's office was as likely a venue as any.

Leconfield House was in what Herbert could only describe as muted uproar; a wildfire of hurried whispers and murmured rumours. The news of de Vere Green's death had already rippled through the building, though to judge from what Herbert heard as he waited in reception, that news was light on fact – the undisputed truth apart, that de Vere Green was dead – and long on speculation, with murder (a frenzied stabbing) and accident (crushed, agonisingly, beneath the wheels of a slow-moving bus) among the candidates.

Patricia, as ever, came to get Herbert.

'What happened?' she asked. She had not been crying, but her usual jaunty air was somewhat flattened. One did not have to like someone – and Patricia had cared little for de Vere Green – to be shocked that they were gone. 'How did he die?'

It pleased Herbert that she had used the word 'die' rather than 'pass away' or some other such euphemism. Death was death; why not call it what it was?

He told her, as quickly and as simply as possible. And then he told her about de Vere Green's relationship with Stensness.

De Vere Green's office had been locked and sealed. But, with a lack of attention to detail that Herbert found all too typical of Five, there was no one actually standing guard. Perhaps everyone was waiting for someone else to take charge.

'Just stand there,' Herbert said to Patricia. Using her as cover, he picked the lock as easily as he had done in Cholmeley Crescent, and he was in.

He had a perfect right to be here, he reminded himself; as far as he knew, the only people who had any idea that de Vere Green's 'suicide' was anything but were himself and Rathbone.

And the killer, of course.

Herbert went into de Vere Green's office, shut the door behind him, and began searching through papers on his desk for – well, what exactly?

He did not know.

Anything relevant to the events of the past few days, he supposed; anything he could add to his report.

Rectum defendere, indeed.

De Vere Green's papers were the usual hotchpotch of espionage bureaucracy. Venona decrypts that Herbert had already seen. Memoranda about expenses and another proposed departmental re-organisation. An envelope marked *Weekend updates, 6–7th December 1952*. De Vere Green could not possibly have seen this before he died, so Herbert did not bother opening it.

Herbert was reminded of the way he had rootled

through Stensness's house after Kazantsev had fled. It paid to be thorough.

His search for pertinent information in de Vere Green's office suddenly seemed much more urgent.

He rummaged through more papers and yet more. Nothing, still nothing, and he had checked everything.

No, he remembered; not quite everything.

He opened the *Weekend updates* envelope which he had previously ignored, and tipped the contents on to the desk.

Two agents' reports, one from Birmingham and the other Cardiff, both concerning trade unions; an agenda for a meeting with Six; and three more Venona decrypts. Herbert shook them free and read them.

The first two seemed nothing special: one an exchange of pleasantries between a *chargé d'affaires* and a second secretary, which may or may not have been code; the other a White House schedule for Truman, consisting of various departmental meetings and a lunch with the Ohio Women's Association.

The third was about Achilles.

It was not long, but then it did not have to be. It had been sent from Washington on 10th October 1946, and confirmed the assimilation of 174 German scientists into the American industrial and academic network. 'Administration unaware' it added; admission that Truman had been left in the dark.

The war had ended in August 1945. De Vere Green had been in Washington for the nine months afterwards; he had left sometime in the early summer of 1946.

The decrypt was dated October, so Achilles could not have been de Vere Green.

Which meant that Achilles had to be Papworth.

Dear God, Herbert thought.

Achilles was a Soviet agent.

Kazantsev was not working for Papworth; Papworth was working for Kazantsev.

And Papworth received the decrypts too. This last one had come over the weekend. Papworth had been at the Embassy yesterday. He would have seen it; he would have known that de Vere Green would see it too, first thing on Monday morning.

'Find me a single Achilles decrypt which you could categorically not have been involved with,' Papworth had told de Vere Green in the church the previous morning, 'and I'll retract it all.'

Had he known, even as he spoke that line, that the proof would be on their desks so soon? Papworth had turned the accusation of espionage back on de Vere Green once; with this proof, he would not have been able to do so again.

So he had killed de Vere Green, before de Vere Green had been able to turn suspicion into evidence.

De Vere Green kept Leconfield House's internal directory next to his telephone. Herbert found the

411

number for the Director-General's office, and dialled.

No, said the secretary; Sir Percy was not in the building at the moment. No, she couldn't say where he was.

It was a matter of national security, Herbert said.

Things tended to be in this building, she replied coolly.

He had evidence that a CIA officer was a Soviet spy and had murdered a senior MI5 man. Wouldn't Sir Percy want to know *that*?

She would let Sir Percy know, she said.

If she didn't tell him where Sir Percy was, Herbert said, he would have her arrested on charges of obstruction of justice.

She was silent, weighing things up; then she said that Sir Percy was at Minimax.

Herbert knew what she meant. Minimax was 54 Broadway, Six's headquarters just south of St James' Park; so-called because, almost thirty years after Six had moved in, the plaque on the door still bore the name of the previous occupants, the Minimax Fire Extinguisher Company.

Herbert had little doubt what – or, more precisely, who – the top brass of Five and Six would be discussing.

He rang Tyce and told him everything that had happened.

'Good Christ, Herbert,' Tyce said when Herbert had finished. 'Good Christ.' He took a deep breath.

'Right. I'll put out an APB for Papworth and Kazantsev – all police, all port authorities. Bugger what Five might want, Six too. We waited yesterday, and look where that got us. What are you going to do?'

'Find Papworth.'

'On your own? After being attacked this morning? Not on your life. You wait there. I'll send a posse of uniforms round, then you can go. No ifs and buts, Herbert, and sod the politics. This is a straight murder hunt now.'

'Fine. Tell them I'll meet them outside the main entrance.'

Herbert hung up, pocketed the Venona decrypt, walked back through the corridors, and went out through reception into the street. The radio had been correct. There *was* light outside, for the first time in four days. Dull and patchy, for sure, but light nonetheless, and its very presence made Herbert start. The sun was showing rather than shining, hanging sulkily in a dirty sky, and Herbert felt on his face the faintest stirrings of a breeze, blowing the fog down the river.

Visibility was still barely more than a couple of hundred yards, but in comparison to what he had been used to, Herbert felt as if he could see to Manchester.

After a few minutes, a car pulled up to the kerb beside Herbert. He looked to see whether it was Tyce's men.

It was not. It was Papworth and Fischer.

Herbert knew that he should run, or shout, or both; but he had enjoyed precious little sleep, his mind was still trying to process the implications of what he had just learnt, and now to see Papworth, the murderer made flesh, was, in his current state, just that last bit too much.

They opened the doors and came for him, one each side, backing him up against a wall – the wall of the headquarters of Britain's security service, for heaven's sake, and there was no one watching who could help.

Papworth reached into his coat pocket and brought out a small switchblade. There was just enough sunshine for the metal to glint dully as Papworth placed it against Herbert's coat, an inch or so beneath his ribs.

'Where is it?' Papworth hissed.

Was this the same man who had come to Hannah's flat in the small hours and asked him the same question? Herbert could not tell.

'Where's what?'

It was not an idle question; Herbert genuinely did not know whether Papworth meant the microdots or the Venona decrypt.

'What Stensness was offering,' Papworth said. 'Tell me where it is, or I'll kill you, and I'll make it slow.'

Funny, Herbert thought, how every person had in them something that one might not see for years, decades even, perhaps never; but when one did, one could never look at that person in the same way again. They were changed, and that could not be undone.

That was how Papworth appeared to Herbert now. The features were Papworth's, the voice too, but the expression and tones into which they were arranged were something Herbert had never seen on him before. Papworth's bluff over-loud American bonhomie was abruptly gone, wiped clean as if from a restaurant slate.

Playing ignorant would no longer work, Herbert knew; nor would holding out.

Was it worth dying for?

No.

Would they kill him anyway?

Perhaps.

But if he continued to resist, they *would* kill him, of that he was sure.

It was no contest, really.

'It's in Guy's Hospital,' Herbert said.

'Guy's?' Papworth said. 'Good.'

Herbert could not see why that should be an especially propitious location, and from the look on his face nor could Fischer, but that was hardly the most pressing of Herbert's problems.

They ushered him into the back seat – no internal locks, he noticed – climbed into the front seats themselves, and set off.

'There you go,' Papworth said, more to Fischer than to Herbert. 'I told you he'd be there.'

'A stroke of luck,' Fischer said.

'Luck be damned! Intuition.' Papworth chuckled. 'Always trust your hunches.'

Papworth drove with skill and no little verve, slicing past the slower cars which had ventured cautiously out this morning.

Herbert looked out of the window and tried to calculate his options.

Papworth knew why Herbert had gone to Leconfield House, that much was clear. He would not have gone there himself otherwise. So should Herbert tell Papworth that he had the decrypt, or should he act as though he had found nothing?

The latter, clearly. The proof of Papworth's treachery was Herbert's only piece of leverage; to let Papworth know that he had it would seal his fate. Herbert's elimination would then become desirable, even necessary.

No; his only hope of getting out of this alive was to give Papworth what he wanted and get away as quickly as possible.

When they crossed Waterloo Bridge, Herbert saw that the river was still shrouded in miasma, and the boats remained at anchor; no surprise, as waterways tended to be where fog settled first and lifted last.

A few minutes later, now on the south bank, they passed the approach road to Blackfriars Bridge.

From this point on, Herbert realised, they would follow the same route he had taken this morning in the ambulance.

In the half-light, seeing all the traffic islands and potholes, he caught his breath. He had been very, very lucky to get away unscathed on that drive.

The road outside London Bridge station was clogged by buses. Herbert counted seventeen in all, halted nose-to-tail in a gigantic red metal caterpillar, doubtless waiting for their drivers to come back and claim them.

Papworth parked as near to the foyer as he could without actually driving in, and they went inside.

The Emergency Bed Service warning was now at yellow, Herbert saw; the ratio of admissions to applications had dropped the wrong side of eighty per cent.

Staccato whispers in the corridor, like bushfire.

There were no longer enough shrouds to wrap all the corpses in the mortuary.

There were more deaths than there had been in the cholera and influenza epidemics of times past.

In flats opposite Battersea power station, windows had fallen from their frames after sulphur dioxide had eaten through the metal hinges. Imagine what *that* was doing to your lungs.

Through corridors Herbert now knew well, walls smeared in blue-green.

They passed two doctors chatting.

'I'm telling you, Reginald,' one was saying, 'the best cure for a haemorrhaged ulcer is a large soluble capsule filled with Dreft washing powder and washed down with a gin and tonic. One every morning, that's the prescription. It worked for Rodgers.'

'Rodgers?'

'Rodgers and Hammerstein. He's the whitest man I know.'

Herbert kicked away the mocking bubbles of their laughter.

They reached the ward Hannah had been placed in.

'It's in here,' Herbert said. 'I'll just get it for you.'

'We're coming in with you,' Papworth said.

Herbert did not want to expose Hannah to any more danger than he had to; but there were plenty of people around, and if he could minimise the time spent there with her, then that would surely be all right.

He pushed open the door and walked in.

Hannah's bed was empty.

'Where the hell is she?' Herbert said, to no one in particular.

'Are you her gentleman friend?'

The question had come from one of the other beds; a young man with a yellowing plaster on his left temple.

'That's right.'

'She's gone to see your mother. She said to tell you if you came back.'

'My mother?'

'Yes. One of the nurses was talking about what a coincidence it was, that they ended up in the same hospital. So she went to see her.'

Typical Hannah, Herbert thought; anyone else in her situation would have stayed in bed, rather than tapped her way through unknown corridors to make friends with a woman she had never met.

Herbert looked at Hannah's bed again. Her cane was not there.

'Let's go and see your mother, then,' Papworth said, his voice sunny for the benefit of the young man and anyone else who might have been listening.

'Yes,' Herbert said, forcing jollity into his voice, 'let's.'

They continued through the warren until they came to Mary's ward.

She was not there either.

Angela was busying herself in the corner with one of the other patients.

'Angela,' Herbert said, 'where's my mother?'

'Oh, hello, Herbert.' She smiled at him, then at Papworth and Fischer. 'Hello.'

They smiled back; Herbert's friends, no need to worry.

'Two doors down, on the right.'

'Why did you move her?'

'A private room became available, and she kicked up such a fuss that we moved her there. More for our own peace and quiet than anything else, you know?'

419

She laughed, to let Herbert know she was joking – well, half-joking – and then turned back to the patient she had been attending.

Herbert was about to ask where Guy's had got the spare room from, since they were on the yellow warning.

Then he realised that the previous occupant had probably joined the ranks of those on whom the fog had taken its toll in the most crowded part of the hospital: the mortuary.

They found Mary and Hannah at the third time of asking.

The room was small and almost dark; a small bedside lamp provided the only illumination. Mary was sitting up in bed, with Hannah wrapped in blankets on the chair next to her.

'Is very simple,' Hannah was saying. 'Marriage is love. Love is blind. So, marriage is institution for blind.'

'Stop it, dear,' Mary said through her chuckles. 'It hurts me to laugh.'

'Hello,' Hannah said, having heard Herbert, or smelt him, or just had some sixth sense of his presence.

'Herbert!' Mary said. 'Told you they'd find me a room, in the end. And your lady friend is making me laugh far more than is good for me.'

She looked at Papworth and Fischer, as though noticing them for the first time. 'Who are you?' she asked.

Papworth closed the door behind him and stood

420

in front of it, arms folded and shoulders out, like a linebacker.

'Hannah, I need your cane,' Herbert said.

'It's in her *cane*?' Papworth asked.

When Herbert nodded, Papworth looked at Fischer, as if to ask, *How could we have missed that?*

Fischer shrugged, and said nothing.

'What on earth is going on?' Mary asked.

'Is not here,' Hannah said.

'It's not on your bed.'

'Must be down side.'

'I've had enough of this,' Papworth said.

'Without your cane, how did you get from your ward to here?' Herbert asked.

'Nurse bring me.'

Herbert turned to Papworth. 'We'll have to go back and get it.'

'She's lying,' Fischer said. 'The cane's here.'

Hannah slumped suddenly, her eyes wide against skin quickly pale; a relapse. Herbert grabbed her under the armpits and held her upright. Her face was slippery with sweat, as though her skin had sprung a leak.

'Get a doctor!' Herbert yelled at Papworth.

'I'm a doctor,' Fischer said.

'A *real* doctor, damn you!'

'I *am* a real doctor.'

Hannah was staring at Fischer. Her gaze was so intense that Herbert could hardly believe she could not see. She was stammering, and Herbert had never seen her so uncollected.

Then, in the split second before she managed to get the words out, he knew what she knew, and what she was going to say.

'Hello, Uncle Pepi,' she said.

Mengele, Herbert thought uselessly; Mengele, Mengele. Mengele was here.

So obvious, when one knew. So obvious, when one put together the pieces.

Genetics, the new frontier of science; the battleground for the next world war.

Mengele, who had vanished from post-war Germany.

The Americans, recruiting Nazi scientists to stop them working for the Soviets.

Operation Paperclip, which had whitewashed the German scientists' records and given them false names if necessary.

Dr Fischer's pursuit of DNA was the natural continuation of Mengele's fiendish work in Auschwitz.

So obvious, when one saw Mengele's unblinking basilisk stare, with all the Biblical connotations, his eyelids so heavily hooded that only half of his greenish-brown irises were visible.

So obvious, when one considered Hannah's reactions.

In Wheeler's, she had excused herself instantly, almost as though she had taken a sudden turn. Mengele had been there. Even though he had not spoken in her presence, she must have sensed something, an injustice whose memory was locked so deep within her that, on reflection, she had simply refused to consider it.

The terror on her face in the small hours as the intruder rampaged through the flat; again, she must have known, even without knowing that she knew.

So obvious, when Herbert thought of the way in which that intruder had threatened to blind him.

So obvious, that here was pure iniquity, pulsing in endless waves of fission.

Hannah's shrinking was almost visible. She had bowed her head and dropped her shoulders, clasping her hands in her lap. Suddenly she was fifteen again, the shy twin who would not have said boo to a goose, all her sparkling defiance – all *Esther*'s stubborn refusals – gone. She looked halfway catatonic; too far gone to speak.

For days, the radio had spoken of little but visibility, or the lack of it. With grudging admiration Herbert had to doff an imaginary cap to Mengele, for what could be more visible than a man hiding in plain view?

Mengele, too proud to go to ground in a Paraguayan jungle. While all those Jewish commandos were tramping round South America, their quarry was going about his unobtrusive daily business at the heart of the enemy.

At school, Herbert had occasionally played a game with an atlas, where each player in turn chose first a map and then a name on it, before obliging the others to guess at his selection.

The name could be anything – village, town, city, hill, mountain, river, lake, ocean, state, empire – as long as it appeared on the motley and perplexed surface of the chart.

The novice would opt for the most minutely lettered names, predictably deliberate in their obscurity and therefore easily deducible.

The adept, in contrast, would nominate words which stretched in outsize letters from one end of the map to the other, and which therefore tended to escape observation simply by being too obvious.

So it had been with Mengele; faced with the grievous nature of his crimes and his consequent need to hide for ever, he had, with magnificent conceit, chosen not to conceal himself at all.

'Uncle Pepi?' Papworth said to Hannah, surprised. 'You *know* him?'

Herbert saw the briefest flash of concern in Mengele's eyes, and he knew instantly how deep the deception had run.

'His name is Josef Mengele, and he blinded her in Auschwitz,' Herbert said.

'What on earth is going on, Herbert?' my mother said. 'Who *are* these people?'

'This man is called Fritz Fischer,' Papworth replied. 'He worked at the Institute of Biological, Racial and Evolutionary Research at Berlin-Dahlen, and at the Frankfurt Institute for Hereditary Biology and Racial Hygiene.' Fischer had told Herbert much the same the night before, but he had been economical with the institutes' full titles, omitting any references to race or evolution. 'He now works at Caltech with Linus Pauling,' Papworth continued. 'He's never been near Auschwitz in his life.'

'This man is Josef Mengele,' Herbert said. 'He was camp doctor at Auschwitz.'

'Impossible.'

'Ask him.'

'Impossible,' Papworth repeated. 'Auschwitz was staffed by the SS. The SS had their blood group tattooed under their armpits. We checked his armpit: no tattoo.'

'He refused to have one,' Herbert said. He, too, had checked Mengele's armpit in the restaurant last night, and now he remembered something Hannah had told him.

'Why would he do that?'

Herbert turned to Mengele, questioning. Why, indeed?

Mengele would deny it, Herbert was sure; he was Fritz Fischer, he would say, and anyone who maintained otherwise was a fantasist.

Papworth, murderer of at least one and a double agent, a man whose entire life was based on the principle that black was white; would *he* believe? Would the arch-deceiver admit, even to himself – *especially* to himself – that he had been conned?

Even for Papworth, Herbert thought, wilfully

consorting with a man like Mengele must have been beyond the pale.

'I refused to have the tattoo,' Mengele said, 'because I was convinced that any competent surgeon would make a cross-match of blood types and not rely solely on the tattoo before administering a transfusion. Tattoos are ugly. I did not want one.'

Papworth ran his hand through his hair and puffed his cheeks; but he did not move away from his guard post at the door.

He had come too far, and was too greedy, to be denied now, Herbert thought.

Papworth looked at his watch. 'Come on,' he said. 'We haven't got all day.'

Once more, Herbert assessed his options.

Hannah was blind and, at least temporarily, stunned into submission.

His mother was sixty-five and bedridden.

Papworth was bigger and stronger than him.

And Mengele was a psychopath.

He had been in better situations, put it that way.

'If this is your idea of a joke, Herbert,' Mary hissed, 'it's entirely tasteless.'

'Right,' Mengele said. 'Give me the cane, and we'll be done with this.'

'The cane is back in the first ward we went to. I'll go and get it.'

Mengele smiled, as though Herbert was entering into the spirit of a game.

'And raise the alarm? You must consider me very stupid.'

Mengele looked around the room and, with a visible frisson of delight, he saw a trolley in the corner.

A hospital trolley, littered with various surgical paraphernalia; the kind of thing that should have been kept in the doctors' quarters, but which during busy periods was liable to be left in odd places at odd times.

He went over to it and rummaged around.

A white coat was hanging from the side. He donned it, flicking at the collar to straighten it, looking for all the world as though it had been tailored for him alone.

Mengele, the *Malach Hamavet*, Angel of Death, assuming once more the form of a brilliant physician in order to continue cutting his endless swathe of destruction.

He turned from the trolley.

'You have heard of the Inquisition?' he said. 'Inquisitors used three degrees of interrogation. The First Degree was questioning the prisoner. So, I ask you again: where is the information?'

'And I tell you again: I don't have it.'

Mengele sighed; the sigh of a disappointed schoolmaster faced with an habitual miscreant.

'The Second Degree,' he said, 'is showing the instruments of torture.'

He picked up a surgical saw, went over to Hannah, grabbed one of her wrists and laid the

427

serrated edge of the saw against it. She did not respond.

'A conundrum,' Mengele announced. 'How do you put out the eyes of a blind person? By cutting off their hands, that's how. What would you do with a pair of stumps, my dear? How would you read? How would you hold your cane? How would you find your way round a room?' A scalpel appeared in Mengele's palm, as though he were a magician. 'Or perhaps I slice off your fingers, one by one? Ten amputations are much more challenging than two, no?'

'Why won't you *listen*?' Herbert said.

Mengele looked at Herbert as if he could not have been less interested, and continued. 'Perhaps the application of water torture would be effective. You know how the Inquisition did this, Mr Smith? They tied the prisoner upside down to a ladder, forced his mouth open with an iron prong, and pushed a strip of linen down his throat. Water was then dripped on the linen until the prisoner, desperate to avoid being strangled, swallowed the strip. Then the torturers gradually withdrew the strip, covered in blood and mucus; and the whole process began again. The amount of water was carefully measured, of course, or else the prisoner might suffocate. Eight quarts at a time, no more.'

It was nastiness for nastiness' sake, Herbert saw, for there was no way that Mengele could possibly put all that into practice, not here and not now; and that made Herbert even angrier.

'Come *on*,' Papworth said, hurrying Mengele forward again.

Herbert knew what face Mengele would show America. He would have embraced Uncle Sam's way of life with apparent eagerness: church every Sunday, popping down the coast to Mexico once in a while, picnics with his Caltech colleagues.

Herbert knew too that it was all a sham, because Mengele hated it; hated the carefree lack of discipline in prosperous, democratic America, where everyone was equal and everything allowed; hated the lack of spine in the new Germany; hated the way the authorities read his mail and dangled the carrot of American citizenship forever out of reach; hated the way the world had exulted at seeing the Third Reich brought to its knees; hated, hated, hated, because hate was the only thing that dried his tears.

Mengele looked again at Hannah. Herbert tensed, too obviously, for suddenly Papworth stepped forward, away from the door, and twisted Herbert's right arm up between his shoulder blades, ripping splinters of pain through his ligaments.

Clearly, Herbert thought, Papworth did *not* consider Mengele beyond the pale; or else he felt himself so near his prize that he no longer cared.

Hannah looked wildly around, as sensitive to atmospheric changes as a barometer, but it was Mary who spoke.

'This is a land,' she said disbelievingly to

Mengele, 'of Goethe and Beethoven, Bach and Kant . . . and you?'

Mengele half-smiled, as though he had, intentionally or otherwise, misunderstood her tone and chosen to take it as a compliment, equating his genius with that of those great men. Then, with deliberation in every pace, he moved across to Mary's bed and took from his pocket a large strip of cotton, which he rolled into a ball.

'The Third Degree is the torture itself.' He turned to her. 'Open your mouth.'

'Whatever for?' she asked.

He hit her in the stomach, a punch that a fit young man might have shrugged off but which was more than enough for an old woman.

What little bronchitic breath Mary had whistled from her lungs. Her head came forward with her mouth wide open, as if trying to catch the escaped air, and Mengele jammed the cotton into her mouth and grabbed both her hands in one of his to stop her from removing it.

It was not Hannah he was going to torture; it was Mary.

She was older and weaker, and the very fact that she was here in the first place laid bare her most basic weakness: the fact that she could hardly breathe.

A good torturer knew his techniques as a mechanic knew his tools. Mengele could clearly judge suffering as an engineer gauged the stresses and strains on a bridge.

He knew too that she was Herbert's mother, and that all else paled before that.

Mary looked at Herbert, her eyes widening in fear.

To try and get air flowing freely through her nostrils, she snorted twice; a measure of her concern, as making such unladylike sounds would usually have mortified her.

Mengele leant in close to Mary, the better to hear how laboured her breathing was. Her eyes swivelled towards him and then back to Herbert.

Herbert saw her cheeks start to redden.

She knew, and Herbert knew, and Mengele knew, that it was a vicious circle. The less air she got, the more anxious she would become, and the more anxious she became, the less air she would get.

'Don't even think about yelling for help, Mr Smith. Papworth would cause you a lot of pain, and it wouldn't do you any good anyway. People cry out all the time in hospitals, and no one pays them the slightest bit of attention.'

Mary oinked again, and a glob of mucus appeared above her upper lip. The folds of her nightdress shifted slightly as trapped air began to push her lungs outwards.

She tried to cough, and gagged on the cotton, making bile flow from her nose and tears spring to her eyes.

Mengele reached into the pocket of his doctor's coat and brought out a small cotton plug, which he held up to Herbert as if for his approval. Then, with quick precision, he wedged it in Mary's left nostril.

'For God's sake,' Herbert shouted, 'don't you think I'd have told you by now? *Why won't you believe me?'*

Even in Herbert's desperation, he could see that the question was rhetorical. Mengele did not believe him because those who deceived for a living never did, and because this was too important for Mengele to take the slightest chance with.

His power at Auschwitz had been transient and limited, but this, the Holy Grail of science, would assure him immortality, a temptation surely irresistible to a man of such vaulting ambition. He must have chafed at working under a genius like Pauling.

This would be his vindication; this the one that put his name in the encyclopaedia.

Josef Mengele, Herbert thought; the one man who had passed through the gate at Auschwitz above which was written *Arbeit Macht Frei* – 'Work Makes You Free' – and believed the legend.

Mary's shoulders were now hunched with the effort of breathing.

The sinews in her neck stood out like steel hawsers, tracing tight lines beneath her skin, and between these ridges the soft tissue was sucked into deep hollows.

Herbert imagined spots of black behind her eyes, an invisible iron clamp around her chest, and the final, coruscating blame, that he, her son, was somehow responsible for all this.

Mengele brought out a second, identical cotton plug, looked at Herbert, saw nothing that would convince him otherwise, and inserted it into Mary's other nostril.

Herbert squeezed his eyes on tears of angry humiliation.

'All right,' Papworth said suddenly. 'He's telling the truth.'

Mengele looked at Papworth, ostensibly for confirmation that he could stop.

But Herbert, ever the Watcher, saw behind the look, and he knew what it had really been: disappointment. That was it; disappointment that Papworth had denied Mengele the chance to inflict more torture.

It had not been – at least, it had not solely been – about finding out where the cane was. Mengele had done it because he could, because he wanted to, because he enjoyed it.

Herbert clamped his teeth together so hard he was sure he would shatter them.

With the physician's swift, clinical hands, Mengele took strips of surgical plaster. He cuffed Mary's wrists to the bedhead and Hannah's to the chair, gagged both women, and grabbed a stethoscope from the trolley, presumably to afford his disguise extra verisimilitude.

Ironic, Herbert thought, that it was the Jews who had the definitive word for that kind of behaviour: *chutzpah*.

Papworth opened the door, and the three of them walked back into the corridor.

Mengele shut the door behind him. There was no way of locking it from the outside, but that would, Herbert surmised, prove immaterial. By the time the ruse was discovered, Papworth and Mengele would be long gone.

They made it back to Hannah's ward without incident.

The cane was there, on the floor by the side of the bed as Hannah had said.

Herbert picked it up and handed it to Papworth, who ushered them out of the room again before unscrewing the top of the cane and tipping the contents into his hand.

'That's it?' he said in astonishment.

Mengele took it from him and examined it.

'Microdots, there and there.' Herbert pointed to the legend *Ho. of Parlt*.

'You're kidding me,' Papworth said.

'Don't be stupid.'

'Prove it.'

'One of them is some sort of X-ray photograph. The other's a code which describes what the photograph represents.'

'And the code is?'

'Doctor!'

It was Angela, coming down the corridor.

'We've got twenty more patients just come in who really need . . .'

She stopped, peering at Mengele; trying to equate, Herbert saw, the white coat with the man she had seen in Mary's ward, when Herbert and his two unwanted minders had first come looking for his mother.

'You're not a doctor,' Angela said.

There was the briefest hiatus while Mengele tried to think of a response.

Then Papworth had his knife out again, and before anybody could react, he had carved a long curving line fast down Herbert's cheek.

It had been done more to distract than to wound, Herbert realised, even as he clamped his hand to his face and felt blood gush from between his fingers.

Angela's first priority, excellent nurse that she was, was to try and hurry Herbert to a tap, in order to wash the gash out and try to stem the bleeding; but Herbert knew there was no time, and he pulled away from her.

'My mother. And Hannah – the girl with her. In her room. They need help.'

Faces bled easily, Herbert knew, but this was merely a flesh wound; he must have been jerking his head away even as Papworth had slashed.

It had been the shortest of delays, but it was still enough. By the time Herbert looked up, Mengele and Papworth were long gone.

*   *   *

435

Herbert ran down the stairs, pausing on every floor to look for Papworth and Mengele, in case they had switched escape routes; but they were nowhere to be seen.

He reached the main entrance, his heart sinking. If they'd made it back to their car, they could be miles away by now . . .

And then he stopped.

The car was still there, parked where Papworth had left it.

Herbert looked up at the sky.

It might have been his imagination, but he fancied that the fog was beginning to close in again. Still, it would be possible to drive through.

So why had they abandoned the car?

And without a car, where could they have gone?

To the train station, obviously.

Herbert went up through the back streets and into London Bridge station.

The concourse was almost deserted. The air in the station was clear enough, and Herbert's vision keen enough, for him to make out faces, and neither Papworth nor Mengele were among the few people standing there.

If not the railway, then where?

The river.

He ran through the concourse, out the other side of the station, and on to London Bridge itself, the downstream side, looking down the south bank of the Thames towards Tower Bridge.

Herbert saw a workmen's café, less than a

hundred yards down; and two familiar faces in the window.

Not Papworth and Mengele; Pauling and Kazantsev.

Pauling was talking to Kazantsev, who was jotting things down in a notebook on the table. It looked as though Kazantsev had got his interview at last.

Except Kazantsev was no journalist; not primarily, at any rate.

Did Pauling know that Papworth was a Soviet agent? Was he aware of Mengele's true identity?

The first was possible, Herbert thought; the second unlikely.

Two men walked past the entrance to the café. Papworth and Mengele.

Tyce's men would surely have been at Leconfield House by now, Herbert thought. What would they do, when they couldn't find him there?

Where was the nearest police kiosk? Or even a public phone box, come to think of it? He needed reinforcements.

Papworth and Mengele stopped alongside a cargo boat, the *Ellen & Violet*, a seventy-footer with a tall central stack and a copious sprinkling of rust throughout. Smoke from her engine was rising to melt into the fog, and a short gangplank connected deck with shore. Two deckhands stood on board, one fore and one aft, looking ready to cast off.

The fog was denser down here than it had been by Guy's, and in the football pitch length visible

Herbert could see no other boats moving. Had the *Ellen & Violet*'s captain got permission to set sail, or was he just going to chance his arm?

Kazantsev and Pauling suddenly emerged from the café, and walked straight up to Papworth and Mengele.

Of the four, only Papworth and Kazantsev knew what was going to happen, Herbert saw.

He had a sudden, sinking feeling that he did too.

The body language gave it away. Papworth and Kazantsev were tensed on the balls of their feet, while Mengele and Pauling were standing with the slightly hunched aspect of the confused.

Papworth may not have known Mengele's true identity, but he had clearly kept one final trick up his sleeve: the reason why going via Guy's had so suited him.

This was what Papworth had planned all along, Herbert saw. The *Ellen & Violet*; that was why he had hurried Mengele in the hospital. The microdots were a bonus, albeit a bonus he had wrenched into being by his hunch that he would find Herbert at Leconfield House. Papworth had spent four days trying to get his hands on the microdots, but, if it had come to it, he would surely have left without Stensness's secret, as long as he had something much more important.

The scientists.

Never deceive a deceiver, Herbert thought, they'll just deceive you right back.

Papworth grabbed Mengele, twisting his right arm up behind his back, just as he had done to Herbert in Guy's.

Kazantsev stepped behind Pauling and wrapped an arm round his neck.

The agents hustled their captives up the gangway and on to the *Ellen & Violet*.

The moment they were on board, the deck-hands cast the ropes off and pulled the plank up, and they were motoring, downstream towards Tower Bridge, the horn sounding a loud, long blast to signal that they were underway.

The Thames flowed east; out past grimy suburbs, through the busiest port in the world with cranes crowding both banks in long lines from the Pool of London to Tilbury, and all the way to the sea beyond Southend and Shoeburyness.

The fugitives might switch boats at Tilbury, Herbert thought, if they had a proper deepwater vessel lined up. Or else they might just keep going in the *Ellen & Violet*, uncomfortable though presumably seaworthy, all the way across the North Sea and into the Baltic.

All the way to the Soviet Union, in other words.

The Pool of London was absolutely still, save for the *Ellen & Violet* chugging up the river, and the lone figure running down the towpath in a frantic effort to keep abreast.

Throughout the fog, Londoners had been bombarded with medical advice: stay inside whenever possible; keep the house shut up tight; put a handkerchief across your face when outside; and, most of all, avoid unnecessary exertion.

Herbert seemed to be in breach of every single one of these strictures, and with something of a vengeance.

The tide was high, and the *Ellen & Violet*'s funnel reached into the brumal skies.

They would have to open Tower Bridge for her.

It was no more than half a mile from London Bridge to Tower Bridge, but with the filthy air scouring his lungs and the screaming worry that he would be too late to stop the *Ellen & Violet*, Herbert felt like Pheidippides running from Marathon, and feared that he would share his fate to boot, dropping stone dead on arrival.

Papworth and Kazantsev had not just wanted the science; they had wanted the scientists too. Pauling, a suspected communist sympathiser and the world's premier chemist, and the man previously known only as Fischer, a former Nazi.

Both would be enormous propaganda victories for Moscow; one man from each of democratic capitalism and Nazi fascism, the two systems of government most implacably opposed to communism.

Both men would doubtless be paraded as ambassadors for peace and harmony, portrayed as having seen the light and defected to the promised land.

Not to mention Papworth, Herbert thought. Like Burgess and Maclean, he was surely never coming back.

The *Ellen & Violet* sounded its horn again; one long blast, two short, another long.

Tower Bridge, invisible for most of the run, had taken on the aspects of a mythical kingdom. No matter how far and how fast Herbert ran, it seemed to get no nearer, until suddenly there it was, with the fog like a cape round its shoulders, the famous Gothic towers and swooping aquamarine suspension chains emerging shyly from the gloom.

He slowed to catch his breath, and at that very moment, the bascules began to rise; the road slicing in half and opening up so that the *Ellen & Violet* could pass beneath.

There were steps up from the towpath to the bridge.

Herbert took them two at a time, and when he emerged on to the roadway, perhaps twenty seconds later, the bascules were already halfway up.

Next to the South Tower, on the downstream side, he saw a cabin that looked vaguely official. There were railings around it, and a gate from which a padlock hung disconsolately unlocked; perhaps it was supposed to have been shut, but this was the first time the bridge had been open in four days, so he supposed security was not as tight as it might have been.

At any rate, he was not complaining.

He banged open the gate, leapt the short flight of stairs up to the cabin, and hurled himself through the door.

Levers sprouted in neat rows from the floor, and the far wall was studded with dials. He had come to the right place.

'Shut the bridge!' he yelled through heaving breaths. 'Shut the bloody bridge!'

There were two men in there, both looking at Herbert in understandable astonishment; with the blood from Papworth's slash running down his face, he must have looked a sight.

'Calm down there, sir,' one said.

Herbert pulled his police badge from his coat.

'Shut the bloody bridge,' he repeated. '*Now*.'

The men moved with quiet economy, but there was no mistaking their purpose, nor their professionalism. They pushed back levers, glanced at dials, and spoke to each other in monosyllables: *pawls, bolts, brakes*.

When Herbert looked out of the window, the bascules were down again.

It had taken less than a minute.

He ran out of the cabin, across the road, and peered over the upstream side of the bridge. The *Ellen & Violet* was within view, and the churning of the water round her hull indicated that she was already hard in reverse, trying to stop in time.

Quite a shock for the captain, Herbert thought, to see the bridge close again like that.

The fog meant that the boat had been travelling on light throttle, and the *Ellen & Violet* stopped with her funnel twenty feet or so from the bridge.

Herbert glanced down. The bow had just about

gone under the bridge, and he was standing directly above her foredeck.

There was a small crowd round him now. Mainly engineers and mechanics, he guessed, come to see what the fuss was, but also two police constables.

Herbert had clean forgotten; there was a small police station on the bridge itself. He turned to the constables and showed them his badge.

'We need to get down to that boat,' he said. 'There are fugitives on board.'

'There's a rope ladder in the north cabin,' one of the mechanics replied.

Herbert nodded. 'That'll be fine.'

A couple of men in overalls ran off.

'Police! Stay where you are!' Herbert yelled down to the *Ellen & Violet*; somewhat superfluously, he thought, as there was nowhere they could go, save for shuttling endlessly between Tower and London Bridges.

The men were back inside a minute with the rope ladder. They fastened one end to the railings and hurled the other out away from the bridge in a tumbling parabola.

Herbert watched it unravel as it fell, swaying in alarmingly wide arcs before fading to slack.

'Is everyone on board a fugitive, sir?' said one of the constables.

'Not everyone.' Pauling was clearly a victim, not just from the evident shock that the abduction had represented, but also because there was a world

443

of difference between challenging US government policy and defecting to Moscow. The crew's guilt was also perhaps debatable, depending on how much they knew about their cargo. 'But arrest anyone you see,' Herbert continued. 'We'll sort out the sob stories later.'

'How many are there?'

Papworth, Mengele, Pauling, Kazantsev, the two deckhands, plus a captain – the boat had set off the instant the ropes had been slipped, which meant that neither of the deckhands could have had time to cast off and then take the wheel. 'Seven, minimum. Maybe more.'

'We'll need more than the three of us then, sir.'

Herbert looked at the assorted Tower Bridge staff.

'Anyone fancy making a citizen's arrest?' he asked.

There was no shortage of volunteers, that was for sure.

Herbert felt they were almost certainly motivated less by the prospect of social justice than by the possibility of a good old-fashioned scrap, and he could not have cared less.

A sailor would doubtless have swarmed down the rope ladder like a monkey. Herbert took his time, making sure that, of his four extremities, at least three were in contact with a rung at all times.

He imagined the bridge staff laughing at him, the landlubber picking his way down as though stepping through a minefield, but he was past caring.

He half-jumped, half-fell the last few feet to the deck. There was no one around.

The constables arrived, followed by the engineers and mechanics.

'One of the fugitives has a knife,' Herbert said.

They shrugged; stout British yeomen, it would take more than that to put them off.

Herbert made them fan out, half down each side of the boat.

It was easier than he had expected. There were only a limited amount of hiding-places on a boat, even one as sizeable as the *Ellen & Violet*, and none of the fugitives had had the time or inclination to conceal themselves very effectively.

Papworth and Pauling were still in the engine room.

Kazantsev and Mengele were further forward in the foc'sle, where the smell was terrible – engine oil, damp cloth, and the high odour of men who had gone too long in close company without washing.

The deckhands looked bewildered, the captain slightly less so.

Papworth shouted that he had diplomatic immunity from arrest. No one listened.

There were other boats downstream of the bridge, queuing up to come through.

Herbert herded all seven occupants of the *Ellen & Violet* back up the rope ladder, ensuring that there was someone he could trust – a constable, an engineer, or a mechanic – both ahead of and behind them on the climb.

One by one they reached the top, and were grabbed by strong and unyielding arms.

Mengele was the last up, Herbert directly beneath him.

On the bridge, two engineers hauled Mengele off the rope ladder; and without warning he slumped in their arms, mouth frothing.

They laid him on the floor, slightly panicked by the way his eyes were rolling; and Herbert, coming up over the parapet, knew even as he shouted that he was too late with the warning.

The moment the engineers' hands were off Mengele, he sprang to his feet and set off down the road, heading south, off the bridge.

The traffic barriers were still down, though he could have leapt them without difficulty.

Beyond, however, fanned out across the road, was a line of pedestrians, waiting for the bridge to reopen. They had watched the others being escorted off the boat, and enough of the onlookers were now shouting for Herbert to know that they would not let Mengele through.

Mengele stopped dead and whirled round. Herbert followed his gaze, and saw a similar phalanx of pedestrians arrayed on the other side of the river, towards the City.

Blocked to the north, blocked to the south, Mengele went the only place he could: into the control cabin.

*　　*　　*

The two men who had shut the bridge were among those who had come to help detain the fugitives, so there was no one in the cabin to stop Mengele.

Shouting at the others to stay where they were – there was no point losing more than one of the escapees – Herbert followed Mengele into the cabin.

Mengele was nowhere to be seen.

The cabin was small, perhaps twenty feet by ten. It took Herbert only a few seconds to be sure that Mengele was not hiding anywhere inside.

There was a flight of stone stairs on the left, leading downwards. It was the only place he could have gone.

Herbert followed, mongoose to Mengele's snake.

The stairs kinked right twice and emerged into a long, low room with concrete walls. Machinery was everywhere, metallic behemoths in black and orange which sprouted pipes thicker than a man's torso and valves as large as a human head.

Had it not been for the door on the far side of the room that was still swinging, Herbert could have wasted minutes hunting Mengele in this mechanical forest.

Herbert ran for the door, wondering as he went through whether it was some kind of trap, but it was too late to worry about that; this was the quick, where one either gave it or one did not.

The door gave on to more stairs, a short flight only, and at the landing where the stairs stopped,

Herbert caught his breath, both literally and figuratively.

Below him was a vast, magnificently forbidding chamber, patched here and there in darkness where some of the metal-grilled lamps had given out.

The chamber was shaped like the quadrant of a wheel. The roof ran horizontal and the nearside wall vertical, but the third side, the one which connected the floor to the furthest extremity of ceiling, described a long, graceful curve, ninety degrees of a circle.

Tracts of jade-coloured slime clung to the wall. Herbert shivered as the dampness wafted up.

Through the silence came a hushed, echoing clanging: the sound of feet on metal.

Herbert ran to the side of the landing.

A spiral staircase span down and away from him, and there was the top of Mengele's head, a quick glimmer of light bouncing off the balding patch on his crown as he moved.

He was no more than a quarter of the way down, a third at the most.

Herbert went after him, taking the steps first two and then three at a time, his outside hand bouncing off the banister with every impact. One misjudgement and he would have turned his ankle, and he was right on the very edge of control, to the extent that stopping seemed a far more hazardous alternative than keeping going.

Down and down they went, the unyielding

rungs jarring Herbert's knees, down into the bowels of the bridge, past gargantuan stanchions and girders studded with thousands of grey-painted rivets, and even as Herbert looked frantically for Mengele, he twinged with admiration for the sheer achievement of building such a bridge.

Mengele was near the bottom now. Herbert was closing, but not fast enough.

Mengele had the secret in his pocket: the helix, shaped exactly like the spiral staircase they were on.

Like the helix, Herbert thought, the staircase repeated its shape again and again, which meant that anywhere more than a full turn in from either end, there were identical spirals both above and below him.

Below him.

Herbert looked down again. Mengele was perhaps two-thirds of a turn ahead.

When Herbert's hand next skimmed the banister, he grabbed at it hard and swung his body up and over, so that he was dangling outside the staircase.

With his right hand still on the banister, he gripped the nearest step with his left, and then brought his right hand down to join it.

Now he was hanging entirely below the level of the flight he had been on.

Jumping straight down would have been pointless, as he would have landed on the banister directly beneath. The staircase ran vertically, so he needed to jump inwards.

With his arms extended to narrow the distance, it was perhaps ten feet, and the only way it would not hurt was if he landed on Mengele as he came round the corner.

Herbert jerked his legs forward, dropped, and hit Mengele like a depth charge.

Mengele crumpled forward and down, and Herbert heard something crack as he did. They rolled the last few steps together, clawing at each other.

Then, by luck or judgement, Mengele smacked Herbert's skull against the central pillar of the staircase at the point where it reached the floor.

The blow was not especially hard, but in the few seconds it took Herbert to clear his head, Mengele was gone again, down a tunnel to the right.

The tunnel gave on to the chamber which Herbert had seen from the top of the staircase. From up close, he saw that the curved surface was not perfectly smooth; in fact, it was ridged across its breadth in regular terraces, each one about eighteen inches high. They had entered the chamber perhaps a third of the way up the curve.

Mengele was limping badly, dragging his right leg behind him. That must have been the crack Herbert had heard.

Herbert jumped on Mengele once more, and once more they rolled downwards, this time down the terraces, all the way to the bottom, where they came to a halt by a low ledge which abutted the vertical wall.

Mengele's doctor's coat was streaked with grime. Herbert rummaged in its pockets, feeling for the material Mengele had stolen, tipping his head back to keep out of range when Mengele tried to punch him.

Mengele was yelling in pain and anger. In his fury he had reverted to German, so Herbert could not understand a word he was saying.

Several stentorian peals rang out high above them, echoing round the chamber.

They sounded like outsize bolts being shot; and, as the first squares of faint grey began to appear at the edges of the ceiling, Herbert realised that they were exactly that. Brakes, pawls and bolts: the mechanisms to lock and unlock the bridge.

Herbert knew with a rush what this chamber was. They were in the depths of the pier under the South Tower.

The vertical wall faced north, across the river. The ceiling was the underside of the road, the outside end of the south bascule. The bascules were far too large simply to hinge, he realised; they needed a counterweight, something to go down as they went up, and what better than the last quarter of their own length?

Hence the curved surface, to accommodate the counterweight in its arc; an arc that would end up against the wall where Herbert and Mengele

451

were. And to judge from the speed at which he had seen the bascules operate earlier, it would take less than a minute.

For a few seconds, somewhat absurdly, all Herbert could think about was why they were opening the bridge. There were other boats which wanted to come through, he remembered; but surely someone would have checked that no one was down there in the chamber?

Then Herbert remembered that it must have been a good minute's walk from the landing above the chamber back up to the control room; in other words, easily enough time for someone to have looked in the chamber, seen that it was empty, and gone back to give the all-clear, while Mengele and Herbert had fought their way from spiral staircase through tunnel to chamber.

Anyway, none of that mattered now. What mattered was getting clear before several hundred tons of iron and steel crushed them.

The counterweight was travelling pretty much flush to the floor, certainly too close for Herbert to pass beneath its leading edge.

Herbert felt again in Mengele's pocket, and this time his fingers found the crumpled papers. Mengele's hand closed over his, and with his free fist Herbert hit Mengele in the face, hard enough to loosen his grip.

Careful not to rip them, Herbert removed the papers from Mengele's pocket, checked that they were all there, and stuffed them into the pocket of his own jacket.

The counterweight was almost a third of the way down the curve; which, given that the tunnel entrance was a third of the way up it, and that they were at the bottom, meant that Herbert had to move faster than the counterweight if he was going to get there in time.

No time to think. Herbert pushed himself upright.

Mengele's hand closed round Herbert's ankle, and pulled him back down.

Herbert kicked Mengele in the chest, twice, but by the time he was free again the counterweight was more than halfway through its arc, and Herbert's last chance to make the tunnel had gone.

Herbert felt as though he was disappearing; and somewhere deep in the most primitive part of his brain, he knew that there was only one way to keep himself in the world, even if it was only for the next few seconds, and that way was violence.

He set on Mengele with all the fury he could summon.

It was as though the insane frenzy of Mengele's attacks at Auschwitz had somehow transferred to Herbert. He punched, kicked, stamped, bit and gouged, each blow some small revenge for all the evil Mengele had done: for blinding Hannah, for shooting Esther, for torturing Mary, and for all the faceless ones too, the hundreds of twins on whom he had experimented, the thousands of ordinary, innocent people whom he had sent to the crematorium with a flick of his wrist.

Herbert felt *alive*.

Dear God; he was about to die, and he had never experienced such vitality.

The counterweight, a monstrous wedge intent on destruction, was almost on them.

Herbert looked from it to Mengele, moaning as he lay limp and bloodied against the ledge.

The ledge was two foot high, two foot deep, and stretched all the way across the chamber. Suddenly Herbert understood why it was there: for safety in cases such as this, when someone got caught down here.

Either the counterweight would pass over the top of the ledge and end up against the wall, in which case Herbert could press himself flat to the floor in the lee of the ledge and let the counterweight pass above him; or it would stop against the bottom of the ledge, in which case Herbert could stand on top of the ledge, flush against the wall, and watch the counterweight come to a halt a couple of feet from his face.

But which one?

It should have been easy to judge; but he was exhausted from the struggle, the chamber was in semi-darkness, and the counterweight was coming fast.

Think.

If the ledge had been a deliberate addition, which Herbert was sure it was, it was surely more logical to have the counterweight stop against the ledge rather than against the wall; for who would want to dive for a damp and dirty crawlspace when they could simply have stood upright?

He had a couple of seconds to decide, no more.

Herbert looked down at the ground beneath his feet, where Mengele lay.

If the counterweight had been intended to pass overhead, there would have been a sudden dip in the floor, an extra step down. There was none.

Herbert jumped on to the ledge and pressed himself flat against the wall, praying that he was right, and thinking that he would not be around too long to find out if he was not.

No time to help Mengele up, even if Herbert had wanted to.

The counterweight, brutally and remorselessly unseeing, right in his face now.

It stopped with an explosion of cracking bones and squelched organs, splattering warm parts of Mengele on to Herbert's face and clothes; and Herbert was shaking, laughing, crying, shouting, teetering on the edge of delirium, but safe and alive.

Whatever break in the fog there had been was over; the mist was rolling over the barges again, and settling like snow on the roads.

Herbert sent two uniformed officers back to the American Embassy with Pauling; he himself took Papworth and Kazantsev to the Borough police station, halfway to the Elephant & Castle.

Papworth was, of course, still protesting his diplomatic immunity; Herbert had no right to do this, he was in breach of the law, Papworth would make him pay for this, and on, and on, and on.

'One murder, maybe two. Kidnapping a police officer – me. Aiding and abetting actual bodily harm: Mengele's assault on my mother. When your government finds out what you've been doing,' Herbert said, 'your diplomatic immunity will go in a flash. But that will be the least of your problems.'

Herbert commandeered an interview room: bare, no windows, but no bright lights in the face either. He posted three constables to stand guard, and instructed them not to say anything to Papworth at all. He would be back as soon as he could.

He rang Guy's and spoke to Angela, who assured him that Mary and Hannah were both OK; pretty shaken, unsurprisingly, but no permanent harm done.

He would try and come by later, he told her; but it looked as if he had a long afternoon ahead of him.

Then he phoned Tyce, and gave him the latest.

'If the film rights to your life ever come up, Herbert, I'll be first in line,' Tyce said. 'You want me to come down there? Or come see Sillitoe with you?'

'The latter, please. And if you can find the Commissioner . . .'

Herbert met Tyce and Sir Harold Scott at Minimax, where Scott's presence allowed them to bypass, in turn, a security guard, a secretary, a Six branch director and then Six's deputy director-general on the way to seeing Sir Percy Sillitoe.

With Sillitoe, Herbert knew, they had one priceless advantage: Sir Percy was a career policeman, and the unofficial brotherhood of Scotland Yard ran deep.

Sillitoe listened, nodded, listened some more while Herbert told him what had happened. At no time did he doubt Herbert's word.

When Herbert had finished, Sillitoe rang the Home Secretary, Sir David Maxwell Fyfe, made an immediate appointment with him and the American ambassador, Walter Gifford, and took the three policemen round to Whitehall so that Herbert could repeat his story.

Herbert anticipated trouble. Maxwell Fyfe was part of the traditional right wing of the Conservative party; Gifford was a personal friend of Eisenhower's. They were hardly the two people Herbert would have chosen to try and wheedle special treatment from.

As it was, he need not have worried.

The moment he said that Papworth had murdered at least one British citizen, he had Maxwell Fyfe's attention.

When he pointed out that Papworth had been betraying the United States for almost a decade, Gifford fell into line as well.

You understand, Gifford said, that a man who did what Papworth had done could be considered American only by virtue of his passport, rather than his mores. That kind of behaviour was the diametric opposite of what America wanted in, and expected from, its citizens. There were many millions of good, solid, upright, God-fearing Americans who would be disgusted at what Papworth had done; they should not all be tarred with the same brush as one man in one department of the American government.

Herbert said that he couldn't agree more. And he meant it.

Under the circumstances, Maxwell Fyfe and Gifford agreed to a temporary waiver of Papworth's diplomatic immunity pending investigation, allowing Herbert to continue his questioning without the Home Office needing to go through the rigmarole of declaring Papworth *persona non grata* and the State Department kicking up seven shades of transatlantic stink. The Agency's own investigators would move in once Herbert had finished.

In other words, a private, semi-unofficial, and eminently sensible solution to what could otherwise have been a knotty problem.

Herbert returned to Borough station bearing the order on Home Office notepaper, and slapped it on the table in front of Papworth.

'Am I supposed to be impressed?' Papworth asked.

'I've been authorised to consider some sort of deal if you co-operate.'

'That's not what it says there.'

'They're hardly going to put *that* in writing, are they?'

Papworth was silent.

Perhaps, Herbert said, he would make it known that Papworth had been fully aware of Mengele's real identity all along.

That wasn't true, Papworth said, and Herbert knew it.

Yes, Herbert did; but who would say otherwise? His mother? Hannah? After Papworth had stood aside and let Mengele do to them what he had done? No way.

Herbert left Papworth and went in to see Kazantsev.

Kazantsev had no diplomatic protection, but he was saying nothing. He had done his job, nothing more, nothing less.

Herbert knew that both men would be hard to break, because spies always were. If a man was trained in interrogation, he would also be trained in resistance to same.

Papworth would fold quicker than Kazantsev, Herbert felt.

With civilians, Herbert would have fired questions seemingly at random, in order to disorientate the subject, confuse him, in the expectation that eventually he would forget what he had said about this or that, because he was bound to have been lying about something, and lies were always harder to remember than the truth.

But this would not work on Papworth, at least not in the short term. Therefore, Herbert had to somehow convince Papworth that his best tactic was to be helpful.

He went back in to see Papworth.

'Kazantsev's making your average canary seem tone deaf,' he said.

'Do me a favour. That's the oldest trick in the book.'

'Except when it's not a trick.'

Herbert put another piece of paper down; an extract from the statute books that the ambassador had given him, specifically Section 2 of the United States Espionage Act 50 US Code 32, which prohibited *the transmission or attempted transmission to a foreign government of anything relating to the national defence.*

The offence carried the death penalty. Herbert had helpfully ringed that bit in red.

'What sort of deal?' Papworth asked at length.

'That depends on what you tell me.'

Papworth considered some more.

Like Herbert, he knew that now, when it was just the two of them, circumstances were as favourable as they were going to be. The more people who were brought in, especially from the American side, the less leeway Papworth would be given.

'All right,' he said.

Papworth and Kazantsev had begun working on the defection plan the moment Pauling's visa for the conference had been approved.

If Pauling's keynote speech had correctly identified the structure of DNA, however, the information would have been out in the open, and all their advantages would have gone.

The night before the conference, therefore, Papworth had laced Pauling's food with small quantities of an antimony-based emetic (freely available from pharmacists). It was nowhere near enough to kill him, or even cause him lasting damage; merely enough to imitate the symptoms of gastric fever, such as vomiting and diarrhoea, thus rendering him sufficiently indisposed that his keynote speech had to be cancelled.

As it was, Papworth need not have bothered. He had read the speech during one of Pauling's more extended bathroom vigils, and even a man who was more spook than chemist could see the flaw in Pauling's argument.

Pauling had gone for three helices on the basis of density – two chains simply left too much space unfilled – and had the sugar phosphate backbones forming a dense central core. But the phosphate groups were not ionised; each group contained a hydrogen atom, and therefore had no net charge. In effect, the structure Pauling was proposing was not an acid at all. He had knocked the *A* off DNA.

It was an error that even a graduate student should have picked up, let alone a genius like

Pauling. It just went to show, everybody could have their off days.

Then Stensness had made his offer, and so Papworth had gone along to the Peter Pan statue. He had taken Fischer – that was how he had thought of him then, so best to call him that, if Herbert didn't mind – along with him to check the veracity of any information Stensness might have brought.

Of course, Kazantsev had told Papworth the time of his own appointment, and together – without Fischer's knowledge, of course; he of all people would have been horrified to know of Papworth's true leanings – they had formulated a hasty plan.

Kazantsev had demanded to see what Stensness had before committing himself to any deal.

Stensness had refused.

Kazantsev and Stensness had argued.

Kazantsev had stormed off, partly for the benefit of Papworth, who had the next appointment. If Papworth behaved reasonably, they reckoned, then Stensness, perhaps shaken by Kazantsev's aggression, might prove more amenable.

But when Papworth and Fischer had arrived, Papworth had seen that the tactics had backfired. Far from shaking Stensness, Kazantsev's attitude had emboldened him. He was just as intransigent with Papworth as he had been with Kazantsev.

Papworth had felt the situation slipping away from him.

He and Stensness had struggled. Fischer had joined in, somehow managing to lose his ring in the process – they'd come back to that in a moment – and then, between them, Papworth and Fischer had dragged Stensness down to the water and held his head under, to try and make him submit.

But the water was very cold, Stensness' gasp reflex had been very strong, and Papworth and Fischer had overdone it.

Then they had been interrupted by someone else arriving.

De Vere Green? Herbert said.

Must have been, Papworth agreed, but they had not known that at the time. So they had high-tailed it.

Herbert realised that Papworth and Mengele had not known that Stensness was still alive, albeit unconscious. Herbert's first intuition when Hannah had found the coat had been spot on: Max must have come to and struggled free, but, fatally weakened, had collapsed again, and this time he had drowned.

But de Vere Green had already been at the statue; so he must have waited in the fog for a while before realising what the splashing meant, and by that time it had been too late.

If only he had been quicker, Herbert thought, de Vere Green could have saved his lover, and therefore himself too, and none of this would ever have happened.

Two murders; and there could have been, should have been, none.

Too late, on every count.

Papworth went on. De Vere Green's accusation in the church on Sunday morning had shaken him, because of course it had been true. Papworth had turned the accusation back with what even Herbert had to admit was quick thinking, but he had also known that this advantage was temporary at best; and all the more so come Sunday afternoon, when he had seen the decrypt concerning Operation Paperclip.

So Papworth had gone round to de Vere Green's, held a knife to his throat – he had known de Vere Green long enough to know that he could not stand the sight of blood, as Herbert himself had seen when he had resigned from Five – forced him to write the suicide note, then chloroformed him, turned the gas-fire valve open, and left, knowing that de Vere Green would be dead long before the anaesthetic wore off.

Of course Papworth had known that an autopsy would pick the chloroform up, but by the time it did, and by the time anyone had assembled all the pieces and put them together, he would have been halfway to Moscow, because the fog was supposed to have cleared by then.

When Herbert spotted Mengele's ring mark, Papworth had left him to continue interrogating Mengele in Wheeler's, while he went back to the

Embassy, took off his own ring, and put it by the side of the bath.

Herbert remembered that he had not looked at Papworth's hands when he brought Mengele back; why should he have? He had been observant, but not observant enough.

Lucky that it had fitted Fischer's little finger quite so perfectly, but a man was entitled to some good fortune along the way, wasn't he?

Then, Papworth added, Mengele had followed Herbert back through the fog to Hannah's flat, waited until Herbert and Hannah were asleep, attacked them and, when he could not find the formula, had set the flat alight, hoping both to cover his tracks and to kill them. Papworth had not known until afterwards. Had he known, he would of course have tried to dissuade Mengele.

Or accompanied him in order to maximise their chances, Herbert thought.

In that particular instance, therefore, Papworth was innocent. But, set against everything else he had done, it would count for precious little.

Had Mengele known who Hannah was before she had identified him? They would never know.

Yes, Papworth said, of course their planning had been imperfect; they had been forced to work some things out more or less on the hop.

But what else could they have done? Stensness had made the offer, and they couldn't have risked de Vere Green getting his hands on it.

It would have been all right if none of them had possessed it, but how could he have been sure that was the case?

That was what the race did to people, Herbert thought. It forced intelligent men to rush things, both through fear that the other fellow was on the cusp of a breakthrough, and through the eternal desire for fame.

Fame was self-feeding; the more one had, the more one wanted, and too much was never enough.

When scientists in the future managed to read humanity's DNA, Herbert thought, they would find everything that Mengele had mentioned the previous night at dinner, but they would also unearth plentiful quantities of man's less appealing qualities: folly, hubris, ambition, and greed.

The fog had thrown up enough of all these, even as it had worked both for and against Papworth and Kazantsev. Against them, in that it had kept them in London when they had wanted to make their escape. For them, in that it had given them the chance to try to get the material Stensness had promised, an offer of whose existence they hadn't even been aware until pretty much the end of the conference.

The microdots had always been a bonus, unexpected but desirable. In the end, it was Papworth's determination to seize them that had got him caught, for without that he would have left this morning when the fog had first partially cleared, and Herbert would never have found him.

466

Had he settled just for the defection and the scientists, he would have got clean away; and that would have been enough, for surely Pauling would have discovered the secret eventually. Scientific progress might not be linear, but it was inexorable.

Herbert looked at Papworth, thinking that something was missing.

After a few seconds, he knew what it was.

Papworth had told him what had happened, and when, and where, and how; what he had not told him was *why*.

Not why he had killed Stensness and de Vere Green – that was obvious. But why he had chosen to spy for the Soviet Union in the first place, why he had chosen to betray his country.

And even as he studied Papworth, Herbert realised where the answer lay.

Not in the merits of communism over capitalism, or in the preference for world peace over Cold War, but in Papworth himself.

Any question of loyalty came down to something very simple. To betray, one must first belong; and Papworth had never belonged. He was a vain misfit for whom there was only one cause worthy of his loyalty: Ambrose Papworth and his God-given right to have the world arranged the way he wanted it.

The answer lay, for lack of a more precise phrase, in Papworth's DNA.

Perhaps deep down Papworth had always wanted to be caught, Herbert thought, if only

467

because now the whole world would know his name. There would be a trial, and even the kind of mass opprobrium he could expect would, for such a man, be better than the alternative: an anonymous exile in a Moscow apartment where, after a couple of years, few people would know what he had done, and even fewer would care.

'So,' Papworth asked, 'what kind of deal are we talking?'

'You'll have to sort that out back in Washington.'

Papworth's jaw dropped. 'But you told me . . .'

Herbert spoke in a language Papworth could understand. 'I lied.'

It was past nine when Herbert made it back to Guy's, and by then both Hannah and Mary were asleep. Loath to wake them, he told Angela that he would be back in the morning.

The fog was a strange patchwork quilt: a black nightmare on the Strand but bright and clear at Piccadilly Circus, fine at Marble Arch and impenetrable in Bayswater.

Three thousand people were queuing for tickets at Stratford tube station because the buses had stopped.

River traffic was locked down again.

The opera at Sadler's Wells had been halted after Act One because the audience could no longer see the stage.

Everybody had a fog story, just as everybody used to have a bomb story.

No one had a fog story as good as his, Herbert thought.

On the way home, Herbert realised what had been nagging him at Rosalind's flat the day before.

Rosalind had been speaking about the way in which she ascertained her facts and fitted the theory round them, and she had compared this with the tactics of Watson and Crick, who started with a theory and saw where the facts fitted.

Herbert had been following Rosalind's path, and he should have gone with Watson and Crick instead. He had let the facts cloud his judgements; no, not the facts, but rather what he had *seen* to be the facts.

Like Rosalind, Herbert had trusted in what he had seen, and he had been mistaken. Time and again, even after Hannah had shown him the error of his ways, he had looked without seeing.

In some ways, he had been as blind as Hannah.

No wonder scientists did what they did, Herbert thought; they preferred science's exactness and the perfection of its truths. Humanity was rather messy in comparison.

Stella was waiting for Herbert when he got back.

He looked at her, and could not for the life of him read the expression on her face.

There could have been admiration, surprise, jealousy, or uncertainty; there could have been all, or there could have been none.

Stella's favours did not come for free, Herbert thought, so why should her emotions? Her make-up was designed to hide as much as to accentuate. Whatever she had learnt in her life had doubtless come the hard way; she wasn't about to make the path of knowledge easy for anyone else.

He felt a strange desire to screen his face from the scorching blaze of Stella's eye.

'Well, my love,' she said at last, 'good luck to you.'

'I'm sorry?'

'Herbert, don't take this the wrong way, it's good that you've found a woman, you know? Now you don't have to come and visit me no more. You understand?'

He nodded numbly, but no, he did not understand; there could be very few men in the world who had been rejected by a whore.

'No,' Stella said, 'you don't see, do you?' She paused, trying to find the right words. 'It's not a personal thing – well, it is, but not in the way you think. It's because I like you, Herbert; you're a good man, you never take me for granted. I like you, so I want you to be happy, and to be happy you need a nice girl, and if you have a nice girl then you won't have to come and see me no more.'

She grinned, a warrior under her war paint, and he smiled back.

'Yes,' she said, satisfied. 'Now you see.'

9TH DECEMBER 1952

TUESDAY

The trial of Bentley and Craig was starting at nine o'clock, so Herbert needed to mind the fort at New Scotland Yard, even though he wanted nothing more than a break. He stopped by Guy's at seven. Even at that hour, Hannah was already back in with Mary.

Mary was still angry and shaken by what had happened the previous day, and nor was she shy of telling him so.

'What the hell do you think you were doing, Herbert, bringing those people in here like that? That man tried to kill me, did you see? I can't eat solids now, just tea or milk, and they won't even put some brandy in it like I asked them to.'

'Mrs Smith, it not Herbert's fault,' Hannah said.

'It's a disgrace, letting . . .'

Mary started to choke, her lungs not up to coping with the force of her vitriol. Hannah reached across and put her hand flat against Mary's stomach.

'Breathe, Mrs Smith,' she said calmly. 'Breathe from stomach, use stomach muscles there. In and out, my hand I feel move . . . good, good.' She smiled. 'There! You get better already.'

Mary's choking subsided to a gurgle.

'Now perhaps you'll listen to me, Herbert,' Mary said. 'Think about some other line of work . . .'

It was a familiar argument, and one that Herbert had no intention of resuming, at least not there and then.

There was a strange silence, as though they were all waiting for something they dared not identify. It was Hannah who broke it.

'Mrs Smith,' Hannah said. 'What did you call him?'

Mary looked from Herbert to Hannah. 'What did I call who?'

'Herbert's twin. The one who died.'

There was a rushing from deep within Herbert, a swelling wave which came breaking up and over his body.

He was gasping for breath, not just through his mouth and nose, but through every organ, every pore in his skin, as though all the air in the world would not be enough for this immense, inner panting. Perhaps this was what being born felt like.

Herbert knew, even without looking at his mother, that Hannah was right.

Reactions flitted like seasons across Mary's face; disbelief, fury, shame.

'Alexander,' she said at length. 'I called him Alexander.'

Who else would have known, but a twin herself? It must have been so clear to Hannah, the girl who could not see; all the things, large and small, that Herbert had revealed to her, while refusing to believe it for himself; refusing, indeed, even to entertain the prospect, except at a depth so distant as to be measureless. The answer had been there all along, and he had erected the thickest of fogs around it.

'I was going to tell you, Herbert, but I never found the right time,' Mary said. 'Perhaps when you got married, or had children of your own; but you never have, have you?'

And the longer she had gone without telling him, the harder telling him had become; the issue no longer simply the secret itself, but also the keeping of it.

He saw in a flash what he had showed Hannah without even realising: the model car with one wheel missing which he used as a paperweight and which she had stood on in his flat; the painting he had bought in Portobello Market, the one of a man banging his fist against a mirror in frustration because there was no reflection in it.

His mother was still talking through the relief of catharsis.

'You were locked together in the womb, Herbert. You came out normally, head first, but

Alexander was a breech birth, and he couldn't breathe. Oh, Herbert, how you pined for him when you were a baby; you cried for two years, never a break.'

He had come into this world a murderer; wrapped around his brother and taking his breath from him. Now he came to this bedside a murderer, having struggled with Mengele the way he had struggled with Alexander; again Herbert had been nearest the air, and again he had survived.

Too much of him, too little of Alexander. No wonder he had cried for two years.

'They wouldn't even let me hold him, Herbert! They gave you to me instead. I had the rest of my life to hold you. I wanted Alexander, just for a short time. Mine! He was mine! They did the postmortem without telling me, and then suggested that I mourn for a while and get over it. How could I mourn someone I hadn't even seen?'

How, indeed? And so she had idealised Alexander, forever perfect in imaginary life; a shining triumph wherever Herbert disappointed, popular wherever he withdrew, pillar of the community wherever he skulked in dingy isolation, husband and father wherever he was neither. Alexander; the invented him, braver, cleverer, more lovable, more daring, more of all the things in which Herbert was less.

'I had never been special, Herbert. Having twins was the only thing that had ever made me stand out; months and months of excitement, people asking every day, sharing in my joy; and then gone, all gone, just like that. An anticlimax; no, a catastrophe. I had been admired; now, I was pitied. No one wanted to talk about it, and those that did said things like "You can always have another one" or "How lucky you've still got one left." *Lucky?* Would anyone dare say that to someone who had lost a single child? Not in a month of Sundays. But they said it, Herbert. They said it.'

And she could never escape her loss, because the reminder was there every day, crying, falling ill, demanding her time and attention, tainted by a million quotidian flaws. Half a pregnancy meant half a child. Herbert's existence was Alexander's absence, Herbert's birthday was Alexander's deathday; how could she celebrate one while mourning the other?

Hannah followed him out of the room.

'When I tell you of Mengele and Esther,' she said, 'it the first time I tell anyone, because until then I feel no one will understand, but I thought you were different, and I hoped you to be worthy of it. The way you react, I know that you *do* understand, and that you *are* worthy; and I know why.'

'So why didn't you tell me?'

'Is not my position. Is for your mother to do so.'

'When you forced her to.'

Hannah laughed. 'A little kick in the backside is not always so bad.'

'When did you first think that – about Alexander?'

'The first night, when I saw your loneliness, your complete isolation, because that only come from losing something in the heart. You the watcher, solid and solitary; me the doer, fiery and independent. They are not so far apart, Herbert; they are just different ways of expressing the same feeling.'

A breeze stroked Herbert's forehead as he walked through the car park; then a sudden gust, skidding pages of a newspaper across the ground like tumbleweed.

He looked up, and there was the sun, back with an insouciant shrug as if it had never been away. Clouds hurried across its face, escorting away the fog and its chemical storehouse of unwanted outriders: soot, ash, carbon monoxide, sulphur dioxide, nitrogen oxides, hydrocarbons, organic acids, methane, acetylene, phenols, ketones and ammonia, all ripped away on the east wind.

Herbert would have liked to think that the complacency and self-interest which had caused the fog in the first place were also disappearing, but somehow he doubted it.

His mother was his mother, he thought. He would tell her that she had betrayed him, and then he would tell her that he would always love her. Why else would that be, except for something as yet undiscovered which had been passed from her cells to his?

She had, at least, given him the reason for his loneliness, perhaps for his life itself, and it was now that he knew the reason – perhaps *only* now that he knew the reason – that he could begin work on redressing it.

In the ambulance the day before, he had seen that he was someone who could love, because he had despaired at what he might lose. No longer would there be the grey choke of emptiness, because love lived too; not as prophylactic but as counterweight, a provider of purpose.

The concourse at London Bridge was half-full, and Herbert smiled, at everything and at nothing in particular.

He was among people, and that was enough.

Perhaps life had brought Herbert more than his fair share of darkness, but without it the light would not have seemed as special as it did now.

They were both as valid as the other, he saw, the darkness and the light; and the only way to deal with them was to endure one and enjoy the other, for as long or as short a time as they lasted.

He had hated some of his life, tried to escape it and push it away; he had rendered himself indifferent to a great deal more of it.

No more. He would embrace it all and clasp it to his hip; so close that they would be, in a manner of speaking, twins.

Herbert walked on to London Bridge.

Around him, upstream and down, north and

south, huge cranes swung across the newly-cleaned sky. Bulldozers heaved, thrust, and grabbed. Buildings sprouted with the promise of a new, spacious city, a matrix of glass and steel and aluminium, of fresh shapes and clean air.

Halfway across, he stopped, leant against the parapet, and looked downstream.

On the river, boats of every size and description had raised steam and were now sweeping past docks and landings; a vast armada of mudhoppers, liners, coasters, colliers, tows and motor barges, tooting their foghorns in joyous cacophony as they ducked beneath the upraised arms of Tower Bridge and headed for the sea, free at last, free at last, free at last.

Afterword

In January 1953, Maurice Wilkins showed – without Rosalind Franklin's permission – her X-ray photograph 51 to James Watson, Francis Crick's colleague at Cambridge. In his book *The Double Helix*, Watson recalled: 'the instant I saw the picture, my mouth dropped open and my pulse began to race.'

Convinced that the helix was indeed a double, Watson and Crick set to work in a frenzy. Within weeks, they had deduced the two crucial elements of the molecular structure that Rosalind had missed; that the chains ran anti-parallel rather than parallel, and that the base nucleotides were invariably paired together, adenine with thymine, guanine with cytosine.

At lunchtime on 28th February, Crick walked into The Eagle pub, just round the corner from the Cavendish laboratory where he and Watson worked, and announced to everyone within earshot that they had found the secret of life. And indeed they had.

They were more circumspect, however, when it

came to publishing the details of their research. The issue of *Nature* on 25th April that year contains one of the most celebrated of all scientific understatements, when, having outlined their theory, they said: 'It has not escaped our notice that the specific pairing we have postulated suggests a possible copying mechanism for the genetic material.'

The magnitude of their discovery is hard to overstate.

Hardly a day seems to go by when some aspect of genetic research is not in the news, be it in the field of agriculture, medicine, forensic science or ethical debate. It is as integral a part of the modern world as electricity or the automobile, and will only become more so as technology continues to advance.

It is therefore Francis Crick and James Watson whose names have entered the history books, as well-known and influential a double act as any in modern times – as natural a pairing as Bonnie and Clyde, Lennon and McCartney, Rogers and Astaire, or indeed their own double helix. Every schoolchild who studies chemistry or biology knows their names.

Together with Maurice Wilkins, Watson and Crick's work on DNA won them the Nobel Prize for Physiology or Medicine in 1962. Nobel Prizes can be shared between no more than three people, but tragically the question of Rosalind Franklin's claim on a place in Stockholm was purely academic; she had died from ovarian cancer four years previously, at the age of thirty-seven.

Francis Crick stayed in Cambridge to continue

work on the genetic code until the 1970s, when he left to take up a post at the Salk Institute of Biological Studies in San Diego, California. His death in July 2004 at the age of eighty-eight was reported on the front page of newspapers in Britain and elsewhere.

Maurice Wilkins, who had been involved in the Manhattan Project during the war, became a prominent figure in the world of scientific ethics, campaigning against the involvement of scientists in weapons research. He died three months after Crick, also aged eighty-eight, and again his death made headlines around the world.

James Watson has worked at the Cold Spring Harbor Laboratory in New York State since the 1970s, for most of that time as its director. He remains one of biotechnology's most senior, active, charismatic and outspoken figures.

Linus Pauling won two Nobel Prizes: Chemistry in 1954, for studies of molecular structure and the chemical bond; and Peace in 1962, for the fight against atomic testing. He is one of four two-time winners, and the only one whose laurels combine a scientific category with a non-scientific one. He died in 1994, at the age of ninety-three.

More than four thousand people died in the London fog of 1952, from three main causes: acrid smoke producing shortness of breath due to bronchial spasm, which put a fatal strain on the heart; carbon and soot getting into lung cells already sticky and congested, leading to low-grade pneumonia and heart failure; and, in patients suffering corpulmonale, stretched lung cells becoming congested and fluid exudating into lungs, causing death virtually by suffocation.

The tragedy led directly to the passing of the Clean Air Act four years later. The last London pea-souper was in 1962, though it was on nothing like the scale of the one a decade previously. There have been none since then.

Mary Smith died in 1954, of complications arising from asthma and bronchitis.

Sasha Kazantsev, who did not enjoy diplomatic immunity, was convicted of attempted kidnapping and spent five years in Belmarsh prison. On his release, he was returned to Moscow. He was never heard from again.

Ambrose Papworth recanted his confessions to the murders of Richard de Vere Green and Max Stensness. He was tried in the United States on counts of treason, convicted, sentenced to death and, in October 1956, was executed at Sing Sing.

The news of Josef Mengele's death in the bowels of Tower Bridge was never made public, to spare the United States both acute embarrassment and international opprobrium at having harboured arguably the most notorious war criminal of them all.

Neither London nor Washington therefore made any attempts to dispel the impression that Mengele had after the war fled to South America, firstly to Paraguay and then to Brazil.

A man widely thought to be Mengele died on a beach near the Brazilian town of Embu in 1979, after suffering a stroke while swimming. In 1992, the results of DNA tests were published purporting to prove that the body was indeed that of Mengele, and this was almost universally accepted as fact.

In truth, however, DNA tests at that time were far from infallible, especially when applied with lax regard to proper procedures, as was the case in this instance. But, as it so often does, the world saw what it wanted to see.

Mengele himself would surely have been tickled pink by the vast irony that DNA, his holy grail, was used to 'prove' that a stranger's body was his.

Stella Chalmers was killed in a car crash in 1967. Herbert read one of the lessons at her funeral.

Both Derek Bentley and Christopher Craig were found guilty of the murder of PC Sidney Miles. Bentley was hanged at Wandsworth prison on 28th January 1953 by the executioner Albert Pierrepoint; Craig was ordered to be detained at Her Majesty's Pleasure, and was released in 1963.

Herbert and Hannah married on Saturday, 30th May 1953, four days before the Queen's Coronation. After Mary died, they moved to America, where Herbert joined the police force in Princeton, New Jersey, and Hannah continued to apply her talents as a polymath.

They had two children, a girl and a boy, and lived in America for more than thirty years, only moving to South Africa in 1977, when Herbert was sixty. Too old to be a policeman by then, he turned his hand to news photography, working on the Johannesburg *Sunday Times*.

It was on that newspaper that I first met him, in 1987, and on that newspaper where he told me the first part of this story. In the years that followed, when I was back in London and he had retired to Knysna on the famous Garden Route in the Cape, we continued to correspond, and gradually two things became clear: that he wanted me to write his story as a book, and that he did not want to be around to see it. He was still bound by the Official Secrets Act, and he was not a disloyal man. But he wanted his story to be told, and he wanted it to be told in full.

The Great Fog of London lifted on 9th December 1952. Fifty-two years to the day later, Herbert Smith died. He was eighty-seven.

Hannah still lives in Knysna, and is visited often by her two children.

They are called Esther and Alexander.

Boris Starling. London, January 2006